**Rosa~~~~~~ as a
teena~~~~, ~~~~~~. For a
~~ily trip to ~~~~~~~~~~~~ she was fifteen, she packed
~~ugh Mills & Boons to last the month! Rosanna's
~~ssion for reading and her love of children resulted in a
~~llar teaching career, with four Best Practice Awards,
~~d she also pursued another passion: writing. She has
~~n published in over a dozen anthologies, and since
~~uring her dream of being a Mills & Boon writer has
~~me true!

New York Times and *USA TODAY* bestselling author
~~irley Jump spends her days writing romance so she
~~ avoid the towering stack of dirty dishes, eat copious
~~ounts of chocolate and reward herself with trips to the
~~l. Visit her website at shirleyjump.com for author
~~vs and a book list, and follow her at Facebook.com/
~~rleyjump.author for giveaways and deep discussions
~~ut important things like chocolate and shoes.

Also by Rosanna Battigelli

Swept Away by the Enigmatic Tycoon
Captivated by Her Italian Boss

Also by Shirley Jump

Their Last Second Chance
The Family He Didn't Expect
The Firefighter's Family Secret
The Tycoon's Proposal
The Instant Family Man
The Homecoming Queen Gets Her Man
Return of the Last McKenna
How the Playboy Got Serious
One Day to Find a Husband
Family Christmas in Riverbend

Discover more at millsandboon.co.uk

CARIBBEAN ESCAPE WITH THE TYCOON

ROSANNA BATTIGELLI

THE MARRIAGE RESCUE

SHIRLEY JUMP

MILLS & BOON

First Published in Great Britain 2020
by Mills & Boon, an imprint of HarperCollinsPublishers,
1 London Bridge Street, London, SE1 9GF

Caribbean Escape with the Tycoon © 2020 Rosanna Battigelli
The Marriage Rescue © 2020 Shirley Kawa-Jump, LLC

ISBN: 978-0-263-27873-6

0320

FSC
www.fsc.org

MIX
Paper from
responsible sources
FSC™ C007454

This book is produced from independently certified FSC™
paper to ensure responsible forest management.

For more information visit: www.harpercollins.co.uk/green

Printed and bound in Spain
by CPI, Barcelona

CARIBBEAN ESCAPE WITH THE TYCOON

ROSANNA BATTIGELLI

For my beautiful daughter, Sarah, a strong, shining star.

CHAPTER ONE

"YOU SIT HERE and don't move, Adrien," Chanelle heard a deep voice say at the table across from hers. She had just been looking out at the coast from the deck of the luxury cruise liner *Aquarius*, a ship she'd never dreamed she'd be a guest on.

"I'll be right back with something yummy for the both of us," the man said with a laugh. "I'll give you a hint: it rhymes with *nice dream…*"

Chanelle looked up, curious to see the face that matched the voice. But she only saw the back of the man's head. And below the golden-brown hair that curled at the ends, a firm neck and muscled shoulders that were distractingly discernible under his turquoise shirt. His perfectly fitting black linen trousers emphasized his strong legs.

Before he turned toward the ice cream machine, a young lady passed by wearing a red bikini and a filmy white cover-up that barely covered anything, and gave the man a big smile. She said something to him, and Adrien's father stopped to talk to her, giving Chanelle a glimpse of his chiseled profile and groomed shadow. And his quirky smile and narrowed eyes.

Chanelle's stomach muscles contracted involuntarily, and her pulse quickened, followed immediately by a feeling of guilt for her physical reaction to a guy who was married and yet flirted with other women.

Despicable. And practically in front of his child...

Her attention was diverted by the *vroom, vroom* sounds of the man's son as he moved his miniature racing car along the table. Adrien was a cute little boy, with bright blue eyes and short, golden brown hair, the same shade as his dad's. At one point, he backed the car up and let it go. The car skidded off to the far end of the table, and the boy immediately jumped on his chair to reach across to get it. Chanelle turned in alarm toward his father, but he was now concentrating on filling two cones, the woman gone.

Chanelle's heart skipped a beat. Adrien was so close to the ship railing… What if he took a tumble over the edge? Her heart leaped into her throat when she saw him begin to straighten, and without any further hesitation, she closed the distance between them in two strides and clasped his arm.

"You need to come down—"

"What exactly are you doing?"

Chanelle heard the deep voice directly behind her. Only this time it lacked the light, playful tone he had used with his son. Before she could react, the child had wrenched himself away and was scrambling off the chair and running to his father.

Chanelle turned to face them awkwardly, feeling a flush bloom across her cheeks. The man had set down the cones and was embracing Adrien with one arm while staring at Chanelle, his eyebrows furrowed above icy blue eyes. "Why were you grabbing him?"

Because you weren't there, making sure your son didn't end up losing his balance and tipping overboard, Chanelle wanted to retort.

She felt her jaw muscles tensing. "I wasn't grabbing him." She looked at the man steadily, willing herself to sound calm and not defensive. "He had jumped up to get his toy car, and I was worried that he'd lose his balance and fall." She gazed at the boy, whose face was puckering as he looked at his shoes. "Or topple over."

"He was in no danger. I had my eye on him." The man's eyes narrowed, and Chanelle felt as if she were staring at two brilliant blue laser beams.

Your eye was on a red bikini, she wanted to retort. She felt her cheeks fire up as the stormy blue of his eyes intensified.

"I was closer to him than you," she said, trying to keep her voice steady, "and from where I stood, he looked perilously close to the edge." Chanelle bit her lip. "Look, I was just trying to protect him. One wrong move and he could have—"

"I get the point," he said, putting up a hand. His tone lacked its previous gruffness, and his eyes seemed to have softened. "Thank you for your valiant gesture."

Chanelle's eyebrows lifted as she stared at the man who was staring down at her. His eyes were a startling turquoise, matching his golf shirt. Gazing at his bronzed features, perfectly shaped lips and a jawline that reminded her of the sculpted perfection of Michelangelo's *David*, Chanelle felt an inner jolt. A series of jolts. As her gaze slipped downward, she had the crazy thought that with his looks and build, he should be modeling for a living. The top buttons of his shirt were undone, revealing an inverted triangle of golden-brown hair. When her gaze returned to his face, she started at the piercing intensity of his eyes. She looked away, her cheeks feeling like molten lava. He stepped forward and took his son firmly by the hand. The child lowered his gaze again, aware that his actions had caused concern.

"What is going on here?" A thirty-something young woman with bouncy strawberry-blond hair, and clothes and shoes that screamed *designer*, approached them and took Adrien protectively by the hand. She threw a concerned look at her husband.

"Nothing to worry about," he drawled. "I'll take care of it."

Chanelle couldn't help glancing at his left hand. *No ring.* She almost snorted. *No wonder.* He obviously preferred to *look* single… Chanelle's gaze flew to the petite woman. Did she have any idea that her husband was a playboy?

A rich playboy, from the look of her diamond of at least two carats.

"I'm going to our stateroom. Come on, Adrien," she said brusquely. She lifted an eyebrow imperiously toward her husband. "Vance?"

"I'll join you shortly, Mariah," he said. He released Adrien's hand.

Chanelle stood by awkwardly as the man's wife strode past her stiffly, ignoring her completely. When she and her son had disappeared past the automatic glass doors, Chanelle glanced warily at the man. *Vance.* Nice name. Too bad it didn't match his character.

He had taken a few steps closer, and his brows were furrowed again. Her nose picked up spicy notes of his cologne. A woodsy and exotic fragrance that reminded her of sandalwood and cedar. Chanelle wondered uneasily if, now that his wife and child were not present, he was about to give her a blast for interfering in their business.

Why *hadn't* she minded her own business? The cruise hadn't even begun, and already she was feeling a surge of anxiety. She took a deep breath, bracing herself for a verbal onslaught.

And then his brows unfurrowed. "Have you considered applying for a job on the ship, watching over the children?" he said with a quirk of a smile, blue eyes crinkling at the corners. "I don't believe this cruise line comes equipped with a guardian angel."

Chanelle blinked, distracted by the way the turquoise of his eyes had darkened to lapis and not knowing how or what she should reply. She patted her hair down self-consciously. It had been rather humid in Tampa, and in such conditions, her hair had a tendency to fluff out and get frizzy.

Her emotions at this moment felt just as frizzy, with the unnerving way that he was gazing at her…

"I—I was just trying to prevent a tragedy," she said, unable to keep the defensiveness out of her voice. She straightened, trying to boost her confidence. She was not going to let this—*this womanizer*—try to appease her with his charm. How many other women had he referred to as an angel? "And I'm not sorry I interfered," she added, jutting out her chin.

He stared at her wordlessly for a moment, his eyes narrowing, before shifting his gaze to her engagement ring. His jaw muscles flickered and he seemed lost in thought, and Chanelle had to resist the urge to whip her hand behind her back. Finally he looked up, and pinned her with a curious gaze. "Your fiancé is a helluva lucky guy to have such a caring wife-to-be. He won't have to worry about your future children, with *you* protecting them like a lioness." He gave a husky laugh and then stared at her intensely. "So tell me, since this is a Zodiac cruise, *are you* a Leo?"

Vance watched the extraordinarily long eyelashes of the woman opposite him flutter over green-hazel eyes that sparkled like gemstones. Her glossy lips parted briefly and then shut, drawing his eyes to their perfect dimensions—not too thin and not too wide. And from having observed her stature as he approached—or more specifically, the way she fit into her white jeans and fuchsia T-shirt—it was obvious she either worked out or was just born lucky. He watched as she ran her fingers through her lustrous auburn hair, the movement sending a hint of her perfume drifting toward him, a candy-like scent of raspberry and plum…

She blinked at him as if his question were the last thing she had expected to hear him say.

What the hell was he doing? He didn't really want to know her sign, did he? *No, of course not.*

Vance wished he could take the question back. It was something he might have asked in a more flirtatious situation. And he had no intention of flirting with this lovely but rather overreactive—*and engaged*—passenger. He shifted as a couple strode past them. He should have followed Mariah back to the stateroom immediately. And now he had to think of an appropriate way to end this—

"Sagittarius."

She said it defiantly, her green eyes flashing a silent warning.

He had no choice but to continue this now. "Ah…the Archer," he murmured. "The healer whose intelligence forms a bridge between earth and heaven." He raised an eyebrow. "Let me guess. You're either a nurse or a teacher…or in some kind of caring profession." He stroked his jaw. "Or I'm completely off the mark and you're an astrophysicist," he added with a chuckle.

She wrinkled up her face and rolled her eyes, an attempt—*possibly?*—to conceal her amusement. A tingling sensation spiraled through him. The dimples that had appeared briefly in her cheeks were charming. Whether he liked it or not, she was igniting feelings that he did not want ignited. He forced himself to come back to earth. "Well, are stars your thing, or what?" he said lightly.

Her lips parted, and she had that look of *Why would you even want to know?* She gave him a measured glance. "I don't have time for stargazing," she retorted, "and my job is much more down-to-earth. With no sparkle or glitter."

She hesitated for a moment, and her eyes seemed to darken. He caught the slight crease of her forehead before it disappeared.

"I'm a social worker," she said matter-of-factly. "In child protection." She took a deep breath, and her eyes seemed to blaze in the late-afternoon sunshine. Her mouth opened slightly as if she were about to say something more but then promptly closed again.

Vance surveyed her flushed cheeks. No wonder she had been so quick to act with Adrien. And he had been too quick to jump to the wrong conclusion, asking her why she was grabbing him… "Protectiveness is in the nature of a Sagittarius," he said gruffly, nodding.

She didn't respond, but something flickered in her green eyes before she lowered her gaze.

Vance knew that Adrien hadn't been in danger, but he could understand that from where she had been sitting, it had looked like Adrien was in a very vulnerable position. And she hadn't hesitated in reacting…

Something in Vance's gut told him that if Adrien *had* tumbled over, this vigilant Sagittarian would have plunged right in after him. He had seen that fierce protectiveness in her eyes as she had quickly reached out to stop him. Vance had no doubt that on the job or not, she saw herself as a champion of children, on constant alert to ensure their safety and well-being.

His gaze shifted again to her hands, where she was unconsciously twiddling her ring.

He felt his jaw tensing. "I should let you get back to your—"

Her head jerked up.

"Fiancé."

Her eyes shot green sparks at him before dropping to her left hand. "Thank you," she replied stiffly, her voice sounding far from grateful. She tossed her hair back and turned away.

It was quite the mane, he thought, watching the way the sun made her auburn hair look like copper gold. He had a sudden urge to run his fingers through it. And to talk to her longer, despite the voice in his head urging him not to.

"Hey, there," he called. He waited until she turned around and then flashed her a smile. "I realize I must have sounded harsh initially," he said. "I apologize. I'm protective, too, when it comes to family."

Her eyes widened. For a moment she said nothing and then shook her head dismissively. "No need to apologize. I probably should have minded my own business."

"Well, allow *me* to at least apologize for addressing you as 'Hey, there,'" he said, smiling. "I'm Vance. And I'd like to make it up to you by buying you a drink. What do you say, Miss—?"

She blinked at him wordlessly. When a few seconds had passed and she still had not responded, he frowned. "Is something the matter?" Was he imagining it, or was she giving him a look of disdain?

"I don't have drinks with married men," she said coolly. "And I believe you told your wife you'd join her shortly…"

Vance blinked, momentarily confused, but before he could reply and tell her he wasn't coming on to her, she had turned on her heels and disappeared.

Way to go, Kingston. How obtuse to be offering to buy a guest a drink, given that she was engaged and that she had presumed he was married. From the look on her face, it was obvious that she considered him a creep. Shaking his head, Vance headed inside and pressed the elevator button for the ship's upper level—Deck Thirteen.

He glanced at the time on his phone. The cruise director would soon be announcing the emergency assembly drill. All the passengers would be called to make their way to their assigned deck to undergo the required safety routine in the event of an emergency. And soon after that, the ship would set sail.

He had enough time to have a quick talk with Mariah and Adrien and then relax with a glass of wine at the Mercury Bar on Deck Ten. No, he would head to the bar first. Mariah would probably be wondering what was taking him so long, but until she texted, he was just going to take advantage of having some time to himself.

As the elevator opened on Deck Eight, Vance caught a flash of auburn hair among a group of people walking down the hall. He felt his pulse jack up. And then another flash of fuchsia above snug-fitting white jeans. It *was* her. He smiled apologetically when he realized that several elderly women were waiting for him to move to the back of the elevator so they could enter.

Moments later, Vance leaned back in a lounging chair in the Mercury Bar, savoring one of the ship's premium wines. It would kick off his week-long holiday after an intense nine months taking over Zodiac Cruises, his parents' company. Even though he had initially balked when his mother had mentioned plans for a special cruise to formally hand over the reins of the company to him, Vance was looking forward to finally having some time to unwind.

Nine months ago, the life Vance had known and enjoyed had shattered. His father had had a heart attack after a family dinner. Before he had taken his last breaths, he had managed to tell his family that he loved them.

Vance swallowed hard. The man who had spent so much

time away from home—and had relinquished parenting to build his business—had looked at him with piercing clarity for a few moments and rasped, "I'm sorry, son. For everything I said or didn't say to you. For not being there for you as you were growing up. I… I wanted to build the company for my family. Now I leave it in your hands… Will you take it on, son?"

Vance had felt a sharp twinge in his own chest at his father's words, and he had instinctively realized that he needed to forgive his father. The wall he had constructed around his heart over the years, brick by brick, had to give. But something had lodged in Vance's throat, preventing him from expressing any feelings, and when his father passed seconds later, Vance was flooded by guilt that he had not given his father the satisfaction of knowing that he had forgiven him—or at least that he would try to forgive him—and that he would carry on with the company.

That was what his dad had always wanted, to have him working alongside him, learning the ropes and eventually taking over when he decided to retire. But Vance had balked from the beginning, always feeling a disconnect with the man who had barely been around in his youth.

And how could the concrete barrier around his heart even begin to give after decades of reinforcement? His father's quickly uttered words to him as he approached the end of his life were too little and too late.

Getting involved in the company had been the furthest thing from Vance's mind. In high school, when his father had urged him—on one of his rare home visits—to do his community service hours at Zodiac Cruises' headquarters, Vance had declined, preferring to volunteer at a nearby art gallery. His time there had reinforced his interest in the art world, and the sketches he had shown his father to prove his intentions to pursue art at university had met with barely concealed scorn.

"You've got to be joking." His father's sharp laugh as he had tossed Vance's scrapbook aside dismissively had struck him as if he had lunged a fist into his chest. Vance still remembered how he had wobbled backward a couple of steps, slack-jawed and speechless.

"Are you telling me you'd rather be a starving artist?" His father's eyes, resembling gray storm clouds, had bored into Vance. "Don't be a fool." And then he had abruptly left, telling his wife that he had lost his appetite and wasn't going to stay for dinner.

Vance winced at the memory. His father had been harsh with him, but Vance had refused to buckle and eventually graduated with a master of fine arts degree, receiving the highest honors and a substantial monetary prize from the department. His mother had been at his graduation ceremony, and the look of pride in her glistening eyes had moved him, but her effusive words of praise and congratulations could not make up for the fact that his father had not bothered to show up.

Within a few months, a prestigious art gallery in Toronto's historic Distillery District had hired Vance as assistant curator, and his work there, along with his travels, had kept him quite occupied, with very little time to visit his mother save for the occasional Sunday dinner.

The dinner that had proven to be his father's last had turned out to be the same as previous occasions—the atmosphere tinged with tension, stilted conversation and a formality that was never present when he was alone with his mother. Seeing his father—whom he had always categorized as tough and uncompromising—reduced to such a vulnerable and conciliatory state had been a shock. His father's deathbed request had immobilized him, and Vance had barely had time to process the request before his father passed.

Vance took a gulp of wine. He had never wanted to get involved in the family business, but the irony was that after the funeral, Vance had spent every waking moment trying to prove himself worthy of following in his father's footsteps. For his mother's sake, he had tried to convince himself repeatedly. He was doing it for her, to keep the business running as smoothly as possible. And maybe to assuage the guilt that had surfaced knowing he hadn't given his father the satisfaction of a positive response to his last request as he had taken his last breaths.

And to do the job properly, it meant that he had had to temporarily give up the lifestyle he had previously enjoyed, which his father had not approved of. And his job at the art gallery.

It had been too late to make a vow to his father, but not too late for Vance to carry out his promise to himself.

So for the last nine months, Vance had worked twelve-hour days at headquarters in Toronto and had undertaken several cruises, mentored by every department head of Zodiac Cruises. He had been surprised at how much he had enjoyed learning the workings of the business, and he had started to think of ways that he could put his art and history background to good use in the company...

His mother had planned *this* cruise to officially acknowledge Vance in his new position. "Your father wanted this, remember?" she had reminded him several times when he had claimed that he didn't have time. "His dream was to pass the reins as president of Zodiac Cruises over to you himself one day..."

Vance felt a fresh stab of grief and the familiar swirl of guilt in his gut. What had he really known about his father's dreams? His feelings toward his father were so convoluted. He was sure that he had felt every possible emotion when it came to his dad: bitterness, disappointment, abandonment, even hate in his adolescent years. He had never understood the man…a man who had chosen work over family.

What's done is done, he told himself. He had another drink of his wine and willed the memory of his father's last moments to vanish. As soon as that image had dissipated, green-hazel eyes flashed in Vance's memory. Why did his thoughts keep returning to *her*? For nine months, he had stayed clear of women, focused entirely on the company. He hadn't agreed to take a break and go on this cruise with the notion of resuming his past lifestyle…

And yet he had impulsively told her he'd like to buy her a drink. What the hell had he been thinking? And he had completely ignored the clear fact that she was engaged. Vance scowled. It was obvious that his playboy habits hadn't been completely extinguished…

He couldn't help wondering what her fiancé was like. Did he run his fingers through that blaze of hair? Did it get wild and tangled when they—?

Taking a deep breath, Vance forced the image out of his mind. He should have never agreed to this cruise. It was frivolous, considering the projects that needed his attention back at Zodiac headquarters…

Vance rolled his neck to one side and then the other. Maybe after the emergency drill, he'd relax in his private whirlpool. He felt tense around his shoulders, and the warm jets would be a welcome relief… A bit later on, he'd either order room service for dinner or they could dine at one of the specialty restaurants if Mariah preferred.

And then they would proceed to the Milky Way Theater, where the ship's troupe of dancers and singers would be performing a medley of songs from the '60s to the '80s.

Classic hits from iconic singers. It was a great first-night show, and he would be giving a brief welcome to the audience before it started.

And maybe the Sagittarian might not be there to distract him…

CHAPTER TWO

CHANELLE STOOD BY the railing on Deck Eleven, her gaze shifting from the lapping waters of the bay to the magenta-and-gold sunset as the Tampa Bay skyline receded in the distance. She had decided against joining the cruise director and other staff and the probable swarm of guests at the Sail Away party on Deck Twelve after the emergency drill. She wasn't in the mood to mingle just yet...

Chanelle closed her eyes, letting the repetitive sound of the waves soothe her. Her thoughts were interrupted by a soft giggle in a far-off corner. Two darkened forms exchanged a kiss and wandered off hand in hand. She sighed. Could she not have picked a holiday where she wouldn't be reminded at every turn of her failed relationship?

She bit her lip. Much as she had wanted to blame Parker for not being sensitive enough to her work commitments, she had had to face the truth: that she had invested more time and energy in her job and not enough with him.

"I've met somebody at the gym..." He had dropped the bombshell seven months ago. And he'd told her he would be back the next day to get his things. Everything but the engagement ring he had given her.

If all had worked out with Parker, she might have been planning her wedding now, or even enjoying her honeymoon...instead of cruising alone, Chanelle mused, taking a deep breath.

But it hadn't worked out, and she had to admit—if she were to be totally honest—that she was relieved.

Not that she had felt that way at first.

Hurt and feeling betrayed, she had wanted to analyze what had gone wrong with their relationship and had checked out the self-help section of a local bookstore. One title had immediately caught her eye, as Parker had often accused her of being overly sensitive. And soon after delving into the book, Chanelle had discovered that she had many of the traits that the book identified…some that she had been aware of and some—she had realized in wonder—that she had exhibited even in childhood.

She'd also learned things she hadn't known: that highly sensitive people had nervous systems that were more easily activated by sensory stimuli. Which had explained why certain smells were unbearable, or why intense sunlight or loud music or people could be so jarring…and why her skin couldn't tolerate certain fabrics. No lace or wool for her! Or most synthetic materials. All this had illuminated her as to why she'd ended up with a skin rash or migraine at times…

Chanelle had learned that highly sensitive people—or HSPs—processed their experiences and feelings with greater depth and emotional intensity.

Given such sensitivities—not only physical, but emotional also—was it any wonder that her line of work had pushed her coping mechanisms to the max? And that Parker hadn't been able to cope? The book had outlined how challenging it could be for others to understand and empathize with an HSP. It was challenging enough for an HSP to deal with their sensitivities, and relationships could present even greater testing grounds…

Her relationship with Parker hadn't passed the test. Neither one of them had been solely to blame, though. She had been too focused on her work—there was no denying that—but Parker could have at least been honest with her and broken things off *before* getting involved with someone else. That would have been the *decent* thing to do.

And it had been this last thought that had finally convinced Chanelle that Parker hadn't been the right man for her. After the initial shock and sting of betrayal, Chanelle had accepted the fact that Parker was not the guy she was meant to have a happy-ever-after with.

He had betrayed her trust. She deserved better.

This realization had come before the acknowledgment that she had burned out on her job. And her parents, who were on the other side of the globe on an extended trip to visit relatives in Australia, hadn't been there to comfort her for either her breakup with Parker or her lingering emotional distress after a traumatic case involving two siblings and their neglectful parents. Meredith, Chanelle's employer, had kindly advised her to consider a leave even months before this particular case, having observed the classic signs of burnout becoming more prevalent in Chanelle. But Chanelle had insisted she was fine, telling herself that she needed her work more than ever after Parker had left…

She had been wrong, of course. She should have heeded Meredith's advice from the beginning. Chanelle sighed. After consulting with her doctor, Chanelle had taken a leave, "to be assessed on a regular basis." This was not a sign of weakness, her doctor had asserted gently, but a step toward ensuring her emotional well-being. Having a job that dealt with the trauma of others required particular diligence in maintaining physical and emotional health and balance in one's own life.

Enough! Chanelle was tired of thinking of the circumstances that had brought her here. And she needed to keep Parker out of her thoughts. She didn't want him on this cruise with her. She was over him.

She had tucked the engagement ring he had left her in her purse months ago and had slipped it on her finger momentarily, wondering what she was going to do with it. And then, before she could put it back in her purse, she had become distracted by the incident with the child and his distracted father.

Perhaps what she really hadn't gotten over was the fact that another man had dumped her. The first one had been her biological father. Her mother had revealed the story to her when she had felt Chanelle was ready. His name was Trevor, and upon hearing that his girlfriend Katie— Chanelle's mother—was pregnant, he had promptly broken up with her, claiming the baby wasn't his. He had accepted a job out of town right after college graduation and never returned, leaving Katie heartbroken. Fortunately, Chanelle's grandparents hadn't abandoned Katie, and Chanelle had grown up missing a father in her formative years, but living with a set of grandparents who cherished her.

She had just turned twelve when her mother married a furniture dealer called Martin, and although Chanelle had initially been reluctant to trust him—there had been a couple of men Katie had dated before him who had caused Chanelle some anxiety—Martin's easy and joking manner and obvious devotion to her mother eventually won her over. Chanelle's faith in men had been temporarily restored, but now she had to admit to herself that Parker's decision to break up had stirred up a flurry of latent feelings that could be associated with her father's rejection of her. Her social work and psychology studies had not been for nothing, she thought, her mood darkening as she watched the swirling waters from the deck.

Two men had abandoned her. One, her father, who hadn't even wanted to acknowledge that he'd had anything to do with her conception. Who had chosen to run away from his responsibilities to her and her mother. And Parker, who had left her for another woman. Both had run away from the promise of what was to come—the birth of a baby and the birth of a marriage, respectively. Neither the baby nor the marriage had been given a chance…

Chanelle's work had helped take her mind off the latter. She had pushed herself to the limit, convincing herself that the children she was protecting, or rescuing from a parent or parents who were unfit, depended on her. And she had no intention of abandoning them.

She had tried to be a superwoman, she realized, and had driven herself into a state of burnout. And she was having a hard time coming to terms with not being able to do her job.

Who am I? She shook her head and gripped the deck railing. Her job had been everything to her. *What do I do now?*

Chanelle squeezed her eyes tightly at the prickly sensation behind her lids but wasn't able to stop a few tears from slipping down her cheeks.

"Hey, there…"

Chanelle didn't need to make the quarter turn to see who the approaching footsteps belonged to.

The distracted father/playboy.

"I can't have anyone on my ship looking so sad." He stopped a couple of feet away from her.

Had she heard correctly? *My ship?* No, it couldn't be…

Chanelle quickly wiped her eyes. How embarrassing that he had seen her in such a state. She looked beyond him, expecting to see his wife.

"Has something happened on board to upset you?"

Why did he care? And what could she possibly tell him?

"I—I'm okay," she managed, her voice wavering.

His eyes swooped down on her and narrowed. "No, you're not."

She stared at him, startled by his directness. Something

thudded in her chest. "It's not something I feel comfortable discussing with—"

"A total stranger?" He raised an eyebrow. "Look, you don't need to discuss anything with me. But now that I'm here, I'd like to set the record straight." He took a step closer. "I wasn't trying to come on to you earlier…and seeing someone in tears on a cruise concerns me."

Chanelle looked beyond him again, the butterflies in her stomach rising in a swirl. What would his wife think if she suddenly showed up? She took a step back. "I appreciate your concern, but you don't need to worry about me." Actually, she *didn't* appreciate his concern, but the words had left her mouth before she could stop them.

"The expression on your face worried me." He rested an arm on the railing and glanced at the water before meeting her gaze again. "It was more than sad—it was almost a look of desperation."

Chanelle's eyes widened as his words hit her. *Hard.* "You thought I was going to…" She glanced at the black depths of the bay. She had been momentarily sad, yes, but desperate, no. *No.*

"I would have stopped you," he said huskily. "Or dived in after you, new suit and all."

"You wouldn't have had to." She held up her chin defiantly, trying to prevent herself from gazing at him from the neck down.

His piercing blue eyes had a hawklike intensity, as if he were trying to determine if she was lying. "Good to know." His brow smoothed out. And then his eyes narrowed again. "I don't mean to pry, but if there is a problem between you and your…" He glanced at her ring finger.

It suddenly hit her. He had noticed her engagement ring during their first encounter…

His words struck a nerve. Chanelle bristled. Was this…

this Romeo…actually implying that she was having issues with her fiancé? What business did he have to butt into her life? She felt an inner heat surge through her veins and upward into her cheeks.

"Look, I hate to be blunt, but I don't appreciate you trying to find out if there is a problem in my relationship. It's really none of your business." She felt her cheeks tingle. Usually the precursor to their becoming flaming red. "And if you don't mean to pry, then don't."

"*Touché.* I apologize, Miss…or Ms.…."

She threw him an incredulous glance. Did he not realize that she didn't want to keep talking to him? He just raised his eyebrows and looked as unruffled as she was ruffled. It didn't help that a portion of her brain was registering how good-looking he was in his charcoal-gray suit and salmon-colored shirt and black tie. She heard herself sigh in frustration.

"Chanelle." There! Now maybe he'd go away and leave her alone.

He opened his mouth to respond but closed it when his cell phone buzzed. He retrieved it from his pocket to glance at it. He messaged back and then looked at Chanelle again. She moved away from the railing, and he did the same. Surely he didn't intend to follow her? She was planning to head over to the Ristorante Mezza Luna for dinner, having made reservations at this specialty restaurant when she had booked her cruise, deciding that she deserved to pamper herself.

And after this double encounter with this playboy, Chanelle was anxious to start relaxing. She nodded dismissively and walked toward the glass doors, deciding to freshen up in her stateroom before heading to the restaurant. She saw his reflection and felt her stomach muscles tighten. Inside, the lights of the chandeliers made her blink.

She headed to the elevator, and when she turned, her heart jolted. Vance was striding toward her, but his phone buzzed again and he slowed down to glance at it. Chanelle hurried into the elevator, but before the door closed, she saw him glance up and across at her, his eyes glittering like the chandelier crystals above his head.

Mariah had texted Vance the first time to say that she was almost ready. He had laughed inwardly. His sister's sense of time was faulty at best. "Almost ready" could mean "I need another half hour." But she had surprised him with her second text that she was in the restaurant and had already ordered them drinks.

Vance had messaged her that he needed a few extra minutes.

He glanced at the closed elevator doors before striding over to a recliner near a lounging nook and thought about what had just happened with Chanelle.

Chanelle… What a soft, feminine name. A name fit for an angel, except that there had been nothing angelic about the look she had flung at him.

Why had she appeared so dejected when he had first spotted her? His heart had begun to thump against his rib cage when he had seen her gripping the railing in that isolated corner of the deck… And at the sight of the tears glistening on her cheeks, the thump had turned into a hammer. He had been ready to leap toward her, and then she had turned to look at him…

Relief had swirled through him like an electric current. He had wanted to wrap his arms around her—an irrational impulse, considering he didn't know her, but he couldn't deny that he had felt a surge of protectiveness that had stunned him.

He had immediately noticed that she wasn't wearing her

ring, which was why he had presumed that she and her fiancé had had some kind of disagreement, or maybe even a fight. No wonder she was sad, especially if she was having problems in her relationship. Had she ended the engagement? Had *he*? Vance's jaw tensed at the thought that Chanelle's ex-fiancé might have cheated on her. Maybe that was why she seemed so irritated with *him*. Maybe she was projecting her anger and hurt on him or any other male who crossed her path or even looked at her the wrong way…

But why was this Chanelle taking up so much space in his thoughts? He squeezed his eyes shut for a moment, then relaxed them. Tensed his shoulders, then let go. He did this a few times, and after a few deep breaths, he opened his eyes.

Vance checked the time and sprang to his feet. He had kept Mariah waiting far too long. At the entrance of the Ristorante Mezza Luna, the maître d' greeted him and led him to a far table, where Mariah was already enjoying a glass of white wine and a plate of cheeses and spiced olives. "Sorry I'm late, sis," he said with a rueful smile. He sat down, and after the waiter had filled his glass, he explained what had happened earlier with Chanelle, reassuring Mariah that Adrien had never been in danger. "How is the little munchkin?"

"Adrien's having room service with Mom, then they're going to watch a movie and go to bed early," Mariah said.

Vance nodded and took a drink of his wine.

"Don't look now, Vance!" Mariah lowered her voice to a whisper. "There's the lady who couldn't mind her own business."

Vance set down his wineglass and tried to ignore the skip of his heart beat. "Mariah, I told you, she was just worried—"

"Okay, okay. I can't fault her for that, *Sir Vancelot*."

She chuckled as he rolled his eyes at her childhood nickname for him.

Vance turned casually. Chanelle hadn't spotted him. She was smiling brightly at the maître d' and nodding. She had changed from casual wear to a long magenta skirt with a shimmer of sequins along its flaring hem and a body-hugging black top that accentuated her slender neck and feminine curves. The maître d' led her directly toward the table next to his and Mariah's.

Mariah's phone rang, and Vance could hear that it was his mother's voice on the other end.

Chanelle suddenly stopped walking. Vance met her incredulous gaze. He held up his glass and nodded with a polite smile. It was obvious from the rosy hue of her cheeks that she was flustered to be seated so close to *him*. And Mariah.

Chanelle gave a brief nod and looked away, focusing on what the maître d' was telling her about the wine selections. She murmured her choice, and he nodded. "Certainly, Miss Robinson."

Vance didn't know if it was the wine or the discovery of Chanelle's last name that ignited a shiver of heat inside him. He said it under his breath. Chanelle Robinson. He liked the way it sounded. Soft. Silky. Just like that mane of hair tumbling over her shoulders.

The next time his glance coincided with Chanelle's, he flashed a smile and nodded. Her eyes fluttered briefly, and she responded with a nod that made him think of a robin giving a tentative peck at the grass. Her cheeks were now almost as red as a robin's breast, and the way her arms lifted and then dropped helplessly made it clear to him that if she could fly away, she would.

"Mom says Adrien feels a little warm. Probably too much excitement today," she murmured, arching her eyebrows in Chanelle's direction. "I'm going to check on him. If he's okay, I'll meet you in the theater."

Vance stood up and met Chanelle's eyes. Even in the dimmed lighting of the restaurant, they were stunning, their green-hazel depths looking like a mystical pool from an enchanted land.

"I hope you're enjoying Mezza Luna's fine offerings, Miss—Chanelle," he said as they approached her table. He gave her a casual smile. "Oh, and please allow me to introduce you. Chanelle Robinson, this is Mariah Kingston… my sister."

CHAPTER THREE

CHANELLE STRUGGLED TO keep her surprise in check. *His sister?* And how did he know her last name? Oh, yes, the maître d' had said it…

Feeling awkward at the realization that she was just blinking back at him, Chanelle turned and offered a tentative smile to his sister.

Mariah held out her elegantly manicured hand. "Nice to meet you. *Again.*" She blew her brother a kiss. "I'm going to go and check on Mom and Adrien and then head to the Milky Way Theater. See you in a bit, *Sir Vancelot.*"

Chanelle watched her leave, a petite swirl of pink silk and ivory linen above shapely legs and stiletto heels that Chanelle wouldn't hazard to wear. When she had walked into the restaurant and had caught sight of Mariah sitting across from Vance, something in Chanelle's chest had deflated, and she had considered making an excuse to the maître d' and filing out of the restaurant. The last thing Chanelle had counted on was bumping into the both of them so soon after the earlier incident…

Discovering that the lady he was with was his sister and not his wife had caused a thumping against her rib cage that almost made her look down at her chest self-consciously.

Vance put his hand on the chair opposite her. "May I?" he said, his blue eyes appearing more like indigo in the muted light of the restaurant.

"Um…" She glanced from him to the waiter. "Okay," she replied slowly, irritated both by his question and by the way her pulse had spiked.

How could she tell him, with the waiter standing right there, that she had been looking forward to a quiet dinner?

Despite feeling flustered, Chanelle couldn't help thinking how drop-dead gorgeous he looked in his gray suit with the salmon-colored shirt making a striking contrast with the extraordinary purple-blue of his eyes. They reminded her of the rich hue of the delphiniums in her summer garden.

"Will you be joining Miss Robinson for a glass of white wine, sir?" the waiter asked Vance, naming the vintage she had selected.

Vance nodded his approval. "I could tell you were a woman of good taste," he said, flashing Chanelle a smile. "May I join you?"

Chanelle hesitated before giving a curt nod.

Vance turned his gaze back to the waiter. "Put it on my tab, Luciano."

Chanelle gazed from one to the other and opened her mouth to protest, but Vance put up his hand firmly. "That wasn't necessary, Mr.…Vance," she said when the waiter had left.

"No it wasn't, Miss *Chanelle*." He leaned forward. "It's just my way of thanking you for looking out for Adrien."

Chanelle frowned. "You weren't too pleased about me getting involved earlier."

He clasped his hands under his chin and gazed at her squarely. "I admit I may have overreacted." His eyes glinted. "I'm sorry. Can you find it in your heart to forgive me?"

Chanelle was at a loss for words. From the slightly amused tone of his voice, she didn't know whether he was being genuine or mocking her. And at the same time, she was trying to process the fact that he wasn't married after all, that Adrien was his nephew, and that his earlier offer of buying her a drink wasn't the act of an unfaithful womanizer.

Which meant that she had overreacted as well.

So maybe you should apologize, too, her inner voice suggested. *And if this hunk wants to treat you, let him! You have a choice—you can tell him to take a flying leap, or let him spend his money on you... Live a little!. And if he flirts with you, give it back to him. You've forgotten how to have fun, girl!*

As she framed some words of apology in her mind, the waiter reappeared with the wine. Vance tasted and approved a sample and nodded for the waiter to fill their two glasses. He held his glass up and waited for Chanelle to clink hers with his, but she ignored his cue and went ahead and took a sip.

"Mmm..." Chanelle closed her eyes momentarily, unable to control a little shiver. She was entering into unknown waters, she warned herself. She felt her nerve endings tingle and realized she could either take this opportunity to enjoy the cruise, or leave it...

The excitement stirring in her stomach gave her the answer. She wasn't going to mope around anymore. She was going to loosen up a little. She had always been too serious growing up and had proceeded with caution in every aspect of her life, even when she had left home. Chanelle breathed in deeply, her chest expanding, and she felt like a Sagittarian warrior, ready to rise up to anything or anyone. Especially one like the Dionysus sitting across from her, twirling his wineglass with a gleam in his bewitching blue eyes.

Vance looked at Chanelle as the waiter asked her if she had decided on her entrée. She chose a seafood risotto, and

Vance decided to order the same for himself. "Excellent choice, Chanelle. It's one of my favorites," he said after the waiter had left. Chanelle paused, her eyes widening as if she had just realized that he was not going to be leaving after he finished his wine. And the slight flutter of those long lashes made him wonder how she was feeling about that…

"This is even better than the wine I had in my room." Chanelle's words came out in a rush. "And I thought that one was superb. I must say I'm impressed with the perks on this cruise. The complimentary gift basket was such a lovely surprise, with the scrumptious chocolates and all those other goodies." She flashed him a smile before taking another generous sip of wine, her eyes a combination of amber and emerald as they blinked at him above the rim of her glass.

Vance certainly hadn't expected this…this about-face. But then maybe Chanelle was trying to drown her sorrows, the sorrows of a broken relationship…

"Cheers, *Sir Vancelot*," she said with a tinkling laugh as she raised her glass and cocked her head at him, her hair cascading down like a shimmering curtain. His heart did a flip, and he had to stop himself from extending his hand to let her rest her head against it.

Vance gazed at Chanelle's flushed cheeks and long eyelashes. He had no illusions that they were fluttering for *his* benefit, yet he couldn't help being mesmerized by their languorous movements, allowing him glimpses of the heady hazel depths of her eyes.

He coughed, and feigned a frown. "Now don't *you* go calling me by that silly name, Chanelle. My sister likes to torment me occasionally with it, with maybe just a *little* less frequency than when we were kids and playing with my medieval castle." His eyes narrowed. "I'm neither a sir nor a chivalrous knight."

Chanelle gave him a shy smile that made his stomach muscles contract. "You were ready to rescue me earlier… That proves you're chivalrous." She averted her gaze to help herself to an olive and immediately exclaimed at its spiciness. She ran her tongue over her lips and fanned them with her hand.

As Vance watched her mouth, a spiral of heat flicked throughout his body. The waiter set down their plates, and after thanking him, Chanelle gave a self-conscious shrug and dug into her risotto. Vance suppressed a smile. It was refreshing to see a woman enjoy food, unlike a couple of the willowy high-fashion models he had dated who had pretended to be happy with a few pieces of lettuce and a couple of carrot sticks.

"Are you a pescatarian?" he wondered aloud.

"No. I just stay away from red meat."

"So no bacon for you."

"I'm into *baking*, not bacon." She laughed, lifting her wineglass to her lips.

He grinned. "Since you've ventured into the world of puns, perhaps you should consider a job in comedy…"

The humor suddenly disappeared from Chanelle's face. Her eyelids fluttered briefly, and she stared down at her plate. He saw her jaw muscles flexing. When she looked back up, her eyes were glistening.

Vance set down his glass. "I'm sorry, Chanelle. Did I say something wrong?"

She put her fork down. "No, I'm… I'm…" She shook her head. "I'm just a little down about my job." She cocked her head at him as if she were trying to ascertain whether she could trust him to tell him more.

"It's a tough job," he said gently. "Dealing with vulnerable children and harsh situations day in and day out. I can only imagine—"

"I thought I would last longer than this…"

"You left?"

"I'm on a leave. Burnout." She sighed. "I love kids, I love seeing bad situations turn out for the better, but it hasn't always worked out that way…and it has affected me off the job as well."

"You're only human." He controlled his impulse to reach out and tap her reassuringly on her arm. "It's obvious you care, and with your background, it's no wonder you were alarmed when you saw Adrien on that chair. Your devotion to children is admirable," he added softly.

"I'm too devoted, according to my fiancé." She bit her lower lip and leaned back. "I mean my ex-fiancé. He broke off our engagement."

"I'm sorry to hear that," he murmured. "You've been through a lot."

"I have to take some of the responsibility," she said, her mouth twisting. "I spent too much time working."

And her fiancé hadn't liked it.

Vance watched as Chanelle slumped forward, her chin resting in one hand. Her earlier levity was gone, and he suspected the wine might have had something to do with her shift in emotions. He couldn't imagine her spilling all this personal stuff to him otherwise.

He glanced at his watch and sprang out of his seat. "I'm sorry to cut this short, Chanelle, but I have to be somewhere else. Five minutes ago, actually," he added ruefully. "I'll let you enjoy your dessert in peace. By the way, will you be catching the opening night's performance in the Milky Way Theater?"

"I—I…maybe," she said cautiously before picking up her fork again to dig into her risotto.

"Okay then," he said slowly, nodding. "Maybe I'll see you there. *Arrivederci.*"

Vance glanced at her left hand. He was about to add something and then decided against it. Feeling a strange tug in his stomach muscles, he rose and left.

Vance sprinted toward the theater. He had been totally absorbed—*distracted*—with Chanelle Robinson. Thank goodness he had looked at his watch or he would have been inexcusably late, missing his cue to address the guests on this special cruise.

In five minutes, the cruise director would be welcoming the crowd, then he'd be introducing him, and Vance would share the reason he and his family were on board the *Aquarius*. They had decided to keep it from the media and had simply wanted to have a relatively small celebration of Vance's official position as president. They had decided on a five-day cruise just to relax, mingle with their invited guests—who had promised to keep the event under wraps—and have a gala evening midweek, when Vance's mother would announce her retirement and formally pass over the business to Vance.

The uninvited guests were in for a surprise, for the gala would be open to them also, in appreciation for their patronage and, for some, their loyalty in returning to Zodiac Cruises for a holiday. In fact, what seemed to be trending was for Zodiac faithfuls to book a different Zodiac ship each time they cruised. Vance had already met a group of nine forty-something women who had already cruised on four of the ships in the fleet. They had been friends since high school, and although they didn't all live in the same town, they reunited every year for their one-week cruise.

Vance had smiled at them earlier in the lobby of the art gallery. As he had strolled by, he had heard one of them whisper, "He doesn't have a ring. He must be unattached…" And one of her friends had chortled. "Lucky gal who gets to attach themselves to *that*. I'll be having sweet dreams tonight…and of course, *I'll* be the lucky gal." And at the resounding laughter, he had stifled a chuckle and had gone to chat with the art rep.

Now, entering the slightly dimmed theater, Vance looked around. Spotting Mariah, he made his way to the third row in the orchestra section. Mariah smiled at him and continued checking her messages on her cell phone. Vance sat back and thought about what the ladies had said.

"He must be unattached."

Well, they were right. For the most part. At the moment he was not seeing anyone. His last relationship had fizzled out after his father had died. Brianna was a wealthy socialite his mother had invited over one night, someone she had thought might be a good match for Vance. They had seen each other for several months, but Vance hadn't been ready for a serious commitment, and Brianna *had*.

If she had been the right one, wouldn't he have wanted to settle down?

His mother had hinted more than once—and not too subtly—that perhaps he should start trying to find someone who could become more permanent in his life. He was thirty-four, after all, and didn't he get tired of dating one beautiful woman after another? Vance smirked at the memory of the comment she had made once—that he changed women as often as he changed cars.

"You're not getting any younger, son, and neither am I. I don't expect to have grandchildren when I'm too old to be able to lift them. Or play with them."

Occasionally she had taken a sterner approach, pinning him with her steel-blue eyes.

"You can't be a playboy all your life, Vance. It's time to get serious…serious about settling down."

Vance had instinctively known that his mother had felt responsible for indulging him and his sister in all ways.

They had grown up spoiled and entitled, he had heard her complain to his father, and now they expected that lifestyle to continue.

Especially Vance. At least Mariah had married and blessed her with a grandson. She could be high-maintenance at times, but being a parent had tamed her somewhat. Now Vance, on the other hand…

A week after his mother had voiced her concerns, his father had died. And the lifestyle Vance had known had come abruptly to a halt. There were matters to take care of, both personal and business, and his mother had been too distraught to deal with any of them. It had been left to Vance to make the funeral arrangements and to be the strong shoulder for both his mother and sister.

Brianna had expressed sympathy, but she was used to a certain pace in her life, and she had expected Vance to keep up with her high-profile social events and private parties a few weeks after the funeral.

But the passing of his father had taken the desire for partying right out of Vance. The immensity of his father's responsibilities and the esteem in which his business associates had held him had made Vance acutely aware that *his* involvement in the company had been peripheral at best. And when it had been time for the last goodbyes, and his mother, sister, brother-in-law and nephew had walked away, Vance had stayed behind to quietly reiterate the vow he had failed to make to his father before he died.

Soon after, when he had told Brianna about his intentions and that he couldn't make a firm commitment, Brianna had skipped out of his life.

Vance checked the time on his phone. One minute before the show… He glanced at Mariah and saw that she was texting her husband, who hadn't been able to join them on the cruise, as he was tending to business in Europe.

Vance glanced around and was pleased to see that the theater was filling quickly. His eyes narrowed as he searched the moving groups for a sign of Chanelle. And then he checked himself.

Why did he even care if she attended the opening or not?

The orchestra started up, and a minute later, cruise director Jake Ross walked out on stage. At his cue, Vance strode to the side door that led to the stage and waited for Jake's intro. Jake warmed up the audience with his jokes and stories about funny experiences onboard, and when the laughter had subsided, his tone became more serious.

"Ladies and gentlemen, I have the distinct pleasure of welcoming you to the *Aquarius* and to our opening night show here in the beautiful Milky Way Theater. You are in for a few surprises this week, starting with the man you are going to meet shortly. He is someone who has taken on the monumental task of leadership of Zodiac Cruises these past nine months since the passing of Mr. Bruce Kingston— Zodiac's founder and president—proving with his unreserved determination, razor-sharp focus and relentless efforts and inexhaustible energy that he has everything it takes not only to continue in his father's fine footsteps, but to leap beyond. He will reveal his vision for the company during this cruise, and I am sure that you will be as excited as the staff of the *Aquarius* and of the entire fleet of Zodiac Cruise ships to hear about his initiatives and to celebrate during this special cruise." He turned toward his right and extended a hand. "And now, please join me in welcoming Mr. Vance Kingston, acting president and co-owner of Zodiac Cruises!"

Vance stepped out to a resounding applause. He was moved by Jake's words and the crowd's enthusiasm, and after thanking them for their presence and participation in

a Zodiac cruise, he explained why he was there, and what
they would be in for.

At the loud cheers of approval and whistles, he gave a
bow, and when he raised his head, his gaze landed on a
guest who was just sitting down on the far end of a middle
row in the right-hand section of the theater.

Chanelle...

Had she arrived in time to hear him from the beginning?
He pulled his gaze away from her. Ordinarily, he had no
problem addressing a large crowd, but somehow, knowing
she was there, he suddenly felt awkward. He hadn't told
her anything about himself, and he couldn't help wondering if she'd be feeling awkward as well when she realized
who he was.

He finished up his address and thanked the audience
again. His gaze swept casually over the crowd, and for a
few seconds, Chanelle seemed to be looking straight at
him. As the orchestra started up with a musical number
that would take the audience through decades of Broadway
theater productions, Vance strode off the stage, the cue for
the *Aquarius* dancers to appear.

He and Mariah had chosen seats near the front on the
left-hand section of the theater. Vance was too far away
from where Chanelle was sitting to even get a glimpse of
her. As he sat down, he exchanged smiles with Mariah,
who squeezed his arm in approval. The chandeliers were
dimmed, and the dancers burst onto the stage in a swirl
of sequins, lights and music. Vance sat back in the plush
seat to take in the spectacular opening, but as the dancers
spun past, it was a pair of hazel-green eyes that danced
before him…

CHAPTER FOUR

CHANELLE HAD ALMOST made up her mind to call it an early night after her dinner and go back to her stateroom. She knew that she had indulged in more wine than usual, and she had been aware that her responses to Vance had been less careful as a result. It made her cringe to think of how she had giggled and made a ridiculous remark about him being chivalrous. And how she had called him Sir Vancelot. And if that wasn't bad enough, she had nattered on about her job and her past.

By the time she had finished the restaurant's signature tiramisu, Chanelle had felt like she could easily go straight to bed. Her appetite had been quelled in the most decadent way, and the rich food and the wine had made her quite mellow. The restaurant had almost filled to capacity and the alternating levels of voices had started to become overwhelming.

She had been wondering whether she could handle sitting for over an hour in the Milky Way Theater when her eyes had started to droop. It had been an emotional day in more ways than one, and she had debated whether she could even take the sensory stimulation of the opening night performance when all she wanted to do was lie on her bed with the balcony door open and listen to the relaxing sound of the waves…

But Vance Kingston will be there, remember?

Chanelle had smiled and thanked the waiter. As she had walked out, the image of Vance's inky-blue eyes as he had said earlier, "Maybe I'll see you there," had made her stop in her tracks. It might have been a totally casual statement, but the thought of encountering Vance again had made her heartbeat quicken, even if he'd be there with his sister.

Why was he on this cruise with his family? Was it a special birthday for his mother? Chanelle had wondered if she'd get the chance to find out more about Vance on the cruise.

She had kept walking, her steps suddenly lighter, her drowsiness gone. Outside the restaurant, she had checked the time. The show had started at nine, and she had already missed ten minutes. But a glance toward the theater doors had confirmed that people were still filing in. She had heard laughter from the audience, and the thought had occurred to her that it might do her a world of good to laugh, especially after spending the last few months dealing with the reality of job burnout and, a couple of months before that, her broken engagement with Parker.

Chanelle's counselor had encouraged her to find opportunities to lighten up her life with events that would bring her joy and laughter. She needed to balance her life, have more fun…

At the next peal of laughter, Chanelle had ignored the voice in her head that told her it had been a long day and she should just go to bed. She had followed a family into the theater and spotted an empty aisle seat to her right.

Settling in her seat, she had caught the last few minutes of the cruise director's comedy routine before he began his announcement. She had started at the mention of Mr. Bruce Kingston, and a few moments later, felt a greater jolt at hearing the name of Vance Kingston, "acting president and co-owner of Zodiac Cruises." Her gaze had riveted to the man walking across the stage.

Her Vance?

What a ridiculous thought. He was not *her* Vance. But he *was* co-owner of the cruise line. She had felt a flutter in her chest as she recalled his earlier words: *"I can't have anyone on my ship looking so sad..."* So she *had* heard correctly.

Chanelle had joined the rest of the audience in clapping their welcome, and when the noise had subsided, she could hear the thumping of her heart against her ribs. Even from a distance, the way he had looked in his tailored suit had caused her to draw in her breath, and her cheeks had flamed at the tingling that had begun navigating throughout her nerve pathways.

Three women in the row ahead of her had nudged each other and exchanged whispers about the "hunky owner" of the cruise line. Chanelle had difficulty trying to listen to Vance while overhearing descriptions about his sexy attributes.

She had been relieved when they had stopped their chatter and focused on what Vance was saying, allowing her to focus as well. She had listened to his deep voice welcoming the crowd, thanking them for having selected Zodiac Cruises for the very first time or for their loyalty in returning.

He had proceeded to give a summary of his father's vision and accomplishments, and then his voice had wavered for a moment when he declared that his focus was to keep his father's company thriving. As the audience responded with enthusiastic applause, Vance had scanned the theater with an intensity that made Chanelle's insides flip. Could he be searching for *her* in the crowd? she had mused. He *had* said, "Maybe I'll see you there…"

She had shaken her head at her silly presumption. Vance

Kingston was for all intents and purposes *president* of the cruise line. He had obviously just been showing her the courtesy he would have displayed to anyone else on the ship. But after her embarrassing behavior in the restaurant, she'd vowed to make every effort to avoid him.

And then she had frozen. For a moment, it had looked like Vance was staring right at her, and the applause and people around her had became muted as she held her breath at the possibility... And then he had shifted his gaze and continued speaking. He had promised the audience that they were in for some special perks and surprises on this particular cruise, and that the cruise director would keep them informed every day of what was happening, along with the daily bulletin they would be receiving.

Finally, Vance had thanked them again, told them to enjoy the opening show and, flashing the crowd a smile that elicited a couple of whistles, had walked off the stage.

Vance was nowhere to be seen as the crowd exited the theater, and Chanelle had to admit to herself that despite her vow to avoid him, she felt a little disappointed. She returned to her stateroom and had a quick shower, her earlier drowsiness completely gone. While her hair was drying, she searched online to see what she could find out about Vance Kingston. Chanelle discovered that he had been a person of interest in the world of the elite for quite a while, frequenting exotic locales and attending high-profile events— dealing with art, cars and entertainment—that attracted the rich and famous, many of them women.

Some of the headlines had proclaimed him to be one of Canada's most eligible bachelors, not only ruggedly handsome, but easygoing and extravagant, indulging in a variety of interests and activities all over the country. One week he'd be seen skiing in Whistler, British Columbia, among

Hollywood celebrities, and the next he'd be at some posh literary or art event in Toronto or at Montreal's jazz festival. From the look of any one of the women in his company, it was obvious that they were happy to share the spotlight with him.

After checking more recent sites, Chanelle learned that Vance Kingston had been employed as head of acquisitions at an art gallery in Toronto's Distillery District until the death of his father nine months earlier. Recent articles described him as almost reclusive now, totally focused on carrying on the family business.

Chanelle turned off her cell phone and ventured out on the balcony. She stared down at the water, swirling and cresting and catching the light of the moon in shiny arcs and squiggles. She could have stayed there longer, but her common sense reminded her that a good night's rest had been what her doctor and counselor had recommended.

Lying under the bedsheets with her balcony door partially open, Chanelle listened to the slurping water sounds and thought about the opening night show by the *Aquarius* singers and dancers. It had been spectacular and as dazzling as a top-rated Vegas show. But the image that kept returning to her mind was that of Vance Kingston. The way he had sounded, his voice velvet smooth. And the way he had looked, tall and male-model gorgeous, his golden-brown hair glinting under the spotlight. Flashing that killer smile at the audience that had made her stomach flip and scanning the crowd with brilliant blue eyes that she knew could change like the waves.

Seeing Vance up on that stage had been the first shock, and learning that he was soon to be the official president of Zodiac Cruises had been the second. The memory of him in that tailored suit and the sensual thrum of his voice as he had addressed the audience ignited a tingle throughout her body.

Although it was a balmy night, Chanelle shivered and pulled up the covers. She nestled into a side position, sinking into the comfortable pillow with a sigh. There *had* been a lot of pulsating lights and energetic musical numbers, but she had left the theater less affected by the overstimulation than she had expected. *And more affected by Vance Kingston.*

Chanelle had hoped for a relaxing holiday where she could shake off some of the built-up stress of the past and try to come up with a plan for the future. She *had to* make a decision where work was concerned. She couldn't remain on a leave indefinitely. Getting away on a cruise had seemed like the perfect opportunity to resolve the issue of whether to return as a front-line child protection worker or to seek work in an area that wouldn't consume so much of her time and energy.

But how relaxing could this cruise be, knowing that she might cross paths at any time with Vance Kingston? Would he be dining at the same restaurant? Swimming in one of the pools? Catching the nightly shows? And what about the gala? Surely he must have a special somebody in his life who would be here to celebrate his new position with him and his family?

So what? an inner voice interrupted her thoughts. *Why wouldn't you be able to relax? Just because he treated you to some wine doesn't mean he's going to seek you out again.*

And why would he? With his family onboard, and probably a group of close friends and associates, he would hardly be intending to pursue *her.* For conversation or otherwise.

Chanelle felt her eyelids getting heavy. She wondered what it would be like to be pursued by Vance Kingston. And then she immediately chastised herself for having such a hare-brained thought. She had other things to deal with now instead of indulging in a ridiculous fantasy about the president of Zodiac Cruises.

She was not interested in anybody pursuing her.

Not. Interested.

The last thing she wanted was to be embroiled in a relationship.

Chanelle exhaled noisily. What a ridiculous notion she had had earlier, that of encouraging herself to flirt with Vance Kingston. The wine had been to blame for that. It had addled her brain, loosened her tongue, and of all the people who could have witnessed her temporary lapse of sanity, it had to have been the *president* of Zodiac Cruises.

She closed her eyes and scrunched them tight before releasing the tension, willing the image of cobalt-blue eyes to disappear from her mind.

Vance tossed his jacket onto his couch and loosened his tie. He ran his fingers through his hair. He was happy with the success of the opening night show, but he would have been even happier if, after the show, he had been able to speak with—

He stopped himself. What was he thinking? Just because he had spent some time with Chanelle Robinson before the show didn't mean that he needed to connect with her afterwards. He gave a curt laugh and shook his head before heading to the shower. He had other things to think about, like the upcoming gala.

Mariah had brought up the subject as he was walking her to her stateroom after the show. She had glanced at him speculatively and said she was surprised that he hadn't invited "anyone special" to accompany him on the cruise.

"Currently, there are no contenders in that position," he had replied wryly, raising an eyebrow. "Taking over for Dad has been my priority… And even if I wanted to, there's no time."

"Mom said that Brianna phoned the house the other day. She said she hadn't been able to reach you on your cell."

"I don't have time for Brianna," he had replied dismissively. "Or her universe." He had had no problem inhabiting her universe in the past, but somehow, he had no inclination to get caught up in it again.

In the shower, Vance let the streams of water relax his shoulder and back muscles. Thoughts of Brianna dissipated as frames of Chanelle flicked through his mind like a slideshow: Chanelle reaching for Adrien, her brow creased in alarm; the way she had cocked her head and smiled at him when she called him Sir Vancelot; the flicker of genuine concern in her eyes when she talked about her line of work; the look of her walking into the restaurant with that curve-hugging black top and magenta skirt that matched the color of her lips exactly; and—

He groaned. Chanelle was a witch, she had to be, to have put some kind of spell over him that had her appearing in front of his eyes even when she wasn't there. *Damn!* He had vowed that he wouldn't let women distract him from what he needed to accomplish at Zodiac Cruises… There was too much at stake, especially his self-respect. He had made a promise to himself, and he had every intention of keeping it.

And for the past nine months, he had succeeded. After Brianna, there had been no one. Oh, he had been all too aware that there were women who still had hopes when it came to winning his favor, but he had not succumbed to their discreet and not-so-discreet invitations.

Despite the fact that he had sometimes felt tempted…

He knew it was guilt over his lack of involvement in the business before his father had passed away that had something to do with it. *Everything* to do with it. And his failure to make a deathbed promise to his father to take over the business. Yes, guilt had put a giant wedge between him and any thoughts of involvement with another woman.

Vance stepped out of the shower, briskly towel dried his hair and wrapped the towel around his hips. He sauntered over to his minibar and extracted a bottle of ice wine. He poured himself a small glass and walked out to his balcony.

Was Chanelle out on hers? Or sleeping?

An image of her lying on the bed with her lustrous hair spread across the pillow sent a shiver through him. Vance finished the wine and went back inside.

He replaced the towel with a robe and stretched out on his bed, his hands cradling the back of his neck. There was something that made Chanelle Robinson different from the women he had dated in the past.

She's not into herself, he realized with a start. She was *real.* No artifice or pretensions. No glossy manicure or designer clothes. Not that there was anything wrong with a glossy manicure or designer clothes. In his experience, it was the *attitude* that sometimes accompanied them that was pretentious.

And Vance hadn't detected any of that kind of attitude from Chanelle. She seemed down-to-earth, and it was obvious she had been dedicated to her job. He frowned as he pictured her walking into a home and having to remove the children because of neglect or worse. Having to deal with belligerent parents…

Vance breathed in sharply. Had Chanelle ever been in danger? A spiral of anger shot through his veins, quickly followed by that surge of protectiveness again. With a groan, he vaulted off the bed. There was no use even attempting to turn off his thoughts and go to sleep. He glanced at the clock. Not quite eleven o'clock.

He considered running around the track on the upper deck and then changed his mind. He tried reading a book, but his mind kept wandering. Frustrated, he put the book down, flung off his robe and slid between the cool sheets of his bed. With a deep sigh, he allowed thoughts of Chanelle to slip in beside him…

CHAPTER FIVE

WHEN CHANELLE WOKE UP, her eyes followed the light to the balcony. This was their first at-sea day, and all that was visible were water, clouds and sky. The clouds were low and tinged pink and coral. So pretty… The sun was just rising, a hazy golden orb veiled by the shifting clouds. Chanelle slid open the door wider and stepped onto the balcony. She stood by the railing, breathing the fresh air and watching the clouds' transformations.

She went back inside and changed into a mint-green swimsuit, deciding to do a few laps in the pool before breakfast. Now that she couldn't use work as an excuse not to exercise, she could invest some time in the physical fitness department. And she rather relished the thought of having the pool to herself. She didn't imagine too many people would be there this early, including…

Chanelle felt her cheeks prickling with heat at the thought of Vance Kingston doing laps in the pool alongside her, his muscular arms and chest—

Stop! She frowned at herself in the mirror. "You, Chanelle Robinson—" she pointed an accusing finger "—are pathetic, daydreaming about the president of Zodiac Cruises. Pathetic and ridiculous."

She stuck her tongue out at herself and, after tying her hair up in a ponytail, put on a peach-colored cover-up.

Grabbing her beach bag and towel, Chanelle headed to the pool on Deck Twelve.

The view at this height was enchanting, and for a moment, she stood at the railing, absorbed in the gentle collision of pink and saffron clouds as they floated across the horizon. She could do this all day, she mused. *This* was relaxation. And she had had too little of it for ages.

The pool water was balmy, and Chanelle floated for a while, eyes closed, concentrating on the delicious feeling of weightlessness. She would definitely have to make this an early-morning ritual.

Breaking into a front stroke, she swam the length of the pool and back six times. After rinsing off, she briskly dried herself with the oversized towel and stretched out on her chaise lounge. She would read for a bit, and then she'd go and shower and dress before heading to the Galaxy Café for breakfast.

Chanelle felt her eyelids getting heavier as she was reading. Despite the comfort of her king-size bed, she'd had a fitful sleep, waking two or three times during the night. Turning the book over onto her lap, she let herself drift off, lulled by the water gushing out of the nearby fountain—an Aquarius water bearer…

Vance had always enjoyed working out in the gym first thing in the morning. Besides keeping him fit, it helped him work out his feelings. Whatever frustrations he had had about his father, by the time he had bench-pressed two hundred pounds or sweated through countless repetitions of weight-lifting exercises, his pent-up emotions had been released, if not completely resolved.

His father had been a workaholic. He had spent his energy on building his company, and he had made a fortune with twelve ships in the fleet, each one carrying the name of a zodiac sign. Zodiac ships were not the largest of cruise ships, but they had the reputation of being among the most luxurious. The first ship to sail had been this one, the *Aquarius*, named after Vance's sign.

Immersed in the growth of his company, his dad had left the rearing of his children to his wife, who had joined him in running the company only after the kids were in school. Vance had grown up missing a father at school concerts, basketball games and tournaments, and sometimes at family holidays and special occasions. Like his birthday. And graduation.

Vance had vowed that he would never become like him. His disdain had manifested in teenage rebellion whenever his father had shown up, and he and his father had clashed incessantly. The more his dad had gotten on his case, the more Vance had acted in outrageous ways.

Like buying himself a Harley when he was eighteen and literally zooming off into the sunset with a motorcycle gang. Not a nefarious gang, just a bunch of wild and moderately rebellious guys like him. They had raced their way west across the Trans-Canada Highway, enjoying the commotion they caused entering every quiet little town or bar. They had especially liked the attention of groups of women in these locales.

They had happened to end up in Alberta just in time for the Calgary Stampede. They had arrived at the beginning of the annual ten-day festival in July and had enthusiastically joined the cowboy and Western-themed party that attracted over a million visitors every year. They had bought themselves cowboy hats and had whooped it up at the rodeos, parades, concerts and chuck wagon competitions. They had taken their fill of pancake breakfasts, barbecues and gorgeous cowgirls in sexy hats, formfitting jeans and pointy leather boots.

Vance had returned to Toronto with two souvenirs, his cowboy hat and an Aquarius tattoo on his upper back. His father had been none too pleased. He had accused Vance of being a spoiled, ungrateful son, worrying his mother half to death and wasting *his* hard-earned money instead of doing something useful, like working his way up in the company.

He *had been* spoiled. Had spent money without much thought. He had taken luxury for granted, having never known anything but fine food, designer clothes, flashy cars and no shortage of women who appreciated such finery.

Though his adventures with motorcycles had eventually waned, Vance had still wanted to travel. Over the last ten years, he had grown accustomed to visiting exotic locations on a whim and acquiring real estate in Canada—an artist's retreat on Salt Spring Island off the West Coast and a spectacular saltbox house in Newfoundland's Conception Bay. His other home away from home was Coral Haven, the island in the Caribbean that his parents had purchased and where they had built a luxurious villa. The island was uninhabited except for the people employed to travel back and forth from Grand Cayman to keep the villa maintained and prepared for the family's visits.

He was looking forward to spending time at Coral Haven during this cruise. While guests enjoyed the excursion to Grand Cayman, he and his family would spend the day at their villa.

After his strenuous workout, Vance was ready for a refreshing dip in the pool, located on the same deck. As the invigoratingly cool water splashed over his heated face and body in the pre-pool shower, he glimpsed a figure on one of the chaise lounges.

He squinted and diverted his head from the spray of water. He could see the woman better now: her long, curvy legs, a book overturned on her right thigh, her silky mint-

green swimsuit with a flounce ruffle top, wet from her recent swim. Her eyes were obscured by ridiculously large
sunglasses, but the ribbons of auburn hair flanking the
curves of her face gave her identity away.

Vance felt a drumming in his chest. The *Aquarius* was
not a small ship, yet it seemed that at every turn, he was
practically bumping into Chanelle Robinson. Vance strode
to the deep end and dived into the pool. When he surfaced,
he shook his head and glanced toward Chanelle, but she
hadn't budged. He began his laps and tried to concentrate
on his strokes, but every time he approached the end of
the pool near the spot where Chanelle was, his heartbeat
seemed to accelerate.

When Vance hauled himself out of the pool, he was
surprised to see Chanelle was still sleeping. Her oversized
sunglasses had slipped crookedly down her nose, and her
shifting had caused her book to tumble over the chaise
lounge onto the floor. He toweled himself quickly and sauntered over to pick up the book with the intention of placing
it on the corner of her chaise, when he noticed her stateroom key card at the foot of her chaise. He couldn't help
glancing at the number on it.

Chanelle gave a sudden vigorous stretch, catching him
soundly on his backside with the back of her hand. He swiv-
eled and met the startled and blinking green eyes that he
was beginning to know so well…

CHAPTER SIX

CHANELLE STARED. WHAT was Vance Kingston doing, standing there wearing nothing but his swim trunks and holding her book in his hand? And standing so close that she had whacked him in the rear? Had he been watching her as she slept?

She was mortified, irritated and embarrassed all at once. The last thing—or person—she had expected to see was *him*. Like *this*. Her eyes swept upward past his trim waist, muscled chest and arms and broad shoulders. And disturbingly amused turquoise eyes.

She straightened in her chaise and pulled off her sunglasses. "Excuse me?" she said pointedly.

"Shouldn't that be a statement instead of a question?" he said with a crooked half smile.

Chanelle gaped at him.

"I mean, I don't know if it was intentional, but your backhand was quite forceful. I'm afraid there might be some bruising…" He patted his backside gingerly and made a grimace.

"It was *not* intentional," she said defensively. "Your rear just happened to be in the way."

She frowned. "Why *were* you in the way?" She stared at the book he still held in his hands. "I can't imagine it was because you wanted to borrow my book."

Vance glanced at the cover of the paperback, and Chanelle wished she hadn't brought attention to it. It featured a blue-eyed frontiersman clasping a brown-eyed heroine with windswept hair by her scarlet-corseted waist. Chanelle felt currents of heat sizzling through her, making her cheeks feel as fiery as the dress on the cover.

"I hadn't intended to." He checked out the back cover and then gazed back at her. "I saw it had fallen, and I was just about to carry out my one good deed of the day and pick it up." Vance's eyes seemed to twinkle at her. "But maybe you can lend it to me once you're finished." He handed it to her. "*If* you think I'll enjoy it."

Chanelle took it and placed it on her chaise. He was teasing her, of course. Or mocking her. She doubted that he was the type to read historical romances. In any case, she was at a loss as to how to answer him.

And at a disadvantage, with him practically standing over her. Chanelle wished she had put on her cover-up. Despite the fact that her swimsuit was a one-piece, she still felt rather exposed, and the tingly sensations within her were causing her to shiver uncontrollably, making her even more self-conscious. She quickly crossed her arms in front of her.

Chanelle heard approaching voices and looked past Vance's shoulder. A family of five was making its way toward the pool attendant. Vance followed her glance. "Time for me to go." He grinned. "Enjoy your book." He turned and strode toward the entrance leading to the elevator foyer. Chanelle's gaze leaped to his broad back, where a tattoo in various blues was splayed on his upper right side. A stylistic double wave design with a realistic-looking splash of water curving below. The same astrological sign as the ship. *Aquarius.* Unable to divert her gaze, she watched the movement of his arm and back muscles until Vance disappeared around a corner.

Chanelle blinked and swallowed and realized she hadn't answered him.

* * *

After her shower, Chanelle changed into a pair of navy capri pants and a sleeveless red-and-white-striped top and sat on the balcony to check her phone messages while her hair dried. Her mother had messaged.

Enjoy, relax and pamper yourself, my darling girl. No one deserves it more than you! Love you!

And her stepdad.

Be well, Chanelle my belle, and contact me day or night if you need to, okay, sweetheart? By the way, I'm bringing back a cuddly friend for you... Love you lots!

And he had attached a photo of himself holding a plush koala bear.

Chanelle smiled and then almost immediately felt a wave of sadness engulf her. It was moments like these when she missed her family terribly and felt so alone... As she stared out at the brightening sky, she felt the prickle at the back of her eyes intensify, and a moment later, tears began to trickle down her cheeks.

She *was* alone. Alone with her fears for the future.

Would she be able to return to her job? The work conditions wouldn't change; *she'd* have to change, or she'd end up in the same boat. Chanelle groaned at the unintentional pun, wiped her eyes and strode to the door. *Stop feeling sorry for yourself,* her inner voice chided. *Get out there and start enjoying this cruise!* Chanelle took a deep breath, tossed her hair back and decided to do just that, starting off with a lovely breakfast in the Galaxy Café.

She opened her door and let out a startled cry at the

man standing directly in front of her, his hand raised in the knocking position.

Chanelle blinked at the same rate as her heartbeat. She willed her eyelids to slow down, but her heart continued racing of its own accord.

Vance Kingston brought his hand down. He lifted his other one and Chanelle recognized what he was holding— her sunglasses. Her gaze flew to his, riveted by piercing eyes that looked more blue-green now, with the teal shirt he had changed into.

"You left these behind," he said drily, "and I convinced myself it wouldn't hurt to carry out a second good deed of the day. I noticed them when I went back to get my towel and gym bag." He chuckled. "I guess forgetfulness is a trait shared by Aquarians and Sagittarians."

Vance gazed into green-hazel eyes that had a luminescence that hadn't been there earlier. She'd been crying…and her cheeks and nose were slightly flushed. He felt the muscles in his stomach tightening. Could it have something to do with her ex-fiancé?

"How did you find out my stateroom number?" Chanelle's eyes bored into his as she took the sunglasses from him.

"Your key card was on your chaise. I couldn't help seeing the number." Something in her expression gave him a jolt. "Good heavens, I hope you don't think my intentions are dishonorable, Chanelle. That would be most unpresidential of me, don't you think?" He waited for her to reply, but she just continued to stare at him.

"Look, I'm sorry if I caused you even momentary worry," he said huskily, raising his right arm to the door-jamb. "I'm not trying to stalk you, Chanelle. I just wanted to get your sunglasses back to you…and now I just want to make sure you're okay."

The way Chanelle was studying his face reminded him of a teacher trying to ascertain if her student was lying. He tried not to make his mouth twitch in amusement and was relieved when her features relaxed slightly.

She cleared her throat. "Okay. *Fine.* I mean, I'm okay and I—I accept your apology." A corner of her mouth lifted briefly. "I'm sorry if I seemed a little testy…"

"Seemed?" he said, raising his eyebrows.

Her eyes widened, as if she didn't know how to take his remark. "Okay, I'm sorry if I *was* a little testy," she said wryly.

"A little?"

She looked at him incredulously. "You make it seem as if I was biting your head off…"

He burst out laughing. "Interesting choice of words." Something flipped inside him when she laughed back, making her eyes take on an emerald hue. "Speaking of biting… would you care to have a bite with me? Breakfast, that is?"

Her eyebrows went up, as if that were the last thing she'd expected to hear from him. She blinked at him as if he had just asked her a complicated algebraic question and she didn't have a clue as to where to start with the answer. "I—I was just about to go to the Galaxy Café," she finally replied.

"I see," he murmured. He looked past her. "I hope you're finding your stateroom to your satisfaction?"

"It's very nice—roomier than I thought it would be." She nodded and shifted awkwardly in the doorway. "Uh… I forgot my sunscreen in the washroom. I plan to enjoy the sunshine after breakfast, but unless I want to end up with a million freckles, I really should—"

"Would you like me to wait here, Chanelle?" He didn't

know what had possessed him to invite her for breakfast, but he had, and there was no way of taking it back.

She hesitated, then shrugged. "You can step inside. I'll just be a minute." She turned and suddenly paused. He followed her gaze to the king-size bed, still unmade, her skimpy teddy tossed on top of the sheets. When his gaze returned to her, her cheeks had already reddened.

He pretended not to notice and immediately sat down on the couch and picked up a magazine. He started leafing through the pages, but out of the corner of his eye, he saw Chanelle walking over and pulling the covers casually over the bed to conceal her teddy. Without glancing his way, she headed to the washroom and closed the door. He heard the water flowing and imagined her splashing cool water over those peachy cheeks.

He was feeling rather heated himself, thinking of Chanelle in that teddy... He tossed the magazine back on the coffee table and leaned back to survey the room. She had some of her toiletries organized neatly on one night table, and there was no sign of her suitcase. He spotted her swimsuit draped over a chair on the balcony and wondered what her reaction would have been if he had been in time to join her in the pool.

The washroom door opened, and Chanelle came out, her hair now held back by a wide navy headband. The casual style emphasized her heart-shaped face and exquisite cheekbones. She had also applied a lustrous red lipstick, and in that snug red-and-white T-shirt and navy capris, she looked like a classic beauty from a bygone era. Innocent and sensual at the same time. Like it or not, that combination sent flickers of desire through him. And the fact that she was unconscious of the effect she had on him made his pulse spike even higher.

She grabbed her tote bag and then suddenly hesitated. "Will you be joining your family?"

He couldn't help chuckling. "Mariah won't be up for a while. And neither will Adrien. As for my mother, she will have already ordered room service at the crack of dawn and is now probably consulting with some of the staff about the gala preparations."

Chanelle nodded, her shoulders relaxing. "I guess we'd better get going, then."

He glanced at the time on his sports watch. "I know the Galaxy Café can get quite busy, especially around this time. How would you feel about trying a spot that's quieter? The Constellation Club, for example."

Her eyebrows shot up. "I… I read that that was for exclusive Zodiac Club members," she said, her cheeks flushing. "I could only afford the basic cruise plan." She gave an embarrassed half smile.

"I can guarantee you won't be turned away," he said solemnly. "If you don't mind going as my guest."

Chanelle blinked. "But…" She looked down at her outfit. "Is there a dress code?"

"Yes," he said with a chuckle. "You have to wear clothes. What you're wearing is absolutely fine, Chanelle. It's not what you think. People aren't parading in black-tie attire and ball gowns." His mouth twitched. "In fact, they're not parading at all. At least not for breakfast."

"I—I don't know. I've budgeted for dining in one specialty restaurant, but this is—"

"On me," he said firmly. "And if you really object, you can offer to do your dishes afterward."

She looked at him hesitantly, then gave a nod, a mix of relief and disbelief in her expression, and Vance felt a warm rush infuse his chest. What he was more accustomed to was seeing a look of smug expectation on a date's face. Not that

Chanelle was exactly a date, but it was refreshing for him to know that a lady wasn't expecting him to pick up her tab.

Vance followed her out of her stateroom, breathing in her perfume—a sweet berry scent—and as they walked side by side in the hallway on their way to the elevator lobby, he greeted the housekeeping staff they encountered with a friendly smile and a few words to thank them for the exceptional job they were doing.

The elevator was empty. As the doors closed, he lifted his hand to press the number to the top deck, and as he did so, it brushed against Chanelle's. Their eyes met, and for an instant, he had this crazy desire to lean down and kiss those fabulous lips. When her mouth opened slightly, it was all he could do to force himself to pull his gaze away from hers and press the button.

Finally, after what seemed like an eternity, the door opened, and he indicated to Chanelle to precede him. Her eyebrows lifted, but she accompanied him down the hall without saying anything. When they came to a door marked Constellation Club, Vance pulled his card out of his pocket and tapped it against the brass plate to the left of the door handle. He opened the door wide and smiled. "Welcome to the club, Chanelle."

CHAPTER SEVEN

CHANELLE GASPED IN AWE, her eyes widening as she entered. She couldn't have imagined anything like the room she had just stepped into. The entire ceiling was a glass dome from which were suspended thousands of stars. Chanelle felt like she was taking in a crystal wonderland.

A waiter in a crisp white shirt, black trousers and aquamarine cummerbund greeted them and led them to an oval glass table with silver legs. The upholstered chairs were ivory damask, and as Chanelle sank into one, she gave Vance an incredulous look. "This place is out of this world," she said, expelling a deep breath. Her gaze returned to the ceiling. "There must be a thousand stars up there."

"Two thousand, five hundred, to be exact," Vance said. "Each glass star is crafted by hand in Murano, Italy. They sparkle with the natural light of the sun in the day, and the dome has a fiber optic star ceiling. But on starry, starry nights—" he flashed a smile at her "—the dome halves retract and the club members are treated to a night under the real stars. And if they're really lucky, they get to see a meteor shower or a shooting star."

"Stunning," Chanelle breathed. She looked around at the gleaming glass tables, each decorated with a multifaceted crystal vase holding a couple of stargazer lilies. In the center of the room, a life-sized and slowly rotating Aquarius statue poured water into a pool from a gilded urn, its gentle gurgling sound adding to the relaxing ambience. The sides of the pool were transparent, and dozens of exotic fish of all colors flitted past each other. Chanelle was mesmerized by their flecks of gold and turquoise, crimson and black, emerald and orange. And their varied shapes and sizes. She could have stood there for hours, enchanted by this giant aquarium. And all around it, the marble floor resembled the ocean, with its varying hues of blue. Sea and sky, she thought. What a heavenly place...

When her gaze returned to Vance, she didn't know what to make of the indulgent look on his face. Was that a flicker of compassion in his eyes? She stiffened. Maybe he was just feeling sorry for her with her limited budget. Perhaps he made it a point to be charitable to a guest every time he went on one of his cruises... She felt a sudden hot prickle inching up her neck.

What had she gotten herself into? She was way out of her league. A few female guests had turned to scrutinize her from head to foot, and from their raised eyebrows and whispered comments to their partners, Chanelle had begun to feel self-conscious. For a moment, she considered making an excuse to leave, but then her inner Sagittarian warrior voice reminded her of her vow to enjoy the cruise and new experiences.

She straightened in her seat and tossed her hair back. Vance was still looking at her with a bemused expression. She picked up her menu and, while scanning it, wished she knew exactly what he was thinking.

She thought she had sensed something more elemental in the elevator, but it must have been her imagination...

The way he was looking at her now was exactly how he had looked at the housekeeping employees. No hint of flirtation in those aqua depths. Yet Chanelle couldn't help feeling conflicted. She hadn't booked this cruise hoping to hook up with some guy to make her boo-boos better. In fact, after Parker had left, she had vowed to focus on work even more and not bother with men at all. And she had certainly succeeded. Except that the consequence of her increased devotion to her job had taken its toll physically and emotionally. No wonder it was called *burnout*. She had felt scorched and withered, like a tree caught in a summer fire.

And now her cheeks were burning as Vance's cool blue eyes gazed at her calmly. Nothing in his expression or body language even hinted that he was in playboy mode. And anyway, why would he be wanting to play with someone like *her*? She had seen the photos of some of the women he had dated, with their perfect features and haute couture.

Some of their handbags had cost more than her monthly salary...

No, she was definitely not his type. All Vance was doing was engaging in a kind act for a guest whom he had caught being upset and in tears over something...and he had considered the fact that she wouldn't want to face a lot of people after that.

Nevertheless, she still felt awkward. He wasn't just *anybody*.

"I usually eat breakfast alone," she said, eyes fixed on the menu. Her words came out more gruffly than she had intended. "In fact, I had almost changed my mind about taking this cruise. I just wanted a holiday where I could relax and be pampered and not have to deal with socializing."

She looked up to see Vance gazing at her quizzically. "You can relax and be pampered here. After breakfast, I can introduce you to our spa professionals..."

Chanelle felt the temperature in her cheeks climbing a few notches at the image that flashed in her mind: Vance lying on a spa bed with hot lava stones positioned down his strong, muscled back. And his Aquarius tattoo on the upper right side…

"Um, thanks, but I'll be fine." Besides, her budget had been stretched far enough. She looked around. The view was stupendous. Endless sea and sky. The clouds had shifted, and the sky was a mix of blues with the occasional ribbon of pink.

Vance had been saying something, but *what*? She looked at him blankly. Her stomach did a flip.

"Coffee or tea?" he repeated.

"Sorry…" She held up her hand. "I don't think I should be here." She bit her lip. "I should go." She caught his frown as she began to rise and then promptly sat down again. She owed him an explanation, at the very least. Her heart thumping, she looked at him squarely. Why be anything but honest? "I have to admit I'm feeling a little out of my element," she said. She glanced toward the other guests before turning her gaze back to Vance.

He leaned forward, both elbows on the table and his hands clasped under his chin. "I think you have all the right elements," he said lightly. "And if you're referring to your bank account, it's not an issue, remember? I'm pretty sure I can cover it, unless you're intending to eat me out of house and home. Or should I say ship and stern?" His mouth quirked to reveal a flash of dimple.

"I—I'm…well…*okay*," she relented. Why was she making such a big deal about the whole thing? She needed to take her own earlier advice and lighten up. "I have to warn you, though," she said, managing a tentative smile, "I do have a good appetite."

Vance nodded his approval as he handed her the menu. "Good. Go crazy. I'm ordering my favorite—buttermilk applesauce pancakes with Ontario maple syrup." He grinned. "Something sweet for a sweet Canadian boy."

Chanelle felt laughter bubble up inside her. She sensed that something was shifting between them. Or maybe it was just *her*. Maybe some of her inhibitions were losing their grip on her. Perhaps it was time to let go of her tendency to control the situation and just enjoy the moment...

She had read enough to know that letting go completely could be a challenge for highly sensitive people like herself. Well, she would rise to the challenge, she decided. Why not enjoy this unexpected turn of events instead of being overwhelmed and feeling out of place? How often would she get the chance to be in the company of a gorgeous guy in a fabulous restaurant on the top deck of his cruise ship? A guy with a dimpled smile that made her stomach swirl in a good way...

"I'll try the crepes filled with hazelnut chocolate and ricotta cheese," she said decisively. "For a sweeter Canadian girl."

He burst out laughing, his eyes crinkling at the edges. "So the Sagittarian has a competitive streak, does she?"

For timeless moments, Chanelle felt like she was suspended in a cloud of pure pleasure as they exchanged smiles. Then the waiter appeared with a carafe of coffee, took their order and reassured them it would be ready shortly.

"So where does this sweeter Canadian girl live?" Vance said, pouring her coffee first.

"Sault Ste. Marie, Ontario," she replied, adding cream to her cup.

He nodded. "Ah, the Soo. Been there. Stopped overnight on my way to Lake Superior for a fishing trip with some guys—let me see—three years ago. Nice little town. Big Italian population, right?"

Chanelle nodded, taken aback that he had come through her hometown.

"We stayed at a hotel by Saint Mary's River. Checked out the Station Mall; one of our absentminded buddies had brought all his fishing gear but had forgotten the important stuff, like clothes and underwear." He chuckled. "While he went searching for his designer boxers, the rest of us waited it out at a pizza and gelato place." He sighed. "I ordered a double scoop of hazelnut and pistachio. *Heaven.*"

Her eyes widened. "You've got a great memory."

He looked at her unblinkingly. "I remember anything that looks good and tastes even better," he said, his mouth tilting up at one corner.

Chanelle felt a warm rush swish through her. Flustered, she looked down and took a sip of her coffee. Her mind was zooming to places she didn't want it to go, and she'd be horrified if Vance even suspected what she was conjuring up in her imagination…

"So after Pete was done, we spent a few hours at the casino, then had some amazing Italian food at the Marconi Club." He chuckled. "*Mamma mia*, just the memory of it is making my mouth water. I'd go back to the Soo again just for the food. Although—" he raised an eyebrow conspiratorially "—I suspect the people are just as appealing…"

Chanelle raised her chin. "Yes, we are. And the Soo is a great place to live. Not too big, not too small. I don't know if I could ever live in a huge city like Toronto or Vancouver. Mind you, I visited Toronto a few years ago. I actually went on a weekend bus tour with a couple of my friends to catch a show at the Princess of Wales Theatre. It was a long trip, though. Eight hours or so."

"So you've been to my hometown. We have great Italian food, too." He grinned. "And every other cuisine you can think of."

"Do you love it? Living in a huge city, I mean?"

"I enjoy all the big-city perks, but I do need the occasional getaway."

"Where do you get away to?" Chanelle asked casually. "Other than Lake Superior."

"British Columbia, Newfoundland, California, the Caribbean…usually a place where there's a large body of water," he said with a laugh. "Do you have any special places you like to escape to?"

"I've stayed pretty much close to home," she said sheepishly. "Worked a lot of overtime hours… But I do have some special spots in and around the Soo. A beautiful beach called Pointe des Chenes. And I've camped up north, Lake Superior way. Batchawana Bay, Pancake Bay. I'm a northern Ontario girl. Love my lakes and forests."

Vance was staring at her with an intensity that made her breath catch in her lungs. *He's genuinely interested in what I'm saying*, she thought in wonder.

The waiter returned with their orders. Chanelle took a first bite of her crepe and closed her eyes. "Heaven," she murmured, before realizing she had used the same term Vance had used to describe his gelato.

"Of course it is." He nodded. "It's the *nocciola*."

Hazelnut. Of course. Her workplace was on Queen Street East, within walking distance to the Station Mall, and she often had lunch at one of the eateries there, ending it occasionally with a gelato at the same place he had been to.

"So we share the same taste in Italian ice cream." Vance drizzled syrup over his pancakes and cut a wedge. "Delicious," he said, and slid the plate closer to her. "Want to try?"

The familiarity with which he spoke made Chanelle's pulse skip. "That's okay, thanks. I think I have more than enough on my plate." Her fork paused in midair. "Literally and figuratively."

Vance looked at her thoughtfully. "Are you thinking you might go back to the same job?"

Chanelle swallowed. "I'm not sure. I loved my job." She heard the defensive tone in her voice.

Vance poured more syrup on his second pancake. "What made you decide to get into social work?"

Chanelle looked down at her half-eaten crepe and tapped it mindlessly with her fork. "I spent my childhood without a father," she said, "and I became self-conscious when there were events at school where parents were invited. My mother came when she could, but most times, it was too hard for her. She was working two jobs to pay the bills. My grandfather had health issues, so he and my grandma couldn't always be there, either." She looked up. "I think subconsciously, I internalized the fact that my father had denied my existence. Even before my mother told me that he had taken off before I was born, I intuitively felt my father's abandonment." She paused, expecting to see a skeptical look in Vance's eyes, but what she saw were his furrowed brows and eyes narrowed in concern.

"I know now that having a sharper intuition is characteristic of a highly sensitive person. Which is why, I believe, I knew early in life that I wanted to help others, starting with my mother. I felt her pain, even though she tried to put up a good front. So I helped around the house without being told, was a high achiever at school, did everything possible to avoid making life harder for her." She gazed away from Vance, recalling how happy she had been when her mother eventually married her stepdad. On the other hand, her unresolved feelings about her biological father had continued to intensify over the years, and she had felt lingering hurt and resentment that he hadn't valued her from the moment he'd known she existed, hadn't deemed her worthy to claim her as his daughter.

Parker's breaking off their engagement and leaving had ignited similar feelings…

Stop thinking about Parker, she chided herself. *He's not worth it.* She turned her gaze back to Vance, who was still looking at her with an intensity that made her heart twinge, but not in a hurtful way.

"I'm sorry, I'm sure you don't want to hear me keep chattering incessantly."

"Don't be sorry, Chanelle. It's obvious that your caring personality growing up under challenging circumstances was a good indication that you'd eventually choose a helping profession."

"Some kids had it worse than I did. One of my classmates came to school with bruises on her arms and face one Friday. I felt so bad for her. She had moved to town about a couple of months earlier, and we were getting to be good friends."

Chanelle gave a shiver. "Kayla had parents, but the rumor was that they were drug addicts. She told the teacher that she had fallen down some stairs, and she was quiet all day. She didn't tell me anything. The teacher told the principal, and on Monday, Kayla didn't show up." They had been in grade nine, and the defeated look she had seen in Kayla's eyes had haunted her all weekend.

Chanelle drew in a deep breath. "We found out that Children's Aid had investigated and removed Kayla from her home immediately. Fortunately, she had a caring aunt out of town who took her in." Chanelle couldn't keep her eyes from blurring. She wiped at them hastily with her napkin. "I knew then that I wanted to become a social worker so I could protect children from abusive or neglectful family members." She sniffed. "I never saw Kayla again, but I have something she had given me for Kris Kringle." Chanelle extended her arm to show Vance the bracelet around her left wrist that Kayla had woven with a variety of colorful threads.

"You've kept it all these years?" Vance looked at her incredulously.

Chanelle nodded. "I became a child protection worker because of her." She smiled. "I don't usually wear it around the clock, only when I'm at work. You could say it's my Sagittarian quiver, loaded with arrows. I know it may sound silly, but wearing the bracelet makes me feel strong, makes me believe that I have the protection I need, especially when I have to rescue kids."

"Wow," he said huskily, shaking his head. "Wow." He reached out to take her hand and stroked the bracelet thoughtfully with his thumb. "It's not silly at all, Chanelle." Suddenly his other hand closed over hers as well. Chanelle's heart flipped and started thumping so hard she missed most of what Vance was saying next.

Her stupefied look must have clued him in. "You're stronger than you think," he repeated, his eyes narrowing. He withdrew his hands as the waiter appeared, asking them if he could take any plates away.

They both nodded, and when the waiter was gone, Chanelle gave a big sigh. "I'm hoping that while I'm on the cruise, wearing the bracelet will help me decide where to go from here…" She let her gaze drift beyond Vance to the sky, now a deep azure that seemed to be an extension of his eyes. "But right now, I just can't see myself in another job."

"Give yourself time, Chanelle," he murmured. "You'll know when the time is right… So while you're on this cruise, I want you to give yourself permission to relax and have fun. Live a little. You deserve it." He stood up. "Starting now. Captain's—no, president's orders. Got it?" He looked at her sternly then flashed her another one of his ridiculously gorgeous brighter-than-sunshine smiles.

Chanelle pulled her chair back and rose. "Got it," she said, flinging her hair back. "I'd hate to disobey and end up walking the plank."

He burst out laughing. "Are you implying, fair lass, that I have the black heart of a pirate?"

Chanelle's pulse vaulted, his words and hearty laugh evoking an image of him in full pirate regalia standing on the bow of a treasure ship, one eye covered by a black patch, the other pinning her with the same crystal clarity as the turquoise waters below.

She couldn't stop the corners of her mouth from lifting. "If not a pirate, then perhaps a scallywag," she said, feigning haughtiness. And flipping her hair back, she strode off toward the exit.

After Chanelle disappeared, leaving him dazed with the memory of her flashing eyes and pixy smile, Vance checked in on his mother, Mariah and Adrien, and then returned to his stateroom to try to sort out some issues that were playing around in his mind as well as the jumble of emotions Chanelle had activated in his gut.

Some of the details that Chanelle had shared about her life had disturbed him. His gaze had been riveted to the shifting emotions on her face as she'd told him about her father abandoning her and her mother's challenges raising her, and he had felt his stomach twist at the difficulties she had experienced. And when she had teared up about Kayla, he had felt a strong urge to wrap his arms around her and hold her head against him.

Her impish smile as she strode off after implying he was a scallywag had caused a different feeling in him—a hammering in his chest that had reverberated throughout his body…

Now, stretched out on the recliner on his balcony, Vance thought again of Chanelle's early years growing up without a father. His own father had been present only minimally, so he could just imagine what Chanelle had felt, especially being so sensitive.

Vance's memory shifted to how he had immersed himself in a new and heavily structured routine after his father had passed. This week—with nothing specifically planned except for the midweek gala—was throwing him off. He might have been more laid-back when it came to work in the past, but that had changed dramatically in the last nine months. He had conditioned himself to get up at 5:00 a.m. every morning, work out at the gym in his condo, shower, have breakfast and be at the office before eight. And most nights, he wasn't back at his condo until after nine.

He'd had no time to think about women.

Until yesterday, after seeing an auburn-haired beauty trying to rescue his nephew from danger.

And after spending some time with Chanelle Robinson in the Mezza Luna Ristorante, and foolishly inviting her to have breakfast with him in the Constellation Club this morning, he was now in danger of losing his resolve to focus on work, not women. Or more specifically, *this* woman.

Vance pursed his lips. He would be on this cruise for three more days after today. And when the cruise was over, he'd never see Chanelle Robinson again. He might not even run into her for the remainder of the cruise.

The important thing to remember was not to seek her out. It would only weaken his resolve. So despite the undeniable way his senses were stirred around her, he had to ensure that he did not act on his feelings. How could he take advantage of her in the vulnerable state she was in, having suffered a broken relationship and work stress?

You've changed, big boy, whether you like it or not.

He froze at the words that had shoved their way into his consciousness. They were true. Before his father died, Vance had never suffered pangs of guilt around relationships, familial or otherwise. He had justified his rebelliousness as a teen and young adult as his way of striking out at a father who was never home. A father who seemed to care more about work than his kids…

The feeling of guilt had sprung up when his father died, knowing he had allowed his built-up resentment to stop him from granting his dad's dying request. Since then, he had been trying to make up for it.

Yes, he had changed, all right.

He had made work his priority, just as his father had done, and slowly, Vance had begun to understand how a person could become consumed with work, with passion, to the point of neglecting everything else.

He could congratulate himself for repressing his playboy ways while focusing on carrying out his father's last wish, but he couldn't deny that certain feelings had been reactivated.

By a fascinating woman who probably wanted nothing to do with him or any other man right now…

But it wasn't just her outer beauty that attracted him. He was intrigued by the depth of her character, her small-town charm and honesty. Her devotion to her job, the children she was so passionate about protecting. Her goodness.

And how could he not be affected by those limpid green pools for eyes, those peachy cheekbones and silky lips? How could he ignore the sleek curves of her body…and that riotous head of hair that he envisioned blowing in the wind as she stood on a rocky outcrop looking out at the endless ice-blue waters of Lake Superior? A Sagittarian warrior, softhearted yet strong and determined, ready to fling her Archer's arrow...

A thought entered his consciousness, shocking him like his very first dip in Lake Superior.

He was falling for Chanelle Robinson.

Falling hard and seeing stars...

CHAPTER EIGHT

CHANELLE HAD WATCHED Vance leave in a swirl of emotions. She had felt some undercurrents in Vance's presence… undercurrents that confused her. Like the intensity in his gaze earlier in the elevator. It had only lasted for a couple of seconds, but the expression in his electric-blue eyes as he looked down at her had galvanized her to the core. And then minutes later, in the Constellation Club, his expression had been genuinely reassuring, making her doubt her earlier assessment.

But the way he had been so attentive, fixing her with that enigmatic gaze, was causing uncertainty in the pit of her stomach about his true feelings.

What true feelings? an inner voice scoffed. *You just met the guy. Do you actually think he has feelings for you? And if you're feeling anything for him, it's because he's gorgeous and rich. And what's wrong with that?*

Chanelle scowled. Yes, how could she not find Vance Kingston attractive? Very attractive. The memory of the Aquarius tattoo on his muscled back made her catch her breath. But it hadn't been thoughts of his wealth that had generated flutters in her chest, that had sent tingles to every part of her. It was the way he had given her all his attention, as if her every word mattered to him. It was how he had validated her by listening to her story, acknowledging her strength, showing concern for her work situation and encouraging her to give it time and to have fun on the cruise.

She couldn't dispute the fact that Vance Kingston was gorgeous and rich. He had asked her to join him for breakfast and he had shown himself to be considerate and thoughtful. But it was just plain silly to think that the president of Zodiac Cruises was at all interested in her in any other way.

And even if he *was* taking a break from his playboy lifestyle for the sake of work—if the articles online were true—Chanelle couldn't imagine someone like him changing his ways after his self-imposed period of solitude.

She shook her head impatiently. Vance had taken up enough of her head space. She was here to relax and enjoy the cruise, just as he had suggested, and not to waste time fantasizing about him or any other man.

Chanelle focused her attention on the Star Guide, an interactive screen that displayed a map of the entire ship and the features on every deck. She decided on a visit to the art gallery on Deck Five. The stunning art collection would be a welcome distraction from her thoughts of Vance Kingston.

There were dozens of international artists featured, not only in the gallery itself, but displayed along the walls on each deck. Chanelle spent close to an hour marveling at the diversity of styles, the vibrancy of the colors and the intricacy and detail in each painting. One particularly captivated her, with its depiction of a moonlit and starry sky mirrored in the indigo-blue undulations of the sea. It was called *Enchantment*, and simply signed *SV*.

A glance at the price made Chanelle's eyes widen. A fairy godmother would have to appear and sprinkle some magic fairy dust in Chanelle's wallet for her to be able to afford it.

Chanelle picked up a complimentary booklet showcasing the artists and their works but couldn't find anything about the artist and his or her painting. An elegantly dressed woman sitting at an ornate French Provincial desk walked over with a smile and told Chanelle that the artist wished to remain anonymous. She gave Chanelle a card with information about the champagne art auction that would be taking place during the mid-cruise gala, and explained that there would be many more pieces featured. And complimentary champagne, of course, a door prize, and some special surprises…

Chanelle slipped the invitation into her handbag and smiled her thanks at the woman before moving on. It sounded like fun, but she doubted that there would be a painting that her budget could accommodate.

Chanelle slowed her pace as she entered the Galaxy Shops. She had splurged on booking the cruise itself and had vowed to be strict with herself when it came to shopping, whether on the ship or during her off-ship excursion. But there was no harm in just looking, she told herself, surveying the luxurious brands of purses and luggage. She checked the price of a coral clutch that caught her eye and sighed before moving on to the jewelry displays. One of the sales staff approached her with a welcoming smile, telling her about the day's special of fifty percent off select brands. Chanelle thanked her, flushing, and told her that she'd have a good look. Which wasn't exactly lying. She *would* look through the sparkly selection.

A pair of ruby earrings in a flower design caught her eye. She noticed the price, then began to walk away. How could she justify spending money unnecessarily, especially when she wasn't one hundred percent sure that she would be returning to her job in a month's time? How was she supposed to recover from five years of intensive work stress in one month? And then what? Would she be ready to get right back into it?

She had rent to pay. And now that she was back on her own, she might even have to look for a new place…or move back in with her mom and stepdad.

Not that she didn't love them, but it would be hard after five years of independence in her own space.

"I'll take these amethyst earrings, dear," a woman said close by. "I think they'll match my violet gown perfectly for the gala."

Chanelle turned and saw a sixty-something woman sporting a smart pixie cut with side-swept bangs that suited her silver-gray hair. She was wearing turquoise palazzo pants and a sleeveless ivory chiffon top. She had removed her turquoise earrings to try the amethyst ones against her ears. On the third finger of her left hand, an enormous diamond sparkled under the ceiling lights.

The woman's open handbag slipped off the counter, spilling some of its contents. Chanelle quickly bent down to retrieve what she could and handed the items to the woman, who gazed across at her with a grateful smile. "Thanks for your help."

"My pleasure," she replied, startled by the crystal clarity of the woman's blue eyes.

Chanelle was about to stand up, too, but a flash on the floor under the counter caught her eye. It was a photo of a child, encased in a plastic folder. A boy with the same arresting blue eyes as the woman.

And the president of Zodiac Cruises.

Something fluttered in Chanelle's chest as she stood up and handed the photo of the little boy she had tried to rescue yesterday to his grandmother. *Vance Kingston's mother…*

No wonder Chanelle had sensed something familiar about her.

After the woman left, Chanelle returned to the jewelry display to look at the ruby earrings. A new voice was telling her, *Relax and have fun. Live a little. You deserve it!*

Foolish or not, Chanelle listened to the voice. Which, she realized as she walked away with her little velvet box tucked away in a Zodiac Cruises gift bag, was the voice of Vance Kingston.

Vance looked over the series of sketches he had been working on for the last hour. There were at least a dozen variations of the logo he was designing for the new cruise line in the Zodiac fleet, its first ship scheduled to launch the following year. His father had initiated the project, and now it was in his hands.

He had to come up with a new name as well, and he had jotted down a half dozen possibilities, including Nebula Cruises, What's Your Sign? Cruises and Stellar Cruises. None of them quite clicked for him, though. He pursed his lips. The logos all had one thing in common—undulating waves. Once he decided on a name, he'd connect the letters with the waves in a flowing forward motion. And maybe add the profile of a sea goddess…

Vance turned to a new page and started another sketch. It was neither a logo nor a name. It was a face with sculpted cheekbones and full, curving lips. Eyes framed with long, feathery lashes. And thick waves of hair cascading down to the shoulder lines.

He took a green and a gold pencil and added color to the eyes. He set his pencils down and took a long, hard look at the result.

Chanelle Robinson was staring back at him…

Time to take a break, he told himself, shaking his head in wonder.

* * *

Vance greeted the art representative at her desk and strolled through the gallery, noticing the new paintings that had been added. Vance enjoyed perusing each one, familiar with many of the artists. He was looking forward to the champagne art auction and wondered if Chanelle planned to attend.

He stopped when he came to the *Enchantment* painting and looked at it thoughtfully.

"It's getting some attention," the art rep said as she joined him.

"Oh?" Vance's eyebrows lifted. "Did someone ask about it, Stephanie?"

"A young lady kept going back to it. She must have stared at it for a good ten minutes." Stephanie smiled at Vance. "She was obviously enchanted by it."

Vance's mouth curved. "But not enchanted enough to buy it," he chuckled.

"Well, perhaps she might consider it at the auction on gala night, Vance. I gave her a card."

"Was she one of our regular cruisers?" Stephanie had been with the *Aquarius* since it launched, and she had become familiar with returning customers, especially the art patrons.

"No, this was a first-timer," she told him. A few guests entered the gallery, and she turned toward them.

"Did you happen to catch her name?" Vance said as casually as he could.

Stephanie looked back. "I spotted her first name on her lanyard. It was different; it reminded me of Chantilly lace." She laughed. "Chantelle. No, *Chanelle*." She walked over and welcomed the guests, and Vance turned back to gaze at the painting.

Enchantment. Why had this painting caught Chanelle's attention? he mused. His gaze swooped over the stars and the waves of blue and indigo before landing on the initials in the bottom right-hand corner. *SV.* His mouth lifted at one corner. He had done this painting while he was working on his masters of fine art degree, and not wanting his father to denigrate it on the rare occasions when he came home, Vance had chosen not to sign it with his own name. He had to thank his sister for giving him the nickname Sir Vancelot…

CHAPTER NINE

CHANELLE PUT ON a light robe and drew the tie around her waist. She had returned to her stateroom feeling over-whelmed at bumping into Vance's mother—and overheated after spending time in the shop—and had immediately taken a refreshing shower.

She inhaled and exhaled deeply, feeling much more re-laxed now, and headed to the balcony. She could stare at the water for ages, watching the cerulean waves change to turquoise and turquoise to cobalt blue. The sun was add-ing magic to the scene, making the water's surface shim-mer with glittering diamonds.

In the next few weeks, she hoped it would be clearer to her what direction to take as far as her job was concerned. This cruise would hopefully give both her body and mind a rest, and then she could decide if she could handle con-tinuing in the same line of work, or if she seriously needed to consider a change of some kind.

But now she didn't really want to think about it. She just wanted to enjoy the glorious view of sky and sea.

Chanelle went back inside and stretched out on top of the bed. She checked the time on her phone. Plenty of time to relax before dinner.

She reached for the daily cruise guide, and while she was checking out the featured events of the day, the daily horoscope caught her eye. She couldn't help skimming the page until her gaze landed on her sign.

Sagittarius, you're in for some surprises. With your ruler Jupiter in retrograde, your inner world is transitioning and spinning you to a higher consciousness. Don't fight it; let yourself enjoy your burgeoning awareness. You may have felt the universe is not on your side after some personal and work upsets, but take heart, Sag. If you stay focused on what's in front of you, what's to come won't be problematic. Go with the flow, Archer, and that arrow will land where it needs to…

Chanelle frowned. It was so *eerie* how much the words could be applied to her situation. And then she scoffed at herself. Parts of the description could apply to tons of people, no matter what their sign was.

Despite her skepticism, she couldn't help reading the horoscope for Vance.

The stars will collaborate to help a business matter come to fruition. Complicated family issues will untangle, and with Uranus guiding you, you will be able to see clearer when it comes to matters of the heart. Concessions may need to be made, and your compliance with the forces of the universe will result in a shower of positive changes.

Chanelle set down the guide and let her gaze drift to the ceiling. Could Vance, despite his calm and collected exterior, have some personal issues of his own he was dealing with? A woman who was waiting for him to ease up at work and shower her with more of his attention?

She shook her head. What was she doing conjuring up possibilities around Vance and his relationships?

Time to get back to reality.

She picked up the guide again. A glance at the time confirmed that she had a few free hours before dinner. Did she really want to spend them lying down on her bed? She was on a spectacular cruise ship and before she knew it, it would be over...

She might as well enjoy every delicious bit of it.

Chanelle perused the activities listed for the afternoon: a tour of the ship kitchens, a magic show featuring a Las Vegas regular, an art class with a high-profile artist, a wine-tasting class, Latin dancing or belly-dancing instruction, a rock-climbing wall, a pool volleyball tournament, a '70s disco party and a dozen other choices.

Chanelle began to reread the list, the times and the locations. She didn't really feel up to doing anything that required dressing up; after all, she'd be doing that for Canada Night. But she really should consider doing something a little out of her element. After all, what would be the likelihood of her going on another cruise any time soon? She might as well try something new. *And exciting...*

As she skimmed down the list, her gaze landed on something that she had missed. The Sky Promenade. It was an extensive course of colorful horizontal rope ladders that were suspended a hundred feet above the skating rink on the top deck, connecting to rope bridges, slopes and descents that had to be navigated by walking while wearing a safety harness.

Chanelle flicked on to the TV channel that featured videos of all the day's events. As the Sky Promenade video started, she gave a little shiver. Heights had always made her feel a little queasy, and this activity would require a stomach of steel, looking down between the ropes to the crystal-clear surface of the ice rink.

There was no way she could do that. No. Way.

She'd be terrified, even knowing that she'd be wearing a safety harness. The motion of the ropes along with the bird's-eye view of the sea on the periphery would throw her off balance with her first step. She clicked off the remote. There had to be something else she could try that wasn't so scary.

Chanelle leaped off the bed and changed into a pair of purple leggings and a thigh-length fuchsia T-shirt before tying her hair up in a ponytail. She'd do something outdoors, she decided, but something less extreme. Perhaps she could try the rock-climbing wall…

Vance's cell phone buzzed, making him start. It was Mariah, reminding him that he'd promised to take Adrien swimming. He checked the time. He'd also planned a quick meeting with the director of environmental operations later in the afternoon for an update on her latest initiative. He smirked. He was supposed to be taking a break from work while on the cruise, but he was realizing just how hard it was to break an established habit…

And after the meeting, he would join Mariah, Adrien and his mother for dinner in the Galaxy Café. Tonight was Canada Night on the ship. The theater would be featuring Canadian singers and comedians, and the Galaxy Café would be serving a signature dish and dessert from every province. There would be wine from the vineyards of the Okanagan Valley in British Columbia and Ontario's Niagara region, cheeses from Quebec, seafood from off the Pacific and Atlantic coasts, organic breads from the Prairies, and more. And sweets galore, like Nanaimo bars, butter tarts and *tarte au sucre*, three of his favorites.

Those who wanted to experience a Canadian winter would have the option of skating on an outdoor ice rink located on the top deck on the opposite side of the Constellation Club. It would be lit up after dark, and there would be blowers blowing in soft imitation snowflakes. And there would be hot chocolate stations and beaver tail pastries made and served on the spot. It couldn't get more Canadian than that.

Vance smiled. The deep-fried pastry, shaped like a beaver tail and topped with anything from cinnamon and sugar to whipped cream and hazelnut chocolate spread, was something he always enjoyed after skating on Ottawa's Rideau Canal, one of Canada's iconic landmarks. There were thousands of skaters and always a line for the beaver tails.

As he changed into swim trunks and a white cotton T-shirt, Vance couldn't help wondering what Chanelle was doing now, and where she would be dining this evening.

Playing volleyball with Adrien in the pool gave Vance a feeling of lightness that he hadn't felt in a long time. Along with a twinge of guilt. He had neglected his godfather duties these past months, and he had missed this. Having fun with a kid. A special kid, who had stolen his heart from the moment Vance had seen his pink and puckered little face in the hospital.

Mariah had asked him if he would be the child's godfather.

"Hell, yes," he had blurted, and then, more cautiously, "Does that mean I have to change diapers?"

"That's part of the deal, Sir Vancelot," she had replied with a shake of her head. "Don't worry, we'll have you practicing on a regular basis. You'll be a pro by the time you have one or nine of your own." Vance had feigned looking horrified, and Mariah and her husband, Chris, had burst out laughing.

Mariah had been true to her word. Adrien had gotten used to Vance being around from the very beginning, and whenever Chris was out of town on business—which was often, since he was the head of a mining engineering company that had projects all over the globe—Vance had gladly stepped up his godfather duties.

Enjoying double-scoop ice cream cones after their swim, Vance felt a contentment that had eluded him after his father had died. He realized that a part of him—maybe a big part of him—had shut down. The part that was all about the enjoyment of simple things, like splashing around a pool and having a cone with his nephew.

But he was determined to change his routine of the past nine months. He would spend more time with Adrien.

And maybe it was time to make some other changes, too…

Vance felt a thrumming in his chest as an image of Chanelle broke through his thoughts.

A coil of desire skimmed through his veins at the memory of her lying on the chaise lounge with that mint-green swimsuit clinging to her body like a second skin.

Yes, he needed to make some changes.

Starting with bringing Adrien back and then seeing if he could find Chanelle.

A flash of pink and purple caught his eye as he leaped up the open stairway to the top deck. From this center point, he could see a number of people clambering up the rock-climbing wall, and a line of others waiting for their turn. The pink and purple lady at the end of the line had auburn hair tied up in a ponytail.

Could it be Chanelle?

She turned slightly, and Vance's pulse leaped. It *was* her. He strode toward her, a strange wave of happiness washing over him. He had decided on a whim to start looking for

Chanelle on the top deck and work his way down. Maybe this was a sign…

"Hey, miss," he called, just steps behind her.

She whirled around, her ponytail flicking him sharply across the chin. "Oh, sorry," she said, her eyes widening. "Didn't mean to strike, but you kinda crept up on me."

"There you go, insinuating that I'm a creep again," he said, smiling at her crookedly.

Chanelle's eyelashes fluttered, and her mouth opened defensively. "And there *you* go, putting words in my mouth again."

An electric tingle radiated through Vance at the teasing tone of her words. He gazed at her wordlessly for a few moments, unable to draw his eyes away from the gleaming hazel green of hers.

Finally the line shifted as another rock climber began his ascent. "So is this your first time?" he said, gesturing toward the wall.

"Yes, I've mustered up the courage to try something new on this cruise," she said with a chuckle. "I considered the Sky Promenade, but after watching the video, I decided to leave that to the daredevils."

"Hmm." He surveyed her thoughtfully. "Are you afraid of heights?"

"Well…" She turned to scan the extensive series of ropes positioned above the skating rink at one far end of the ship. "I'm afraid that with *my* luck, *I'll* be the one whose safety harness breaks."

"Not gonna happen," he said, shaking his head. "I think, Miss Robinson, that there are some trust issues here that we have to deal with." The line moved forward again, leaving two more people waiting in front of Chanelle. "Come on, let me show you that you can do this. Conquer your fear, put your trust in the universe…"

"The universe isn't going to catch me if I fall," she retorted.

"But *I* will." He heard the words jump out of his mouth. "Look, Chanelle, you don't even have to worry about me catching you, because you won't fall. Safety is our number-one priority onboard this ship. Trust me."

Vance saw her forehead crease. "Okay, here's the deal. I haven't actually tried the rope walk myself. And to tell you the truth," he murmured, leaning forward as if to share a secret he didn't want anyone to hear, "*I'm* not exactly crazy about heights. I'm a water guy, remember?" He patted himself on the back, where he had the Aquarius symbol tattooed. "So how about we both try something new and scary together?"

Chanelle was gaping at him as if he were delusional. "You've got to be kidding." She was momentarily distracted as the person in front of her went to get fitted with her safety harness. She turned back to Vance. "You're *not* kidding."

Vance grinned. "Come on, Chanelle. It's now or never. If you can do *this*, you can do anything."

Chanelle blinked at him. Then her gaze shifted upward to the Sky Promenade.

She took a deep breath and slowly exhaled, her eyes meeting his again. "Fine," she declared. "Lead the way!"

From her platform, strapped into her safety harness, Chanelle scanned the view around her with a fluttering in her stomach that continued downward into her legs. The sky was a calm blue with the occasional fluffy cloud drifting nonchalantly by. The sea below was a deeper blue and not as calm, the froth of whitecaps disappearing and reappearing with every undulation. Lined against the side of the ship was a series of lifeboats. Chanelle breathed in and out slowly, hoping she wouldn't hyperventilate.

What on earth had made her agree to this?

Her gaze shifted to the colorful system of thick rungs that resembled a giant crocheted doily suspended above the ice rink. Each stretch of ladder led to a post with a circular platform where you stopped and gathered your courage before attempting the next rope ladder. Some ladders were horizontal, some slightly vertical, with vertical ropes suspended on either side.

Chanelle held her breath as Vance took his first step. She watched the rope ladder swing with his every movement, and she gasped when his foot seemed to be slipping. And then Vance gingerly made his way across the next half dozen rungs before stepping onto the circular platform and turning around to give her a thumbs-up sign.

Chanelle looked above to the metal track into which her safety rope was inserted, so she could glide along as she maneuvered the swinging steps. She could either cling to this rope, which was attached to her body harness, or grasp the cord dangling on either side of her to help her keep her balance.

Why am I doing this? she asked herself again. Vance had encouraged her to conquer her fear, put her trust in the universe…to trust him.

Perhaps she *did* have trust issues, as he had suggested. Maybe deep down she was afraid that history would repeat itself when it came to men, and that whoever came into her life would eventually abandon her… Maybe she was afraid of letting go of her job and trying something new. Maybe she was afraid of letting go of the HSP safety net that kept her cautious and protected.

But maybe it also kept her from experiencing life fully. When had she last felt adrenaline pumping in her veins like right now? Yes, she was afraid, about to step out onto the rope ladder, but she felt an exhilaration at the thought of doing it anyway. She looked across at Vance, who nodded at her with a confident smile and gave her another thumbs-up.

With her heart clanging against her ribs, Chanelle clasped the vertical ropes on either side of her and planted her foot on the first rung. The view below her made her knees tremble. She forced herself to focus on the rung, and gripping the ropes even harder, she put her left foot forward.

The sway of the ladder made her give a yelp. There was no way she could continue…

"You can do it, Chanelle."

Vance's calm voice reached her, and her head snapped up to look at him. His expression was just as calm, as if he knew that that was what she needed instead of a loud exhortation or cheer.

She had to believe that the harness wouldn't let go, that she wouldn't plummet to the ice rink. *Trust me*, Vance had said.

With whatever ounce of courage that still remained in her, Chanelle wobbled across the ladder and stepped up on the platform and into Vance's arms.

Vance tightened his arms around her. "I knew you could do it," he murmured close to her ear. Chest to chest, the heightened pumping of his heart—and hers—made him wish they were alone somewhere so he could savor the sensation that was flooding him.

He felt something primal, instinctive…a desire to protect this woman who had been brave enough to go against her own natural instincts and put her trust in the universe. *In him.* And the way she was clinging to him made him wonder if she could sense his feelings.

Out of the corner of his eye, he could see the attendant waiting for him and Chanelle to proceed before allowing the next guest to take a step forward. There were still plenty of ladders and bridges to navigate. They had to move on.

"Okay, Chanelle, one step at a time. Ready?"

She looked up at him, and his heart swelled at the look in the misty green depths of her eyes. This was not going to be easy for him, either. He would rather be in the pool than up in the air. Taking a deep breath, he released his arms around Chanelle and grasped the vertical ropes. "I'll be waiting for you," he told her huskily before stepping forward.

With open arms.

"My legs feel wobbly," Chanelle said as they left the Sky Promenade. "In fact, I feel wobbly all over…"

Vance nodded. "Join the club. It's the adrenaline rush." He put his hand under her elbow. "How about we sit down for a few minutes with a nice refreshing drink?"

"No alcohol for me," Chanelle protested. "That would finish me off. You'd have to carry me the rest of the way."

"I meant something fruity. Like a tall, cool glass of freshly squeezed lemonade. Or a mango-peach power drink. And by the way, Chanelle," he added with a grin, "my knees are wobbly, too, but not too wobbly to carry a Sagittarius warrior." He raised a hand to give her a high five. "You killed it up there."

She lifted her chin. "I did, didn't I?" She gave a little laugh. "So yes, I'll let you buy me a drink. Mango-peach sounds yummy."

"Mmm. I don't recall offering to foot the bill. But since I'm such a chivalrous guy, I'll do the chivalrous thing. *This time.*"

"Thank you, *Sir Vancelot.*" She beamed at him. "And by the way…you killed it up there, too!"

CHAPTER TEN

CHANELLE WANTED SOMETHING a little more dressy for Canada Night. The captain of *Aquarius* and some of the senior officers and staff would be greeting guests on Deck Five from eight to nine, and those who wished could have their professional photo taken with the captain during the last half hour. Not that *she* was interested in a photo…

Stop kidding yourself, an inner voice taunted. *You may not be interested in meeting the captain of Aquarius or getting a photo, but there will most certainly be a certain Vance Kingston there to impress…*

Did she want to impress him?

Maybe, a small voice admitted.

Something had happened between them up on the Sky Promenade. She wasn't sure if it was the moment when she had looked across at him on the circular platform, and he had nodded for her to proceed, his eyes as calm and blue as the sky above them. Or when she had made it across the first ladder and had literally sunk into his arms. All she could hear against his chest was his heartbeat along with hers.

She had accomplished a feat she had never thought herself capable of. And she would have never done it without Vance's encouragement. Every step of the way. His arms around her had given her such a wondrous feeling of support.

Or maybe something more...

She felt excited about the evening ahead. She was here on a cruise, and she intended to enjoy as much of it as she could.

Chanelle sifted through her dresses in the closet for something that might go with the Canada Night theme. She stopped when she came to a white cotton dress with splashes of red poppies. Well, they were as close as she could get to the red maple leaf on the Canadian flag. The dress was sleeveless, with a fitted bodice, snazzy red belt and skirt that flared from the waist, reaching to above her knees. And her new ruby earrings matched perfectly. As Chanelle swirled to look at herself in the mirror, she felt like a different person. A carefree, much younger person, without the preoccupations that had clung to her while at work.

Chanelle took a deep breath. She hadn't made much time to go out in the evenings when she had been working. She had usually come home late, exhausted, with thoughts only of getting into a shower and pajamas. Had Parker ever even seen her dressed up like this?

The thought of Parker vanished as quickly as it had come. All she could picture in her mind was the expression she hoped to see on Vance's face when he caught sight of her in this gorgeous dress... She swirled around, loving how the skirt swirled with her. The words of her horoscope came back to her:

Your inner world is transitioning and spinning you to a higher consciousness.

She smiled at herself in the mirror. She was spinning, all right.

And she liked how it felt.

Chanelle chose a black purse that matched the black

centers of the poppies, slipped on black high-heeled sandals and headed to the Galaxy Café. She looked forward to enjoying some of the featured dishes—like Digby scallops and other maritime delights—and then she'd make her way to Deck Five.

The place was bustling. As Chanelle looked around for an empty table and didn't see one, she regretted not arriving earlier. Pursing her lips, she considered leaving and trying one of the other dining spots but was blocked by a passing group.

"That's the nice young lady who helped me today," a voice came out of nowhere. "Invite her over, Vance. There's an empty spot at our table."

Through the shifting throng, Chanelle turned and caught sight of Mrs. Kingston, who was smiling directly at her while nudging Vance gently on the arm. Vance's sister and nephew were staring at Chanelle openly, and as Chanelle met Vance's enigmatic gaze, she felt a flush travel up her neck to her cheeks, which she was sure were now as red as the poppies.

"That's the lady who tried to rescue me," Adrien cried, pointing directly at Chanelle.

Chanelle wished there was a way of rescuing herself. She hadn't expected to meet Vance's family, let alone dine with them. Now she had no choice but to wait for Vance to approach. A few moments later, the group had moved on and Vance was striding toward her. Before her eyes met his, Chanelle just managed to scan gray straight-leg trousers that fit impeccably and a baby-blue fitted shirt and a Canadian-themed tie with alternating rows of loons and maple leaves. Under other circumstances, she might have joked about it.

"The Archer—slash—good fairy strikes again," he said, a glint in his blue eyes.

"It happens when I least expect it," she replied, unable to keep a note of defensiveness from creeping into her voice.

Her pulse spiked when Vance cupped her elbow to direct her toward his table. "I believe you've met everyone in my family but haven't been properly introduced to my mother. Chanelle Robinson, Elizabeth Kingston."

"Nice to see you again, Mrs. Kingston." Chanelle noticed that they had started on their meal, but Vance's spot was empty. "I'm sorry to disturb your dinner."

"Please call me Betty." The older woman smiled as they shook hands. "And it's not a disturbance. Is this your first cruise, Chanelle?"

Chanelle nodded.

"And you're traveling alone?"

She nodded again, feeling a prickling sensation at the back of her neck. It happened whenever she became anxious, and right now she was very apprehensive about being questioned about her personal life. If there was anything she was highly sensitive about, it was either about work or *that*.

"That's very adventurous of you. Well, since you were so kind to help me today, Chanelle, I'm sure Vance here will be happy to help you in any way during the cruise. Right, son?"

Chanelle groaned inwardly. She was afraid to look at Vance. He must be feeling even more cornered than *her*.

"It would be…my pleasure," he drawled. He grinned as Adrien took a huge bite of a butter tart. "Would you care to join me for dinner, Chanelle? My family started without me, as I was at a meeting. They'll be leaving shortly and I'll be all by myself." His eyes glinted at her expectantly.

Chanelle's heart flipped. "Oh…um…sure," she said and, nodding to the group, she strode toward the nearest buffet, her nerve endings tingling knowing that Vance was right behind her.

When they returned to the table, Vance's family was ready to leave. "Goodbye, Chanelle," Betty said. "We'll be heading to Deck Five for the captain's event. Perhaps we'll see you there?"

"Perhaps." Chanelle didn't want to commit; *this* encounter had already made her feel somewhat overwhelmed. She smiled her goodbyes and tried to focus on enjoying the famous scallops from off the Nova Scotia coast while Vance dug into his *tourtière* and poutine. She glanced at him as he was licking a dribble of the cheesy gravy before it slid down to his chin, and the split second that he caught her gaze, she felt her insides quiver. He ran his tongue over his lips and then flashed her a grin. *"Je m'excuse,"* he apologized. "I adore Quebecois cuisine, and it adores my face." He slid his empty plate away and reached for the dessert plate. "And now for the pièce de résistance…"

Vance bit into his butter tart. It was sweet, but not as sweet as the woman sitting across from him, munching delicately on the lacy cookie she had chosen. Her auburn hair was gleaming in the sun that streamed through the window, and with the stunning dress she had chosen, she could easily be the subject of a painting.

Vance was convinced now that fate was deliberately making them cross paths.

It was impossible not to notice someone as beautiful as Chanelle. But being with her again, something deep inside him was telling him it was more than just her looks that was drawing his attention. It was her actions, whether it was the way she had sprung up for Adrien or how she had readily helped his mother.

He was seeing glimpses of her highly sensitive qualities, he realized. And he liked them just as much as her physical qualities…

They hadn't exchanged much conversation over dinner. She had seemed very pensive, and he hadn't wanted to disrupt her thoughts. As he bit into his second butter tart, a drop of syrup began to slide down one corner of his mouth. He saw Chanelle's mouth twitch and he laughed. "I told you, French Canadian food and I have this mutual attraction..."

Vance wiped his mouth with a napkin. Chanelle was gazing at him enigmatically, and he felt something shift inside his chest. He wanted to reach out and squeeze her hands and impulsively tell her that sharing her company had been another treat for him, and that he had also enjoyed their time together in the Sky Promenade and afterward at the fruit bar.

It was crazy, but despite his intention earlier to not seek her out, Vance suddenly wished he could take hold of Chanelle's hands and get her out of that chair and into his arms. Right or wrong, he wanted to taste her lips, and trail kisses down her neck to that lovely spot at the base of her neck where her pulse was softly beating.

His eyes burned with longing as he held her gaze, and a flicker in Chanelle's green hazel depths made him wonder if *she* could possibly be feeling the same way...

CHAPTER ELEVEN

CHANELLE DIDN'T KNOW if she should feel relieved or upset at the sudden appearance of a waiter with a jug of water to refill their glasses. For a moment there had been something in Vance's expression that had made her want to catch her breath. But when she transferred her gaze from the waiter back to Vance, whatever she had seen—or imagined—was gone.

He rose and asked her if she would be going to the captain's event. Unsure if he was leading up to asking her to accompany him, or if he was just being polite, Chanelle hesitated. Maybe that look in his eyes had just been a figment of her imagination. Like a mirage for a desert traveler seeking water...

So what had she been seeking? An indication that Vance Kingston—a seasoned playboy—had feelings for her? Feelings that went beyond a physical attraction?

You're delusional, her inner voice mocked. *Do you actually think this Zodiac magnate would be interested in you in that way? Wake up and smell the sea air, honey.*

She saw Vance glance at his watch.

He was obviously anxious to get back to his family.

She stood up. "I think I'll just go back to my stateroom," she told him. "I've developed a bit of a headache, and if I rest awhile, it may not develop into a migraine."

Vance frowned. "Do you suffer from migraines often?"

"When I've been under a lot of stress, or if when the barometric pressure changes. Usually before my head starts pounding, I get a warning, an aura."

He raised his eyebrows. "What do you mean?"

"Auras can vary. For me, it's a zigzag that flashes in my eye, making it hard to focus," she said. "So if I'm looking at you, I don't see you the way you are. I see you like a Picasso painting…"

"Wow, I had no idea," he said. He peered at her closely, as he were expecting to see an aura develop right then and there. "Will you be okay to go back to your stateroom alone?"

"My vision is fine at the moment," Chanelle said drily. "Your features are perfectly in place."

And perfect, she added silently.

"If you *do* end up with a migraine, please don't hesitate to dial the medical facility. And if you want to de-stress, you might want to consider a spa treatment while you're here."

"Thanks. I'd better go. I'm keeping you from the captain's event," she said lightly.

"Not at all," he murmured. "Take care of yourself, Chanelle. And if you *do* feel better, I hope you consider coming back to the event."

She nodded and started to walk away. Of course she would take care of herself. But she had no intention of going to the captain's event with Vance. Even though she had seen something in his eyes moments earlier that had ignited a spark of excitement in her veins…

No, she tried to convince herself as she entered her stateroom and plopped down on the edge of her bed, she had only imagined something in Vance's eyes.

Chanelle caught sight of herself in mirrored panels on either side of the television unit. Her cheeks didn't need blush; they never had. They were quite rosy right now, a telltale sign of the anxiety caused by her ambivalent inner voices: *Vance Kingston is interested in you. There is no way Vance Kingston is interested in you.*

Chanelle couldn't imagine finding someone who would understand her sensitivities and the demands of her work. Her previous relationship had crumbled because she had made her work a priority.

Maybe she just didn't know how to be in a balanced relationship.

She had things to work out about herself…her job…her future. So how could she possibly entertain even the remotest idea of being with another man? It hadn't even crossed her mind when she had booked this cruise…

Chanelle shook her head in frustration. Here she was, stuck and feeling restless in her room, while people were enjoying themselves at events all over the ship. She could be at the featured artist event or magic show, or at the '70s disco party, or maybe trying out her luck at the casino…

Who was she kidding?

She probably didn't have the concentration to sit through a gallery presentation, she didn't know if her head could take the blaring disco music and she didn't even gamble. Chanelle sighed and impatiently grabbed the pamphlet showing the evening's events. This was apparently the other side of Sagittarians. The negative side. Restless and impatient. Yup, that was *her* right now.

Chanelle tossed the pamphlet down. Being highly sensitive hadn't always worked in her favor over the years. She had taken herself out of play in many situations—often social ones in high school and university, and later, with work colleagues—because of her HSP sensibilities. Which meant she had missed out on fun opportunities because of her inhibitions and inability to loosen up. She hadn't given herself the chance to explore new friendships, new possibilities.

And in worrying about the negative, she had missed out on the positive.

She was still doing that.

It was time for her to stop second-guessing herself and start taking chances.

Take a leap of faith.

Chanelle stood up and smoothed down her dress. She would not stay cloistered in her stateroom and miss out on the fun on the ship. She freshened up, took a pill for her headache and, after applying a new coat of lip gloss, she grabbed her purse and made her way toward Deck Five.

Her brain might be trying to convince her that Vance Kingston had absolutely nothing to do with her decision, but deep down she knew the opposite was true.

And she was willing to risk everything to discover how he really felt about her by looking into his eyes…

The captain had welcomed everybody on deck, introduced some of his crew, and was now engaged in the photo session with guests. He'd be at it for a while, Vance thought, eyeing the line. In the meantime, the jazz musicians had begun their repertoire, and couples were already moving toward the dance floor. His mother, Mariah and Adrien had said their good-nights. They would be getting up fairly early to board the tender for Coral Haven, and so would he, but he had told them that he wanted to stay behind for a bit to enjoy the music and relaxed atmosphere.

That had been a white lie. He was waiting to see if Chanelle would come back. His anticipation had caused a tensing of his stomach muscles as he directed regular glances toward all the possible entry points she could take to Deck Five. He had almost finished his brandy, and he'd have to make up his mind whether to order another.

Occasionally a couple or small group of women would come up to chat with him. Some of the women glanced at him with undisguised interest, and he satisfied them with a generous smile and a group selfie if they asked.

The dance floor was filling up. The deck had a patio atmosphere, with strings of multicolored suspended lights that provided a soft illumination under the starry night. And sensual music that made you want to slow dance for hours…

If you had the right woman in your arms.

A waiter came by, and Vance ordered another brandy before walking to the railing to look out at the shifting waves. He couldn't help thinking that taking a cruise by oneself could be difficult emotionally, especially when couples were dancing nearby, their arms clasped tightly around each other.

Vance felt a jab in his gut. For the first time in his life, he had a feeling that there was something—no, *someone*—missing in his life. Not that his life had been devoid of women before his father had died. Far from it. But they had all been superficial relationships, with no commitment. He had never *pretended* to be committed. Wasn't that the reason he had earned the title of playboy? And he had enjoyed it for quite a while.

But those relationships were over. He didn't want superficial any longer, he realized. And as Vance stared at the expanse of sea under the stars, he realized something else: he needed to let go of the coping mechanisms he had subconsciously constructed in the past that had affected his relationships.

If he wanted more than just a temporary fling with a woman, he'd have to break down the walls of distrust around his heart and allow himself to be vulnerable. To not withhold his emotions in order to prevent himself from getting abandoned.

And hurt. Like he had done with his father.

His dad was gone.

And after his death, Vance had risked everything for the business. Yes, he had done it initially out of guilt, but as the weeks went by, the sense of guilt had diminished as his interest and passion for the company had grown.

And now his gut was telling him that he needed to take a new risk and allow himself to be open to a serious relationship...

He gulped back the remainder of his brandy. Turning around, his pulse spiked at the sight of Chanelle making her way past a group of couples who were chatting with drinks in hand. Vance saw every movement she made as if his vision had clicked to slow motion mode: the toss of her shiny auburn hair, the tentative smile on her poppy-red lips, the gentle sway of her hips in that fabulous dress and the even more fabulous curves of her legs. And how could he fail to notice the glances directed her way, both male and female?

Chanelle looked more enchanting than ever. And Vance was more than ready to be enchanted. With his heart drumming so loud he couldn't hear the music around him, he headed toward her.

CHAPTER TWELVE

AT CHANELLE'S FIRST SCAN of the guests on deck, she didn't see Vance, and disappointment hit her like a cold wave. And then she spotted him leaving his place at the railing and walking toward her, and that cold wave turned into warm and bubbly surf.

Vance extended his hand and she took it, letting him lead her to a table for two further away from the musicians. He asked how she was feeling, and Chanelle told him that she was feeling better. She accepted his offer of a drink, and a waiter returned with a virgin Caesar for her and a coffee for Vance.

"I had my drinks before you arrived," he told her. "While I was sticking around to see if you'd come back." He looked at her with those intense blue eyes, and the warm feeling inside her climbed up a few notches.

They sat companionably as they listened to the music and watched the guests dancing. When the jazz musicians took a break, two new performers proceeded to the stage with their Latin guitars. And when they began their second song, Vance asked her to dance.

She could hardly believe that here she was on the second night of the cruise, in the arms of Vance Kingston. *Slow dancing...*

Chanelle couldn't blame the drink for feeling as if she were up in the clouds, floating toward heaven. So the only thing she could blame was Vance Kingston, and his touch that was making her pulse throb erratically. And his spicy cologne that was driving her to distraction. She caught her breath as he pressed her closer, and her forehead brushed against his jawline. If she turned to the right, his lips would be close enough to…

This was madness. How had this happened?

Chanelle had not envisioned a man in the picture—*her picture*—for a long time. And a known playboy, who was doing what he did best: flirting and making her fall for him like every other woman he had played with in the past. Only, unlike those women, Chanelle was neither glamorous nor wealthy…

Chanelle stiffened as the stark truth hit her. The stars in her eyes dissipated and left a dark, black void full of doubts.

"Are you okay, Chanelle?" Vance said huskily against her ear, and she realized that she had stopped dancing.

How could she possibly respond?

She didn't want to be rude, but she had to protect herself. These were dangerous waters she had entered. And judging from her body's reaction to the man who had led her there, she had to make her way back to safe shores before something happened that she would regret. In a few days, the cruise would be over. She was delusional if she thought this shipboard flirting could lead to anything else. She had to put a stop to it.

Now. She was way out of her league.

"My headache's back," she lied. "I think I'll just return to my stateroom."

Vance's blue eyes pierced hers. He didn't release her hand, nor his arm around her waist.

"We can go somewhere quieter…"

"I don't think—" Chanelle hesitated as a couple, locked in an embrace, bumped into them.

Chanelle and Vance broke apart, and after the couple apologized and continued dancing, Vance said brusquely, "Okay, let's go."

Chanelle felt his arm around her as he ushered her inside and she was conscious of a few curious gazes following them. Were they thinking that she and Vance…? Her cheeks burned. She hadn't expected Vance to accompany her.

When they got to her stateroom, Chanelle unlocked the door, opened it a crack, then turned to Vance. "Good night," she murmured.

His eyes glittered down at her. "How can it be, when you don't trust me?"

Chanelle's eyes widened. She opened her mouth and then shut it, completely at a loss for words.

"Chanelle, I haven't known you for very long, but from the time I *have* spent with you, I have picked up on a few cues. Like how your lovely cheeks flame up when you're feeling stressed or distressed." He cocked his head at her appraisingly. "Now I could be wrong, but I have a wild hunch that you were worried about my intentions and therefore had to come up with an excuse to leave."

Chanelle's cheeks were burning. She heard voices approaching from the end of the hall and quickly opened the door wider. The last thing she wanted was people seeing who was at her stateroom door at this time of night. "Please come in for a minute," she urged.

A few moments later, she had no choice but to face him. And be truthful.

She sighed. "I'm sorry I had to make up a fib this time. I was telling the truth earlier, though, and I did take a pill before going to Deck Five." She looked up at him warily.

Vance's mouth quirked, and he reached over to take one of her hands. "Chanelle, I'm not your confessor," he said huskily. "But please tell me if I'm right. I can handle it." His eyes met hers without wavering.

Chanelle bit her lip. He had spoken candidly and hadn't sounded as if he were playing games with her or trying to manipulate her in any way. "You're right," she conceded. "I don't know you very well, and I'm not sure I can trust your intentions. And if you want me to be honest—" she eyed him defensively "—your reputation precedes you."

Vance's eyes narrowed. "Ouch. But thanks for being honest." He looked down at her hand in his and was silent for a few moments. When he looked up, there was regret in the depths of his eyes.

Chanelle felt a twinge of guilt. She hadn't intended to hurt his feelings. *So now what?*

"The past is the past," he said quietly. "I can't undo that, Chanelle. But I'm not the same man I was nine months ago, and the years before that." He gently let go of her hand. "The death of a family member changes you…"

Chanelle felt a lump in her throat as Vance's voice wavered. Maybe it had been wrong of her to bring up his reputation, but it had slipped out before she could think clearly.

She realized the stateroom was dark except for the dim light in the entrance. She should turn on the other lights.

"Now that I know how *you* feel, Chanelle, would you want to hear the truth about *my* feelings?"

"You must feel that I'm judging you…"

"No worries. I have a thick skin. Or rather, a layer of chain mail under these clothes." He suddenly grinned at her. "I'm not called Sir Vancelot for nothing."

Chanelle couldn't help smiling, and some of the tension in the air seemed to dissipate.

"So may I have your ear, Lady Chanelle?"

"I suppose I can spare a minute or two," she murmured. "But then you'll have to go. I've booked an early excursion tomorrow on Grand Cayman." She strode into the room and turned on a light. She sat on one edge of the couch and Vance sat down beside her.

"Swimming with the stingrays?"

"*Not!* With my sensitive skin, I'd probably break out in some kind of a rash."

"Going to Hell?"

"*Pardon?*"

Vance chuckled. "It's a town named for its unique rock formations. It's part of the island tour and includes the turtle center."

Chanelle laughed. "For a moment I was about to tell *you* where to go!"

Vance burst out laughing. "And I called you a *lady*?"

Chanelle pretended to look at him with disdain.

"Well, where will you be heading, my lady?"

Chanelle felt something flip in her chest at the smile in his voice and eyes as he said *my lady*. "I'm heading to a beach with the name of some kind of alcohol. Whisky Beach or something to that effect."

He chuckled again. "Rum Point Beach."

"Yes, that's it! Rum, whisky—it's all the same to me, since I indulge in neither."

"You're a funny lady."

"Why? Because I don't drink much?" Chanelle frowned at him, confused.

"Because you make me laugh."

"Is that what you wanted to tell me? That you find me amusing?"

Vance gazed at her without responding for a few moments. And then he placed his hand over hers. An inner voice told her to move her hand away, but a stronger voice said the opposite. She couldn't tear her gaze away, either.

"I want to tell you a lot of things, Chanelle. Yes, I

find you amusing. And kind. And dedicated. And—"
he squeezed her hand gently "—and beautiful." His eyes
seemed to darken as they gazed into hers with such intensity that she caught her breath. And then he was leaning
toward her, and the magnetic force that his eyes had ignited
seemed to be pulling her toward him as well.

When their lips touched, her eyes closed automatically
and she was unable to process anything else but the instinctive need to respond. She felt Vance release her hand,
and a moment later both his hands were cupping her face,
deepening his kiss until her whole body tingled. Had a kiss
ever felt this sweet? This…delicious?

When he finally pulled back gently to look into her eyes
again, Chanelle felt like she was swimming in their dark-
est, deepest, most pleasurable depths.

She traced her fingers against the stubble of his jaw.
Vance caught his breath and suddenly brought her hand
down. "I need to go now, Chanelle," he said gruffly. "I'm
sorry, but I don't want to stay and have you regret it later."

Vance felt like an absolute heel, leaving Chanelle with that
look in her eyes. The look of a dejected puppy. But how
could he stay without knowing for sure that she wasn't just
caught up in the moment and later wouldn't blame him for
taking advantage of her?

Kissing her had been his first big mistake. Yes, she had
responded, and yes, he had wanted to continue, but something inside him had tugged on the reins of his passion and
made him stop. Chanelle Robinson was vulnerable. She
had had two big changes in her life in the past year and
had booked this cruise to relax and make choices about her
future, not get involved with *him*.

Vance returned to his stateroom and walked out to his
balcony. He watched the waves rising and cresting, and

he felt a similar agitation inside. A swell of happiness that Chanelle was attracted to him, and then a sense of deflation that somehow he had handled it all wrong.

He should have kept it light. They had been laughing, caught up in a play of words, and he had to go and spoil it by letting his testosterone take over.

Vance groaned. He could have even stopped after he had told her that she was beautiful. But he hadn't been content with the sparkle that had lit up her eyes at his words. He had wanted further proof of her feelings...

Well, he had gotten proof, all right. But when Chanelle had demonstrated her desire, his inner voice had abruptly broken through the sweetness of her kiss to tell him to slow things down, that she was vulnerable and that she needed space to work things out in her life.

He started to unbutton his shirt when a tentative knock on his door made him freeze. His heart jangled against his rib cage. He leaped to open it, but it wasn't Chanelle standing there. He tried to control his emotions and smiled at the environmental director he had met with earlier. He and Pauline had become friends since he had started working at Zodiac, and she would be leaving the next morning for her upcoming wedding on Grand Cayman Island at the end of the week.

She handed him a gift box. "Since I won't be at the gala to celebrate your new position, *President Kingston*," she said, hugging him.

"Thanks, Pauline. And I have a surprise for you when we're all back in Toronto."

"Sounds good," she said with a laugh. "I like surprises."

He wished her the best, gave her another hug and watched her leave. Turning to reenter his stateroom, he started at the sight of Chanelle halfway down the opposite hallway, her face as frozen as her body. She had intended to come to his stateroom, he realized, only to find him hugging another woman who was just leaving.

He had to explain…

But before her name had finished leaving his lips, Chanelle had turned around swiftly and disappeared around the corner.

CHAPTER THIRTEEN

AFTER VANCE HAD left her stateroom, Chanelle had remained transfixed on the couch, her face feeling as numb as her brain. What had just happened?

Vance had ignited something within her that she had never experienced in her previous relationship. A combination of feelings that had produced an alchemy that was powerful, magical.

A desire to know Vance to the core.

The magic had been sparked by his touch, his kiss, his words…

And then he had pulled away.

Because he had thought that if he stayed, she might regret it later…

He couldn't have been more wrong.

Chanelle had stared woodenly at the door, considering a swirl of other possible reasons for his decision. Farfetched though it seemed, could it be that deep down, he was worried about her motives?

That she was really after his money and was trying to ensnare him?

Chanelle did not want to accept the excuse Vance had used. He had pinned his decision on *her*, making it look as if he was considering her feelings before his own. Feelings that she *might* have regrets if they had allowed their passion to play out…but then, she *was* terrified of getting hurt again. Did she go into self-protection mode whenever things got serious? Maybe…

But *he* had decided to play it safe and deny them both what they had been close—*so close*—to experiencing.

And he hadn't given her a say about it.

Chanelle had felt shortchanged. With an unexpected surge of warrior determination, she had leaped off the couch and decided to talk to Vance, thinking that at the very least, she could ask him to open up about his true feelings, just as she intended to be about *hers*.

And then, whatever would be, would be…

Minutes later, the elevator had opened to the lobby on Vance's deck. Chanelle's nerve endings were practically crackling, and she had breathed deeply to try to steady her heartbeat. She had turned into the long hallway, only to spot a woman wearing the familiar Zodiac employee blazer hugging Vance. And then he was telling the woman that he had a surprise for her when they were back in Toronto. She had laughed, and then Vance had given her another hug.

At this point Chanelle's feet had felt cemented to the floor. Like in a nightmare, with her vocal cords frozen as well.

Seconds later, Vance had gazed *her* way, and Chanelle had clearly seen the dismay on his face.

She hadn't wanted to stick around. Nothing he attempted to say would have mended the gash in her heart.

Once a playboy, always a playboy, she had thought bitterly as her gaze dropped to his unbuttoned shirt. And she had turned and fled, taking the stairs instead of waiting for the elevator. It was only when she had arrived back in her stateroom, and she had bolted the door, that she had burst into tears.

Damn him, she thought now between sobs. He had played her for a fool. No wonder he hadn't wanted to stay.

He had planned an *encounter* with an employee he was obviously involved with on the ship and back in Toronto.

Well, he could have her. And while he was at it, he could also go to hell.

Vance had considered running after Chanelle but had decided against it. She would not have wanted a scene of any kind in front of other guests. He would wait awhile and then go and knock on her stateroom door. And hope that she would let him in and give him the chance to explain.

Would she hear him out after what she had witnessed? Being highly sensitive, Chanelle would have arrived at the worst possible conclusion about him. And he couldn't blame her.

Putting himself in her shoes, he could understand why she wouldn't want to face him. She had been on her way to see him—that alone made his heart twinge—only to find him hugging another woman. And Chanelle must have heard the exchange between him and Pauline as well. His promise of a surprise when they were back in Toronto...

He had to talk to Chanelle. Make her understand...

Vance had another thought. Chanelle was probably not only thinking the worst about *him*, but also about herself. That hurt even more. He groaned. Chanelle had had a rough year personally and professionally, and the tenuous feelings of trust that she had shown him must have immediately shattered. He had seen it on her face.

She would be blaming herself for having allowed him to get so close...and feeling humiliated...

Vance rose and strode to the door. It was almost midnight, but there would be no rest tonight unless he got through to Chanelle. He did up the buttons on his shirt and headed to her stateroom, his pulse as fast as his footsteps.

CHAPTER FOURTEEN

CHANELLE LOOKED AT herself in the bathroom mirror. Her eye makeup had smeared from all the crying she had done, and her eyelids were puffy. *Absolutely beautiful*, she thought bitterly, using Vance's earlier words.

Chanelle was too upset to even attempt sleeping, so instead of changing into her teddy, she put on a pair of shorts and a T-shirt. Knowing that her thoughts would just continue to torment her, she turned on the TV and started flicking the channels mindlessly. Propped up on pillows against the headboard, she felt a flutter of anxiety at the thought of having to spend three more days on the cruise with the possibility of crossing paths with Vance.

If she did run into him, she would not let him see how shattered she was. She had her pride.

And she had absolutely no intention of seeking him out. *Not a chance in hell.* She had allowed herself to succumb to his charms and had ended up feeling like a complete fool.

As she continued changing the channels, Chanelle realized she was clenching her jaw again. And watching TV wasn't helping. She pressed the off switch and turned off all the lights except the lamp by her bedside. She breathed in deeply and tried to focus on the sound of the waves from the open balcony door.

Her attempt at mindful meditation was interrupted by a soft tap at her door. Chanelle felt her stomach coil instantly into a hard knot. She remained motionless. Had it been her imagination?

The knock came again. "Chanelle? Please give me a chance to explain…"

Chanelle's heart tumbled crazily against her rib cage. She couldn't believe that Vance had the nerve to think that she would give him the time of day. Or night. The last thing she intended on doing was opening the door and letting him in. She had made that mistake once, and she wouldn't be so foolish as to allow him in her space again.

"Chanelle? I know it sounds like a cliché, but it's not what you think. You'll understand if you let me in."

Vance was keeping his voice low, but Chanelle could hear both urgency and frustration in it.

"I don't want to explain out in the hall… Please answer, Chanelle."

Chanelle turned off her lamp and pulled the covers over her head.

There's your answer, Mr. Kingston.

She woke up to a baby-blue sky that was painted with soft brushes of pink. It was such a peaceful sight and a sharp contrast to how she felt inside. She couldn't get the memory of Vance and the woman out of her mind. She had had a troubled sleep, waking up every two to three hours, and at one point, she had almost been tempted to go to an upper deck to walk around and clear her head.

Chanelle was glad she had set her cell phone alarm. She couldn't wait to get off the ship and spend the day by herself on Rum Point Beach. Sure, there would be other guests who would be thinking along the same lines, but she was determined to find a quiet spot and just forget everything that had happened to her so far.

She stepped into the shower and tried to keep thoughts

of Vance from following her in. *Fat chance.* How could she forget the feel of him as they danced? The muscled shoulders, his hand firmly clasping hers…and then later, the heady sensation as his lips took possession of hers…

Stop! He used you!

Chanelle turned off the shower. *That's* what she should be focusing on, not his body or his lips, she thought, scowling. She wrapped herself in the guest bathrobe and a few moments later changed into a navy bikini before slipping on a knee-length yellow cotton dress with eyelet accents and spaghetti straps. The multicolored wrap bracelet Kayla had given her was her only accessory.

Chanelle prepared a large beach bag with the essentials and then checked the time. Room service should be arriving shortly. Another smart decision she had made yesterday. She would have her coffee and toast and then make her way down to the tender station on Deck Two. She would at least enjoy the beach today, Chanelle promised herself. And there would be nothing or nobody to prevent that from happening.

Least of all Vance Kingston.

Chanelle took the elevator down to Deck Two. She had received a call from Guest Services while she was having her coffee, advising her that her time to board the tender had changed. For unspecified reasons, she would be leaving half an hour later than she had planned.

When she arrived, there was a group just about to get onboard. She rushed to join them and presented her identification card to one of the security officials. A whistle sounded, and a few moments later, the group proceeded to board. There was a substantial breeze, so Chanelle opted for the covered lower deck. She made her way carefully down the steps, glad to see there were plenty of good seats.

She made her way toward the back, and a sudden shuffling made her look to her right. Her heart felt like it was about to rocket out of her chest…

Chanelle swayed sharply as the tender started moving, and she plopped down hard on the seat closest to her, just arm's length away from where Vance Kingston was standing. And at the far end of the tender, his family was smiling and waving at her.

Vance wished Chanelle would have heard him out last night. He had stared at the door of her stateroom for a few minutes after his last appeal, hoping that Chanelle would change her mind. He had gotten the message loud and clear when he saw from the space at the bottom of the door that she had turned off the light. Giving up, he had headed back to his own stateroom.

He had felt like a total jerk to have hurt Chanelle, even if it *had* been unintentional. And none of it would have happened if he had just continued kissing her instead of leaving her at such a vulnerable moment.

But where would they be now if he had let himself give in to the passion that had been steadily building inside him?

He had to make amends to Chanelle.

For several hours, Vance had racked his brain as to how he should handle this highly sensitive situation with an even more highly sensitive person. Staring up at the ceiling above his bed, Vance had come up with a few ideas and then scrapped them. And then he remembered that she was heading to Rum Point Beach. And he and his family would be taking one of the tenders to Coral Haven. The passengers would all be getting off at Grand Cayman, and Vance's tender would continue on.

The only thing he had to do was to ensure Chanelle boarded the same tender he would already be on. That could be arranged with a quick call. And then Vance would attempt to make another appeal for Chanelle to hear him out. And if he couldn't convince her, she'd still have the option of getting off at Grand Cayman. If Chanelle continued to Coral Haven, it would have to be entirely of her own free will.

Vance met Chanelle's incredulous stare with a polite nod. He had known that it would be as awkward as hell trying to discuss the matter between them with people all around, but he had no other option. He would give it his best shot, and if Chanelle could be convinced to remain onboard instead of going with her original plan, they would be heading to a place that Vance considered heaven on earth. While Mariah, Adrien and his mother relaxed in one section of the rambling villa his father had had built five years ago, Vance would have a better opportunity to set things right with Chanelle.

And if the stars and planets were all aligned in his favor, he and Chanelle would spend an idyllic day together before the tender arrived to take them back to the *Aquarius*.

Vance closed the distance between them by sitting opposite her. He leaned forward. "Chanelle, I can't say a lot now, but I promise you'll understand if you let me explain."

Chanelle's cheeks were like smoldering coals, but her eyes flashed ice. "Oh, I understand," she said stiffly, keeping her voice low.

She turned her gaze away from him to look out at the scenery. He felt bad that her first excursion off the ship had to be tainted by bad feelings. If only she would gaze into his eyes and see the genuine tenderness he felt for her. But of course she couldn't, with the thorn-covered glasses she was wearing…

Vance gazed at Chanelle's profile and felt his heart expanding. It wasn't just *tenderness* he felt for her, for God's sake, it was more than that. It was a truly happy feeling that had eluded him in the past, even when he had thought he was enjoying himself with other women. It was the feeling that he had found a rare treasure when those green-hazel eyes had sparkled under the patio lights on Deck Five.

It was the way his heart had vaulted when she returned his kiss…

Maybe he wasn't quite ready to put a name to it just yet, but if it was what he thought it was, he'd find the right way to let Chanelle know…

Before time ran out on him.

CHAPTER FIFTEEN

COULD *ANY* MAN be trusted? Chanelle tried to focus on the enchanting views of palm trees and charming villas as the tender sped past, but Vance's proximity made it impossible. The lump of bitterness and disillusionment that had settled in her throat and stomach after last night's discovery hadn't lessened any, and now, facing Vance but unable to express herself with so many people around them, Chanelle felt frustrated. And angry.

Chanelle swayed forward as the tender hit a choppy patch of water, and she caught her breath as Vance's arms shot out to steady her. His face was inches away from hers, and now she could see the faded blue of his eyes and the shadows beneath. His Adam's apple bobbed as he swallowed.

He hadn't slept much, either, she thought. Could it have been the result of a guilty conscience? *Good.*

As Chanelle stared at him defiantly, something in Vance's expression made her falter.

There was something there that was different than the way he had looked at her in the past. A look of…of *sadness* that seemed to reach across and connect with something in her own eyes.

And then he smiled at her as he released his hold, but the sadness remained in his eyes.

Chanelle felt a vague urge to let him explain. Her heart started drumming.

Should she relent and at least hear him out?

A chorus of excited voices distracted her. A group of passengers around her rushed off to get a better view of something in the waters.

"A pod of porpoises," Vance said. "Always a delight for tourists."

Chanelle started to rise, but she hesitated as Vance touched her arm. "Can we talk? At least while this diversion lasts?"

Chanelle looked down at his hand at the same time that he withdrew it. His touch, although gentle, had sent a sizzle along her nerve endings. She felt a flush creep up her neck. Taking a deep breath, she sat back down.

He was leaning forward, his brow creased above blue eyes that startled her with their clarity. "Chanelle, I know you're planning to go to Rum Point Beach. But I don't think you'll be able to enjoy it fully with this misunderstanding between us. If you give me a chance, I will clear everything up."

Chanelle raised her eyebrows. How much could he clear up with her before the passengers returned to their seats? "This—this is awkward," she admitted. "I should never have—"

"No, Chanelle. I take full responsibility. I want to explain—better than I did last night—why I needed to leave. And that the person you saw at my door is not who you think she is."

They both turned at another wave of excited shouts from the passengers.

"Look, Chanelle." His voice had a sudden note of urgency. "In a minute—or less—they'll be back and we won't be able to talk. I need more time. I'm asking you to trust me and to stay on the tender. Come to Coral Haven with me instead of going to Rum Point Beach. There will be time and space to make things right." His eyes bored into her like blue spears. "I want to make things right with you, Chanelle."

The passengers started clapping. "That's the end of the porpoise show," Vance said. "And we're almost at Grand Cayman…"

Chanelle had no time to respond as the passengers made their way noisily back to their seats. Her eyes met Vance's as a couple of teenagers zipped past them. No, there was no time—or space—to hear him out.

Do you want to?

She bit her lip, the thrumming in her chest increasing as the tender neared the shore. Moments later, the passengers started to file up the stairway and out, and Chanelle knew she had less than a minute to make a decision. She glanced at Vance's mother and sister, who were absorbed in something Adrien was saying.

Chanelle glanced quickly at the family now exiting the tender. She stood up, her knees feeling wobbly. If she was going to leave, she'd have to go. Now.

Her gaze flew to Vance. He hadn't moved, but his eyes were fixed on hers like lasers. Her brain willed her body to start walking, but her feet were rooted to the floor of the tender.

Chanelle opened her mouth to say something, but the whistle of the tender operator startled her. She bit her lip and, feeling a tremor of anticipation course through her, she promptly sat down.

Vance's heart had jolted when Chanelle had stood up, but when, timeless seconds later, she sat down, his heart had started pumping so hard that he almost put his hand over it to try to calm it down.

This was big. He had seen the indecision on Chanelle's face, the flicker of a frown as she debated in those few seconds whether she should leave and proceed to her excursion on Rum Point Beach or stay and give him the chance to explain. He was both stunned and elated at Chanelle's decision.

He wanted to say something, but his words were stuck in his throat. Chanelle had turned slightly to look out at the activity on Grand Cayman, and he was relieved to have some time to process the impact of her decision. And his reaction to it.

Vance hadn't taken it for granted that she would choose to continue on to Coral Haven. And he had felt a current of indecision himself before he suggested it to her. Was he doing the right thing? Why was he choosing to make things right with a woman he had known for less than two days? And why was he bringing her to Coral Haven? He hadn't brought Brianna there, despite her not-so-subtle hints that she'd love to see his island.

He knew he was complicating things. He had sacrificed so much of the last nine months to the promise he had made to lead the company. He had made it his top priority. Nothing had competed with his razor-sharp intentions. Nothing and nobody. Especially a woman. He had instinctively known that to succeed, he had to suspend his playboy inclinations. At least until he had proven himself at Zodiac Cruises.

But something had changed since he had stepped onboard the *Aquarius*. In his previous relationships, Vance had played it safe, controlling the extent of his emotions. He hadn't allowed himself to become emotionally entangled with any woman. And they had seemed satisfied—for the most part—with the limited scope of his intentions.

It was different with Chanelle. No other woman in the past had intrigued him the way she had. Instantly. And after two days of spending time with her, something deep inside was telling him he needed to take a risk with this woman. Risk showing her that he genuinely cared about her feelings. About her.

He wanted more with her.

And he had to find out if there was any chance that she wanted more with him. If she would let him teach her how to trust.

He couldn't play it safe anymore, and he couldn't toy with Chanelle's emotions. The only way to discover what she wanted was to act now, before the cruise ended and she went back home.

Which was why he had had to provide an opportunity for them to be together.

He wanted more than just work in his life. He didn't want to end up like his father. And he knew now that he wanted—needed—more than just a physical relationship.

He wanted love.

Vance gazed at Chanelle's profile. He felt an ache in his chest, but it wasn't painful. It was an ache of longing, of anticipation, knowing he had to make a conscious decision to take a risk. A risk at letting love in.

He watched the breeze ruffling the long, thick waves of Chanelle's hair. Her complexion was peach soft, with a rosy glow on her cheekbones. He caught a whiff of her perfume, its sweet peach scent making him feel like he was in an orchard in BC's Okanagan Valley or in Ontario's Niagara-on-the-Lake. He breathed in deeply, and at that moment, she tossed her hair back and met his gaze.

She blinked at him wordlessly, the sweeping motion of her eyelashes over green-hazel eyes mesmerizing him, the curve and fullness of her lips making his pulse quicken. He wanted to talk to her, but they were a few minutes away from Coral Haven, and he didn't want to start something he couldn't finish.

He would get that chance soon enough…

CHAPTER SIXTEEN

CHANELLE HEARD ADRIEN shout something excitedly. She pulled her gaze away from Vance's and saw that they were approaching an island. Coral Haven. She drew in a breath, already enchanted by what she saw. The surf cresting on the whitest beach she had ever seen, leaving what looked like the scallop-edged lace hem of a wedding gown. Lush vegetation and palm trees swaying in the breeze. And glimpses of a sprawling villa beyond with its coral facade, canopied windows and elegant balconies.

"Pinch me," she murmured, and then realized she had said it aloud.

"I would," Vance replied huskily. "But I'd get into trouble with my mother."

How was she supposed to respond to that?

Fortunately, she didn't have to. Vance answered his cell phone, and Chanelle couldn't help hearing his responses to someone called Valentina, thanking her and Carlos for looking after the villa and preparing it for their visit. He told Valentina the tender was approaching and just minutes away, and her response made him chuckle. "I'm sure 'the little breakfast' you prepared for us is more like a banquet, Valentina." He glanced over at Chanelle. "So it's a good thing I've brought an extra guest."

Another pause followed by a deep laugh. "No, Valentina, the only Mrs. Kingston with me is my mother. My *other* mother besides *you*," he joked.

Moments later, the tender was moored near a large boathouse and Chanelle waited for Vance's mother, sister and nephew to precede her as they stepped onto the long dock. Vance followed behind her, and as the rest of his family strode briskly toward the path that would lead to the villa, Chanelle slowed her pace to gaze around her. The view was stunning, with the clear azure water lapping at the pristine shore, changing to various hues of turquoise in deeper waters.

"Do you still want me to pinch you?" Vance's amused voice behind her made Chanelle realize that she had stopped walking altogether.

"Thanks, but no thanks," she returned with a slight edge. "I can usually bring myself back to reality without having to be pinched." She quickened her pace.

"Chanelle, you know I'd never hurt you." His voice was soft as he stepped up beside her.

"Well, you have," she blurted, forgetting her earlier intention of not letting him see how shattered she was. She felt a prickle behind her eyelids but couldn't bring herself to look at him.

"Uncle Vance!" Adrien left his mother's side to run back toward them. "Can you come and swing with me in the gazebo? Mommy's going inside to help Valentina, and Grandma's going to check on the rose garden..."

Vance bent to catch Adrien as he approached and lifted him high over his head. Adrien squealed, "Let me down, let me down," but as soon as Vance complied, he cried, "Lift me up, lift me up!"

Vance burst out laughing, and Chanelle couldn't help smiling. Their gazes met when Vance, holding a giggling Adrien up in the air, turned to glance at her. Despite her comment moments earlier, Chanelle felt a sizzle run through her at Vance's boyish grin. The rest of him was anything but boyish, she couldn't help thinking as he brought Adrien back down. Her gaze took in his strong shoulders and muscled biceps, enhanced by his tan T-shirt. His well-fitting jeans couldn't disguise his muscular legs, either.

The dock ended and a charming stone walkway began, flanked on both sides by agave and other exotic plant species that made Chanelle catch her breath with their vibrant colors. An artist's paradise, she thought, her gaze flitting from the brilliant multicolored crotons and hibiscus varieties to the giant pink-and-coral peony blooms that perfumed the air as they walked past. She caught her breath at the variety of orchids. She had read up on the flora of the islands and had learned that there were twenty-six varieties of native orchids, and one in particular called the wild banana orchid, which was the Cayman Islands' national flower.

Chanelle gasped when the sprawling two-story villa came into full view, with bougainvillea spilling over balconies and yellow-green canopies adding charm above the windows of the coral stucco walls. Absolutely enchanting.

Her gaze wandered to a courtyard featuring white rattan furniture with red-and-yellow floral cushions and giant glazed pots bursting with flowers of the same color. Four umbrella tables were set with cut flower arrangements in decorative clay vases, and two hammocks swayed slightly in the breeze at one edge of the courtyard, near the rose garden that Vance's mother was now inspecting.

"The pool and gazebo are on the other side of the villa," Vance told her, as Adrien pulled him in that direction. "Why don't you join us, Chanelle?"

They disappeared around a bend before Chanelle could reply. She gazed toward the beautiful rounded door of the villa. It was painted the same green as the window canopies and looked like an illustration from one of Chanelle's childhood fairy-tale collections.

Chanelle strode quickly toward the path Vance and Adrien had taken. Things might be strained between her and Vance, but she didn't really want to put herself in a position where she would be open to questioning by the women in Vance's family.

And at least Adrien would be a buffer. She wasn't ready to be alone with Vance again. *Not just yet…*

The other side of the villa was just as breathtaking, with its wraparound porch and massive sunroom. The pool area, with its outside bar and elegant chaise lounges, was an oasis in itself, with potted palms and water fountains and an outdoor shower at each end. The center tiles at the bottom of the pool featured the Zodiac Cruises name and logo, and the twelve zodiac signs were displayed on the outer tiles.

Chanelle felt like she was in another world. Vance's lifestyle was so far removed from her own. Why, her entire apartment could fit in the sunroom. She sighed. It wasn't that she was begrudging any of the Kingstons their material possessions. Vance's parents had worked hard to achieve their success, making many sacrifices at the beginning, according to the online articles she had read about their rise to success in the cruise business. And now Vance was leading the company, showing initiative and a fierce commitment to its continuing success.

Chanelle watched the soon-to-be official president of Zodiac Cruises swinging away with his nephew in the gazebo, grinning as if he were a kid at the midway. It was a huge white structure on a solid foundation, with an overhanging roof and rolled-up canvas panels between its twelve wooden posts. On the end opposite the swing, there was a hammock big enough for two people, a bistro set and a bar-size refrigerator.

Chanelle couldn't help wondering if Vance had made use of the gazebo with any of his female friends on sultry island nights… All he'd have to do was to roll down the canvas panels and he'd have a summer bedroom…and a bottle of wine in the fridge waiting to be savored…

Vance's gaze met hers as she stood a few feet away from them, and he waved her over, bringing the swing to a stop. "Come and join us," he called. "There's nothing more relaxing than an old-fashioned ride on a swing."

Chanelle eyed the swing. She would sit across from Vance and Adrien. She could handle *that*.

But could she handle having those blue eyes continue to look at her that way?

Vance tried not to make it obvious, but he couldn't help gazing at Chanelle and the striking picture she made. No, *striking* wasn't the perfect word. She was eye candy in her yellow dress with its eyelet sections, revealing glimpses of navy and bare skin underneath. And her bare shoulders—under the thinnest spaghetti straps—and curvy legs elicited thoughts that made his heart drum an erratic beat against his ribs.

He couldn't believe that she was actually here on Coral Haven, especially after he had basically given her the brush-off last night. The excuse he had tried to convince himself with was that Chanelle might have regretted it later if he had stayed. And that had been a valid supposition, but there had also been another reason why he had backed off. *Fear.* Fear that making love to Chanelle would force him into a commitment, and he hadn't been sure that he had it in him to commit to a serious relationship.

He didn't exactly have a good track record when it

came to commitment… But then again, he had never met a woman he had wanted to commit to.

He had screwed up with Chanelle. But now he had the opportunity to make things right. Explain his reasons. *His fears.* Show Chanelle that he wasn't playing with her emotions or with anyone else's.

As soon as he could get her alone…

Valentina had prepared a feast. The gleaming modern sideboard displayed platters of croissants, pastries, steaming omelets and sausages. She had put on the strong coffee that Vance and Mariah preferred and Earl Grey tea for their mother.

Minutes earlier, Valentina had sounded a bell, and after rolling down the canvas panels of the gazebo to keep it cool, he, Chanelle and Adrien had gone inside. Vance had introduced Chanelle, and Valentina had given Vance a wink and an approving nod before leaving for the day.

Breakfast was not as awkward as Vance thought it might be. Mariah was treating Chanelle like a longtime girlfriend. And his mother was chatting easily with Chanelle about her rose garden.

Vance reached for another custard-filled croissant. There was no rush to do anything but enjoy the moment. And he certainly was enjoying how things were playing out with Chanelle and his family.

It shouldn't be too long before he had Chanelle all to himself…

CHAPTER SEVENTEEN

AFTER VANCE'S MOTHER and sister had left to go up to their respective rooms, Vance turned to Chanelle. "Look," he said, "we're here for a good stretch. I *do* want to explain what happened last night…and apologize for any misunderstanding… but could you just indulge me for a few minutes and let me show you around the place?" He tilted his head at her—if she wasn't so upset with him, she'd find his puppy dog look humorous.

Chanelle pursed her lips. Maybe he was trying to ease into it…and maybe she needed a few moments to mentally prepare what to say to *him*. "Fine," she said coolly, wishing those baby-blue eyes weren't so easy to look at. She couldn't let them distract her from the reality of his true nature…even though he had made her feel things she never thought she would feel again…

Despite her intentions to remain indifferent, Chanelle found herself captivated by the beautiful rooms and eclectic furnishings. She found herself listening as Vance explained how his mother's love of antiques was reflected in areas like the main floor living room, with its mahogany Chippendale highboy and gleaming secretary desk, along with more traditional floral upholstery.

His preference for elegant simplicity was the inspiration for the sunroom, he told her, indicating the ivory Italian leather couches and scarlet cushions positioned around a red-lacquered circular coffee table. Chanelle's eyes widened at the massive bay window that overlooked the pool and gazebo area and provided a stunning view of the beach a short distance away.

Vance had selected many of the paintings throughout the villa, and he gave Chanelle a blurb about each artist and the inspiration behind the work.

"Wow," she said. "I didn't expect you—"

"To be so smart?" His mouth twisted wryly, and he gazed down at her with raised eyebrows.

"That's not exactly what I meant," she said, flushing.

"I *did* major in art history and design, and before stepping into my father's shoes, I curated an art gallery. Although I sadly neglected my own art after discovering the art of being a playboy," he added wistfully.

Chanelle's eyes widened. How could he be so...so *casual* about it?

"Forgive me for being blunt, Chanelle, but it is what it is. My parents weren't very happy, as you can imagine. My mother wanted me to use my degree in some capacity in the company—designing and overseeing the art galleries and auctions, for example—but I was caught up in my own self-indulgent world. And I couldn't see myself working for or with my father."

"You didn't get along?" Chanelle ventured.

Vance gave a curt laugh. "Ah...*no*. He was barely around. He was a workaholic. And when he did come home, he made it clear that he had no use for my art."

Chanelle felt a pang at his words. She understood what being a workaholic was all about. And now she could see how that had affected her relationship.

"Both sides lose out," she murmured. "It must have been hard having a father but hardly ever seeing him. And having him not take your art seriously."

"I had a hard time investing any emotions—positive ones, that is—in an absentee father," he said, his voice steely. "And I swore I'd never turn out like him."

His gaze shifted to a stunning landscape on one of the walls of the sunroom. She had recognized it immediately as a painting by one of the iconic Group of Seven upon entering the room. Now at close range, she saw that it was one of J. E. H. MacDonald's scenic landscapes. Vance turned to Chanelle. "I like to have a bit of Canada with me when I'm away." He smiled. "I also have a Lawren Harris in my bedroom. I was inspired by the Group of Seven. I started sketching and painting in high school and had filled a sketchpad with my drawings to show that I was serious about pursuing art at university." His smile disappeared. "My father got angry. Tossed it aside. For him it was get involved in the company or nothing. And back then, I chose the nothing."

"Our past experiences and choices help make us who we are," Chanelle said. "When we're young, we subconsciously tell ourselves stories in order to cope with our situation. You internalized the fact that your father put his work before you and probably concluded that he didn't love you. But now, as an adult, having stepped into his shoes for the last nine months, your perspective has probably changed a little. Maybe you can see that he was focused on building a future for you, possibly because his father wasn't able to do that for him. And maybe he was worried, knowing how hard it is for artists to make a living…"

Chanelle hesitated. What was she doing? She had no business speculating on his personal situation or feelings toward his father. She was here to listen to what he had to say, not to give him a social worker's take on his relationship with his father.

A muscle flickered along Vance's jawline. His eyes had

narrowed and he was looking at her intently, but Chanelle had a feeling he wasn't really seeing her at that moment. And then he turned abruptly and strode to a curving alabaster staircase that led to the second floor.

Passing the closed doors of the bedrooms where he said Mariah, Adrien and his mother were resting, Chanelle followed Vance through a long hallway to a central foyer with an antique drop-lid desk, built-in bookshelves and two recliners. When he gestured to Chanelle to sit down, she complied, her pulse quickening.

Okay, here it comes, she thought, trying not to look as cynical as she felt. *The excuse for kissing me like the ship was about to go down, then leaving me in the lurch to take up with a Zodiac employee.*

She bit her lip. Despite the rather personal exchange between them a few minutes ago, the fact remained that he had some explaining to do.

Why was he staring at her like that? He wasn't waiting for her to begin, was he? Because if that was the case, she had plenty she could say to him, starting with—

"Chanelle, before I get into what I really want to say, I have to thank you…"

Chanelle couldn't help making a sound that came out as a half laugh, half cough. "You're kidding me. For *what*, exactly? For providing you with some onboard entertainment?" She tossed her hair back and stared at him pointedly.

She was satisfied to see his eyebrows furrow and a hurt expression cross his features.

"Ouch," he said softly. "Chanelle, you've got it wrong. And I promised to explain—"

"I think I can figure it out," she said, raising her eyebrows. "As I might have mentioned before, your reputation precedes you. Leopards can't change their spots."

Vance clutched at his chest. "That's another arrow to the heart, Sagittarius. Didn't you see the sign on the tender? No archery allowed…"

"This is not a joking matter," Chanelle said curtly. She shook her head and stood up, heat sizzling through her veins. She strode to the French doors and stared out. The sun had disappeared, and the swiftly moving clouds were darkening. Just like her mood. She was already upset at *him*, but now she was upset with herself.

Vance sprang up from the recliner and strode over to stand beside her. "Look, Chanelle, please let me explain, okay?"

Chanelle turned to face him as a few drops of rain began to plop against the panes.

"I wanted to thank you for giving me your take on the situation with my father. My perspective has changed," he said huskily. "I gave up the playboy lifestyle after my father died." His gaze shifted to the view. "I was too stubborn to promise my dad on his deathbed that I would carry on the business. And when he died, I was filled with guilt." He gazed back at Chanelle. "I realized I had to let go of some things. First of all, years' worth of resentment for a father who had spent more time at his job than with his kids. And second, life as a playboy." His eyes pierced into hers. "This leopard *has* changed, Chanelle. No spots in the last nine months. And the woman you saw me with is our director of environmental operations. She came by to drop off a gift for me since she wouldn't be at the gala."

Chanelle raised her eyebrows, remembering Vance's unbuttoned shirt and the hug he and the woman had shared.

"I was hugging her because she was leaving this morning to meet her fiancé in George Town," he said, as if he had just read Chanelle's thoughts. "They're getting married at the end of the week and then going on their honeymoon."

He gave Chanelle a few moments to digest this information. "She's not only a great employee, but she's become a good friend. And in case you heard mention of a surprise in Toronto, I was referring to a surprise party from the staff to congratulate them on their wedding."

Chanelle pursed her lips. So if Vance had given up his playboy ways, why had he paid any attention to *her*? Kissed her so...so—

Vance stepped closer to Chanelle. Her pulse rate had increased exponentially as Vance had proceeded with his explanations and now, with him standing so close that she could feel his breath on her forehead, she was overwhelmed by a feeling of light-headedness. She looked up at his firm jawline and curves of his mouth, and when her gaze met his, the intense look in his blue eyes startled her. She inhaled sharply as Vance leaned down to kiss her.

She had wanted to ask him why he had left her stateroom so abruptly, what he had meant when he had said, "I'm sorry, but I don't want to stay and have you regret it later..." but his kiss blocked her words. And now his lips were moving over hers with a gentle pressure that was sending a swirl of desire throughout her. When he suddenly clasped her and deepened his kiss, Chanelle felt her thoughts and unspoken words scatter.

She wanted to believe him.

And she wanted this fantasy to continue...

Chanelle felt her sense of caution dissipating with the intoxicating pressure of his lips on hers. She wrapped her arms around his neck, and with the deliberateness and precision of a skilled Archer, she slid her fingers under his T-shirt to where the Aquarius waves were tattooed on his back. Pressing him closer, she returned his kiss with the passion that he had ignited, confident that her invisible arrow was hitting its mark.

* * *

Vance could feel his heart thumping erratically as Chanelle responded to his kiss, and when they finally broke apart, he realized the extra pounding was coming from the fat drops of rain pelting the French doors. A flash of lightning appeared, followed by a crackle of thunder that made Chanelle jump.

Sudden rain showers were common enough in these parts, and he was sure that this one wouldn't last long. He was disappointed, though. He had hoped to walk along the beach with Chanelle and show her around the island…

He wrapped his arm tighter around her. Her face had paled and her green-hazel eyes were blinking. "My, what big eyes you have." He smiled at her. "Don't worry, Chanelle, the house won't blow down. It's a good thing we're here, though, and not out on the water."

"I'm not worried… I guess. But I think you're referencing two different fairy tales."

He laughed. "But there's a wolf in both, right?"

"Yes, and I'm hoping there are no wolves in sheep's clothing around here."

Vance couldn't resist leaning in to nibble Chanelle's neck, his pulse spiking when she gave a little shiver. "And what would you do if you came across one?" he teased.

"I'd distract him with custard-filled croissants," she shot back with a grin. "I'm sure he'd find them much more tasty…"

"I don't know about that," he murmured, leaning toward her again. Another clap of thunder reverberated around them, and Vance heard the alarmed voices of his mother and sister calling him from down the hall. His mother was probably worried that some windows were open and that the rain was pouring in. "I'd better check the windows," he said, squeezing Chanelle's hand.

"You're not leaving me here," she said. "I'm coming with you, Vance. I don't like big storms." She looked up at the ceiling as if she were afraid that it would cave in from all the rain. "Shouldn't we be hunkering down in the basement?"

Vance couldn't help chuckling. "You're in the Caribbean, Chanelle, not Canada. We don't have basements here."

They met his mother and Mariah in the hallway. Mariah rushed to him, grabbing his arm.

"I can't find Adrien," she cried. "I peeked in on him earlier and he was napping, so I had a snooze, too. When I heard the storm, I went to get him, and he wasn't there." She started shaking, and Vance took hold of her arms.

"Stay calm, Mariah. He must be in one of the rooms. You check the rest of the rooms on this floor, and we'll start on the main floor."

She ran down the hall toward the central foyer and where Vance's bedroom was located, calling Adrien's name. Vance turned to his mother. Her face was pale as well, and he felt his heart, which was already drumming over Adrien, twinge. "Mom, you and Chanelle wait downstairs. Chanelle, maybe put on some herbal tea for my mom, okay? I'll search for Adrien. He's probably doing a puzzle in the family room."

He gave them both an encouraging smile and descended the stairs two at a time. He hadn't wanted to show how worried he was, but as he filed through room after room with no sight of his nephew, a feeling of dread enveloped him.

By the time he returned to the kitchen, Chanelle was pouring the tea, and Mariah was running into the room. She burst into tears when she saw that Adrien wasn't with him.

"He—must be outside," she sobbed, trembling. "I'm going to go find him."

"No!" Vance said brusquely. "I'll go."

CHAPTER EIGHTEEN

CHANELLE POURED CHAMOMILE TEA into a cup as steadily as she could, not wanting to show how distressed she was. A child was in danger. Someone she knew, and someone who was precious to Mariah and her family. To the man she was losing her heart to.

"I'm going out to help Vance," she told them and rushed out of the kitchen as Vance's mother was formulating a protest.

Chanelle couldn't just sit there. She wasn't programmed that way. She had been trained to act with lightning speed when alerted to a dangerous or volatile situation involving a child. And right now, the storm was a danger. An enormous danger, with the intermittent lightning, slashing rain and what seemed like gale-force winds. She forced her mind not to think about any number of frightening possibilities as to where Adrien might be.

Chanelle was relieved to find another raincoat in the foyer armoire. It was oversized, but at least it would keep most of her protected. As she put it on, she decided that since Vance had gone out this way, he'd probably be checking the front of the villa and the covered boathouse. She would check the back.

As soon as Chanelle stepped outside, the wind whipped the hood of her raincoat back, and she knew it would be hopeless to even try to put it back in place. She wished she had at least put her hair up in a ponytail, which would have prevented her from being blinded at every turn by stinging strands of her hair along with the lashing rain. It was just early afternoon, but the sky had darkened ominously, and in the heavy downpour, Chanelle could barely discern what was two feet in front of her. An icy fear gripped her.

She prayed Adrien was safe…

Her sandals were soaked, and since the raincoat just came down to below her knees, her legs were drenched as well. It was hard to keep her eyes open, and she had to concentrate on which direction she was going. At one point she slipped into a flower bed that the deluge had reduced to a muddy soup, and she let out a cry at the stab of pain as her knees crashed into a decorative stone slab.

Her legs coated in mud, Chanelle regained her balance and continued toward the gazebo. She reached the pool area first, and her heart twisted at the thought that Adrien might have ventured into the pool.

But surely he wouldn't have dared without an adult with him…

With the reduced visibility, Chanelle had to skirt around the perimeter of the pool, peering in for any sign of Adrien. He had been wearing a red T-shirt…

Thank God, she murmured under her breath, seeing nothing. She plodded on toward the beach. She thought she heard a voice as the rain continued to pelt down, but the sound was quickly swallowed by the wind.

Chanelle was thoroughly soaked through. The raincoat had not been able to prevent the rain from streaming down her neck and drenching her dress right through to her bikini. She pushed her hair away from her eyes as a streak of lightning lit up the sky and made the area around her seem like something out of a supernatural movie. At the next boom of thunder, she made a dash for the gazebo, her heart responding with its own boom.

As she scanned the darkened interior, she spotted a hump in one corner of the gazebo. It looked red… She yelled out his name, and Adrien ran crying to her and wrapped his arms around her waist.

Vance ran as far as the boathouse, the blood pumping so hard in his veins that he was oblivious to everything but the sound of his own heartbeat. Who could have known that the weather would flip? And that Adrien would impulsively venture out of the villa?

He was five years old. And a boy who loved to explore around the island…

Vance backtracked and sprinted toward the shed near the rose garden. He glanced at the roses his mother had admired earlier, now flattened, with petals scattered all around the lawn.

Would Adrien have gone to seek shelter in the shed if he had been playing in the nearby sandbox when the storm had hit? Vance faltered at a sudden muscle cramp in his leg and came to a stop. He swore under his breath and bent to massage his calf, wincing at the pain. When it eased, he continued toward the shed, walking as quickly as he could instead of running to avoid the risk of cramping up again.

Vance called out Adrien's name and looked inside the shed. Disappointment lumped in his throat. He prayed that Adrien might have made his way to the gazebo, the only other outside structure on that side of the property.

As Vance passed in front of the villa, the front door opened, and his mother called out.

Had she and Mariah found Adrien in some unsuspected place inside?

He stopped, chest heaving, only to hear his mother say worriedly that Chanelle had gone out to look for Adrien as well, and she had seen her heading toward the back of the villa.

The lump in Vance's throat slid and landed in his gut like a boulder.

In heaven's name, why hadn't Chanelle stayed put? Now he had two people to worry about. *Two people he loved.*

Cramp or no cramp, Vance sprinted around to the back, yelling out Chanelle's name. His hood had flown off long before, and he couldn't be bothered to keep it over his head. He clenched his jaw as thunder rumbled around him, and he prayed that Chanelle and Adrien were nowhere near areas vulnerable to lightning strikes.

He reached the pool and scanned the water that was agitated by thousands of needlelike raindrops. Now he knew what *desperate* felt like. With an ache in his heart that made him cry out, he made a run for the gazebo.

Vance knew that he had only been outside for minutes, but somehow it felt like an ordeal of hours. He reached for the canvas flap, and seconds later, he wanted to collapse in relief as his eyes made out the huddled figures of Chanelle and Adrien in the corner near the hammock.

Vance called out Chanelle's name at the same time that she called out to him. He ran to her and Adrien and hugged them tightly. "Thank God you're both safe," he said hoarsely, not having the heart to scold either one of them.

"I just got here," Chanelle told him, her voice trembling. "I couldn't just stay inside—"

"We'll talk later," Vance said brusquely. "Let's get out of here. Wait," he stopped her as lightning illuminated the canvas panels. "Okay, Adrien, come with me," he urged when the flashes stopped. "Chanelle, stay right beside us.

We'll go in the sunroom door." He took off his raincoat
and put it around Adrien before lifting him up and carrying him across the property and past the pool, looking over
his shoulder at Chanelle every few paces.

Vance set Adrien down once they were in the sunroom.
He called out to Mariah, and in moments, she was running
toward them, crying in relief.

Adrien hadn't said anything up to this point, his face
frozen in shock, but when he saw his mother, he ran into
her arms. "Mommy, Mommy. I was so scared."

"I know, baby. Mommy was scared, too."

Vance's mother was close behind, and when she reached
them, she hugged Adrien tightly, despite the fact that he
was dripping wet, the raincoat dwarfing him. "Run a nice
warm bath for him, Mariah, and I'll get him some milk and
cookies after I grab some towels for these drenched souls."

Mariah turned to hug Vance and then Chanelle, despite
their dripping state. "I can't thank you enough," she said
tremulously.

"Chanelle found him in the gazebo," Vance said, keeping his voice steady.

"You're an angel." Mariah hugged her again. "A true
guardian angel." She stepped back and then looked down
with a frown. "Chanelle, you're bleeding."

Vance turned to look. Below Chanelle's raincoat, her
legs were smeared with mud and trickles of blood. "I'll
take care of her, Mariah."

When they had gone, Vance helped Chanelle out of her
raincoat. Her clothes were just as plastered as his, the only
difference being that her knees and legs were bare and his
weren't. He frowned upon closer inspection of her scraped
knees. He wrapped a towel around Chanelle and brushed
the last towel quickly over his hair and body before flinging it onto a wicker chair.

"You leave me no choice, Chanelle," he said firmly, "but to play doctor with you." And before Chanelle could respond, he lifted her up in his arms and made his way through the villa and up the alabaster stairway to his bedroom.

CHAPTER NINETEEN

AS CHANELLE FELT herself being whisked up by Vance's strong arms, she had no choice but to clasp her arms around his neck, her heart thudding like a jackhammer. She closed her eyes as he proceeded up the stairway, anticipating a very uncomfortable landing should he lose his balance and fall…

But he didn't miss a step or even falter, as if carrying a woman up the stairs this way was something he was used to doing.

Chanelle opened her eyes and let out her breath. They passed the center foyer where they had been sitting earlier, and after a few moments, Vance paused at a set of double doors and reached for the handle. Chanelle caught her breath at the sight of the four-poster king-size bed and the stunning Lawren Harris painting above, a winter landscape that didn't seem at all out of place in this villa.

Vance's bedroom.

He carried her to a roomy walk-in closet revealing a row of shirts and pants and shelves with at least a dozen pairs of footwear below. "I hope you see something you like in here," he said, setting her down, and although she couldn't see his face just then, she could tell he was smiling. "Because you're going to have to get out of your wet clothes."

Chanelle's mind whirled. "Maybe Mariah has something I could borrow?" She looked down at her yellow dress, its thin cotton material plastered to her body and revealing the navy bikini underneath. Her neck started prickling with discomfort, and she pulled the towel more snugly around her.

"Maybe," he said, his gaze telling her that he had observed the revealing state of her clothes. "But she's busy now, and I'm not going anywhere until we fix up those knees. Before they get infected…"

He motioned for her to proceed into the ensuite bathroom and to sit down on a black leather chair near the marble-sided shower stall. Chanelle was dazzled by the gleaming luxury of the room, with its sleek granite countertop, floor of diagonal white and black marble tiles, and crystal spiral light fixture.

"I can take care of them," she told him. She winced. "I'll just need—"

"Don't move, Chanelle," he said firmly. "I have everything I need in my medicine cabinet. Now just hold tight and it will be over in a few minutes…" His mouth quirked. "You look like a wet little duckling in that yellow dress. And no, not the one in the fairy tale," he added quickly. "Quite the opposite."

She flushed. He was delusional if he thought she looked *pretty*. She had caught a glimpse of herself in the large vanity mirror above the black granite countertop. Her hair framed her face in tangled ropes, and her eye makeup had smeared and run under her eyes in black and navy streaks.

Yeah, real pretty.

Vance strode over to a gleaming white cabinet, withdrew a few items and deposited everything on the side table next to Chanelle. "I'll be back in a second," he told her.

She was tempted to start cleaning up her knees on her own. He had brought over a bottle of antiseptic, some sterile cotton gauze sponges, a couple of wide bandages and some antibacterial ointment. But as she went to grab the bottle, he returned with a chair from his bedroom.

He wagged a finger at her. "Now, now, Miss Robinson…" He deposited the chair opposite her, grabbed a lined waste-paper basket and set it down beside his chair. He washed his hands in the sink, and Chanelle felt like squirming when he glanced in the mirror a couple of times and caught her watching him. After drying his hands, he sat down on the chair.

"Okay, let's do this." He took a deep breath and poured some of the antiseptic on a gauze sponge. He leaned forward and was eye to eye with Chanelle. "I'll need your leg, miss," he murmured.

Chanelle stared at him. He raised his eyebrows. "Oh…" She blinked.

Did he want her to stretch out her leg on his lap?

He held out his hand. "May I?"

"Okay."

What else could she say?

She was already barefoot, having removed her soaked sandals in the sunroom. She extended her leg slowly and tried to keep her breathing steady as Vance put one hand under her calf and the other under her ankle before placing her right leg on his left thigh.

"Okay," he repeated. "Now this might just sting a lit—"

Chanelle let out a cry as the antiseptic soaked into the scraped areas, and her arms flailed, throwing the towel off her shoulders.

"I'm sorry, Chanelle. I know it must sting like hell. But we have to clean it out."

"Just hurry," she replied through gritted teeth and gripped the sides of the chair. Chanelle closed her eyes as he poured and dabbed, using a new gauze pad for each area. She felt like her knee was on fire, and it took all she had not to jerk her leg and accidentally kick him in the face.

"Okay, there, there. Your wound is clean. I'm just going to put some of this antibacterial ointment on the bandage and cover it lightly."

Despite the throbbing in her knee, Vance's soothing voice was helping her to relax a bit. But he still had her other knee to tend to…

He set her leg down gently and lifted her other one onto his thigh. "Okay, here goes. We're almost done."

"You haven't even started the torture," she retorted, her eyes already closed.

"You're being very brave, Chanelle," he said solemnly before applying the antiseptic.

This time she did jerk her leg as she cried out, and when her foot made solid contact, she opened her eyes to see Vance holding his hands over his mouth and jaw.

"Oh, my God," she cried. "I'm so sorry. I didn't mean to kick you."

"I think some teeth are loose and are about to fall out," he said, his voice muffled behind his hands. "Oh, well, it's a good thing I've given up my status as a playboy." He shrugged. "Because I'm pretty sure being toothless is not one of the prerequisites."

Chanelle watched anxiously as he moved his hand away, expecting to see blood and teeth spill out. He gave her a sudden grin, and she saw that his teeth were intact.

Perfectly intact.

She glowered at him. "That was not necessary. You scared me."

"I'm sorry, Chanelle." He gave a soft laugh. "I just couldn't resist…"

She pursed her lips and then smiled. "Apology accepted.

I'll *try* to resist kicking you again." She closed her eyes and then reopened them. "But I can't promise."

"Duly noted. Now let's finish this operation. My other patients are waiting."

Chanelle felt a warm stirring inside at their banter. And then clenched her teeth as Vance proceeded with the next round of dabbing. When the second bandage was in place, Vance looked at her quizzically.

"I've cleaned all around your knees," he said, "but we still have to get some mud off you." He looked pointedly at the streaks on her lower legs.

"I can do that myself," she told him. "I'll sit on the edge of the tub and wash it off." She eyed the streaks her feet and legs had left on his jeans. "And I think you'll need to wash up as well, Dr. Vancelot. And dry."

She felt a warm rush as he smiled at her, his eyes a startling azure. "Um… I'll just need a clean towel," she added.

"Right in the tall cabinet," he murmured. "And I'll use the guest washroom in the room next door." He strode to the door. "You should change into dry clothes right away, Chanelle." His gaze dropped to her legs. "My pants certainly won't fit you, but I do have a pair of light pajamas with a tie belt." His mouth curved. "I'll leave them and some T-shirts on the bed for you…and Mariah can find something for you afterward."

Vance let the warm jets of water pulsate over his body in the guest room shower. He felt some of the tension ease out of his neck and shoulder muscles. For all his levity with Chanelle a few moments ago, he hadn't been as relaxed as she might have thought.

First of all, the fear of what might have happened to Adrien had made every nerve and muscle in his body so tight that he could still feel a residual ache. And then learning that Chanelle had gone out…

Discovering them in the gazebo had made Vance almost collapse with relief. But he had had to be strong for the both of them. Strong physically and emotionally. The physical side had been the easy part. Carrying Adrien inside and then carrying Chanelle upstairs, no sweat. It had been the emotional part that had drained him. Staying calm when he wanted to scream his frustration at every minute of his search that had proven fruitless.

In these past nine months at the helm of Zodiac Cruises, Vance had taken his position seriously, and as he had vowed after his father's death, he had stepped up to the plate and taken control. Out in the storm, he had felt all control slipping away from him. He had not been able to control either Adrien or Chanelle from going out and potentially putting themselves in danger.

He could have lost either one of them.

A lightning strike, a heavy falling tree branch, a misstep causing them to slip into the water or hit their head on something and pass out—any of these situations could have happened.

Vance had experienced the feeling of pure helplessness out in the storm.

And it had shaken him to the core.

But despite this feeling, his instinct to protect his family had kicked in. Every last neuron in his body had been primed to battle the elements and bring his loved ones back home safely.

Home. It wasn't the villa, beautiful though it might be. Home was the people in it, the people you loved.

His home was his family.

And Chanelle.

The storm had shaken up his thinking, too. His thoughts about commitment, about trust.

And if he had hesitated in the past about commitment, it was simply because the right woman hadn't been in his life at the time.

Chanelle was the right woman. He felt it in his gut. And he was ready to shift the scales in his life and find a balance between work and love.

Images of Chanelle flashed in his mind, from the first time he had seen her grab hold of Adrien with her white jeans and fuchsia T-shirt, to her elegant skirt and black top in the Mezza Luna Ristorante, and to that sexy white dress splashed with red poppies… And the yellow dress she was wearing now, wet and clinging to her body, revealing her bikini underneath…

Yes, her physical beauty had aroused his senses, but it had been her inner beauty that had touched his soul. Chanelle was kind, sensitive, courageous, funny, hardworking…and she loved kids.

His pulse quickened at the thought of having children one day…a thought he had never seriously contemplated until now.

But that would mean having a woman—Chanelle— being as committed to him as he was to her.

Aren't you jumping the gun a bit? His inner voice shoved its way into his consciousness. *You haven't even told Chanelle that you want to be in a committed relationship. You just told her you've given up your playboy lifestyle, explained about Pauline, and then you kissed her. Get with the program, buddy. If you want her, you'll have to get more creative. A kiss alone isn't going to do it.*

Vance smiled ruefully. No, he *hadn't* made it clear to Chanelle how he felt. But the storm had made his feelings clearer to *him*. Now he just had to figure out how and when to communicate those feelings to Chanelle.

Vance stepped out of the shower and dried himself brusquely with a large, plush towel before changing into white Bermuda shorts and a turquoise shirt.

In the shower, Vance had come up with a crazy idea that would show Chanelle how committed he was to her… but he needed to sketch out his ideas on paper. And once he was satisfied with his plan, he would present it to her.

When Vance returned to his room, he was disappointed that Chanelle had already gone. He checked the time on his phone. They had about an hour and a half before the tender returned to pick them up to head back to the *Aquarius*. Looking out his balcony doors, he was relieved to see that the storm had diminished significantly to a light sprinkle, and the skies had brightened. There was no danger that they wouldn't be able to return to the ship.

He sat down at his desk. He would work on his idea before going downstairs. And if he didn't get the chance to share it with Chanelle before heading back, he'd save it until later tonight at the gala.

CHAPTER TWENTY

Chanelle had felt a little strange, sitting on the edge of Vance's bathtub in her bikini, rinsing off her legs. How could she *not* imagine him soaking in it, with the jets sending water swirling all over his body?

It was so unnerving…

He'd laid out three T-shirts and a pair of pajama bottoms with alternating loons and red maple leaves—that reminded her of the tie he'd worn for the Canada evening—and the words *Loony for You* on the rear.

Really? In any other situation, she would have found the Canadian-themed pajamas amusing, but all she could think about was how ridiculous she would look in them. With a sigh, she changed into a black T-shirt and the pajamas and headed downstairs.

At least her face and hair no longer looked like she had come out of some lagoon, she thought. Chanelle found Mariah and Adrien in the kitchen. Mariah laughed when she saw the loony pajamas. "Don't mind me," she said. "I can't help cracking up every time I see those. Can you tell Vance is a proud Canadian? Right down to his pajamas. And boxers. But don't tell him I told you." She laughed again.

"Don't tell me what?" Vance said, entering the room. "That Adrien's eating all my cookies?" He winked, ruffling Adrien's hair.

"Nice pants, Chanelle," Vance continued, chuckling. "You're welcome to keep them as a souvenir."

Chanelle's mouth dropped, and Mariah burst out laughing. "I can see how thrilled you are, Chanelle. Come on, let's go wash and dry your clothes and see what we can find for you in my room."

Chanelle was aware that Vance was watching them as they walked out of the room. Or more specifically, *her*. His gaze had swept over her T-shirt, and she had a feeling that his gaze was now taking in the *Loony for You* on the rear of the pajamas.

Upstairs, Mariah waited for Chanelle to get her wet dress and bikini and then proceeded to the laundry room. "They shouldn't take long," Mariah told her. "I'll put them through the quick cycle."

"There's no point in me borrowing your clothes, then."

"Okay, well, do you want to come back downstairs or wait in the guest room? There's a fabulous window seat with a great view, and a pile of books and magazines."

"I can wait in the guest room, thanks."

"No, thank *you*, Chanelle. Please know that you're welcome to visit us here any time."

The guest room was bright and roomy, with coastal decor. The linens were done in white and sky blue, with big accent pillows in a fresh butter yellow. Chanelle sat down at the window seat and looked out at the brightening sky, trying to figure out why she felt a sudden sense of foreboding.

Soon they would be back on the ship, and Coral Haven would be just a memory. She just wished she had been able to explore the island a little more, walk on the beach, swim in those jeweled waters...

It had been kind of Mariah to invite her to come back

and visit, but what reason would she have to come back to the Kingstons' private island?

Soon the cruise would be over, and she would have to make a decision about her job. That was the reality she faced. And sharing passionate kisses with Vance Kingston wasn't going to change that reality. How could it?

The anxiety she had felt searching for Adrien made her realize that she had also been anxious about returning to the same job. Important though it was, it was also highly stressful, and she had had more of her share of stress these past years.

You're stronger than you think, Vance had told her. *You'll know when the time is right.*

Maybe it was time to look at a career change.

No, there was no maybe about it. It *was* time. Time to find something in a related field that wouldn't take all her energy. That would allow her to lead a more balanced life.

There! She had come to a decision! As soon as she returned home, she would start her search for a new job. And a new life. Chanelle automatically reached for her bracelet and realized with a jolt that it wasn't on her left wrist. And then she remembered…she had left it on one corner of the tub.

She would run in and retrieve it before Vance came back upstairs. And then she'd grab her clothes, dry them, get dressed, return to the ship and enjoy her remaining time on the cruise before getting back to reality.

A reality that didn't include Vance Kingston.

While she was exploring other job options in Sault Ste. Marie, Vance would continue his job as president of Zodiac Cruises in Toronto. He had said that his playboy lifestyle was finished, and maybe it was.

But the way he kissed you…

So Vance had gotten carried away after some emotional

sharing about his father...and so had *she*. But that didn't mean Vance wanted anything more. She had been a temporary diversion. He had encouraged her to have fun on the cruise. Live a little.

She would be crazy to think that Vance Kingston could figure in her life after the cruise.

Chanelle bent forward to pick up her bracelet, trying to ignore the sudden heaviness in her chest.

"Nobody ever showed me they were 'loony for me' quite like that before."

Chanelle froze outwardly, but inside, it felt like a lava flow.

She straightened and turned around, holding out her bracelet. "I came back for this," she said as evenly as she could. The room seemed to be closing in on her. She couldn't breathe. She needed air.

She wanted out. Out of the room, out of the villa, and off the island.

And away from Vance.

Away from the man she knew would only ever be a fantasy...

Chanelle was too hot in Vance's black T-shirt. It was making her suffocate. She wished she could just tear it off. And the stupid pajamas, too. She needed to go and get her clothes.

Now, before she...

Vance leaped to catch Chanelle as she fainted. Her face had been flushed, and he had thought it was embarrassment at his comment—which he had instantly regretted—but he suspected that it was something else. Perhaps something to do with the barometric pressure, since she *was* highly sensitive to changes in temperature.

Vance's heart began to pound.

Was she breathing?

Her body had flopped onto his chest, and her head was drooping to one side. He placed his cheek against Chanelle's neck and felt the fluttering of her pulse. Relieved, he lifted her and carried her to his bed, where he set her down gently.

Vance raised both her feet and stuck a pillow underneath, while watching her mouth and eyes for any sign of movement. Had she been too hot? He couldn't very well remove her shirt, though. He put her feet back down and felt for Chanelle's pulse on the side of her neck.

Thank God, or he would have had to initiate CPR…

Vance leaped to the minibar fridge for a bottle of water. She'd need it when she regained consciousness. He set it down on his night table before leaning forward to feel for her pulse again. Watching her filled him with a sudden feeling of tenderness that made the backs of his eyes sting.

And a feeling of terror.

She needed to come to. Calling for emergency services would take far too long.

"Come on, Chanelle, my love. Wake up. *Please*." He brushed a kiss on her forehead.

She gave a soft moan, and her eyes fluttered. And opened.

Vance let out a deep breath. *Thank God.*

Chanelle tried to move.

"No, Chanelle. You have to stay still for at least fifteen to twenty minutes."

"Why?" Her eyes widened. "Where am I?"

"Shh. You're on my bed and you've just regained consciousness."

"From what?" Her eyes widened. "We didn't…"

"No, silly. From fainting. And you scared the hell out of me," he said gruffly. "For the second time today."

Her brow wrinkled. "Why?"

"Why are you asking so many questions?" He felt her forehead. "Just relax. You might be dehydrated. Here, have some water."

He put the bottle to her lips while supporting the back of her head with his other hand. She lay back down, and her hazel-green eyes pierced his. "Why?"

"You're a stubborn one, aren't you? Okay, do you really want to know why, Chanelle? It's because I…I—"

"Vance?" Mariah called from the hallway. "The tender is here."

CHAPTER TWENTY-ONE

CHANELLE WATCHED THE island recede until she could no longer make out the coral walls of the villa. In reality she had only been there for hours, but it had seemed so much longer...and now she was leaving with this inexplicable feeling that she had lost something before she had had enough time to figure out what it was.

When Mariah had called out to Vance, his mouth had clamped shut, and whatever he had been about to say was left unsaid. He had left quickly, and a moment later, Mariah had entered his room to keep an eye on Chanelle. Chanelle had closed her eyes, not feeling up to chatting. After ten more minutes of lying still, she had risen slowly to find that Mariah had retrieved her dry clothes. "Come down when you've changed, Chanelle. The tender is waiting for us."

As they all left the villa moments later, Vance tried to catch her eye, but Chanelle deliberately avoided his gaze. He offered a hand as she was about to step into the tender, but she ignored it with the pretense of helping Adrien. Vance frowned and looked sideways at her, but she continued moving on.

Now, heading back to the *Aquarius*, Chanelle focused on the shifting blues of the sea.

Better than focusing on the shifting blues of Vance's eyes, she thought cynically.

It was choppier going back, a residual effect from the

storm. By the time they boarded the ship, Chanelle's stomach was feeling unsettled. She couldn't wait to go back to the privacy of her stateroom. She'd order a soothing pot of herbal tea and maybe a bite to eat later, if she was up to it. As they waited in the lobby for the elevator, she said as much to Mariah, who quickly reminded her about the gala later in the evening and the champagne art auction. "Have your tea, Chanelle, and a rest, too, but please come to the gala. It's the highlight of this cruise! We'll save you a place at our table, okay?"

Chanelle felt a heat searing her nerve endings, knowing that all eyes were on her. Especially Vance's. It was even worse once they filed into the elevator. His breath fanned her neck, and the spicy cedar notes of his cologne tickled her nostrils. When the bell sounded and a couple excused themselves to exit, there was more shifting, and Chanelle felt Vance's hands encircling her waist to gently indicate that they needed to get by. Chanelle started and took a step sideways while her heart did a somersault.

She held her breath as the door closed, expecting Vance to move his hands away, but as the seconds ticked by in her mind, they stayed put. Chanelle felt sure everyone could see her flaming face, and she was just as sure that Vance could feel her erratic breathing reaching the span of his hands.

Another group needed to exit, and this time, Vance complied with Chanelle's silent wish. Hers was the next stop, she thought, breathing out her anxiety. At the ding, she stepped out and turned to wave. "Thanks again." She smiled, focusing her gaze on Mariah and Vance's mother. "Have a good evening." She turned away quickly, letting out a big sigh of relief as she heard the elevator doors close.

Chanelle repositioned her beach bag over her shoulder and started to walk toward her stateroom when she heard footsteps behind her.

"Chanelle…"

Chanelle turned slowly and stared into cobalt depths that made her feel that she had just entered the eye of a storm.

"You're looking at me like I'm a boogeyman, Chanelle." Vance ventured a crooked smile.

"I—I just wasn't expecting you to follow me," she said without smiling back.

Vance was puzzled. Was she upset at him about something? It was obvious that the dynamic between them had changed. Maybe her fainting spell had something to do with it.

"You looked like you wanted to be alone in the tender, so I didn't want to bother you, Chanelle. I figured you had a headache." He took a couple of steps closer to her. "How are you feeling now?"

Vance saw confusion flitting across her face.

"I'm fine," she said curtly.

"Well, I'm glad I was there to catch you before you hit that marble floor," he told her huskily.

"Yes," she said, her voice softening slightly. "I don't think I thanked you for that." She nodded. "Thank you."

"You're very welcome, Chanelle." He paused as the elevator opened and let out a family. When they had filed down the corridor, he closed the gap between himself and Chanelle. "I'll walk you to your stateroom."

Vance was convinced there was something bothering her.

Why else would she be treating him so indifferently?

Her kiss before the storm hit had been anything but indifferent… It made his stomach flip just thinking about it.

What had changed? Certainly not *his* feelings. If anything, they had intensified when he saw her lying on his bed and thought of how devastated he would have been if he hadn't been there and she had fallen to the floor and seriously hurt herself.

Vance realized with a jolt that Chanelle had stopped walking and was at her door, looking at him pointedly, her hand on the doorknob.

"Chanelle, I wanted to talk to you back at the villa before we left…" He looked at her earnestly. "There's something I need to say to you." He watched as her eyebrows furrowed. His gaze lowered to her lips and to that tiny turquoise vein pulsing at the base of her neck. Vance felt his jaw tensing. He wished he could just kiss her now and leave no doubt in her mind as to how much he wanted her…

"I'm sorry, Vance," Chanelle said stiffly, turning the door handle. "I think it's best if you go."

CHAPTER TWENTY-TWO

OUR LIVES ARE galaxies apart and always will be.

Chanelle hadn't had the nerve to tell him that to his face. But since she had woken up from her fainting spell, it was as if the fairy-tale fog she'd been in had lifted from her mind and now she could see the situation for what it was. She had thought about nothing else during the ride back to the *Aquarius*.

Chanelle closed the door firmly and plopped herself down hard on the couch, wincing as the muscles stretched in her knees.

Nice shape you're in, girl. Your knees are scratched up and now your heart is broken.

It served her right. How ridiculous to have fallen for Vance Kingston in the short time she had been on the cruise. What had she expected? That the president of Zodiac Cruises would be captivated by her brooding disposition and declare his undying love and affection for her?

Yes, they had shared a passionate kiss, a kiss that had had her yearning for more. Vance had swept her off her feet—both figuratively, sending her into wispy clouds of fantasy, and literally, carrying her up a grand flight of stairs like in some old-fashioned movies she had enjoyed watching before life had gotten too busy with her work.

But she had to listen to the voice of reason in the back of her mind. The niggling voice that was telling her that this physical attraction between her and Vance wasn't going to end up like a fairy tale. How could it? In a few short days, she'd be stepping off the ship and making her way back home. The idea that Vance Kingston was contemplating anything more than a casual flirtation with her was simply ridiculous. *A fantasy.*

And *she* had to make it clear to him that she wasn't going to encourage any further contact with him. Because although she had every intention of staying rooted in reality, she knew that there was always a chance that being alone with him could weaken her resolve…just like the spicy cedar scent of his cologne weakened her knees and made her want to—

She was obviously more vulnerable than she had thought.

Chanelle let the tears well up, feeling sorry for herself and even more sorry that she couldn't cry on anybody's shoulder. When her tears were spent, she walked out to the balcony to watch the sky and the sea as twilight began to set in. Since she wasn't hungry and had no intention of attending the gala, she would take this time to explore some options about her future.

Chanelle placed a hand over her bracelet. Becoming a social worker hadn't been a bad choice. Working in child protection had just become too much for her. Maybe a highly sensitive person like herself would have a difficult time thriving in such a stressful, emotionally charged job for her entire career…and maybe the five years she had devoted to this area of social work was all she was meant to do. But what other job *could* she do?

Chanelle looked up at the sky, a palette of blue, pink and magenta. Something deep inside told her that she would discover the answer if she kept open to new possibilities.

Send it out to the universe!

How often had she read *that* advice in self-help books?

"Okay, I'm sending it out to you, universe!" she called out to the sky before going back inside.

She couldn't let this thing with Vance destroy her peace of mind. She was stronger than that. She had to accept the fact that they had been physically attracted to each other and that was all. And if she wanted to be open to new possibilities, she needed to get herself out of her stateroom and allow herself to live a little.

Maybe she'd go to the gala after all.

What would there be to lose? She could handle it. She'd enjoy the musical entertainment and the complimentary champagne at the art auction, and then she'd sleep in tomorrow and enjoy one last sea day before they arrived back in Tampa the morning after.

And then she'd be ready to start a new chapter in her life.

Do you really think you can handle going to the gala? You're taking a risk—

Chanelle squeezed her eyes shut, as if the action could put a stop to her HSP voice. It had worked for her in the past, allowing her to be cautious, be safe. Protecting her from frightening possibilities…

Her eyes flew open. What was there to be frightened of? Yes, she was taking a risk. But that wasn't going to stop her. She was a Sagittarian, wasn't she?

They had chosen to have the gala on the top deck. A section of the Constellation Club had been cleared for the ship musicians, and after the official announcements, they would be performing a medley of popular tunes from the last four decades.

Vance clapped along with the guests after his mother thanked them for joining the staff of the *Aquarius* in celebrating her retirement. Her tribute to Vance's father had moved the audience.

After the applause subsided, she called Vance up to join her. She looked at him for a moment, her mouth quivering slightly. "I can only imagine how difficult it has been, son, for you to have accepted the challenge of taking over where your father left off…" She bit her lip, and Vance felt a lump form in his throat.

This was difficult for her, too. It had always been difficult for her, raising him and Mariah single-handedly most of the time. He hadn't been the only one who had suffered… and now he could see that she had also suffered for him, lacking a proper relationship with his father.

"I'm so very proud of your commitment, dedication and hard work, Vance. You've proven yourself—as I knew you would—not only to your family, but to the entire company, and there is no doubt in my mind that your father would have been just as proud." Her voice trembled at her last phrase, and Vance felt his eyes begin to mist along with hers.

"So, with all my love and pride, I congratulate you for your leadership, and I'm absolutely thrilled to officially name you president of Zodiac Cruises."

Vance blinked a couple of times to keep his emotions in check as he and his mother embraced. When his vision cleared, he looked beyond the clapping hands to his sister's table. Mariah was there with Adrien, but she was not looking in his direction. She was waving at someone. He followed her gaze and spotted Chanelle standing near a column.

She stepped forward, and what he saw took his breath away. She was wearing a floor-length deep purple satin gown with a filmy silver shawl over her shoulders. And she had arranged her hair in a side-swept style, held back with something that glittered under the string lights. His pulse hammered against his veins as he watched her walk over to sit next to Mariah. She waved to Adrien and said something to make him laugh.

Vance heard his name again, and he turned and saw that his mother was looking at him with raised eyebrows.

It was his turn to speak.

He hadn't written out a speech; he knew exactly what he had to say. After thanking his mother for trusting him to carry on the business, he announced his new plan: a new cruise line that would cater to social service organizations, offering their employees a special discount for a Zodiac R&R Cruise. Not only would the employees get the rest and relaxation that they so greatly deserved, Zodiac would treat them with special perks and discounts in all areas of the ship. The first ship in the fleet would be in operation by the following year.

"Society doesn't always recognize the tremendous work and sacrifices made by social workers, nurses and teachers, to name a few," he said, scanning the crowd. "Zodiac Cruises wants to support those who support others." He paused as the guests applauded enthusiastically and, glancing in Chanelle's direction, saw that her attention was riveted on him.

Great—if he could figure out a way of speaking to her alone, he could tell her the rest of his plan…

Vance thanked everyone for choosing Zodiac Cruises and for sharing in the celebration. He guided his mother toward their table, relieved that the entertainers would now be in the spotlight before the art auction began.

He had some unfinished business with the beautiful lady in purple…

As they approached the table, he saw a man stooping to talk to Chanelle, and a moment later, he was leading her toward the other dancing couples.

Where had this guy come from?

Vance tried not to make it obvious that he was watching them as he helped himself from the hors d'oeuvres tray that one of the waiters was holding out to him.

Vance had no idea what he had just swallowed. His thoughts had returned to Chanelle's abrupt manner after her fainting spell.

As he had changed into a white shirt and black suit, he had wondered why Chanelle's behavior toward him had shifted from sizzling hot to disturbingly indifferent. Could she be deliberately repressing feelings for him that went deeper than the physical chemistry that they had both felt? She was probably holding back, believing that they would never see each other again after the cruise.

He would find out tonight, he had vowed, adjusting his tie. And if Chanelle decided not to attend the gala, he would find a way to see her and clear things up with her. Make her understand that he wanted *her* in his life after the cruise. And forever. With that resolution, Vance had made his way to his mother and Mariah's stateroom, feeling much lighter than before.

It wasn't going to be easy to approach Chanelle now, though, with a man having suddenly appeared out of nowhere to whisk her away to dance. They seemed to be chatting easily, and Vance felt a stab of jealousy. *He* should be the one holding Chanelle. He rose, intending to cut in for the next dance, but a few guests stopped to congratulate him and his mother, and he had no choice but to engage with them for a few minutes.

When they moved on, Vance strode toward a less crowded section of the deck, where the smooth operator had managed to lead Chanelle.

Luck was on his side this time, he thought smugly as the song came to an end. But the fellow did not let go of Chanelle.

And had his hand slipped down to her hip?

"May I have this next dance, Chanelle?" Vance gazed at her first, but before she could answer, he turned to stare pointedly at the guy, his mouth curved slightly but his eyes sending a clear "Back off" message.

The guy released his hold on Chanelle, smiled awkwardly and told Chanelle he'd see her in a bit.

Like hell you will, buddy.

Vance nodded with a congenial smile and took Chanelle's hand.

His other hand settled around her waist. He felt her stiffen, and when his gaze met hers, her eyes seemed to be shooting sparks at him from their hazel-green depths.

And then she pressed closer and went on tiptoe to place her cheek against his. His pulse leaped as her lips brushed his cheek and earlobe.

"I *don't* want to dance with you," she hissed in his ear.

CHAPTER TWENTY-THREE

CHANELLE FELT VANCE'S body tense up. She hadn't meant to sound so rude, but the words had escaped before she could think of another way to give him the message.

"Why not, Chanelle?" he said, with genuine curiosity in his voice.

Chanelle was taken aback. She didn't know what she had expected him to say, but she certainly hadn't expected him to ask her to explain. Now she had to answer. And there was no point mincing words. She turned to meet his gaze. "I—I don't want to dance with someone who…who makes me want more…when I can't have more." Chanelle felt her neck prickle with heat at the intensity in his eyes. They had some kind of magnetic pull that kept her from looking away. And to make it worse, the musicians started performing "Stairway to Heaven." The string lights suddenly dimmed, and Vance drew her closer.

"What makes you think you can't have more, Chanelle?" he murmured against her ear as he initiated the slow dance. "You've got your facts wrong."

Chanelle's heart was jumping hurdles. "But the cruise will be ending in two days…" She felt his lips brush against her earlobe and rest there as they danced. The touch made her nerve endings sizzle and her body shiver at the same time.

"Chanelle, let me say what I wanted to tell you at Coral

Haven. You're an enchantress—who looks absolutely stunning in purple, I must say—and someone whom I'd like to continue to see even after the cruise ends."

Chanelle froze and as Vance's words sank in, her feet and arms feeling woozy. The couples dancing around her became blurred, and the music seemed to pulsate right through her body. And then she felt Vance's arms tighten around her, and her arms rose of their own accord and wrapped themselves around his neck. Her cheek grazed his chin, and when their eyes met, it felt like nobody was on deck except them and the music was playing for them alone.

Vance's gaze was intoxicating, and when he pulled her tightly against him, she marveled at how her body fit right into his. They slow danced for what seemed like forever, and when the song finally came to an end, Vance nuzzled her earlobe again and whispered, "Chanelle, do you believe me?"

She opened her eyes with a start, and as some of the couples dispersed, she saw Mariah walking up to them. She broke away awkwardly from Vance.

"Hey, you two," she smiled. "We're heading back to our stateroom. Adrien's starting to nod off. But don't stop dancing on our account. Good night, Chanelle. Good night, *Sir Vancelot*. Don't drink too much champagne…"

As they left, there was an announcement that the art auction would begin after the next mix of songs, and the champagne would start to flow. At the beginning of a classic rock song that everyone started singing to, Vance lifted an eyebrow. "Stay or go?"

"Go," she told him. "I want to end the evening on a quiet note."

"It's quiet in my stateroom."

Chanelle felt a moment of panic. She was at a total loss as to what to do next. Here she was, having just danced as close as two people could possibly get, and she couldn't seem to process Vance's words that she was someone he'd like to see after the cruise, let alone his invitation to go to his room.

He had asked her if she believed him. *Maybe...a little...*

There was no doubt in her mind that there was chemistry between them.

Incredible chemistry.

But he hadn't said *I'm in love with you* or *I want to spend the rest of my life with you.* He had just said she was someone *he'd like to continue to see...*

And there was no guarantee that came with the Vance Kingston package, the guarantee that he wouldn't leave her in the future. Just like her father and Parker had done...

Chanelle's mind filled with doubts.

Maybe they had both been swept away by their physical attraction to each other...and that was the extent of it.

"Chanelle, you're frowning. Are you okay?"

"I—I'm just tired," she said.

She was tired of exhausting herself by trying to analyze Vance's every word or action.

She knew that this was part of her highly sensitive nature, and sometimes—many times—she wished she could just sail along in life without her brain getting twisted up in knots about everything.

What was wrong with her? She was sure most women would jump at the invitation to join Vance in his stateroom.

"Chanelle, if you're too tired, can you just come to my room for a few minutes? There's something I've been designing for Zodiac Cruises, and I'd love to get your input." Vance's eyebrows lifted as she waited for his response.

Chanelle searched his eyes and saw nothing but earnestness in them.

But what if—?

No! She wasn't going to let her doubts control her this time. She was just going to allow herself to sail along for once. Vance's words popped back in her mind: *You're stronger than you think.*

Yes, she was strong enough to handle anything the future had in store for her. But it had taken a little help from Vance to remind her of her inner strength. Her sense of self. She needn't be fearful of anyone abandoning her anymore, least of all herself. She was a Sagittarian, wasn't she? Vance had called her that enough times to make her come to the realization that she had power over her life, her choices, her loves…

And no one could ever take that away from her.

"Sure," she said decisively. "I can spare a few minutes."

Vance led Chanelle toward the sliding doors leading to the elevator lobby. The gala was in full swing. The captain and some of his crew were drawing a lot of attention, so Vance knew his absence wouldn't be obvious. The guests were drinking, dancing and having fun, and they would be happy about another photo opportunity with a handsome man in uniform. Or three. The art auction would begin shortly, then more music, followed by an unexpected surprise: a spectacular display of fireworks. Mariah and his mother would be watching from their balcony, and maybe Adrien would be, too, if he was still awake.

As he and Chanelle approached his stateroom, Vance felt his stomach contract with anticipation. He had thought long and hard about how to tell Chanelle about his feelings. About how he couldn't imagine her stepping off the ship and never seeing her again. About how he couldn't stop thinking about her, and how she had inspired him…

And now, he finally had the opportunity to show her. As he swiped his card against the door plate, he glanced at Chanelle. She was holding her clutch purse and looking down, biting her lip. Was she having second thoughts? His heart hammered softly. She was the kindest, most sensitive woman he had ever met. And the only one who had managed to break through the defenses around his heart. The heart that was finally ready to let someone in.

With any luck, he'd convince her tonight that they belonged together. *For life.*

CHAPTER TWENTY-FOUR

CHANELLE SAT DOWN on the edge of the couch and watched as Vance strode over to his desk. She wondered if what he was designing had something to do with his plans for Zodiac's new cruise line. His announcement that the latter would cater to social service organizations, offering their employees a special discount for a Zodiac R&R Cruise, had jolted her.

In a good way. How could she fault him or his company for being sensitive to people like her?

And when Vance had added that Zodiac Cruises wanted to support those who supported others, Chanelle had felt a stirring in her chest, pretty sure that he had been looking right at her. And then moments later a gentleman had appeared and asked her to dance...

Chanelle hadn't really been in the mood, but her nagging inner voice had reminded her about her intention of enjoying herself tonight.

She sat back on the couch now and tapped her fingers on the cream-colored leather hand rest. The sky's earlier brilliance had faded to dusky blues and pinks, with fading ribbons of gold and magenta. She tried to stifle a yawn.

"Hey, don't fall asleep yet," Vance chuckled, sitting beside her. "First I'd like your two cents about my design."

"Sorry, it's been a day."

"You *are* tired." He gazed at her for a moment and added softly, "This won't take long."

Chanelle looked at the sketch pad in his hands. "Does this design have something to do with your new cruise line?"

Vance's eyes crinkled as he smiled. "It sure does."

"That's a great idea to offer special packages to service organizations." She had to give him that.

"Thanks. I've been working on the idea of a new line for months now," he murmured. "But I was stuck on the purpose behind the line. I wanted to find a new angle, and I did…because of *you*, Chanelle."

Her eyes widened, and her heart started a gentle drumming. "Wh—what do you mean?"

"You made me see what can happen to a dedicated employee in your line of work. How important your job is, and how you give your all to help others. People like you need to be rewarded, not get to the point where they burn out. But sometimes burnout happens, to social workers, teachers, nurses, etcetera." He tapped her gently on the arm. "So *that* became my angle. Supporting those who support others."

Chanelle watched Vance open up his sketchbook and prop it up so she could see what he had done. She gave a soft gasp at the first drawing. *Of her.* Her thoughts swirled, and she couldn't bring herself to look up from the page. As he turned the next few pages slowly, the drumming in her heart became magnified. She saw a series of rough sketches with variations on the new name for the R&R cruise line. And then he turned to the last page with a finished sketch.

Chanelle's heart stopped.

She saw two intertwined Cs in the words *Chanelle Cruises*, with each C extended to represent waves in the sea and an archer's arrow zooming upward. She stared at it for a few moments, and when she looked up, Vance's face was blurred. She wiped her eyes and saw that his eyes had misted also. And then Chanelle remembered what she had thought earlier, that Vance hadn't told her he was in love with her or that he wanted to spend the rest of his life with her. No, he hadn't told her.

But he had just shown her.

Chanelle gazed at him in wonder.

Was she dreaming? She must be dreaming…

Vance closed the sketchbook and placed it on the coffee table. She felt immobilized as he reached over to grab something leaning against his side of the couch. He turned it toward her and she gasped. It was the painting she had admired in the art gallery. *Enchantment*.

She was speechless as Vance stood up and propped it against the back of the couch.

"Is that…" Her gaze dropped to the initials, and her eyes widened. "Did *you*—"

"Yes, it's one of mine." He gave her a sheepish smile. "The art rep mentioned that a guest was admiring it. And she noticed your name on your lanyard." His blue eyes gleamed. "It was going to be in the art auction, but I replaced it with another painting when we returned on the ship. I wanted you to have this one."

She gasped as he suddenly dropped to one knee.

"I have fallen under the spell of your enchantment, my lady," he said huskily, taking her hand and kissing it. "Will you do me the great honor of bestowing me with your hand?"

"You already have it, Sir Vancelot," she murmured with a soft laugh.

"I was speaking of your hand in marriage, my haloed beauty." He grinned, caressing her hair with his other hand. "In anticipation—and hope—of your positive response, I have begun to design your engagement ring…but in the meantime, I hope this humble handmade gift will suffice."

Several loud pops filled the air. "Come with me, Chanelle," he said urgently. He led her to the balcony, and as they stood at the railing, they heard a whizzing sound and more popping as the sky sparkled with the most dazzling fireworks display Chanelle had ever seen.

They watched for a few minutes and then Vance turned her toward him and, wrapping his arms tightly around her, kissed her thoroughly, sending sparks to every last inch of her body. When he released her, his eyes pierced hers, reflecting the flashes in the sky.

"Do you believe me, Chanelle?" he said huskily, repeating the question she hadn't answered earlier. "And will you—"

"I do," she breathed, and reached up to show him with her own kiss.

Vance gave a moan of pleasure. "I almost forgot to add," he said, while brushing soft kisses along her neck, "Zodiac Cruises will be in need of a director of children's activities. Someone who loves kids and can plan year-round events that are fun and safe." He paused to gaze deeply into her eyes. "I must warn you, though. Job hours vary and may require some night shifts…and plenty of cruising."

Chanelle felt a sudden flutter in her gut. Was she actually ready to leave her small-town world and take such a leap? To a new city, new job and, most important of all, a new relationship? Her gaze melded with his. What she saw in the depths of Vance's ocean-blue eyes was a bright promise…

Yes, she was quite ready to take that leap.

"I'll cruise with you anywhere and everywhere," she sighed, slipping her hand underneath his shirt to caress his back. She felt him shiver as her fingers brushed over his Aquarius tattoo.

"I love you, my Sagittarian angel," he murmured against her ear as the boom in the sky intensified. Without waiting for her to answer, he scooped her up in his arms and carried her to his bed, where Chanelle knew the fireworks were only just beginning…

* * * * *

THE MARRIAGE RESCUE

SHIRLEY JUMP

To Joe—may every day going forward
be as happy and wonderful as our first date
and that moonlight stroll through town.
You're my forever.

Chapter One

At five years old, Grady Jackson had climbed up the makeshift diving platform that reached out like a hand over Stone Gap Lake, damned near giving his mother a heart attack. She'd yanked him back, then she'd sat him down on a wooden picnic bench and lectured him long and hard about not being a foolish, headstrong boy. As soon as her back was turned, Grady had scrambled up the ladder a second time and jumped. When he hit the cool, deep, dark water, he'd spent a long moment submerged, so deep he wasn't sure he'd be able to get back to the surface. He had kicked and flailed and clawed his way to the top, and when he took that desperate breath of warm summer air, he'd learned his first life lesson—that taking risks was the adrenaline that fired his brain. Until it wasn't, and everything went sideways.

Now here he was in North Carolina with his tail between his legs. He'd been asked—ordered—by his COO to "take a break from the stress," as Dan Samuels had put it. His COO's loyalty almost cost the man everything, and yet he'd stayed, like a sentry who couldn't leave his post. Of all the people in Grady's employ, Dan should have hated him, told him off, stormed out of the office. In a way, it stung more that Dan had stayed to the bitter almost end.

He'd even taken the task of gently telling Grady the company had lost faith in him.

Hell, he'd lost faith in himself. Grady had ruined everything.

The resources he had left were going to pay Dan's salary and keep the health insurance current. Grady had sublet his apartment, liquidated what he could, and poured everything into Jackson Properties. That money would last another month, maybe two, if nothing changed. If he cashed in the rest of his retirement assets, Grady could buy a couple more months.

A far cry from nine months ago. Once upon a

time, Grady Jackson had made the pages of *Forbes* magazine as an upstart who was heading straight to the top.

What did being at the top mean, anyway? That he got to stand on a towering pile of regrets and look down at the lives he'd ruined?

Grady pulled into Stone Gap a little after three in the afternoon, not in the Maserati he had given back to the bank two months ago, or in the Mercedes convertible he'd bought for fun and sold to keep the lights on at the office, but in a two-door economy rental that shuddered whenever he pushed the accelerator past fifty. The downtown area had barely changed in the past fifteen or so years, as if time had decided to stand still right there on Main Street. The same shops with the same cutesy names sat in the same spots, and the same neighbors strolled along the sidewalks, some now with grandkids in tow. Grady could still see shadows of memories of times with his brothers in the ice-cream shop they'd frequented, the Catholic church basketball court where they'd spent hundreds of afternoons, and the rolling green grass of the park that had been like a second home.

It was all so charming and quaint, a small town filled with families and hopes and dreams. The kind of world that would relax anyone other than

Grady. The closer he got to his destination, the faster his heart hammered and the shorter his breaths became. His vision narrowed, and his chest began to ache.

It's your fault... If you'd only thought before you leaped into that deal... They were counting on you...

He cursed and pulled at the neck of his shirt. There was not enough air in this damned car. Grady pulled under the wide branches of a shady oak tree and parked. He opened all four windows, and for a split second he couldn't feel any air at all. There was nothing to breathe, nothing...

A whispering breeze tickled his face, then picked up steam and whooshed through the car. Grady closed his eyes and concentrated. *Inhale.* One long, deep breath in. *Exhale.* Let the air go gradually, a degree at a time. *Inhale. Exhale.* Repeat. Until the vise on his chest loosened.

This was a temporary setback. He needed just a couple weeks, maybe three at most. He was going to fix this.

He *had* to fix this.

Yet the doubts lingered in the thudding of his pulse. Was this decision, like so many others in the weeks since he'd lost that government contract, just another mistake waiting to happen?

Grady put the car in gear and kept going, until Main Street yielded to trees and space, and brought him to the T junction with Oak. He turned right, then took a left and another right, and finally pulled into a driveway as familiar as the back of his hand. For a second, he was five again, and bursting through the front door and into a world unlike any he had known.

The tar surface had rippled and cracked over the years, and weeds had seized the opportunity to sprout from the crevices. The yard was less overgrown than he'd expected, considering Grady had had to cancel the lawn service last month, which meant some neighbor was probably running his John Deere over the grass a few times a month, just to keep the neighborhood looking nice. That was the kind of place Stone Gap was—do unto others, regardless of whether they do unto you in return.

He got out of the cramped rental and inhaled again, drawing in the scents of fall. Grady stood there, inhaling, exhaling, focusing on the ground, until his heart slowed its frantic hammer.

The two-story house, flanked by a detached one-car garage on one side and a flower garden on the other, cast a long shadow over the driveway. He'd spent many a summer afternoon here, running in and out of the kitchen, hearing the screen door slam behind him and his grandmother's voice reminding him to be careful. The smell of fresh-baked bread, or of warm chocolate chip cookies, would bring him back for a few minutes of still-ness in the kitchen before he was off again, explor-ing the woods behind Grandma's house and the creek that wound its way through the trees like a trail for Hansel and Gretel.

Finally, he was here. He'd come back. To what, he wasn't sure. Amends, at the very least.

He was reaching for his bag when a movement caught his attention. A flash of beige fur, a rus-tle in the shrubs, then the flick of a tail. Grady dropped the bag on the driveway and crossed to the bushes—overgrown and thick and apparently not on the do-gooder neighbor's list of things to do—and bent down. "Hey, you."

Another flash of fur, a couple feet high, then two big brown eyes peered through the twined branches. A yip, then the eyes were gone, the shrubs trembling. Little guy was terrified. Grady could relate to that.

"Hey, buddy, don't worry. I won't hurt you." He straightened, then slipped through a break in the bushes and into a small bare area too heavily shaded by trees for anything to grow. Just on the other side of a massive oak that must have been a hundred years old stood a yellow Lab puppy.

Grady approached slowly, his hand out, talking in soft tones. "What are you doing here? You lost?"

The puppy nudged forward, cautiously sniffing the space between him and this unfamiliar human. He didn't have a collar, and his ribs rippled beneath his fur. If this dog was someone's pet, they were doing a crappy job taking care of him.

"I have half a sandwich left in the car," Grady said to the animal. "Ham and cheese, nothing fancy, but I bet you don't care. Want some?"

The puppy kept on wagging and approaching. Grady bent down, keeping his hand extended, letting the dog sniff and make an assessment. Whatever he smelled, he approved of, because the next thing Grady knew, the puppy was pouncing on his knee and licking his face. Grady had never had a dog as a kid, and never had time for one as an adult, but this pup apparently didn't care about a human's pet-care résumé.

"I'll take that as a yes." Grady scooped the dog under his arm like a football—thing probably didn't weigh more than fifteen pounds—then cut back through the shrubs and over to his car. The puppy squirmed and twisted, trying to lick Grady's face every step of the way. Grady retrieved the sandwich, unfurled the paper wrapper, then stood back and watched the puppy gobble it in a few bites.

"That your dog?"

Grady turned. A hunched, elderly man with a Charlotte Hornets cap pulled low on his forehead waved at the puppy. The man had sharp blue eyes, and a scruff of white beard on his chin. He was carrying a copy of the *Stone Gap Gazette* in one hand, and a coffee mug in the other.

"No. I just found him in the yard," Grady said.

"Thing's been wandering around here for weeks. Every time I tried to catch him, he took off. Called the dogcatcher, but that guy's about as useful as a rhinoceros in a swimming pool."

Grady chuckled. He extended a hand toward the man. "Grady Jackson. I'm one of Ida Mae's grandsons."

The man had a firm grip, and his blue eyes brightened at the mention of Ida Mae. He leaned in closer, studied Grady for a moment. "You're that little wild child who was here every summer, tearing up the woods."

"That'd be me." His two younger brothers had both been studious and quiet, the kind who preferred books to dirt bikes, almost as if they'd had different parents, except when they were at Ida Mae's, and the tight hold they held on their lives loosened. Even today, Grady had little in common with Nick and Ryder, who'd settled into IT careers, until Nick moved down here last year. The brothers had been close at one time, but as they got older and the two-year-plus age difference had made more of an impact, the three of them drifted apart. Nick and Ryder had stayed close, while Grady had fallen into the new role of loner—and it had stuck.

Nick lived a couple miles away now with his new wife. Grady couldn't even remember her name or when they got married. Showed what kind of brother he was. He hadn't even told Nick he was coming to Stone Gap.

He wasn't so sure Nick would care. All their communications for the last few years had been via text. Maybe Grady could remedy that. Maybe not.

"Pleased to see you again. I'm Cutler Shay." The old man studied Grady some more. "You might not remember me, but I'm the one who fixed the flat tire on your bike that time."

Grady had been seven, maybe eight, when he'd gotten that flat. He remembered standing there in the middle of the road, stumped. His father had never been the kind to show his boys how to do much of anything, and certainly not how to change a bike tire. He had exacting expectations for grades and decorum, which didn't include skinned knees or broken bikes. Cutler—he'd been heavier, darker haired and taller then—had given Grady a mini tire-changing clinic on the sidewalk in front of his house.

"I remember that. You taught me more about that bike in one afternoon than I learned the rest of my life."

"Well, that's probably because I've got a head full of useless facts and I'm known for talking the ear off an elephant." Cutler chuckled. "So…now that Ida Mae, God rest her soul, has passed on, are you here to stay or sell? Saw your brother living here for a month or so, with that pretty lady he married. Nice couple."

At Christmas, Nick had asked if he could use the house for a few weeks. Grady had said yes, figuring it couldn't hurt, and would keep the place from falling apart during the winter. He'd worried about damage and decay with each passing week of Atlantic winds and North Carolina sun. And yet, even though the pale yellow paint had faded and one of the dark green shutters was hanging askew, overall, the house didn't seem to need a major facelift. Ida Mae had been fastidious about her home, and that attention to care and maintenance probably meant what was inside was in equally good shape.

"Sell," Grady said. Ida Mae had left the house

to him and divided her life insurance between his brothers. Leaving him the place had been some act of sentimentality, he was sure, but in all honesty, he'd rather have gotten full right to the insurance, which, as cash in hand, would have been a hell of a lot handier and wouldn't have required a real estate sign, sale and deed signing. Still, the house was what he'd gotten, and now he hoped it held the key to a financial reboot and a second chance.

Cutler shook his head. "That's a shame. That house has been in your family for three generations. Ida Mae sure would have wanted it to stay that way."

Yeah, well, unlike him, Ida Mae wasn't broke and out of options. Grady loved his grandmother dearly, and had loved the time he had spent here with her, but that didn't mean he was sappy enough to hold on to the house out of sentiment. Not when he needed the money so desperately. "Well, nice talking to you, Cutler. If you find out who owns this dog, let me know."

"You should take it to Beth Cooper. That girl knows about every dog in this town, and if someone lost that little guy, she'd be the one to hear about it."

Beth Cooper. The name hit Grady like a brick. Last time he'd seen her, he'd been sitting behind her in math class on the last day of sophomore year, trying to work up the courage to ask her to the end-of-year dance. Young Grady had been a risk taker in every area of his life—except with girls. The teenage Grady had gotten tongue-tied around pretty girls, and around Beth Cooper in particular. He could still see the curve of her neck exposed by the lift of her blond ponytail, the bright blue of her eyes, and the grace of her smile.

"Beth has a little shop on First," Cutler went on. "She's a groomer, dog trainer and rescuer of pretty much anything lost or hungry."

That fit the Beth he remembered, but it didn't answer his real questions. He wondered if she was still single, if she still had that melodic laugh he'd loved, and if she remembered him half as well as he remembered her.

Grady scooped up the puppy, which had finished eating and was now sitting beside him, expectant and still looking hungry. "Thanks, Cutler. I'll take this guy down to her now. I'm sure some family is missing him."

Cutler nodded. "Nice to see you again. Don't be a stranger."

Considering Grady wasn't planning on staying in town after the house sold, he didn't know how to answer that. So he didn't answer at all. He just opened the car door, deposited the puppy on the passenger's side, then shooed him back when he scrambled onto the driver's seat.

"Hey. Can I ask you one favor?" Cutler said.

Grady paused, his hand on the door. "Sure."

"Don't rush into selling right away. Stay in the house for a while. See how it feels on you. Sometimes a house grows on you when you spend some time with it. You know, like a new friend."

Grady wasn't about to agree and there was no diplomatic way to refuse, so he just said goodbye, got in the car and then pulled out of the driveway. Regardless of what one sentimental neighbor thought, the chances of him keeping this house— and taking away his only option for starting over and making it up to all his employees—was about one in the millions he used to have.

For a Pomeranian, Lucille was one strong dog that had firm opinions about baths. Beth Cooper grabbed a thick white towel and swiped the worst of the water and suds off her face. Unfortunately, the towel didn't do much for her soaked jeans or shoes, past Beth's waterproof apron. "Okay, so now we've both had a bath," she said to Lucille.

The little white dog wagged her tail, sending another spray in Beth's direction. Beth laughed, picked her up, then put her in the small pen in the back of the shop, to let Lucille run off some of her postbath joy before Beth attempted to brush her and give her nails a trim.

A couple other small dogs scampered around Lucille, in a circle of yips and tail sniffing. It was like a preschool, except with fur and wet noses. Beth loved the dogs, though, and loved the hours she spent in her shop. There was just something about a dog—the way it loved unconditionally, gave without needing in return—that made the worst days she'd ever had seem a little better.

The chime announcing a customer sounded in the back room, surprising her, given the odd hour. She didn't have a ton of walk-in traffic—usually just clients coming in for drop-offs and pickups. Beth glanced in the mirror as she headed to the front, though it was pretty much a useless exercise. She spent her days giving baths to dogs, so dressing up was pointless. As per usual, her hair was wet, tendrils plastered to her cheeks and neck, and soapy water blotched the parts of her bright pink Happy Tails shirt that weren't protected by the apron. She smoothed the errant hairs in the direction of her ponytail, then pushed on the closed bottom half of the split swinging door, making sure none of her doggy customers were underfoot.

A man stood just inside the front door, looking uncomfortable and out of his element. He was tall, broad shouldered, and wearing a pale blue button-down shirt with the cuffs rolled up, exposing strong hands, defined forearms. Jeans hugged his hips, outlined long, muscular legs and, she was sure, one hell of a nice looking butt. Aviator sunglasses hid his eyes. In his arms, a squirming yellow Lab puppy kept licking the man's cheek.

Damn. She should have at least put on some lipstick or something before she came out to the front. It wasn't every day that a hot man came into her shop. Not that she was on the market for dating or even anything close to it. Right now, she didn't need another man in her life besides the one who already took up every second of her spare time, but it didn't hurt to be admired once in a while and feel more like a girl and less like a wet dog.

"Hi! How can I help you?"

"Beth." He shook his head. "Wow. You look… grown-up."

How did he know her name? Her gaze swept over him again. Nothing familiar registered. "Do we know each other?"

He took off the sunglasses, deftly avoiding the puppy's attempt to nibble on the frames. Deep brown eyes met hers. And still no ring of recognition. "You don't remember me?"

"I'm sorry, I don't." But something nagged at the recesses of her memory.

"Grady Jackson. I sat behind you in Advanced Geometry sophomore year. Also sat on the other side of the room in English III with Mrs. Delaney." He grinned. "Hawkins Prep was a pretty small school, so we were in a lot of classes together, but never really talked."

His name rang a bell, but she couldn't place his face. Her life in high school had been…a mess, to say the least. It was a wonder she'd graduated. But that wasn't something she talked about, then or now. For Pete's sake, she was almost thirty-two. She was way past taking some stroll down that section of Memory Lane. "That was a long time ago."

"It was." He hoisted the puppy a little higher. "Anyway, I just got back to town, and I found this little guy in the woods behind my grandmother's house. Cutler Shay thought you might know who he belongs to."

She came out from behind the counter, once again wishing she'd taken a bit more time in front of the mirror. She might not remember Grady from high school, but was acutely aware that he had grown up into a mighty hot-looking man. She highly doubted he was equally impressed with her.

She reached out and gave the puppy a little head rub. In response, he licked her palm, the roughness of his tongue tickling her skin. "He looks like he might be one of the Wells family's pups. Their Lab had puppies about three months ago. I thought they found homes for all of them before they moved to Seattle."

"Apparently, they missed one." Grady thrust the dog toward her. She had to admit the puppy was cute, but the guy holding him was even cuter. "Maybe you can ship him up there or something?"

Beth put up her hands and laughed. "I don't think the post office ships dogs that young, for one, and for another, I've got my hands full right this minute." She gestured toward the back of her shop, which had erupted in a constant cacophony of barking at the sound of voices out front, and most likely, the scent of the puppy. "Besides, he seems to really like you and is already attached to you. Maybe you should keep him."

"I have way too much on my own plate to worry about a dog." In answer, the puppy resumed licking Grady's face in earnest. Grady laughed. "Hey, hey, don't argue with me, buddy."

She liked his laugh. Liked his smile. How had

she missed him in high school? But even as she asked the question, she realized she knew the answer. Back then, her entire life had been consumed with raising herself and making sure there was food in the fridge when her mother was drinking and her father was checked out. A marching band leading a herd of unicorns could have paraded through her classes without her noticing. Just holding herself together had taken all her concentration.

For years, Beth had thought graduation would bring her freedom, a life of her own. Then her mother died, and her father fell off the edge of the earth in his grief. If anything, things had become more complicated than before. Nowadays, her life revolved around her father's declining health and keeping her business running.

Kind of ironic, actually, that she was now devoting so much time and energy to being there for the man who hadn't been there when she'd needed him most. When she was a little girl, she'd loved her father fiercely. She still remembered him taking her to the zoo. Teaching her to ride a bike. Hoisting her on his shoulders. Then his career had taken off—and so had he.

As much as she'd wanted her life to be different, taking care of Dad and building a fledgling business meant she didn't have time for a romantic relationship. She barely had time to breathe. And as much as she loved dogs, she definitely didn't have time for a puppy, not with the hours she spent at her dad's and here.

"Seems like you've been outvoted," Beth said. "How about this? You keep him for now, and I'll let my customers know you're looking for a home for this cutie." She rubbed the puppy's ears again, and he caught her hand with his paws. "He's one happy dog."

"That's because he ate my lunch." Grady shook his head. "I've never had a dog and don't know the first thing about them. I'm dealing with a lot of problems right now, and a dog will just be a distraction I can't afford. So I'm probably not the best choice to be a pet's foster father. Plus, I don't think I'll be in town that long."

In other words, don't get attached to this guy's eyes or voice. Which, of course, she'd already decided.

"I'm sure someone will scoop this little one up—" she tickled under the puppy's chin, and he gave her a happy pant "—before you know it. I really would take him for you, but I…can't."

She didn't go into details. Even if Grady wasn't practically a stranger, few people knew about her father's illness, about how much Beth worried, how her entire life centered on making sure he was safe and comfortable. A man who had done his best in the last few years to make up for his daughter's childhood, and who was losing his battle against heart disease. Dad was all she had left, and she couldn't add one more thing into an already complicated life.

"The shelter in town is full, and though they have foster families take dogs from time to time, I'm pretty sure all of them have dogs right now." Beth frowned. "When it comes to pets, there's not enough people to love the ones that get abandoned. So if you can keep him, at least until there's an opening…"

Grady looked wary, then finally nodded. "Okay, but only for a couple days. I really do have a lot on my plate."

"Great!" She might have said that with a bit too much enthusiasm. "I've got plenty of extra dog food and leashes and stuff here, so I can get you set up with supplies."

"I'd appreciate that, Beth."

The way he said her name sent a little tingle down her spine. She didn't know why; she didn't remember him from school, except in a vague oh-yeah-someone-had-that-unique-name way. If Grady had been interested in her, she probably wouldn't have noticed even if he'd put up a billboard in her driveway. Beth had become mother and father to herself, not to mention a worried, hovering mother to her own parent. She'd spent way too many hours searching for bottles, dumping them out, trying to stay one step ahead of the bad days.

Grady met her gaze. "You know, if you're free later today, maybe we could grab a drink. Catch up on the years in between."

Was he asking her on a date? She didn't know what to do with that. The last time she'd been on a date…

Well, she couldn't remember when that was. The hours in between work and Dad were rare, and frankly, no one wanted to date a woman who had weird little two-hour pockets of time available. *Oh yeah, we can grab coffee while the visiting nurse is there. Or outside the doctor's office on Tuesday afternoon at three.*

"Uh, my time's a little crowded right now. But let me grab those supplies for you." She spun on her heel and went into the grooming room, shutting the lower half of the door again, a habit born out of one too many wily pups getting out. Beth grabbed a box off a shelf and loaded it with a bag of dog food, a leash, two plastic bowls for food and water, and a couple chew toys.

"Let me get some of those."

She jumped at the sound of Grady's voice. The toy in her hand tumbled to the floor. He was right behind her, less than a foot away, and in the close quarters of the back room, she could catch the dark, woodsy scent of his cologne. See the gold flecks in his brown eyes. The slight dusting of stubble on his chin.

"I'm, uh, good here." She held up the box and nodded toward the door. In the other room, the trio of dogs in her care today kept on barking. "Can you open that? And check first to make sure I don't have any runaways."

"Runaways?"

"I keep the dogs I've groomed in a pen in the grooming room, but every once in a while one gets past me. Some of them are pretty resourceful climbers."

He held the door for her, but the space was close, and she ended up brushing against his arm as she passed. A whoosh of attraction ran through her. Insane. She had no time or desire for any man in her life aside from her father.

Grady followed behind her, then reached over, plucked the leash and collar out of the box and attached them to the puppy. He put the Lab on the floor, and the little guy scrambled across the tile, sniffing and exploring in a fast circle. Grady looped the leash over his wrist, then took the box from her. Their hands brushed a second time and that crazy whoosh ran through her again.

"Uh, thanks."

"No problem." He took one of her business cards out of the holder on the front counter and tucked it in his pocket. "I'll call you, Beth."

"Um, like I said, I don't have time for coffee or dinner or—"

"I meant about the puppy. Then you'll have my number, in case someone wants to adopt him."

"Oh. Oh, yeah."

"But I would also like to call you about going out to dinner. I can work around whenever you're free."

That was definitely asking her on a date. No question about it. "I'm…really busy. I'm sorry."

She glanced up at Grady. He was handsome, interested and single. And she was turning him down? God, she was a moron. But it was far better to not date Grady at all than to try to schedule a man into those two-hour time blocks.

"Maybe another time." He started to head for the door, with the box in one hand and the leash in the other.

"Grady, wait."

He pivoted.

She reached in her back pocket and pulled out

her phone. "Before you go, let me get a picture." When he raised an eyebrow, she hurried to say, "For the ad. Not for… Well, for the ad."

Now he had her even more flustered. A guy she didn't remember, didn't know. Maybe she hadn't had enough protein for breakfast or something.

Grady set the box on the glass case at the front of the shop, then picked up the puppy. "Should I set him on the counter?"

"No, right there is good." She snapped the picture. Of Grady and the dog. She'd crop Grady out, of course, before she posted it. In the meantime, maybe she could find her yearbook and figure out who he was. Because as much as she knew she shouldn't be, she was intrigued.

And that interest was one more thing that would distract her from what was important.

Once Grady was gone, Beth cropped the picture, put it on the shop's Facebook page, then sent an email out to her client list. Focusing on the puppy needing a new home, not the fact that she needed a new life.

Chapter Two

Once upon a time, Reggie Cooper had been a force to be reckoned with. Six-foot-two, barrel-chested, an amateur welterweight champ in his twenties. He'd made an impression everywhere he went, this bear of a man with a booming voice and a friendly word for pretty much every man, woman, child and dog he encountered.

But now, in his midsixties and worn down by a life of hard living, Reggie had become a shadow of his former self. A translucent oxygen line snaked into his nostrils, but still he struggled to breathe, to battle against the crushing weight of congestive heart failure. He'd quit smoking a decade ago, but the cigarettes had done their damage, and ever since two back-to-back heart attacks a couple years ago, his health had been on a rapidly declining path. The worst part was that along with his health and strength, he'd also lost will to do anything more than wait to die.

"Hey, Dad," Beth said. She set the grocery bag in her arms down on the table and crossed to her father, who was in the same place he had been this morning: in his leather recliner, feet up, remote in one hand, and the TV blaring some Alaska-set reality show.

"How's my girl?" He gave her a smile, then thumbed the volume down. "How was work?"

"Great. How was your day?"

"Good, good. Quiet."

She nodded. It was the same conversation they had every day, with the same answers. They both danced around the truth—that her father was dying and there was nothing either of them could do to change that fact.

He had months. At most, a year. Every time she saw him, she felt the pressure of that ticking clock, the passage of time. Many days, she didn't even want to go to work because she hated the thought that she'd miss out on moments with her dad. Time she hadn't had when she was little, when her father's success and the adoring crowds took him away from her and her mother.

Beth had built up almost three decades of resentment toward him, bricks in their relationship formed as she'd watched her mother cry herself to sleep at night, then drink the next day away. The days Beth had had to get herself dressed and out the door, even as young as six years old, because Dad was gone again and Mom was passed out. The times Beth had smiled and nodded when people talked about her father like he was part superhero, part celebrity, and she'd had to pretend she actually knew that man.

Reggie had paid for private school and a weekly maid and a new car every two years, but he hadn't been there in any way that counted. Then came the ironic twist of congestive heart failure, which had felled her active father and forced Beth into the role of his caretaker. Now she worried if he was eating, how much he slept, whether he remembered to take his medications. And every time she looked at him or even thought about him, she stuffed down the anger and hurt, just like she had when she was young.

"Do you want spaghetti tonight, Dad? Or do you

want me to heat up the leftover soup from Monday?" she asked.

"Come sit with me for a minute first." He patted the side of his chair. "I have something I want to talk to you about."

Her stomach twisted. Had the doctor called? Had her father's condition worsened in those hours she'd been at work? Or had he opened the mail and seen yet another astronomical medical bill stamped with an overdue notice? The money from his fights had long since run out, spent in a decade and a half of chasing his fading fame after the big checks stopped coming in, continuing that life of travel and celebrity until the world forgot his name and his record was replaced by another man's.

Beth kept the bills a secret from her father, not wanting to add the strain to his overtaxed heart. She grabbed the mail before he saw it, took the calls from the doctors and the hospital's billing agents, and did her best to pretend this whole thing was a hiccup. Some might say she was enabling him to live in denial, but he was the only parent she had left, and that overrode everything.

Beth dropped onto the ottoman that flanked her father's chair. She'd sat here dozens of times in the last few months, talking to him more than she had in the twenty-nine years before that. During her childhood, on the rare days when he was home, he'd spent his hours in the den, watching tapes from his fights or following some golf match, while Beth was on her own and Mom sat in the kitchen nursing drink after drink.

One day, while she was sitting at the kitchen table with a cigarette in one hand and a glass in the other, Mom's liver had given up fighting the vodka. After the funeral, Beth hadn't spoken to her father for three years. There had been ugly words in the cemetery that had expressed only a fraction of the simmering anger in her heart.

Then he'd had a heart attack that nearly killed him. And another. Beth had brought her father home from the hospital, and in tentative baby steps, they'd begun to build a real relationship, forced by his reliance on a daughter he hardly knew. The more time she spent on this ottoman, the closer they had become, and now she lived with a constant worry in her gut for a man who had never worried about her.

Her father coughed, deep, racking coughs that shook his too-thin body and colored his face cherry red. Beth waited, her hands clenched tight in her lap.

After a while, he drew in a deep breath, then

turned to her. "You do too much for an old man who doesn't deserve such kindness."

"I don't do enough, Dad. If I hadn't had to work late—"

"Don't apologize." He covered her hand with his own. It was cool, the skin pale, but his touch was as firm as his words. "Leave me be, and go live your life. You're thirty-one. You should be out with your friends, having fun, meeting men."

"I hang out with my friends, Dad." Which was a lie because she couldn't remember when she'd had time for more than a quick cup of coffee with Savannah Barlow, never mind drinks with the girls. Savannah was busy enough with her new husband and her one-year-old baby, not to mention the real estate division Mac had started, which meant keeping in touch was doubly difficult.

"Go find yourself a man," he said. "You're as beautiful as your mother was. You should have men falling all over themselves to be with you."

The reference to her mother made Beth bristle. "I'm fine in the dating department. I don't need to meet anyone new."

"Really? Because I haven't seen a man around here or heard you talk to one. You should find one before I die."

Like a man would solve all her problems? If

anything, in Beth's opinion, men only created complications she didn't need. She'd had the fiancé and lots of unforgettable dates, and found herself much happier without a man in her life, especially right now. "Dad, don't talk about that. You're doing great. The doctor said—"

"I have months." He sobered and drew in another deep breath. The oxygen tank whispered the truth in the background. "You know it and I know it, even if that idiot doctor of mine keeps telling me I have plenty of time."

Beth busied herself with straightening the clutter on the small table beside her father so he wouldn't see the guilt in her eyes. "You're doing fine, Dad. And I'm fine, really. I've got a great guy in my life." She flashed him a smile.

"Let me meet him and I'll size him up."

She half expected her father to put his dukes up. "I can take care of myself." *I have been, pretty much all my life.*

Reggie leaned in and studied her face. "This fellow you're with…he's a good man?"

If she told him the truth, that she hadn't dated anyone in longer than she could remember, he would get upset. Lately, even small things had the potential to seriously upset him. Like a favorite TV show being preempted by breaking news. Or his doctor's appointment running late. Or the newspaper boy forgetting their house. The depression he felt over his diagnosis lowered his spirits more every day, even as he refused to accept the truth of his inevitable death. So she did what she had been doing for months about the bills and the doctor's words—she lied. "Yes, Dad, he's awesome."

"Then how come he hasn't been around here?"

Because he doesn't exist. "He's working a lot, and you've been…under the weather. I just didn't want to burden you with company."

"Have him over for dinner this Sunday." Reggie nodded, as if that settled it. "I'll check him out and if he meets my standards, you'll have my blessing for whatever you do in the future."

"I'm not thinking about the future. I've got enough to do in the present."

"All the more reason you should think about a life after this—" he waved at the oxygen tank and the recliner "—is all empty. I'll be gone someday, Bethie, and I want to know you…" He cleared his throat and shook his head before the emotion showed in his voice and eyes. The man who had once knocked out another boxer with a single hard right hook, and who had once had his jaw broken in two places and refused to go to the hospital until the end of the fight, maintained that stoniness every day of his life. "Sunday, six o'clock."

How could she say no when her father was looking at her like that, with a mixture of hope and expectation? How could she break his heart and tell him she didn't have a boyfriend, and wasn't going to have that bright future he wanted for her? All her life, she'd wanted her father to notice her, to ask about the boy she had a crush on or the speech she'd made in debate class. She'd wanted his advice, his support and most of all, his interest. Now, finally, Dad wanted to be part of her life. How could she push that away?

There might not be another chance, the oxygen tank whispered.

"He'll be here, Dad," she said. Maybe by then, her father would forget about the invitation. Or maybe she could manufacture Sir Galahad out of thin air. "Now, what do you want for dinner tonight?"

Grady tossed a third Italian leather dress shoe into the trash, then turned around and faced two big brown eyes that pleaded innocence. "I know you did it. Just like I know you chewed the last two."

The puppy stared at him, his tail swishing back and forth on the tile floor. Behind him sat a pile of

shredded toilet paper, dragged into the kitchen earlier today, and a yellow puddle from two minutes
ago. A puddle that had occurred exactly five minutes after Grady took the puppy into the backyard.

"You are incorrigible." Grady shook his head.
He reached for the roll of paper towels, then bent
to clean up the mess. The puppy scrambled over,
thinking it was a game, and started tugging on the
edge of the paper towels. "No. No! Sit!"

The puppy ignored him. Grady pushed the
Lab back a few inches, then finished cleaning
and tossed the mess into the trash. On top of the
shoe he'd already dropped there—the right shoe
again, because the dog seemed to have a distaste
for left shoes.

Not a single person had called about the pup
in the three days since Beth had put up the ad.
Grady texted her a couple times a day—usually
right after the fur ball of trouble got done destroy-
ing something—and she always sent back short
"No, sorry" responses.

After the first day of being distracted by working, and the disaster with his shoes, Grady hadn't
left the teething monster alone for more than a
minute. Just making sure the dog didn't chew
through an electrical cord or scrape up a door was
taking all of Grady's time, so much so that he had

barely had a chance to get anything done. He'd met with two Realtors about selling Ida Mae's house, but each had left in a hurry, after the furry monster peed on one man's shoe and chewed the strap off one woman's handbag. Grady was pretty sure there was a WARNING email circulating around the Stone Gap realty community about him and his wayward dog.

He let out a deep breath and faced the large kitchen window that looked out over the yard. What was he going to do? How was he ever going to make things right? His chest tightened, and he closed his eyes, counting to ten, then to twenty, then to thirty, until his heartbeat slowed.

Never in his life had he been an anxious person. He'd jumped off diving platforms and plunged into multimillion-dollar deals without a second thought. Maybe he'd believed he was invincible, some King Midas corporate giant who could never make a mistake.

Until he did.

That government contract was a sure thing, Grady had been told over and over again. *The money is there in the budget*, his contact on Capitol Hill had said. Grady's COO and CFO had warned him not to sink so much of the company's assets into funding the building of a ten-story defense-research facility. *The government's decisions shift like summer winds*, Dan had said.

Grady had been so sure this would be a success. He'd had a run of great successes in building or renovating facilities for companies, creating exactly what they needed to take their business to the next level—and generating huge returns for himself in the process. This had been his first entry into the often lucrative and always competitive world of government contracts, and he hadn't wanted to be hesitant or risk missing the deadlines. He'd wanted to exceed their expectations and wow the government with a sparkling new facility ahead of schedule. So he'd fronted the money for the land and building, customizing every floor to the government's needs, then had sat back and waited. Month after month, he'd asked about the budget, the funding for the facility. And month after month he'd heard a new excuse every time: *caught up in red tape*, *held up in appropriations*, and then—

Cut from the budget.

Just like that, the sure thing was axed in some cost-saving measure by a new administration. Grady was left with a staggeringly expensive customized building that he couldn't sell, even at a loss. Even now it sat there, empty and draining the rest of his resources. Grady's company had imploded, unable to withstand such a massive financial hit.

When he'd stood in that room and looked at the faces of people who had been by his side—people whose advice he had ignored—and realized he had failed himself, his company, and most of all them, the first waves of anxiety had started. It wasn't until a week later, when a heart attack rushed Dan to the hospital, that the anxiety became full-on panic.

Grady stood beside that hospital bed and knew his decisions, his mistakes, had been the reason for Dan's near-death scare. From there, Grady began to second-guess every decision. When Dan had found him at the end of the day trying to decide which toilet paper brand would cost the least, he'd told Grady to take some mental health time.

So far, this time off had been more stressful than his job. He fished his phone out of his pocket and instead of texting, he called Beth. If he could get rid of this dog, maybe he could think. Or at least not drive away every Realtor in a three-county area. Grady sent the pup a glare while he waited for the connection. The dog just gave him the same hapless, tongue-lolling grin.

Beth answered on the first ring. "Happy Tails. How can I help you?"

"You can train this dog not to eat my shoes, for starters," Grady said. Okay, so not exactly the greeting he'd been planning, but damn it, the dog was back at it already. Grady waved his foot and the puppy backed off, sat on his butt and wagged his tail.

Beth laughed. "Hi, Grady. I take it things are a little rocky with your new friend?"

"A little? He's chewed up half my house, won't listen to a thing I say, and apparently has no idea what the word *housebroken* means."

"Aw, he's just a puppy. He'll get better."

"Didn't your sign say you do dog training?" he asked. "Because I will gladly drop him off for puppy school. In fact, boarding school for puppies would be even better."

"Well, I don't have a puppy school per se. I prefer to work with the owner and the dog together. It doesn't do you any good if I train the dog to take commands from me, but then you don't know how to get him to behave. Sometimes the owner needs the training more than the dog."

"Well, I can assure you that's not the case here. I'm pretty well housebroken."

That made her laugh, and this time the sound of it eased the tension in his chest. The whoosh of relief surprised him. Was it just the familiar connection of someone from the past, or something about the light tones in her voice that drew him away from that dark place?

Dogs barked in the background, and he heard the sound of running water. "Listen, I have to get back to work," she said. "Do you want to make an appointment for some puppy lessons?"

He didn't have much money, but at this point, he'd find a way to pay her to train the dog by herself—since he wasn't keeping the monster anyway—but then he realized (a) he couldn't afford to pay her that much until he managed to sell something off and free up some working capital, and (b) doing one-on-one puppy training would be a way to see Beth, this woman whose voice gave him a sense of ease he hadn't experienced since his world crashed, without the formality of a date. And he wouldn't have to leave the four-pawed destructor at home alone. "Sure. As soon as possible."

"I have an opening this afternoon at three. Does that work?"

His schedule had already been blown to hell anyway, and the sooner he got this puppy to behave, the better. Maybe then someone would adopt him and remove one more problem from Grady's plate. "Perfect."

After he hung up with Beth, Grady left the dog in the kitchen, barricading the exit with a big piece of cardboard and a chair shoved against it. Maybe that would buy him five minutes of nondestruction to take a shower and get cleaned up.

He was wrong.

By the time he arrived at Beth's shop that afternoon—twenty minutes early, because he was pretty sure he was going to have to buy a whole new wardrobe if he waited any longer—the puppy had managed to wriggle under the cardboard, chew a chair leg, claw down a curtain, open his bag of dog food and scatter it all over the floor, and take a nap on Grady's clean laundry. The anticipation Grady had been feeling ever since the phone call was being edged out by a whole lot of frustration.

He couldn't seem to get the house on the market. Couldn't find any of his former "friends" who wanted to invest in his comeback. And he couldn't figure out a way to get back to work without getting funds from one or the other.

He'd found a great medical-device firm with a commercial property for sale in Lower Manhattan—a bargain-price deal from a colleague who took pity on him and gave him a preemptive crack at a purchase—but only if he could come up with the cash for the down payment in the next couple weeks.

Dan, who had taken an 80 percent pay cut and kept showing up at the empty office, had been the lone cheerleader in the woods. *This could be a quick flip*, he told Grady. *Fast cash. We'll be back on top in no time.*

What was the old saying? Pride goeth before a fall? That was Grady nine months ago, so cocky, so sure. Now, Dan's enthusiasm compounded Grady's guilt. Dan saw him as some wunderkind who could always find a miracle to save them all. What if Grady was just an idiot who'd gotten lucky a few times?

The dog was making it hard to get a damned thing done, which meant he was going to miss this opportunity and his best chance at restoring his career.

Yeah, blame it all on the dog. That was easier than wondering if maybe he'd lost his touch. Or if the fear of making a mistake had become paralysis that would keep him from ever being certain or decisive again.

He stepped inside the shop, to the sound of dogs barking and…singing? He paused in the entryway, the puppy at his feet—for once, sitting quietly—and listened to Beth belt out a damned good rendition of "Lean on Me."

He'd never known she could sing. Of course, he knew very little about Beth Cooper, besides the fact that she was beautiful and better at geometry than he was. She'd been a crush in high school, nothing more. But he suddenly found himself very, very intrigued by this woman with the velvet voice. This woman who loved dogs, laughed easily, and who seemed to have no interest in him whatsoever.

Beth's singing made him forget all about the stresses waiting back at Ida Mae's house. The dulcet tones drew him farther into the shop, around the counter, then into the dog-grooming room. A giant stainless steel tub mounted waist-high flanked one wall, and a half dozen empty dog crates of various sizes sat against the opposite wall, with fans attached to the backs. Another handful of crates had already washed and dried dogs waiting to go home. To dry the dogs after their baths, he assumed. In the center of the room was a wide stainless steel table with a pole to hold a leash, and a variety of grooming tools on the shelf before it. The walls were a cheery yellow, the shelves a bright white and the tile an ice cream–parlor combination of pink, white and yellow. Beth was standing at the sink, washing a Jack Russell terrier while she sang.

She had a nice rear view, outlined by a pair of faded jeans and a pale pink T-shirt that hugged her curves. Her ponytail swung as she launched into a hearty chorus. The dog in the tub stared up at her, seeming just as enamored with Beth's voice as Grady was.

Grady cleared his throat, and as soon as he did, he regretted it, because she stopped singing. The dog in the tub barked. Beth started and spun around. "Grady. I… I didn't hear you come in."

"That's because you were doing your best Bill Withers." He grinned. "You can really sing." The Jack Russell, no longer entertained by Beth, began to wriggle and whine. Beside Grady, the Lab puppy began to whine in sympathy.

"Oh, well…" She blushed. He liked that moment of vulnerability. Very much. It gave him this weird kindred-spirit feeling, as if he could confide in her, tell her that he was terrified of screwing up again. Insane. Admitting weakness only created more weakness.

She glanced at the clock. "Um, are you early or am I running late?"

"I'm early. I'm sorry. I—"

The Jack Russell made a break for it, scrambling across the counter beside the sink and toward the edge. Beth spun back, reaching for the dog just as Grady crossed and did the same. The two of them got a handle on the terrier, close enough for their arms to touch. A blaze of heat ran through Grady's veins, kick-started his heart and damned near bowled him over. His gaze cut to Beth's and held for a heartbeat, then she broke the eye contact and shifted away.

Holy hell. What was that about?

"Uh, thanks," Beth said, her gaze on the dog, not on Grady. "I've got him now."

"Yeah." Grady stepped back. Awkwardness filled the space between them. He hadn't felt this off-kilter around a girl since...well, since he'd had that crush on her back in high school. "The dog seemed like he was enjoying his bath before."

"He only likes it when I'm singing." She blushed again. "Hence the little karaoke show there."

"Don't be embarrassed. You sing really well." He wondered if she'd been involved in chorus in high school. Except for seeing her in class, he couldn't remember much about Beth from back then—no memories of seeing her involved in sports or arts programs. It was as if all she'd done was go to classes and leave right after. Grady, who'd been on the football team and basketball team, and later Future Leaders of America, had been at school so much he'd practically had his own parking space in senior year.

"My audience is entirely canine, so they don't

notice if I'm off-key or make up a few words I've forgotten." She pivoted back to the dog, turned on the faucet and began to rinse him off. Without the musical accompaniment, the Jack Russell squirmed and protested. "Let me just finish up and then we can start the obedience lesson for you."

For him? Or his dog? Because Grady got the feeling he'd crossed some invisible line when they'd touched. All of a sudden she was as distant as Idaho. He knew he should go back out to the front of the shop, take a seat in one of the hard plastic chairs by the door and wait for her like any other customer would. But he wanted that feeling of connection back. "Need any help? Or a really bad bass for backup?"

She laughed. "You sing?"

Laughter was good. Laughter meant she hadn't entirely blocked him. "Badly, but yes."

She glanced down at the dog. He'd started whining again, and was pawing at the edge of the tub. "What do you think, Rudy? Want to hear another song while we finish your bath?" The dog let out a yip. Beth turned to Grady. "How about a little Eagles? Say…'Hotel California'?"

"I'm in." He tugged the puppy's leash and shifted closer to Beth, near enough to catch the floral notes of her perfume, dancing just above the light fra-

grance of the dog shampoo. To be this close to her,
to hear her laugh again, he'd sing the whole score
from *Oklahoma!* if need be.

When Beth started singing, he joined in, stum-
bling over the words a few times, but mostly keeping
up with her. They had their heads close, their voices
winding in and out together, while Beth finished
washing the now-compliant terrier. Even Grady's
puppy seemed mesmerized, because the little monster barely made a peep or moved while they sang.

Beth turned off the hose just as they finished
the song. As if on cue, the terrier shook off the
worst of the water, spraying Grady and her. Beth
had a plastic apron over her clothes, sparing her
from the impromptu shower, but Grady wasn't
prepared. Within seconds, his shirt was plastered
against his chest and his jeans weighed another
five pounds.

Beth glanced at him and bit back a laugh. "I'm
sorry. I should have warned you."

"I'm not melting, so I think I'm good." He
grinned. "It's just water."

"Here." She grabbed two towels from the shelf
above her head, handing one to Grady and using
the second to dry off the dog. Rudy groaned as Beth
rubbed his back and belly, talking softly to him.

Grady stepped back, watching Beth with the

dog. She clearly loved animals, and they loved her just as much. He was pretty sure none of the dogs that Beth groomed would dare eat her shoes or pee on her favorite sweatshirt. "You definitely have a way with dogs. Rudy is half in love with you."

"You just have to know how to speak their language." She finished with Rudy, then put the short-haired dog in the big pen on the other side of the room. Rudy ran around in fast circles, yipping and chasing his tail, clearly overjoyed to be done with his spa treatment.

Grady had met a lot of women in the course of his lifetime. Smart women, strong women, determined women. But he'd never met one who had this soft, intriguing edge to her, or that hint of shy vulnerability that he'd seen when he complimented her on her voice. Everything about Beth drew him closer and made him wonder why she was single.

She hung her apron on a hook, then turned to him. Grady expected her to say something about their singing or how they'd brushed shoulders a few times, but instead she bent down in front of him. "I hear you've been a brat."

A brat?

Then it hit him. She didn't mean him, she meant the dog. Oh yeah. The whole reason he was here. He'd forgotten all about the puppy, who'd barely moved since they'd arrived. Maybe there was something to this singing thing.

Beth ruffled the dog's ears. "Okay, let's get started, while we wait for Rudy's mom to get here." She straightened and turned to Grady. "What'd you name him?"

"Name him? Why would I do that?"

"Because it helps your dog to know when you're talking to him. You can get his attention, and it also helps deepen the bond between you two."

Grady scoffed. "I don't need to bond. I need to get him to stop chewing my shoes and peeing on my clothes."

She laughed. "Well, first you have to establish that you are the alpha dog. And you have to get him to care about you. Hence bond. So…name?"

He glanced down at the puppy, who looked up at him with cute, wide, melt-your-heart eyes and a happy tail wag. He swore this dog turned on the charm the second they left the house. "Monster?"

Beth laughed again. "He's not a monster, are you, little guy?"

The softer, more lyrical tones caught the puppy's attention. He wagged his tail and let out a short woof. The dog was just as captivated with her as Grady was. He couldn't blame the puppy; Beth had a smile that lit her eyes and brought life to the room.

Damn, he wanted to get to know this woman better. Except he had a lot in front of him right now—resurrecting a dead company, filling an empty bank account and restoring dozens of jobs—and he wasn't planning on staying in Stone Gap much longer. Was it even sensible to date someone he'd have to soon say goodbye to?

His number-one priority was the puppy from hell. Once he got the dog under control, everything else would fall into place, like it had a thousand times before. This was just a bump in the road, nothing more. "You don't live with him like I do," Grady muttered. "I think Monster fits."

"Then Monster it is," Beth said. She held his gaze for a second, mirth still dancing in her blue eyes, and he forgot all his very good reasons for not asking her out again.

Then her expression became all business, which raised a great big stop sign. "Shall we get started?"

Chapter Three

The singing had been a mistake.

She'd gotten altogether too close to Grady while they were at the tub, washing Rudy, and ever since, she had been thinking too much about him. About touching him. About kissing him.

Which was all insane. She needed a man in her busy, crazy life like she needed the proverbial hole in her head.

Except...she technically *did* need a man right now. Her father hadn't let the idea of dinner with her "boyfriend" go. He'd brought it up again just this morning before she left for work, and for the first time in a long time, he'd seemed excited and happy, asking her questions, talking about what to have for dinner. Dad was acting involved, connected, and most of all, he was behaving like a typical father for the first time ever. How could she disappoint him?

Yet how could she manufacture a boyfriend in the next three days?

Two years ago, Beth had thought she had her life all aligned. She'd been engaged to the guy she'd been dating for two years, an accountant who lived just outside Stone Gap, and she'd been running a fledgling business that had just started to take off as she built up a steady clientele. She'd recovered from those lonely, difficult years of high school when her mother had died and her father had checked out, and Beth had pretty much been on her own.

Then Dad had had his first heart attack. In those initial weeks, as Beth poured everything into helping her father convalesce, her engagement had fallen apart and her business had begun to lapse. It became abundantly clear that she couldn't juggle all three. The man she had thought would love her through thick and thin had asked her to choose, and she'd opted for her family over someone who would put her in such an impossible situation. Her dog grooming and training business had suffered and almost died. It took a solid year after she'd missed or been late for so many appointments to rebuild trust with her clientele and convince them that she wouldn't let them down again. That rebuilding had happened only because she'd dedicated every waking hour to either her father or her clients. Spare time didn't exist in her world. Ever since, Beth had been alone, except for the occasional blind date arranged by her friends.

Given how her relationship with her father had shifted, Beth knew she would make the same choice all over again. Even though they had never really talked about the past or worked through the pain she still felt over those lost years, she'd found a connection with him that filled in some of the gaps in her heart left behind by her childhood, and as the days he had on earth began to tick down, she knew where her priorities lay. Which meant any kind of real dating relationship had to wait. She was too busy trying to build one with her father.

"Let's try this again," Grady said, drawing her attention back to work. He gestured toward the puppy, who was standing beside Beth on the grassy lawn behind her shop. Rudy's owner had picked up the terrier, and Beth had locked up the store so she and Grady could work with Monster outside. So far, they'd mastered…nothing.

Monster was a typical puppy, sweet and affectionate and a little ADHD. He skittered from thing to thing, his attention never lingering long before he discovered a new smell, a new mystery to investigate.

Beth could hardly judge. Her attention had skipped between Grady and the dog a hundred times in the last few minutes. The scent of his cologne, or the way he flexed his hand, or the deep notes in his voice all frazzled her brain.

"Sit, Monster. Sit." The puppy yipped in reply to Grady's directive.

"Be a little sterner," Beth said. This was her comfort zone, with her focus on an animal, not on a six-foot-two charmer. "Not angry, just firm. So he knows you're the boss."

Grady tried it again, deepening his voice, narrowing his gaze at Monster. He made the sweeping hand gesture Beth had taught him, to go along with his verbal command. *"Sit."*

And…it took a second, but Monster sat.

Grady gave Beth a wide-eyed look of surprise and broke into a wide grin. "He did it. I'll be damned."

The man had one hell of a nice smile. She stood

there a second, smiling back like some lovesick high school freshman, before she remembered her job. "Yeah, uh, all puppies learn eventually, with enough patience and work. Now, reward him." She nodded toward the treat in Grady's other hand. "Then Monster associates doing the right thing with a positive result."

"Sort of like kissing a man when he brings you flowers?" Grady arched a brow in her direction.

Beth's face heated. Had he been reading her mind? And damned if her brain didn't picture her kissing Grady over a bouquet of daisies at that very second. "Uh, yes. Positive reinforcement works for pretty much all mammals."

"I will keep that in mind, Beth Cooper." He bent down and held out a little doggy treat to Monster, who ate it in one bite, then yipped, expecting more.

Grady was a seriously good-looking guy. It wasn't just the button-down shirt he had tucked into his jeans, or the way his dark hair had one unruly wave in it, or the sharp lines of his jaw. It was the way he connected with the dogs—first Rudy, now Monster. For a guy who said he didn't want a dog, and claimed not to even like Monster, his clear affection and indulgent attitude toward the wayward puppy were pretty attractive.

Beth's attention veered to his lips. She could

definitely imagine kissing him. And maybe doing a lot more than that. Good Lord. How long *had* it been since her last date? Way too long, clearly.

She didn't have time for daydreaming like this. She needed to finish this lesson with Monster, then hightail it across town to Dad's house. The visiting nurse was supposed to come today, and Beth always tried to get home in time to talk to her and get a status check. Dad always claimed that he was just fine, when she knew he was anything but. If she didn't stay on top of his doctors' appointments and meds and tests, he'd forget all about them and end up worse off. Her father still had that tendency to assume others would take care of things—and right now, "others" meant her. So she did her best to be at every single appointment and to keep a careful record of her father's medical history.

"So, is there any way we can speed this training thing up?" Grady said. "Maybe find him a foster home or something? I have…a lot on my to-do list, including trying to sell my grandmother's house if I can find a Realtor the dog won't pee on."

Before her father got sick, she'd taken dogs home with her and done one-on-one training all the time. That part of her business had been fairly lucrative, but she'd stopped offering it once her father became ill and she began spending every spare hour at his house. She'd stayed the night so many times, worried about her father's labored breathing, that there was surely an inch-thick layer of dust over everything in her own tiny cottage. If she was going to take on a training project, she'd have to do it at her father's house, to stay close to him. But the last thing Dad needed was some rambunctious Labrador knocking over his oxygen tank.

"I'll keep asking about a foster or adoption option," she said. "I can't take Monster into the dog training school I used to run at my house, but I could slot you two in for a few more hours this week." Which would mean a few more opportunities to see Grady. She wasn't sure if that was a good thing or a bad thing, but she did know she was already feeling bittersweet that their first lesson was coming to an end.

Damn. Why hadn't she paid closer attention in high school? He'd been a star in the yearbook, involved in pretty much everything in school. She remembered Grady being on the periphery, but Beth had been so involved at home that she'd barely noticed anyone in school. Missing out on Grady might have been a mistake.

Looking at him now, and seeing how patient he was with the dog, she felt Grady had Mr. Potential written all over him—assuming she had the hours to explore a potential anything.

"Great. I appreciate you doing that. My budget is a bit tight, though, so…" A flicker of emotions ran across his face. Stress, embarrassment, frustration. "If there's anything I can do in return as a kind of barter, like sing a few bars of 'Desperado' or—"

"Come to dinner at my father's house on Sunday night." Had she just said that out loud? But the more she thought about it, the more she could see the sense in the idea. Grady could pretend to be her boyfriend for a few hours to make her father happy, and in exchange, she'd help Grady with his dog. Just a little even trade, nothing more.

Which would mean she'd have to stop thinking about kissing him. And she would…soon.

Having Grady at dinner would take all the pressure off about how to maintain the facade of her fictional boyfriend, and it would give her father some peace of mind. That alone was worth more than whatever Grady could pay her for dog training. It was a good idea, wasn't it?

"Since you said your budget is tight, I won't charge you for the training," she said, "if you'll just come on Sunday."

"Come to dinner? And as a way to pay off my

training bill?" Grady looked at her askance. "I thought you were too busy to date."

"I am." She sighed and ran a hand through her hair. What kind of thirty-one-year-old woman was too busy to date? Most of her friends were already engaged or married, and some even had kids. Beth couldn't see that kind of future for herself, no matter how far she tried to look ahead. "But I need a boyfriend."

"I'm assuming it's not because the senior prom is coming up and you're dateless." He leaned in again. "And for the record, I totally would have asked you to the prom if I'd had the guts."

Was he being sincere, or was that just empty flattery? The man before her practically oozed confidence and strength, but maybe in high school he hadn't. She barely remembered him, or any of the other guys in her class. How might things have been different if he had asked her? Didn't matter. Those days were so far in the past, they weren't even in her rearview mirror anymore. "Well, if you'd asked, maybe I would have gone instead of staying home and watching reruns of *Happy Days*."

"Why didn't you go to prom?"

"I was…busy." Sitting at home, worried about her father, who was supposed to be in South Dakota for a fight, but was instead out with the guys, pretending he wasn't grieving. Losing his wife had sent him spiraling worse and worse every month. For about five minutes that May in senior year, Beth had considered saying "to hell with it" and going to the prom, but every single time she'd debated doing so, she'd heard her mother's words. *Take care of Dad for me, Beth. Please?*

And so Beth had stayed, because that, apparently, was what she did. Stay and help, even when she wanted to be somewhere else.

"Well, maybe someday we can remedy that missed prom situation," Grady said.

"Are you going to rent a pale blue tux that's too big for you and slap a giant corsage on my wrist?"

"Only if you promise to wear one of those dresses with the giant hoop under it and put those little white flowers in your hair." He winked.

She tapped a finger on her chin. "I think I have one of those in my closet. Leftover bridesmaid hell."

"I believe I have an ill-fitting tux for the same reason. We would make quite the pair."

For a second, she pictured herself next to him, striding into some overdecorated banquet hall with a DJ in one corner and a bowl of secretly spiked punch in the other. How different would her high school years have been if she'd noticed Grady, and he'd asked her out? Would she have had those experiences everyone else had had? The make-out sessions at the top of the hill that overlooked Stone Gap, the middle-of-the-night diner runs after a party, the ridiculousness of prom, followed by a kiss under the stars?

She shook off the thoughts. She was well past the age where she should care about making out with a boy or slow dancing to some Mariah Carey ballad. She had a business to run and a father to worry about. A father whose one wish was to see his daughter happily paired with a good man. Grady could fit that bill for one night, couldn't he?

It would make her father happy, and from there, maybe the rest of a bridge between them could be built, resulting in conversations about something deeper than what happened on a *Survivor* rerun.

"I know this sounds like a crazy idea," she said. "But it can work out for both of us. You need someone to help you train Monster, right? And you need to sell your grandmother's house. My best friend is a Realtor, and she's fantastic at it. I'll connect you with her, if you pretend to be my boyfriend in front of my dad. Just for one night, I swear."

He cocked his head and studied her. "Why me?

You're a beautiful woman, Beth. I'm sure you have dozens of men lining up at your door."

She scoffed, but inside a part of her whispered, *He thinks I'm beautiful?* "For one, I haven't dated in so long, I don't think I remember how. For another, this is a small town, in case you forgot, and I know pretty much every man who lives here. And third, I don't want a relationship or some kind of entanglement. I want an agreement."

"A business arrangement? That's my specialty. Or…used to be."

She wanted to ask about that last part, but doing that would feel invasive after what she'd just said about entanglement. *Keep it professional, not personal.* That would be the smartest course of action. "Yes. A business arrangement only."

Monster leaped against Grady's legs, begging for attention. Grady brushed him off, his gaze on Beth. Assessing. Considering. She felt as if he was running an assets-and-debts check. "I have done a lot of business over the course of my life, and I have to say I have never had an offer like this one."

"It is unique, I agree with you on that." She opened the back door to the shop and ushered Grady and a still-rambunctious Monster inside. She put the box of treats into the cabinet, and then leaned against the counter in the grooming salon.

"But it's a win-win for you, because you get the shoe chewer there under control."

Grady glanced down at Monster, who had clearly gotten bored with all the human conversation and was now gnawing on a shoelace.

To another person, the puppy's constant need for attention and amusement—and an interesting texture between his teeth—might have been a little cute and a bit irritating. But Grady glanced at the dog, then his watch, and a line pinched between his brows. Stress tensed his shoulders and jaw.

"Hey, Monster, no. Leave it." Beth shooed him away. The puppy backed up a few steps, slid onto the floor, and had the sense to look contrite. "Good boy."

Grady cleared his throat and the tension in his features lessened. "You still haven't told me why you need a pretend boyfriend to meet your father. Either that's one hell of a pickup line or you have some ulterior motive I can't see."

"My father is very sick," she said, because that was so much easier than speaking the word *dying*, "and he worries about me a lot. He wants to make sure I'm okay. Part of his recipe for my happiness is a man in my life. And I...sort of told him I have one."

"So you're lying to a man who is sick?"

She winced. "Yes, but…" Her eyes welled. "My dad just wants to know I'll be okay after he…well, when he's gone. I can't give him the diagnosis he wants, but I can give him peace of mind."

"That, I think, is very sweet. Even if it's a bit of a lie, it sounds like you're doing it to ease his stress."

"I know it sounds terrible, but I don't want worrying about me to be added to all my father has to deal with. So if you can just help me out with this little thing, I'd be forever grateful."

"I don't know many people who are like you. You're…refreshing, Beth."

She flushed at the compliment, even though she knew he'd misjudged her reasons. This wasn't about being sweet. It was, deep down inside, about a need to establish a connection with her father before she lost that chance. For him to say, just once, *I'm proud of you, kid.* "I'm just trying to make things easier for him. He doesn't need to worry about me, but every time I tell him that, he just worries more. Hence, the pretend boyfriend. Only for one night, I swear." She'd now said that twice. Desperate much?

"I can do one night, but we should kind of hash out a story line for how we met first. In the meantime…" Grady shifted closer to her. The puppy wandered around them, twining his leash around their legs. Beth tugged him back into a sitting position, but every ounce of her attention remained on Grady. The two of them didn't speak for a moment. "If I'm pretending to be your boyfriend... does that mean I get to kiss you?"

Her heart stuttered. Her face heated even more. "Well... I—I don't think my dad is going to need..."

"You want it to be believable, right? And if a man is dating a beautiful woman like you, he's going to kiss her every chance he gets."

Grady was closer now, so close she could feel the warmth of his skin, catch the scent of his cologne, feel the temptation to put her hands on his hard chest, or the broad muscles of his back. "He might, but it's really not necessary."

"Maybe not, but I don't think we can accurately portray a dating relationship without demonstrating obvious attraction between us."

She parked a fist on her hip. "And who says I'm attracted to you?"

"Who says you're not?"

"I told you, this is business only." Except nothing in this moment felt businesslike or professional. She'd crossed some lines here, mixing her livelihood with...whatever was happening between them.

"That you did," he said. "More than once. However, if this is a business-only deal, then us kissing shouldn't affect you. Or me."

"It won't." If she said it out loud, that would make it true, right? Because at the moment, with Grady only inches away, and the shop quiet and still and intimate, she was pretty sure she would melt if he kissed her.

His mouth curved into a wide smile. "Care to put a wager on that?"

"I don't gamble." She raised her chin, tried her best to look determined and strong and unaffected. "I operate on facts. And the fact is—"

Grady kissed her—cut off her words, cut off her breath and kissed her. Beth's heart skipped a beat, and before she could think twice, she kissed him back. His mouth slid over hers, slow and gentle, a whisper of a kiss. One hand came up to gently cup the back of her head, fingers dipping into that sensitive hollow at the base of her neck. Damn. He'd found that spot that got her every time, and she let out a soft mew, then leaned into him. Grady deepened his kiss, a little hungrier and harder now, his body shifting into place against hers, and any common sense Beth had evaporated. She clutched at his back, feeling hard, dense muscles, imagining for a fleeting second what he would look like naked and on top of her—

And Grady stepped back, breaking the kiss. She heard the jingle of his phone, and just like that, the warm, teasing man became the stressed, steely one again.

He pulled the phone out of his pocket and glanced at the screen. "I have to take this." He turned to go, then pivoted back. "I shouldn't have kissed you. I'm sorry. Sometimes my impulses get ahead of my smarter thinking."

Then he picked up his dog and walked out of her shop. Leaving Beth wondering if she'd just made a smart trade—or a huge mistake.

One thing was for certain—that man definitely understood the use of positive reinforcement.

Chapter Four

The world was dark and quiet, the moon a silent guard over Stone Gap, and Grady lay in a bed that he'd spent a good chunk of his childhood in, half-way to sleep. It was in that twilight space between waking and dreaming that the regrets and doubts plagued his thoughts, catapulting on top of each other, until a sharp catch in his breath jerked him fully awake. His heart thudded so loudly he could hear it, and his breath became a panicked rush.

He kicked off the covers and sat on the edge of the bed, his chest tight and his breath wheezing. He stared at the dappled white specks of moonlight on the wood floor as he drew in a breath, let it out. Drew another in, let it out. His heart kept galloping, and he pressed his hand to his chest, as if that would slow the rapid beats.

What had he been thinking yesterday, kissing Beth and agreeing to be her fake boyfriend? For a second, he'd been his old self, leaping ahead, heedless of the risks of his decisions, allowing his instincts and desires to pull him around like a bull with a ring in its nose. Then Dan had called, and splashed him with an icy reminder of Grady's entire reason for being in Stone Gap. A reason that had nothing to do with a pretty groomer who smelled like spring flowers.

Jackson Properties had become a ghost of the multimillion-dollar company he'd built. The offices were still there, empty and silent, the lights off. Dan, the only employee left, had taken to working mostly from home to save the few dollars on electricity bills. An hour ago, he had texted and asked if there was any possibility of a paycheck advance. *My doctor won't see me again unless I catch up on some of the overdue bills,* Dan had written. *I don't want to add to your stress but I don't know what else to do.*

Grady didn't know, either—but he had no option but to try to figure it out.

Somehow, he managed to get back to sleep. The
next morning, he got started bright and early, spending the day culling his list of contacts, trying to
broker a deal to flip the medical-device company's
property as soon as he bought it, or even better, before he bought it, saving him the scary prospect of
floating the loan in between purchase and sale. A
few people returned his calls and emails, but gave
him nothing more than platitudes and vague promises. Most ignored him. No one, it seemed, wanted
to be near a failure.

Now he stood on Beth Cooper's father's doorstep, clutching a bouquet of flowers in one hand
and a bottle of white wine in the other, and tried
not to break a sweat. A few hours at her dinner
table, then he'd get the name of the Realtor, get
Ida Mae's house sold and get the hell out of town.
Monster pranced in as much of a circle as the leash
would allow, then stopped to paw at the front door,
as if saying, *Come on, ring the bell and get it over
with.*

Grady pressed the button, then waited. He'd
opted for a button-down shirt and khakis. No tie,
no sport jacket. Something casual that said *boyfriend.* Not *guy pretending to be a boyfriend who
is actually in it to get rid of a dog and a house because he doesn't have time for a relationship with*

a woman who deserves more. Last he checked, Macy's didn't stock that outfit.

Beth pulled open the door. Her eyes widened and a smile fluttered across her face. Apparently, his choice of attire met with her approval. He loved the way she looked—always had, ever since she'd sat across from him in high school. But the adult Beth had a sexy, girl-next-door edge to her that he liked even more. She had her hair down, long blond tendrils skating along her shoulders, curving across the top of her breasts. She'd put on a simple pale yellow sundress that left her arms bare and belled below her narrow waist.

Holy hell. Maybe he should have gone for the tie. Because Beth looked like the kind of woman a man should spoil. Whisk off to dinner in Paris or a candlelit dinner on a beach at sunset.

Just a year ago, Grady could have done that. Now, the best he could offer was a bouquet and a charade. He thrust the flowers at her. "These are for you."

She buried her nose in the daisies and inhaled, then lifted her gaze and smiled at him. "Nice touch. Thanks."

He held up the bottle of wine. "And I'm hoping this will take the edge off." For him, mostly, because the last time he'd had this much riding on a date had been, well, never.

"Good thinking." She laughed, then bent down to greet a wildly enthusiastic Monster. The puppy pawed at Beth's legs, but she gently reprimanded him and told him to sit. Monster listened to her, his big brown eyes filled with the same rapt attention Grady suspected his own eyes showed.

Beth glanced up at Grady. "I take it you're as nervous as I am?" she said softly. "For the record, I've never done anything remotely close to this."

He nodded. At least he wasn't the only one with jitters in his gut. "I've never exchanged dinner for dog training and a business card."

Hell, he'd never gone out with someone like Beth. There was just something wholesome and sweet and enticing about her that had Grady off-kilter and wondering if it would be better for both of them if he bailed on the whole thing.

"I really appreciate this, Grady." She rose, took a look over her shoulder, then turned her attention back to him. When she spoke, her voice dropped to a whisper. "Remember the story we worked out by text earlier today. I don't think my dad will be sus-picious, but just be prepared. My father gets tired easily so you only have to stay for a little while.

My dad is also very protective of me, so be prepared for an inquisition. He won't go easy on you."

"You make it sound like dating you is a hardship," Grady said. "I find that difficult to believe."

"Not a hardship. Just…complicated."

Complicated. What did she mean by that? Because everything about Beth read simple and easy to him, like floating down a lazy river.

Behind her, a male voice called out, "Am I going to meet this young man or are you just gonna leave him standing on the porch like a wet newspaper?"

Beth drew in a breath, then opened the door wider. "Come on in," she said. "And don't say I didn't warn you."

Grady entered the Cape Cod–style house, with Monster at his feet, all gangly puppy paws on the smooth wood floors. Beth led the way down a short hallway, flanked by a dining room on the left and a guest bath on the right. The hall spilled into the living room, a crowded space dominated by a massive TV and a recliner. Dozens of pictures hung on the dark wood paneled walls, above a pair of floral sofas and a set of end tables filled with more pictures. In the corner sat an upright piano, the lid closed, bench tucked underneath.

In the recliner sat a man whose body held the echoes of a hearty frame. His cheeks were sunken, his eyes darkened by circles from sleepless nights. An oxygen tube draped over his ears and into his nose, connected to a dark green canister at his feet. He gripped the arms of the chair and shoved himself to his feet, his face pinching with the effort. He stuck out a shaky hand. "Reggie Cooper."

The name immediately struck a bell. A former fighter with a pretty damned good record. Grady stepped forward. "Grady Jackson. Pleased to meet you, sir."

"And what are your intentions toward my daughter?"

"Dad!" Beth's face reddened.

"I don't want you thinking my only daughter's heart isn't worth a little hard work." Reggie leaned forward and gave Grady a glare.

He couldn't blame her father for starting off with that question. If he had a daughter like Beth, he'd be keeping a loaded shotgun by the front door to scare off every man who got within ten feet. "Your daughter is an incredible woman."

"You better not forget that, son." Reggie wagged a finger in his direction and Beth's face turned a shade darker.

"Dad, why don't you sit down?" Beth didn't wait for an answer, but helped ease him back into his chair. Her touch was easy, loving, tender, and some weird part of Grady felt envy. "Can I get you anything to drink, Dad?"

Reggie shook his head. "Get something for that poor boy over there. He looks as nervous as a cat on a lawn mower."

Maybe Grady should have brought tequila instead of wine. Now that he was here, confronted directly with Beth's father and the reality of the situation, pretending to be her boyfriend, even for a minute, felt wrong. This was a man who clearly loved his daughter. Pulling the wool over his eyes when he was sick as hell left Grady's gut twisting, no matter how kind the motives behind the deception. "Let me help you," Grady said to Beth.

"She's got it. Leaves you and me time to chat," Reggie said, waving Beth toward the kitchen before he gestured toward the couch. He waited while Grady took a seat on the worn floral sofa. A solid thirty seconds passed while Reggie sized Grady up, the oxygen tank hissing all the while. "So... how did you meet my daughter?"

When he and Beth had worked out their "history" they'd decided basing it on some truths would be the easiest and best course. It didn't make sense to create a huge fictional account if he was only here for one night, one dinner. "I went to Hawkins Prep, too."

"You grew up round here?"

Yes, he had—in a house as cold as an iceberg. "In Raleigh. My brothers and I used to stay at my grandmother's in Stone Gap from time to time."

"And your parents, where are they?"

As uninvolved in their children's lives as they could be, last Grady had checked. "They're both attorneys in Raleigh."

"Attorneys." The look on Reggie's face told Grady what he thought of that career choice. Grady couldn't disagree, not when his parents fitted in with most of the stereotypes. His mother was as career driven as her husband. He had been the more exacting and demanding one with every element of his life, including his family. It had served him well as an attorney, but not so much as a father. While they were growing up, Grady and his brothers had often said they felt like they were living with a warden, not a dad.

When Grady had gone into business for himself— and struggled the first couple years—his father had used that as an opportunity to call him foolish and impractical. Yet another reason Grady rarely spoke to his parents.

"And you? Do you have a job?" Reggie asked.

"Uh, yes. Sort of." A complicated answer to say he'd laid himself off so he wouldn't drain the company any more. The only one technically employed at Jackson Properties was Dan. Grady didn't want to tell Beth's father about the millions he had made—or the millions he had lost. Or the long story behind the planned government facility that had lost funding before the doors ever opened. "I'm self-employed, sir."

"Code for unemployed," Reggie muttered.

Grady flicked a glance in the direction of the kitchen. Whatever Beth was doing was taking a year and a half. "I, uh, sell corporate real estate in Manhattan."

Or used to. Before he made a bad investment that cost him everything. Yeah, probably not what Beth wanted her fake boyfriend to share.

"You got a college degree?" Reggie asked.

Grady nodded. "MBA from Northwestern."

Reggie let out a low whistle. "Well, that's impressive. My daughter is smart as hell, and she should have gone to college, but with what happened senior year and—"

"Dad, no need to retread history." She handed Grady a glass of wine, then sat on the sofa beside him. Close enough to touch, but still far enough for the gulf of unfamiliarity between them to be palpable. She patted Grady's knee and flashed him a smile. "Both Grady and I prefer to focus on the present, not the past."

What had happened senior year? He searched his memory, but nothing came up. Granted, in senior year he'd been busy with college applications and maintaining his GPA. His world had revolved around a very tiny set of goals and objectives, mainly getting out of the house and away from his suffocating father. He and Beth hadn't had any classes together that year, though it was a small enough school that he'd still seen her around.

"What brought you back to Stone Gap?" Reggie asked. "Doesn't exactly seem like the kind of place a Northwestern grad would choose."

Not at all, which was why Grady didn't live here. Stone Gap was great, as small towns went, but he missed the heartbeat of New York City. Soon, he'd be back there. "I inherited my grandmother's house," he said. "In fact, you might have known her. Ida Mae Jackson? She worked at the corner market in downtown Stone Gap for most of her life. It's where she met my grandfather, and where she retired from, too, about fifteen years ago."

"I wasn't around much in my younger years," Reggie said. "Can't say I got to know anyone in this town much more than in passing. This was my wife's hometown, not mine. I met her when I was on the road, the first year I was fighting. She had such deep roots here, with her parents and grand-parents, getting her to move would have been like trying to uproot a sequoia. In fact, I've spent more time in this chair in the last two years than I spent in Stone Gap in the last three decades."

"My father was a boxing champ and fought all over the world for a good portion of his life," Beth said. She pointed to the photographs on the wall above Grady's head.

Dozens of images of a younger, burlier Reggie in various boxing poses, from the raised fist of a champion to the lightning-quick draw of a south-paw, filled the space. Several pictures of Reggie holding a winner's belt above his head, a few others of him with famous boxers from years ago—George Foreman, Rocky Marciano, Joe Frazier, and even one with crazy-haired promoter Don King.

"I've heard of you," Grady said. "You had a hell of a career."

"Yeah. Those were the days." Reggie sighed, then dropped his gaze to his hands, as if he could still see the gloves on his fists, the mat beneath his feet. He shook his head and cleared his throat, wiping away the cobwebs of memories. "Anyway,

I retired almost fifteen years ago, after I lost my wife, God rest her soul."

Beth's mother had died? Grady immediately felt bad for not even asking about her mother when she'd brought up her father the other day. Was that what happened in senior year?

He realized he knew virtually nothing about her life, about her, and for the hundredth time, he questioned the wisdom of what he was doing. He was sitting here beside a woman who was essentially a stranger, trying to fool a sick man. Albeit for a good purpose, because it was clear Reggie loved his daughter and worried about her. Grady's own father wouldn't have been half that concerned. Hell, he felt that he had more of a relationship with Beth's father in ten minutes than he'd had with his own in the past ten years.

Illness had winnowed Reggie into a shell of the man in the photos. Grady found himself wishing he could do more than just feign love for Beth for a single dinner, if only to give a sick man a bright spot in what seemed to be a pretty gray existence. Because Grady knew what it was like to lose everything, and to have to face the truth of a life that had disappeared in a blink. If he'd been here under different circumstances, he'd want to ask Reggie about winning and losing, and how he got out of bed on the mornings after he lost.

Beth's father might be a difficult man to impress, but Grady had to admit he liked him. Reggie Cooper was direct and frank, not at all the kind of guy to dance around a subject. Maybe that was what had made him such a good boxer—he went straight for the punch, with his fists and his words.

"So what kind of corporate real estate are we talking?" Reggie asked. "You selling diners or department stores?"

"Well, neither. I specialize in medical and technology properties. Most of the time, I find and renovate facilities for clients who are looking for a home base."

"Most of the time?" Reggie's gaze narrowed. "What do you do the rest of the time?"

"Dad," Beth interjected, laying a hand on his arm. "We should probably sit down to dinner."

Beth picked up Monster, putting him into one of those playpen things she had in the grooming salon, and gave him a couple of peanut butter–filled treats that looked like they were going to keep the puppy occupied for a long time. Good.

But Reggie didn't listen to his daughter's request. "So you're like a manager. Selling the boxer to the promoter, pocketing your cut and never getting in the ring yourself."

Did Reggie think there was no risk in Grady's business? If so, he was wrong. Grady had gotten into the ring every time, taken every chance. And the one time he'd overstepped and forgotten to protect himself, he'd gotten the takedown of his life. He tried not to think about Dan, and how much the other man was depending on him. Trusting Grady to pull off a miracle. "When you get in the ring, sometimes you get knocked out."

"Yeah, and sometimes you win it all. If I'd been smarter, I'd have decided to be a manager or promoter, so I could make money off of someone else's knucklehead." Reggie tapped his temple. "But I was young and full of piss and vinegar when I started boxing. Which means I thought with my fists instead of my brains."

Grady could relate. How many times did he wish he'd listened to the sense of others instead of following his own gut reactions?

"Hey, guys, I made a roast chicken with potatoes for dinner and now it's getting cold," Beth said, getting to her feet. "Do we want to take this inquisition into the dining room?"

"Sure, sure," Reggie said. Once again, he waved off his daughter's attempts to help him out of the chair even as he coughed and wheezed, the struggle obvious in his features. He shuffled out to the dining room and sat at the head of the small table. "Grady, you sit right here, next to me."

Grady did as he was told. Beth sat across from him, the two of them flanking Reggie. Her father passed the platter of chicken and potatoes to Grady. The scents of garlic, onion and roasted chicken wafted across the table. Grady's mouth watered at the sight of the browned hen and cubed red potatoes. He'd eaten in many five-star restaurants, but none of the meals he'd had looked or smelled as good as this one. Maybe it was just the thought of sharing the homey dish with Beth, the fact that she'd made it with him in mind. It almost made him wish, just for an instant, that their facade could be real.

Whoa. Where had *that* thought come from? That was a little more of a hearth-and-home road than Grady traveled. And anyway, Beth had probably just been thinking about her father when she made dinner, not him. He didn't need to get all "relationshipy" over a damned chicken. But as he glanced around the dining room, taking in the photos on the buffet, the china settings in the hutch, the floral tablecloth with embroidered edges, he felt like he was back at his grandmother's table.

The setting warmed him, settled his stress…and gave him pause.

What was he doing here? Playing house? Or helping a friend? Or serving his own interests?

The return to the simpler world he'd left behind in Stone Gap was simply…uplifting. A temporary feeling, he was sure, one that would pass in a few days. He'd be itching to get back to the frantic pace of New York before long.

"Looks delicious, Beth." After filling his plate, Grady gave the platter to her. He laid his napkin on his lap, picked up his fork and speared a piece of chicken.

Reggie cleared his throat. "We say grace in this house," he said.

Damn. Grady put the fork down. In that moment, he felt like a five-year-old caught with his hand in the cookie jar.

Beth looked as surprised as Grady. "Dad, we don't—"

"Yes, we do." Reggie nodded in Grady's direction.

"Uh, yes, sir. My apologies. It's been a while since I had a family meal." And an eon since he'd said grace at the table. Ida Mae had been the only one in the Jackson family to insist on pausing before eating. Grady's busy, workaholic parents rarely ate dinner with their sons at all, saving family dinners for major holidays. Even then, they were quiet affairs, where the loudest sound was the scrape of a utensil against the china, a socially unacceptable noise that earned a sharp glance.

"You want to do the honors, Grady?" Reggie asked.

Grady exchanged a *what do I say to that?* glance with Beth. She gave a slight shrug and dipped her head, leaving him on his own. Sink or swim.

There was no way Grady was going to sink, not again, and not at a family dinner with people who weren't even his family.

He cleared his throat. Then cleared it again. "Uh, dear God, thank you for this meal and for the people around this table." He paused. What else was he supposed to say? He tried to think back to his grandmother's prayers, and hit upon the one she said most often, letting the words babble out of his mouth before he thought them through. "Season our lives with goodness and my words with salt in case I have to eat them later."

Beth snickered. Reggie let out a huff. Grady vowed to never, ever, ever participate in impromptu prayer again.

"Amen," Grady said, before he added any more of Ida Mae's pearls of prayer.

"Well. That was different." Reggie raised his head and opened his eyes. "Can't say I've heard that one before."

Thankfully, he didn't seem offended, just… amused. That was good. "It was one my grandmother always said," Grady said. "She didn't believe in taking anything too seriously."

"And I suspect that kind of thinking got her in trouble sometimes?"

Grady chuckled. "More than once. But that was part of what I loved about her. My grandmother was…refreshing. Honest yet loving. I've never met anyone quite like her."

Refreshing. That was the adjective he'd used for Beth a couple days ago. Two women in his life that were a far cry from all others.

"I didn't know Ida Mae that well," Beth said. "I wish I had spent more time with her. She sounds amazing."

"I didn't realize you knew her at all," Grady said. Ida Mae, he was sure, would have loved Beth. She was the kind of girl a boy brought home to meet his mother, Grandma would have said. That was, if the boy had a mother who cared about the kind of girl he brought home. Grady often wondered why his parents had had children, because they seemed to forget their three boys as soon as they were born.

Beth nodded. "I met your grandma a few times at the general store. Every time, she was so sweet to me and never forgot what my favorite candy was."

"That's a good thing for a man to remember, too." Reggie wagged a finger in Grady's direction before he turned back to his daughter. "I might not have been the best husband in the state of North Carolina, but I always remembered how much your mother loved Almond Joys. If we had a fight, I'd bring home a handful of them. I swear, she liked those better than flowers."

A soft, melancholy smile filled Beth's face. "I remember that. Whenever I went trick-or-treating, I'd be sure to get a few to bring back for her."

Father and daughter sat in silence for a minute. "There were some good days, weren't there, Bethie?"

"Yes, Dad, there were. Before..." Beth's voice trailed off. "Well, before."

Grady sat in the middle of a private moment between Beth and her father. A thousand unspoken things hung in the air, questions in Grady's mind that he had no right to ask. What had happened to Beth's mother? What did Reggie mean by "there were *some* good days"? Was it connected to whatever had so consumed Beth Cooper's life that she didn't have time to date? Surely her father had a visiting nurse or something, right?

For a few minutes, there was only the sound of eating and the occasional cough from Reggie's ravaged lungs. Then Reggie said, "Pass those damn-near-amazing rolls, please," and the tension at the table eased. Grady handed him the basket of warm Parker House rolls, and then slid the butter his way.

"So, Grady, quick quiz," Reggie said. "What is my daughter's favorite candy?"

"Dad! That's not fair to ask."

"He should know it. He should know everything about you. Any man who dates my daughter better damned well be paying attention to more than her curves." Reggie gave an emphatic nod. "My own dad used to say that to me when I started dating, and it's good advice."

The older man turned to Grady and stared at him. Grady squirmed in his seat. Beth's favorite candy? How was he supposed to know that? He wanted to look at her for some kind of hint, but Reggie's attention was laser focused, and Grady was pretty sure he'd get caught if he tried to cheat. He'd already messed up grace. He had a feeling he better get this right, or he'd be failing some kind of invisible test. Grady scrolled through his high school memories in a rapid microfiche of images.

"Reese's peanut butter cups," he said.

Beth's eyes widened. "That's…that's right."

"Well, good. Glad to see the boy is paying attention. Pass the potatoes, please." Reggie put out a hand. After he'd refilled his plate, he took a few bites, then turned back to Grady. "It seems to me that you care a great deal about my daughter. When are you planning to make it official?"

Grady nearly choked on the bite of bread in his mouth. *Make it official?* He'd signed on to be a boyfriend for a night, not a lifetime. "Uh, I don't know, sir. Beth and I haven't really talked about that."

Reggie's face pinched with disapproval, then the wrinkled nose and furrowed brow yielded to worry and something that looked like regret. "I'd like my daughter to be settled with a good man before I'm gone—and not to upset this lovely meal, but we all know that's not far away. Heart disease is a cruel mistress who wants her due," Reggie said. "Don't start smoking, son. Not now, not ever."

Grady dropped his gaze to his plate, because all he could see was the flashing ambulance lights and Dan being loaded in on a stretcher. Heart disease was a cruel mistress indeed. Dan's doctor had given him a prescription for three things: more activity, no smoking and less stress. The longer

Grady sat in this town without working capital to get the company running again, the more stress he added to Dan's life.

"I want my daughter to have a happy life," Reggie went on, "one that doesn't revolve around caring for a bitter old boxer who takes ten thousand pills a day."

"Dad—"

"Let me say my piece, Beth. I was a terrible father. A worse husband." He eyed Grady. "Tell me you won't be either of those."

"I won't." That, at least, was the truth. Grady had no intentions of continuing this charade after tonight. And even if he ever did settle down, he vowed to be better than his father had been.

Then he glanced at Beth. Worry creased the space between her brows, shimmered in her eyes. Despite the big show of taking a second helping of potatoes, Reggie had barely touched his meal.

Everything about the man, from his skeletal frame to his lily-white skin, said he was on borrowed time. The hiss of oxygen every time he took a breath added an exclamation point. His gaze as he'd spoken had been filled with entreaty. *Please let me know my most prized and precious person will be okay after I'm gone.*

Grandma Ida Mae had been one of those people

who showed up at the neighbors' house with a casserole when someone in the family was sick. She was first on the scene after a storm to help someone clear their driveway of debris. She'd volunteered to feed the hungry, and set flags at the base of headstones on Memorial Day. She was the kind of person other people aspired to be.

The kind of person Grady had never been. His entire adult life had been focused on building his company, amassing a financial stockpile to fund his ventures and his personal excesses. He'd accumulated things, not friends, and when he'd lost damned near everything and saw the eyes of the people he had hurt, he'd realized how empty that kind of life could be.

Sitting beside him was a man who had a life with real value—a town he loved, a home, and a daughter who loved him fiercely. A man with one simple dying wish. Maybe it wouldn't be so bad to give Reggie a little comfort. Grady didn't have to actually act on his promises—just keep them until...

Well, until. Even after just an hour spent at his table, Grady didn't want the man to die anytime soon. He liked Reggie, a man who came across as frank and stubborn, two qualities Grady looked for in employees, in friends, and in himself. And he liked Beth. More and more every minute he spent with her.

Even now, the worry and desire to keep her father calm and healthy was evident in her words, and the way she glanced at her dad from time to time or gave him a light touch as she got up to refill his water or retrieve more rolls from the oven.

Maybe it was the homemade food. Or the floral sofa. Or the crazy idea that he couldn't fix the big things in his life, but he could fix this small one, that made Grady veer left when he'd been on a decidedly right-turn-only course.

"Sir, I care very much about your daughter," Grady began. Where was he going with that statement? There was still time to change the subject, to talk about candy bars or favorite cookies. "And… and I'd love to make that a permanent relationship."

Beth's fork landed with a clatter on the stoneware plate. Her eyes widened. "You…what?"

"Wonderful!" Reggie's face transformed from pale and tired to flushed and excited. "This is such wonderful news. Best news I've had…well, in a long time. It deserves a celebration! Bethie, remember that champagne we keep in the bottom drawer of the fridge? Why don't you grab that? I can't think of a better reason to uncork that bottle."

"Dad, I don't think—"

"I have one child, and I want to celebrate her engagement. Or soon-to-be engagement." Reggie gave Grady a wink. "I expect you're going to give her the full experience with a ring and a formal proposal, right?"

Grady nodded. He couldn't have formed an intelligible sentence right now if someone offered him a million dollars. He glanced at Beth's shocked face, then at Reggie's ecstatic one, and wondered what the hell he'd just done.

"What. Was. That?" Beth whispered under her breath. She'd dragged Grady into the kitchen to "help open the champagne." Behind the refrigerator door, she gave him a little shake. "What were you thinking?"

"Just trying to give your dad some peace."

"By offering to *marry* me? I'm not getting married, Grady. Not to you or anyone. Not even—"

"To give your dying dad one less thing to worry about?" Grady reached down and retrieved the champagne from the fridge. "Listen, I'm not really asking you to marry me. We'll just pretend for now. I can't…" Grady shook his head and looked away. "I just think it's the least I can do."

"The least…" She shut the fridge door, opened

a cabinet and retrieved three champagne flutes. The last time anyone had used these had been her mother's fortieth birthday. That had been one of the last times she'd seen either of her parents truly happy.

She ran a finger along the delicate curve of the flute. *This is such wonderful news. Best news I've had...well, in a long time.* Her father had been smiling. Laughing. Talking in exclamation points.

"We don't even know each other," Beth said.

"Ah, but I know your favorite candy."

She propped a fist on her hip. "How *did* you know that?"

"Whenever we had a big test in geometry, you'd have a handful of those bite-size Reese's cups on your desk and down them like they were speed." Grady laughed.

"I forgot all about that." Beth shook her head. She was oddly touched that he could remember a detail like that from fifteen years ago. "I hated that class. And tests made me nervous, hence the chocolate binge."

"For me, it's junk food." He leaned against the counter. "Whenever I get worried about something, I'm all about burgers and fries and pizza. As a matter of fact, I had pizza for lunch today."

"You did? What were you nervous about?"

He hesitated before answering, and she wondered what he wasn't sharing. "This whole 'pretend boyfriend' thing."

Somehow, that didn't ring true to Beth. Grady might have been shy, as he'd said, in high school, but he was an accomplished, capable businessman now. What could possibly have him stressed?

And why did she care? This was all pretend and all so very temporary. "These glasses are dusty. I should wash them." She turned away to the sink. "You don't have to do this. I'll give you the referral to the Realtor and train your dog. You did your part, Grady."

Now you can leave me to handle the rest on my own, like everyone else in my life has.

He grabbed the dish towel from where it hung on the oven door, put his back to the counter and dried the glasses as Beth washed them. "My grandmother was the kind of woman who would invite a perfect stranger to dinner or let some down-on-his-luck man stay at her house for free. She was generous to a fault. I…well, I haven't been. I've made more than a few mistakes of my own, mistakes I can't rectify, at least not yet. It's been a long time since I've done anything I can feel really good about. But I can do this."

"How are we going to pull it off? A dinner

is one thing, an engagement…" She shut off the water and lowered her voice. "We barely know each other."

"True. But the charade won't be for long. I'm only staying in town long enough to get Ida Mae's house on the market. Then our 'engagement'—" he gave it air quotes "—will all be long-distance. When I'm not here, you can tell him whatever you want about calls or texts you're getting from me. Your dad will feel better that you're going to be taken care of, and maybe the little reduction in stress will…give him more strength."

The unspoken words: *give you a little more time with him.*

Tears filled Beth's eyes. All these months, she had shouldered the burden of her father's illness alone. The weight of those responsibilities and worries seemed Herculean. Now Grady was offering to help, in a tiny way, by alleviating her father's biggest worry, and giving her a gift she couldn't refuse. And if relieving this stress truly did help her father…it could pay off in an increase in days she'd get to spend with him. Maybe weeks. Dare she hope, months?

"You really think we can pull this off? I mean, I don't want to put you out or add to what you have going on right now." She didn't even know much about what that was, except for Monster, who had curled up in the ex-pen beside his treat and fallen asleep. The fact that she knew so little should have been a red flag. There were stresses and worries in his eyes that he wasn't sharing. Little doubts that told her she should ask more questions. "We're pretty much strangers. It'll be awkward and weird."

Awkward and weird didn't even begin to describe it. *Insane* was a better word. Everything she knew about Grady she could fit on a grain of rice, and her acting skills were about zero. Not to mention she was going to be lying to her father.

Beth glanced over her shoulder at Reggie, sitting at the dining room table, the remote in his hand as he caught some of the baseball game while he waited for the champagne and celebration of a lie. She noted his hunched shoulders, his too-thin frame. For the last year, she had watched her father's eyes slowly shift from warm and optimistic to depressed and worried. Sadness filled the air around him, a cocoon he had lost the strength to escape. But tonight at dinner, for one short moment...

He had been happy. Engaged. Part of her life. There'd been a lightness in his features, a smile dimpling his cheeks. "Maybe..." she said softly, "if we could make my father believe it, he would become more involved and less distant."

"I've only been here an hour or so," Grady said, "and I'm not always the most observant man on the planet, but I can see how much work you're doing to take care of him. The medicine dosing, doctor appointments, cooking, cleaning. On top of that, you're running your own business, which I know is incredibly time-consuming. Maybe this... relationship we're sorta having can make it easier for both of you, just because your father will feel more...settled."

She thought of the restlessness and worry he'd shown in the last few months, how much time he spent worrying about her instead of himself. "He would. But still, pretending to be engaged is a lot harder than pretending to be dating."

Engaged couples touched. They flirted. They kissed. They even...well, pretend engaged couples might not do *that*. Surely she could handle a little flirting and kissing. Couldn't she?

"And there's...the physical part." There, she'd said it.

He gave a slight nod. "True. But we have kissed once. Hell of a kiss, if I remember right."

She raised her chin. "I've had better."

He chuckled, then shifted closer to her. The heat

in the kitchen ratcheted up a thousand degrees. "Oh, really?"

"You're not the only man I've ever kissed, you know." But he was the only man whose kiss had left her unable to think about anything else. Even now, just glancing at his mouth as he spoke quickened the warmth in her belly. The one other long-term relationship she'd had, with a guy she'd been engaged to for a split second, never distracted her like this. She had finished washing the glasses, but the water kept on running behind her.

"Right now, Beth Cooper, I'd like to be the only man you're kissing. Because I liked kissing you…" he shifted closer still "…very…" another step "…very…" he put a hand on her waist "…much."

Was he pretending? Being real? Did she want to know the answer? She opened her mouth but no words came out. Instead, she leaned forward a few degrees, and before she knew it, they were kissing again. Grady's lips skated across hers, featherlight, kissing the edges of hers, with care, almost…reverence.

Damn it. She wasn't going to fall for him. Nope. Not gonna happen.

Of their own accord, her arms went around his waist, and she shifted into his body, sliding into place as if she was the missing yin to his yang.

"If you two kids are done making out in my kitchen, I'd sure like to toast this happy news."

Her father's teasing voice jolted Beth back to reality. She stumbled back, hitting the counter with her hip. A sharp pain ran down her leg. "Ow. Uh… We should—"

"Get back in there." Grady cleared his throat, grabbed the champagne flutes, then tucked the bottle under his arm and headed back into the dining room.

Beth stood there a second longer, her fingers on her lips. What had just happened?

Chapter Five

It was raining cats and dogs and elephants, as his grandmother would say. Heavy, fat raindrops slashed against the windows of his car, darkened the sky and made Grady's already foul mood even fouler. He opened Ida Mae's refrigerator, only to remember he had bought just enough groceries for a week, and he'd been in town for ten days now. Long enough to get the yard work done, the paint touched up and the broken shutter fixed.

And apparently get engaged.

A moment of compassion. And insanity. Of course, it wasn't a real engagement and certainly wouldn't lead to an actual marriage, but still, the whole idea was crazy. It left him thinking about Beth more often—as in, almost nonstop—and made him wonder about things he had no justi- fication to wonder about. His mind would drift, skating between trying to figure out what she was doing and circling back to what it would be like to truly marry her.

Just as quickly, those thoughts were chased by guilt. He should be focused on the company, not on a woman who was a detour, not a destination.

The doorbell rang and Monster launched into a cacophony of barking, as if Jack the Ripper himself was at the door. "Stay here, Cujo." Grady climbed over the baby gate, which had been a godsend idea from Beth, and crossed to the front door. A tall blonde woman in a crisp pantsuit stood on the porch, shaking the rain off her umbrella. Thank goodness. Right on time and right when he needed a reminder of where to refocus.

Grady pulled open the door. "Thanks for com- ing by in this weather."

"A little rain never hurt anyone." She stuck out her hand. "Savannah Barlow. Nice to meet you in person."

Beth's friend Savannah, who had recently added a real estate division to her home renovation business, was about Grady's age, and looked as friendly as a sunflower. He hoped that what she lacked in experience and exposure in real estate she made up for with ambition and hard work. From what he'd heard, Savannah was enthusiastic, motivated, and eager. "Grady Jackson. Come on in. Ignore the killer mutt in the kitchen."

She laughed as she crossed the threshold, leaving her damp umbrella on the porch. Once inside, she looked up the staircase, then swept her gaze across the foyer. He'd oiled and buffed the hardwood floors, and they gleamed, even on a dreary day. "This is a great house. I've always loved it."

"Yeah, it is." Grady didn't want to stand here and reminisce. If he did, he suspected some crazy kind of sentimentality would make him consider holding on to his only legacy from his beloved grandmother. As if he needed a house he wasn't planning to live in more than he needed to rebuild the company he'd staked his—and Dan's—future on. "Let's take the tour, then talk about how long before it can be put on the market. I want to price it to sell."

"It shouldn't be sitting on the market for very long. Places like this, with all this character and the view of the lake—everyone wants a house like this. It's a great place to raise kids."

A memory of him and his two brothers dashing down the lawn in the middle of a Nerf-gun battle on a hot summer day flashed in Grady's mind. What would it have been like to have grown up here all year round, instead of in the cold, sterile mansion the Jackson boys had dubbed the Mausoleum? Or living here and raising a family with Beth—

Whoa, whoa. Talk about derailing his thoughts.

Grady cleared his throat. "Uh, so let me know if you think I need to update anything." He and Savannah walked through the house, and he made notes as she pointed out some chipped paint, a few pieces of furniture to rearrange, some scuffs in the second-floor hallway, and a missing electrical cover. He'd done the outside work yesterday, thankfully before the rain started.

"Overall, this is in almost perfect shape," Savannah said. She turned a slow circle in the dining room, taking in the floor-to-ceiling windows and built-in hutch. Monster had finally settled for sitting in the kitchen and whining in displeasure about being left out of the tour. "Can I ask why you're selling?"

Because I need a restart. Because Dan is sitting in that office in New York, stress beating up his heart a little more each day. "I don't live here. I live in New York."

Savannah gave him a curious look. "Really? Because when Beth put the two of us in touch, I guess I just assumed, well, that you two were together."

"My business is in New York." Or what was left of it. He chose not to address the part about being together with Beth. That answer was as complicated as the one about why he was getting rid of his legacy. "So how soon can you sell it?"

She tapped her lip as she thought that over. "To give you some time to take care of those little things, I can get my photographer out here in a few days, and get it on the market a day or two after that. I'll schedule an open house—"

Too slow. Too much time. Grady shook his head. "I want it on the market now. Today."

"You're the seller and I work for you, but any place sells faster and for a better price with quality photography and some ads. Especially for this house, a well-placed ad campaign can reach that out-of-state buyer looking to settle down here."

"Just get it on the market now, with or without photos. I'll do these—" he held up the list "—tomorrow. Send your photographer at the end of the day."

"Well, that's an ambitious schedule, but sure. Either way, I hope whomever buys this house creates lots of happy memories in it. But I guess I'm just a romantic." Savannah handed him a business card. "Let me know if you have any questions. And say hello to Beth for me."

He thanked the Realtor, and after she left, Grady released Monster from kitchen jail, pulled out his phone and leaned against the door to get a better signal in this middle-of-nowhere town. He would have gone out on the porch, but the rain was still beating hard against the house. A few seconds later, Dan picked up. "Hey," Grady said. "House is going on the market tomorrow at the latest."

"Good. You think it will sell fast enough? Because I just heard Jim Givens is looking into that property in Lower Manhattan, too."

The mention of Grady's biggest competitor made him jerk to attention. "How did he find out about it? I thought we had an early window."

"That window's closing, Grady." Dan sighed. "I didn't want to tell you, but Bob told me he's officially listing it at the end of next week."

Grady cursed. He'd thought he'd have more time. How the hell was he going to get this house sold, closed on, get the money and buy the property that fast?

"And there's more," Dan said. "I need to take a couple days off. Doctor's orders." He chuckled like it was a joke, but Grady knew the truth. Dan's heart, already fragile, couldn't take the eighty-hour work weeks and constant worry being COO of a sinking ship demanded.

Being CEO was no walk in the park, either, but the stress and pressure Grady felt were multiplied by the guilt in his chest. Dan had had that heart attack because of Grady's choices. He never should have taken that big of a risk with the building, one that wasn't a definite flip. Never should have put other people's livelihoods on the line. "You okay?"

"Nothing a little R & R can't cure." Dan paused, then seemed to read Grady's mind. "Quit blaming yourself. Businesses fail. It happens."

"You warned me, Dan. I should have listened."

At his feet, Monster pawed Grady's leg, whining to go out, so he headed down the hall behind the mutt. As soon as Grady opened the back door, the puppy ran into a puddle, then circled the yard, spraying mud behind his paws. Great.

"I think I've got two interested buyers in this new property. I've been calling pretty much everyone in my contacts list who would be a fit for that place," Grady said. "I'll speed things up over here. See what I can do."

"Sounds good. Also…while we're on the subject of Jim…" With Dan, who was usually confident and decisive, pausing was never a good sign. "He's offered a buyout. Said he'll take that empty building off our hands."

Jim Givens competed with Grady for many of the same properties in New York. He'd known Jim off and on for years, and they got along well on the golf course, not so well in negotiations. More than once, Grady had been quicker on the draw or better in the selling game, which pissed Jim off no end.

"Here come the sharks, circling the fresh bait." Grady cursed under his breath. "What's his offer?"

"Less than it's worth, but enough to pay most of the debt."

Monster leaped into a puddle, then popped back, surprised at the splash in his face and the depth of the water.

"And if he can buy this new location before we do—"

"He can offer even less," Dan finished. "Jim's a smart guy. But you...you're smarter. You jump off cliffs I'd never even climb. So yeah, maybe the last decision you made was a total turkey, but you're going to come out of this."

But would he do it soon enough? If Dan had been ordered to take some time off, what wasn't his COO sharing? "If you want to find another job, Dan, I'll write you a hell of a recommendation. Call in some favors. You'd be a valuable asset anywhere you go."

"If you keep making me that offer," Dan said, "eventually my feelings are gonna get hurt. I'm right where I want to be."

Grady's chest was tight and his breath was thin when he hung up with Dan. Standing on the porch, watching Monster chase his tail in the rain, Grady concentrated on breathing deeply, slowing his rushing pulse, while conflicting thoughts pounded in his head.

The puppy finally grew tired of his tail and made a beeline for the house. Grady tried to block him, but the wet dog wriggled out of his grasp and then danced around the kitchen, down the hall, into the living room and back again, leaving a muddy trail across the kitchen Grady had cleaned an hour ago and the floors he had buffed yesterday.

Great. Just great. But at least the distraction of the dog's path of destruction had taken his mind off work and the panic that caused nowadays.

"You are officially off my Christmas list," he said to the dog. Monster yipped, jumped up and left two paw prints on Grady's sweatpants before charging off down the hall again.

Damn it. That dog was going to be the death

of him. As if he didn't have enough to deal with already.

Instead of chasing after the mud machine, Grady pulled out his phone and hovered his thumb over Beth's name. He pressed it, and as soon as she answered and he heard her voice, the aggravations and regrets moved aside to make room for something that felt like…happiness.

"Do you want to meet for breakfast?" he asked. They talked on the phone a couple times a day, but only chatting about the dog and her dad. They'd met for a few more training sessions, and every time, she'd been matter-of-fact, focused on the job and gone the minute they were done.

In this moment, hearing her voice wasn't enough. He needed to see her, see that smile and those eyes that saw past the man he had been. "I'm starving, my fridge is empty, and I figure we can talk about how to get this puppy to avoid puddles."

Yeah, that's why he wanted to see her. To talk about the muddy mutt. Not because she'd lingered at the edges of his every thought ever since that kiss. When she hesitated, he filled in the pause, like a nervous teenager. "I'll meet you anywhere Monster can't go."

"Okay, sounds good," she said with a little laugh. "But we will have some puppy-and-you time later.

You can't train him if you always leave him at home." Beth gave him the address of a café downtown and agreed to meet in half an hour.

Grady put Monster back into puppy jail. "You stay here. I'll be back. And for the love of all that is holy, please chew this—" Grady grabbed a Kong toy that he'd filled with peanut butter, then frozen per Beth's advice yesterday "—and not my shoes, my chair legs or the molding. Deal?"

Monster wagged his tail, and gave Grady a *sure, Dad* bark. Grady was pretty damned certain he'd come home—no, not home, to the house he was selling—and find more destruction and chaos. He drove across town, parked outside the Good Eatin' Café, and wondered if it was too early for a beer. It was barely past nine in the morning and already Grady's frustration level was off the charts.

He sat in the car, replaying the conversation with Dan. The level of anxiety in his chest began to spike again, curling a tight fist around his lungs. Was he moving too fast? Too slow? Should he have tried harder to get a loan? Should he take Jim's offer?

Uncertainty and *hesitancy*. Two words that would never have described Grady Jackson a year ago. But every time he tried to make a decision, he saw the faces of the people he had been forced to let go, and saw Dan in that hospital bed, hooked up to a heart monitor that beeped way too.fast.

Grady ran a hand through his hair and let out a deep breath. He'd fix this, somehow. He had promised Dan. Promised everyone, really.

In front of him, the tiny diner had four bricked stairs that led into the restaurant. Beth could be in there right now. What he had with her was as temporary as a summer storm, and yet just the thought of seeing her eased that fist open.

Inside the diner, bright white speckled tiles were offset by deep red bench seats and bar stools. A neon-pink open sign flashed in the window, and lush, thick English ivy plants lined the shelf above the tables. It was all shiny and new, with chrome accents and an open kitchen that sparkled. A wiry, gray-haired woman rushed up to greet him as soon as he crossed the threshold. "Welcome to the Good Eatin' Café. I'm Viv, the owner." She waved toward an open booth beside one of the plate-glass windows. "Come, come, have a seat. Let me get you some coffee."

He barely managed a "yes, thank you," before Viv was gone and back again with a steaming mug of rich, dark coffee. "I haven't been here in a long time," he said, as he took a seat and gave the diner another appreciative glance. "I like what you've done with the place."

"Why, thank you! We just finished renovating. Had some help from the Barlows. Are you from Stone Gap? If so, you must know them."

Savannah was a Barlow and he knew from Beth that she was a house restorer. Undoubtedly the same family. "I don't, but I'm not really from here—I only used to visit in the summers. My grandmother, Ida Mae Jackson, brought me and my brothers to this café on Sunday mornings."

The smile fell from Viv's face. "Oh, you poor thing. I heard that she died. She was such a wonderful person. I'm sure you're heartbroken."

"She was one of a kind, that's for sure." There were still moments when Grady couldn't believe that she wouldn't be there when he opened the door, with a ready plate of cookies and a hug. Her presence was in every inch of the house, in the apron hanging on the hook by the back door and the black line scuff down the kitchen tile from where she'd successfully tried riding his skateboard one June afternoon. Ida Mae had been a big part of what Grady and his brothers had missed in their childhood, and now that she was gone…

He'd never have her fun, loving and adventurous spirit around him again. The same spirit that had flowed in his blood for as long as he could re-member, then lost the day the business crashed and burned. The only time he'd come close to finding that again was when he was with Beth.

Temporary. It would pass, he was sure. That was a good thing, wasn't it? He couldn't be getting hung up on a woman who lived half a country away.

He settled into the booth while Viv studied him for a minute, an order pad in one hand and a pen in the other. She tapped the pen against her lip. "Wait. Ida Mae Jackson… You must be Grady, the one who's marrying Beth Cooper."

Grady froze. "Uh, how did you hear that?"

"Honey, this is a small town. If you put down a welcome mat, I guarantee you'll have fifty people on your doorstep before the sun sets, bringing you casseroles." Viv smiled. "Reggie Cooper is so ex-cited that his little girl is getting married that he called about half the town. Says to be prepared for the biggest and best wedding Stone Gap has ever seen. Why, he's even talked about having the shin-dig over at the inn. They have a real pretty lawn area, and that Della Barlow can put on one hell of a party. She did it for her son's wedding, and for Katie and Sam Millwright. It's so nice to see Sam get a happy ending after what happened, with his wife dying and all."

The names and places came at Grady in a blur, but they all spelled one thing—this simple little masquerade he'd proposed was no longer quite so simple. "Uh, sure." Which wasn't really an answer to anything, but Grady wasn't certain there was an appropriate response that didn't include *we're just pretending, so don't buy anything from the non-existent registry.*

"So, what can I get you?" Viv asked. "We've got an omelet special. Three eggs with cheese—"

"Yeah, sounds good," he interrupted, his mind still grappling with what she had told him. How did a simple favor for Beth turn into a major shindig at the inn, whatever that meant? "Thanks."

Viv gave him a curious look, then shrugged and headed to the kitchen, calling out something about a "triple bypass" to the chef by the stove. She greeted a couple who entered, and seemed to forget about Grady for a while, which was just fine with him. Maybe she—and the rest of Stone Gap—would also forget about this whole wedding thing.

Then Beth walked inside, hesitating in the doorway as she scanned the room. It seemed like everything came to a halt, and the only thing his attention zeroed in on was her smile. She had left her hair down, long blond waves that curled at the ends. She had on jeans and a T-shirt, which clung to her in a way that made his hands jealous.

Across the way, he could see Viv grinning as she pointed the two of them out to another woman. The Stone Gap Gossip Train was running at full speed. God help him.

Beth spied him and came walking down the aisle. "Good morning." She settled across from him. "Viv gave me the strangest look when I walked in. I'm here all the time, but today it was like it was Christmas and my birthday."

"Or your fake wedding." Grady arched a brow. "Which isn't so fake around here. Apparently there's going to be a shindig, and Reggie has invited the whole town?"

Beth's cheeks pinked and she sighed. "Oh no. Really? When I left his house yesterday, my father was pretty excited, but I didn't think he'd actually start planning anything. I was going to tell him that it wasn't real but…" She bit her lip. "It's the first time he's truly taken an interest in my life. And I… I guess I selfishly want that. I'm sorry. If you want, I'll tell him the truth today."

Half the diner was watching them talk, rubber-neckers curious about their relationship. Viv was standing by the register grinning like the Cheshire cat, as if their romance had been all her idea.

Grady barely noticed. The look on Beth's face, the craving for something she'd needed all her life, trumped the gossip and whispers and stares.

"I spent my life with parents who didn't care what I did, as long as I brought home a perfect report card and behaved in public like the perfect son." He shrugged, as if it no longer bothered him. It did, but he wasn't going to change anyone at this stage of his life. According to Nick's text a couple months ago, Dad had started a tentative relationship with Nick, and reached out a couple times to Grady, but he hadn't replied. The last thing he needed when he was barely managing to tread water was recounting, to the most judgmental man he'd ever known, a list of all the ways he had failed. "I can understand that, Beth, and don't want you to break your father's heart by admitting it was a lie. Besides, what's a little shindig planning? We'll make up some excuse to delay it later."

She reached across the table and took his hand in both of hers. The simple gesture eased the knot between his shoulders and the iron grip on his lungs. "Thank you."

He nodded, then pretended to study the menu, because if he didn't, he might turn around and thank her for helping to lift the albatross he constantly carried. Too bad he couldn't just put her in his pocket and bring her back to New York, for those moments when he panicked about his business tanking. "Anyway, I, uh, hope the food is good. I ordered something called a triple bypass."

Beth laughed. "It's the most delicious thing on the menu. Don't tell my doctor, but I usually order that or apple pie when I'm here for breakfast."

He liked that she was a pie-for-breakfast kind of girl. Liked that a lot. "I'll have to remember that," he said, then realized just as quickly that there was no reason to remember. He'd be leaving town in a few days at most. He wasn't going to be taking Beth with him or even coming back for her. As soon as the house was on the market, he was back on his own, trying to yank the *Titanic* up before it sank to the ocean floor.

He needed more coffee. Viv seemed to read his mind, because she brought the glass carafe over along with his omelet. The egg dish before him was stuffed with sausage, cheese, ham and bacon. The omelet sat atop a pile of cheesy, chunky home fries. Not a vegetable or piece of fruit to be found anywhere.

Beth grinned. "Now you can see why they call it the triple bypass."

Viv laughed. "It's hearty, that's for sure. Enjoy. Oh, and I was talking to Della Barlow about you.

Told her to stop by your table and introduce herself. That Stone Gap Inn really is a masterpiece. They have a fabulous menu and a great rolling lawn for events. It's a nice setting for a wedding. Just sayin'." She gave him a wink, then walked away.

"I'm surprised she didn't bring a preacher over to the table, get the whole thing done while we have a built-in audience," Grady said.

Beth laughed again. "I'm so sorry. I never intended this to become such a thing. I really only meant to invite you for a simple dinner."

Had it ever been simple? Kissing her and pretending to be her boyfriend—*fiancé*—had added a level of complication Grady usually avoided. How was it that he had multiplied the number of things in his life, and instead of activating the panic that had been his constant companion for months, he instead felt weirdly peaceful sitting here, at the center of a town-wide rumor mill?

"So tell me more about your dad, your childhood, things like that," Grady said. "You know, so it looks like we've been dating if someone asks me a question." Not because he was curious about her. He took a bite of the omelet and had to admit it was even better than he'd expected.

"I don't know much more than anyone could learn from the media," she said. "He was never home when I was young. It wasn't until he had the heart attack and needed someone to care for him that I truly got to know him."

"It must be hard on him, not being able to do the things he used to do. From what I remember, he was a hell of a fighter."

"He was." She smiled. "He is. Our relationship is just…complicated."

"Aren't all parent-child relationships like that?" He took a sip of coffee, then debated his next bite—cheesy egg or grilled sausage or both? There was such an overload of food on his plate, much too much for him to eat alone. "Why don't you have some?" Grady nudged the plate across the table. "I'll never finish this myself."

"Wimp." She winked. "I finish it every time. But then I don't eat for a week afterward."

He chuckled. "Well, if you're ordering these regularly, it doesn't show. You look amazing and beautiful, Beth."

She dipped her head and concentrated on spearing a piece of potato. "Thank you."

Clearly, Beth Cooper wasn't used to compliments. Why not? She was a stunning woman, and any man worth his salt would see that, and hold on to it. What did it say about Grady that he was already planning to let her go?

"So what about your family?" Beth took a bite and swallowed. "I know your grandmother was awesome. I read in the *Stone Gap Gazette* that the town council is talking about building a gazebo in the park and naming it after her. She always did so much for the people here."

That was his grandmother. A giver to a fault. It didn't surprise him that people would erect a monument to her. Once again, a flicker of something like jealousy ran through him. What would it be like to live in a place where neighbors treated each other like family? The house where he and his brothers grew up had been far from busy Raleigh, up on a hill, as remote as their parents. His apartment in a high-rise in New York was thirty stories from the hustle and bustle of Manhattan. Ida Mae's house and the dozens of others that ringed Stone Gap Lake had been the closest thing to a neighborhood he'd ever known.

"She was the kind of grandmother everyone wished they could have. I'm glad you knew her."

That shared connection linked him to Beth in a different way than the puppy training or the feigned engagement. She'd known the person he loved most in the world, and admired her just as much. Maybe that was part of why being around Beth eased every tense muscle in him.

"I am, too. She was an incredible person." Beth negotiated through the eggs for a bite of cheesy home fries. The two of them exchanged small talk for a while about favorite teachers and classes, and how awful outdoor gym was in North Carolina in the sun.

"Did your parents live nearby then?" she asked. "I don't think I ever met them if they did, and Ida Mae was always kind of vague about them."

"My parents live in a big house and spend their days recounting all the ways their sons are disappointments to them." He opted for a bite of toast this time, but the bite just sat in his stomach. It was no wonder his grandmother rarely mentioned them. As soon as his father had his driver's license, he'd left Stone Gap in his dust. Even when he came back for the annual visit, he'd stayed in town only long enough to drop off the boys. Every time Ida Mae's son drove away, Grady had seen her heart break a little more. Maybe that was why she'd poured all her love into her grandsons. "I don't really talk to either of them. Nick, my youngest brother, who lives here now, does. I think he's the optimist in the family."

"You have a brother here? We should invite him to the wedding that isn't going to happen." Beth grinned and popped another bite into her mouth.

"That would be appropriate for my family. We never really celebrated holidays or graduations. My grandmother did all that. Life with my parents was all very…staid. Buttoned up."

"Boring."

He laughed. "Exactly. Maybe that's why I was the kid leaping off the diving platform or zip lining. I wanted to escape that stifling house. Wanted to pack all the excitement and fun I could into short intervals, because I never knew when I'd get another chance."

"And so you did. Going into business for yourself is a risky proposition."

He didn't mention where his risks had gotten him thus far. "Which you have done, too."

"I just groom and train dogs. I'm not dealing with millions here. It's a small business in a small town, which suits me fine."

"Don't downplay it, Beth. Your worries about your business are the same as mine. Just because there are less zeroes attached doesn't mean they're different. You've taken as much of a risk as I have."

Except he'd gotten too cocky when his risks had always panned out. And the latest one…

Why hadn't he waited to start construction until he had the contract in hand? Sure, there were plenty of projects he'd done without a specific buyer in mind, just predicting what the market might need next, but those were smaller builds, generic facilities that could work for any number of companies. For something that big, that specific... why had he thought he could understand and predict the movements of a mercurial government?

"I guess I never saw it that way," Beth said. "You're right, though. When I lose a couple of regular clients, it impacts my bottom line a lot. Some of my business is seasonal, with the snowbirds who stay in town to avoid the winters up north. I have to make sure to plan ahead for the other months."

"Smart and amazing. You are quite the combination, Beth Cooper."

She dipped her head again, picking at the last few bites of egg. "We demolished that breakfast."

"Hey." He waited until she looked up at him. "You keep changing the subject when I compliment you."

"I'm just...not used to that." She shrugged.

"As in not used to men finding you beautiful? Because you must be dating only blind guys, if that's the case."

That made a smile flicker across her face. "I never dated much. I never had the time. There was always someone to take care of. Someone to worry about."

"Is that why you didn't go to prom?"

She sighed. "Can we not talk about this? I don't need a running reminder that Beth Cooper's life sucked. It is what it is, and right now, Grady, I'm just trying to get through it without falling apart."

He could certainly relate to that. Half the time he felt like Humpty Dumpty, about to topple and shatter at any moment. He pushed the plate aside and reached for her hand. "You don't have to go through all that alone, you know."

"What, are you going to be there? Sit beside me while I watch my father die?" She yanked her hand out of his. "Thanks for breakfast. I have to go."

"Beth—" But she was already up and out of the diner before he could throw a twenty on the table. She darted out into the rain, and was gone in a blink.

Beth glanced out into the front of her shop ten thousand times on Monday morning. All day Tuesday. Every time she heard the door, or even noticed the shape of someone walking toward her building, she paused. Waited. Hoped. When she came into work on Wednesday, she told herself she didn't care if Grady showed up or called her or had any contact with her. There'd been a few texts back and forth, but she'd kept everything focused on the dog, not on whatever this thing was between them. He was just her pretend boyfriend—fiancé—and she didn't need to spend any time with him.

Although that kiss in the kitchen a few days ago had left her wondering. Well, not just wondering. Tossing and turning and reliving.

Maybe it was just that it had literally been forever since she'd been on a date. And that her last one had been with a balding lawyer she'd met on a dating site, who had not matched his profile in height, weight or hair volume. She could have overlooked all that, but he'd also had this nasally laugh that drove her insane. At the end of the night, when he'd gone to kiss her, she'd feigned a sneeze and ducked into her house. Her fiancé had been a nice guy, but rather dull, and self-centered in the end. Maybe she should have seen that coming when he got aggravated at the time she spent working or caring for her dad. When he'd kissed her, she'd always felt like he was holding back or thinking about something else.

Yeah, so her comparison pool for kissing was pretty shallow. That was all. Added to that, Grady was one hell of a good kisser. Who took his time, made her feel treasured—

The golden retriever she was brushing let out a yelp. "Oh, I'm so sorry!" Beth soothed the dog and went back to grooming, determined to pay more attention to the fur than to the man who wasn't even here.

Still, she wondered why Grady had asked about her family and her past. Why he kept telling her she was pretty. This was all supposed to be quid pro quo—he got the Realtor he needed, and some dog training, and she got a way to cheer up her dad. Why would Grady do so much more than she had asked, for the sake of a temporary and pretend relationship?

Once she was done, she put two pink bows in Daisy's hair, then helped the dog down to the floor. The golden trotted over to the corner and lay down to take a nap, not at all interested in showing off her newly groomed look to the world.

The door to the grooming salon tinkled. Could it be Grady? Or her ten thirty, arriving early? Beth smoothed a hand over her hair, checked her reflection in the mirror—damn that man, she'd started wearing makeup to work just in case—then headed out front.

And there he was, wearing black pinstriped dress pants and a white shirt with two undone buttons that damned near made her faint. He looked so good, like a man walking into his home at the end of the day, that it made her want to curve into him and say something crazy like *how was your day, dear?*

She played it cool and casual, as if he was the mailman or a neighbor she hadn't seen in a while. Not the man she had kissed and was now "engaged" to.

"Grady. What brings you by?" No dog by his feet, so it couldn't be about Monster.

"I wanted to see you."

It was the second time he'd sought her out for something other than the dog. Her traitorous heart skipped a beat. Her much-more-practical mind whispered that this wasn't a real relationship. It was a business arrangement. But that didn't mean her body got the message, because when Grady took a few steps closer, her pulse raced and her lips tingled with their need to be kissed again. By him. For practice, yeah, practice. Just in case her dad questioned the validity of their engagement or something.

"Did you have an issue with the dog or…?" She left the question open-ended. Because she didn't want to assume he was here to see her for a romantic reason, especially after she'd bailed from the café the other day. And she wasn't interested in that, anyway. Right?

"Nothing with Monster. Although we're still on for a training session tomorrow, right?"

She had to stop staring at the inch of his chest she could see past the parted panels of his shirt. Her fingers itched to undo the rest of the buttons, to learn if he looked as good out of his clothes as he did in them.

"Tomorrow?" Grady prompted, when she didn't reply. "Did I get the day wrong?"

She jerked her brain back to the present. "Yes, tomorrow. But…" She bit her lip. "My dad is bugging me about when you're coming over again. He wants to get to know you more. So I was thinking maybe we could do the training session at his house? Just for a half hour and then—"

"Of course. That's not a problem."

Until her shoulders relaxed, she hadn't realized she'd been bracing for pushback. Was it because she was more used to disappointment than agreement with any of her wishes and plans?

But Grady agreed as easily as saying yes to chocolate sauce on his ice cream. He really was making this whole crazy thing simple for her. He hadn't just made a promise and then broken it, which was, to be honest, what she'd come to expect from most people in her life. "Oh, good. Uh, thanks. So…what did you need to see me about?"

"You ran out of the restaurant the other day, and you haven't replied when I asked you about it on

the phone or in texts, so now I'm here in person."
He took a step closer. "Why?"

"I had appointments to get to." It was a lie and
they both knew it.

"And you've avoided seeing me." He took another step. "One would almost think we weren't
engaged."

"We're not."

"As far as this town is concerned, we are. But to
make it visibly official…" He fished in his pocket,
pulled out a velvet box and turned it to face her as
he opened the lid. A round-cut engagement ring
in a platinum setting stared back at her. Not too
big or flashy, but elegant in design, with a halo of
smaller diamonds encircling the main stone.

"Oh, God, Grady, it's—"

"Cubic zirconium. Because, well, I didn't want
you to feel pressured and this isn't…" His voice
trailed off.

*Isn't real. Isn't meant to be a proposal. Is sup-
posed to be a business deal.* Nothing more. Then
why did she feel so disappointed? Did she really expect him to get down on one knee and pop the question with a giant diamond?

"Yeah, that makes sense."

He stood there for a second, shifting his weight,
then thrust the box at her. "Uh, here."

"Thanks." The whole thing was surreal and sad, as if she'd been dropped into a Dali painting. Beth took the ring out of the box and slid it onto her left ring finger. The ring nestled into the space as if it had been meant to be on her finger all along.

"I had to guess on the size. I should have asked."

"It's perfect, Grady. And beautiful." And fake. That shouldn't bother her—but it did. Not the cost or size of the stone, because Beth had never been one of those girls who cared about Coach purses or Manolo shoes. But she realized she'd imagined the moment of getting engaged very, very differently in her head.

"Are you sure you're not disappointed? I mean, I know it's not supposed to be a big deal, because this is all temporary. Still, I wanted something that your dad would believe. Not too big or small. I wasn't sure of your taste, but I thought simple might be best. Easiest. I mean, prettiest, you know, for you. Not that I'm saying you're simple…oh, hell. Sorry. I'm screwing this up."

"You're not, Grady. I get it, I do." He was babbling on and on. Could he be as unnerved by this moment as she was? She splayed her fingers, glanced at the ring, then back up at him. "It's not exactly the moment little girls dream of when they're playing with Barbies," she said. "Not that

I thought we would do anything real. I mean, we hardly know each other and—"

He kissed her. Took her in his arms and kissed her, just as she had imagined him doing, just as she remembered. Soft and sweet, then harder and deeper. Desire ignited inside her and Beth's arms went around his back, pulling him closer. His lips skated across hers, tasting, nipping, teasing, and made her imagine what it would be like to have his mouth on her body, between her legs.

She could feel his erection between them, and that only fanned the fire inside her. She wished they were in her bedroom, wished they were naked, wished this was real. Their kiss deepened, and Beth arched into him as his hand came down to press against her backside. Her nipples hardened, and she both cursed and thanked the thin bra and T-shirt that told Grady exactly what he was doing to her.

His other hand snaked under her shirt, cupping her breast in one broad palm. His touch made her ache inside, and when his thumb brushed against the nub, she nearly cried with need. Then a dog barked and Beth jerked herself back to reality.

What was she doing? This wasn't real. This wasn't anything other than…confusion.

She stepped back, and her body screamed defiance. "We shouldn't do that. We're not... This isn't..."

"What if it could be? Just while I'm in town?"

"You're leaving?" Of course he was. It was a silly thing to say. The house he'd inherited was on the market—he'd come to town for the sole purpose of selling it. His business—his whole world—was more than five hundred miles away.

He nodded. "In a couple days. I should have been gone already, but I..." He brushed a tendril of hair off her face, and damn it all, she leaned into his palm. "I can't seem to leave."

"I'm glad." Then she caught herself, and drew back the emotion that had escaped. She hated showing weakness, especially to someone she barely knew. Except a part of her felt like she knew Grady already. When he'd sat across from her at the dining room table, his eyes had been filled with...

Longing. As if he'd never had something as simple as a family dinner. She'd wanted to explain that her life hadn't had much of that, either. Instead, she'd had a mother who was checked out, a dad who was gone almost all the time. Beth had been on her own. Her mother had vetoed pets, although Beth did dog walking and pet sitting for extra money and to get that pet fix she couldn't get at home. Was it any surprise she'd ended up working with dogs?

Animals didn't let her down or leave her alone when she'd been struggling through her teen years or trying to navigate life after her mother died.

"I'm happy for my dad, I mean," she finished, babbling on like an overflowing brook. "He's like a different person now. For weeks, whenever I'd go over after work, he'd be sitting in the same place with the remote in his hand, watching game show number 783 for the day. But this week, every time I went over there, he's been up and about. Organizing things, dusting. Saying he wanted to get the house ready for guests. You know, for when we..."

The wedding was never going to happen, but she'd deal with telling her father that later. Maybe once her bond with him was stronger, and they'd laid a deeper foundation for the relationship they'd never had. For now, the lightness in his face and the pep in his movements had brought sunshine back into a very gloomy situation.

"You..." Grady shook his head. "You are something I never counted on. I'm a leap-before-I-look kind of guy. Too much so, sometimes." His face clouded, then he shook off the shadow. "But this, well, this thing with us is a little out of my wheelhouse."

"Mine, too." Beth glanced at the diamond, so gorgeous it easily passed for real. "I'll wear the ring for a while, then quietly tell everyone the distance between us was too hard to overcome and… with time, we'll all forget about this."

That was what she wanted. No entanglements, nothing beyond this short-lived charade. There wouldn't be any date nights and kisses under the stars—

What was wrong with her? Since when did she want that kind of thing? She was practical, level-headed. Not some silly romantic who dreamed of a knight on a white horse. She had a business to run, a fake fiancé to pass off and a father who was gravely ill. Foolish romantic clichés didn't fit on that list.

Like Grady, she hadn't thought of all the contingencies, such as the way he kissed her and made her melt. The touch of his hand against her face, almost heartbreakingly tender. How much she missed him when he wasn't here.

"Before that happens, I think we should go out again," Grady said.

For a second, she dared to hope he'd had the same thoughts and regrets. Just as quickly she chased that thought away with a hard dose of reality. His interest was as fake as the diamond on her finger. "We are. Sort of. You're coming to my dad's house for the dog training tomorrow night."

"I meant a real date, Beth," he said. "Like where I pick you up and take you somewhere and everything."

"That's not necessary, Grady. We've already convinced my father—"

"After that kiss, do you find it so hard to believe that I might want to date you for real? That just maybe there's something between us that neither of us should be ignoring?"

"I…" She tried to form a sentence. Couldn't. "I don't really have time for that." Because she couldn't say the truth. *I don't want to believe that and have you break my heart down the road.*

"As you've said, repeatedly. Is it time…or fear?"

She raised her chin. "Fear? What could I possibly be afraid of?"

"That you might actually like me, too. Not a little, but a lot." He grinned. "I was there for that kiss, too, you know."

Daisy got up from her nap and padded over to nose Grady's leg. He leaned down and rubbed the dog's ears, not at all bothered at getting dog hair on his pants.

Beth had to admit that gave him serious brownie points. Any man who loved dogs—even when he said he didn't—got an automatic boost on her list. Which meant, yeah, she did actually like him. A lot. But that wasn't the issue. Nor was that kiss, which had been, by all rights, holy-hell-amazing. She straightened her spine and focused on reality, not foolish dreams. "You said yourself that you're going back to New York as soon as the house is sold, if not sooner. What's the point in going out?"

"To have fun." He took her left hand, his thumb skating across the back, dancing close to the ring and then away. "When was the last time someone took care of *you*, Beth Cooper?"

"I don't need…" But then her throat clogged and she couldn't look at him, and damn it, not a single customer came in to save her from a conversation that she didn't want to have. "I can take care of myself."

"I don't doubt that for a second. But why should you have to all the time?" He tipped her chin up until she was looking at him. "Are you busy tonight? How does dinner and dancing sound?"

"Where? There's no place like that in Stone Gap." Why didn't she just say no? Why did she keep letting herself get tangled up with a man who was going to leave? She had had enough disappointment for one life, and here she was, knowingly walking into more.

"Ah, my dear Beth…" His gaze softened, and

his thumb stayed on her hand. "There's an entire world outside of Stone Gap. Let me show it to you."

My dear Beth. She was sure it was only a turn of phrase, but boy, did it sound nice rolling off Grady's tongue. She started to say no, because she had her dad to worry about, but he'd been in such good spirits lately and doing so well that she was sure she could spare an evening to go out with Grady. Especially since her dad would be thrilled to hear about their plans. "Okay. You can bring Monster with you, and he can stay at my house. I have a doggy door and everything, from when I had pets of my own, so he'll be able to go out whenever he needs to and we won't have to rush back or anything." The guy had just asked her out and she was going on and on about dogs?

A soft smile curved across his face. His hand lingered on hers for one more moment, then he placed a tender kiss on her forehead. "I'm going to do my best to make this an unforgettable night. Because I get the feeling no one has ever treated you the way you deserve to be treated, Beth Cooper."

Chapter Six

When Grady bought his first company, he'd done the whole deal on a wing and a prayer. He'd graduated with his MBA two weeks earlier, and had a stack of cash he'd made working at a factory over the summers. He'd spent months sweating his ass off, assembling lighting kits for operating rooms, and thinking there had to be a better way. Then he'd heard about a start-up company using robotics to do the exact job he had, and six weeks later, he'd brokered a deal to buy a vacant lot and later sell it to the start-up.

He'd leaped, working on instinct, and it had

panned out. So had the next deal and the one after that.

When the money started rolling in, he'd thought it would never end. And here he was, ten years later, once again with an empty wallet and a head full of dreams, but this time with the intention of winning over a woman, not a stubborn CEO. If he'd had the deep pockets of a year ago, he would have booked a private jet, whisked Beth off to some faraway locale for a weekend with room service and five-star meals and an on-site spa.

Instead, he showed up with a rental car and a full tank of gas. He'd thought of buying flowers again, but figured Beth was more practical than that. At two minutes to six, he was on her doorstep, ringing the bell. Beside him, Monster started prancing at Grady's feet, as if he was just as anxious to see her.

Beth opened the door and Grady took in a quick, deep breath. The pale yellow sundress he'd seen her in before had been gorgeous, and tonight's just as much so. She'd opted for a navy blue dress that narrowed at the waist and belled over her hips. It had an iridescent trim that reflected in the blue of her eyes, and skinny spaghetti straps, one looser than the other. The single thin strap draping over the edge of her shoulder drew his attention, and made him want to follow the path with his mouth, down, down, down…

"You are stunning."

Her cheeks pinked and she dipped her gaze. "Thank you."

She didn't just clean up good, she became a cover model. He'd known Beth Cooper was beautiful, but this went beyond that. "I feel like I underdressed," he said.

She stepped forward and put a hand on the lapel of his black suit jacket. "I think you look stunning, too, Grady."

He covered her hand with his, and he would have stood there a long time, just drinking her in, if Monster didn't pick that moment to jump up and nearly knock Grady out of the way. "Hey, you, quit that."

"Monster, sit," Beth said. And Monster, of course, sat. She bent down to ruffle the dog's ear. "What's this?"

"A present. Better than flowers, I'm thinking."

She laughed as she untied the bag of dog treats that Grady had hooked on Monster's collar earlier. "And one that will make a whole bunch of puppies happy. Come on in."

He followed her down the hall and into a bright yellow kitchen with white countertops and bright white tile. Beth's cottage was tiny—he could have put the whole house in his old master bedroom closet—but seemed to suit her. It also felt a hundred times more welcoming that his multimillion-dollar apartment ever had.

Once again, that feeling of calm came over him. In the hours between last seeing Beth and arriving at her house, he'd paced the floors so much he was sure he'd worn a groove in the wood. Dan's two days of rest, away from work, had turned into a full week, because his blood pressure refused to come down. The bill collectors had started calling, and Grady paid what he could, but always, his priority was paying Dan.

He'd called Bob, the guy selling the property, and begged him for an extension before he put it on the market. He'd spent most of yesterday on the phone with two of his regular buyers, selling the property as a must buy. *I don't know, Grady,* they'd said. *We heard you went under. Maybe another broker...*

Another broker, like Jim Givens. Grady had hung up the phone and realized his hopes of selling before he bought—saving himself the prospect of floating his own money—were very unlikely. His best shot at proving his worth again was quickly selling Ida Mae's house, using the cash to buy the building and lot in Manhattan, and then reselling it for a tidy profit. All of which would take time that Grady didn't have. So he'd paced and stressed and worried, until the moment he'd stepped into Beth's cozy cottage. Then, almost instantly, the tension evaporated, and for a second, he wanted to sink onto the love seat in the living room and watch the world go by out the front bay window.

"This is a great place," he said.

"Thanks. I like it—but I'm hardly ever here. I'm mostly at work or at my dad's, taking care of him. That's why I don't have any dogs of my own anymore." She bent down and rubbed Monster's head. "But you're a great substitute, Monster, aren't you? Want a treat?" The dog yipped. "Okay, then sit."

He sat.

"High five." She knelt before him, put her hand above his head and gave a little wave. Monster stared at her. She repeated the command and did it again. On the fourth try, Monster got the message and raised his paw, not quite close enough to touch, but close enough to earn lots of praise and two treats.

"You're so patient," Grady said. "I'd have gotten frustrated and given up after the second try."

She glanced up at him. Her skirt spread around her like a dark blue puddle, and she looked so damned sweet, he found his heart melting a little. When had he become such a softy?

"You?" she said. "You're not a quitter. I did a little reading about you last night, and wow, you've pulled off some incredible business deals. Dealt with more money than I'll see in my entire lifetime. I'm impressed."

"I think what you get these dogs to do is ten times more impressive. You even have me wanting to high-five you for a dog treat."

She stood, then smirked at him. "Do you want a liver-flavored cookie?"

"Not particularly. But I would like another kiss." He grinned. "Assuming it's not liver flavored."

She laughed. "Not at all. More like peppermint."

He shifted closer, invading her space, inhaling her perfume, then resting his hands on her waist. His mouth hovered over hers. "Sounds like a perfect treat."

"Perfect for you...or for me?" she whispered, so close that her lips brushed his with each word.

"Both, I hope." Heat climbed in the space between them, sending his pulse running high. His grip on her waist tightened, and for a second, he considered grasping her hand and leading her to her bedroom, to take his time exploring every single peak and valley of her body. Yeah, probably not a good idea for a first date.

So instead, he gave her a soft, quick kiss, then pulled back. "Your chariot awaits, m'lady."

The words broke the tension, which was a good thing, Grady told himself. Beth laughed. "Let me put the doggy gate up for Monster and grab my purse." She spun out of his reach, threw a couple dog toys on the floor, then latched a wooden gate into place, keeping Monster in the kitchen, where the doggy door led to a fenced-in yard. She had set up a crate for him, and the puppy ducked inside and settled down. Beth grabbed a small purse from the table in the hall, then followed Grady down the steps to the car. He opened the door, waited for her to settle in the seat, then leaned in and stole one more quick kiss before going around to his side.

He hesitated before putting the car in gear. "Are you sure that's enough to keep Monster contained? That dog can get in a lot of trouble in not a lot of time."

Beth laughed. "My house is fully doggy-proofed. I watch my friends' dogs from time to time, so I keep the gates and things in place. And I left him some treat puzzles to keep him occupied while we're gone."

"Treat puzzles? Like that King Kong thing you

have me give Monster? That does work wonders—
for, like, an hour."

"Yep, just like that." She settled back against her
seat and crossed her legs, the fabric of her dress
making a soft whooshing sound.

Grady tore his gaze away from her incredible
legs and concentrated on leaving Stone Gap and
getting on the highway. The hour-long drive to
Beaufort passed almost too quickly. Grady had
always used car rides as a mobile office. In the
back of a car service Cadillac, he'd be reviewing
documents, making calls, returning emails. On
the rare occasions where he drove himself, he had
the phone on speaker for negotiations, researching
and following up with the dozens of people who
worked for him. He wasted little time enjoying the
scenery or exchanging small talk.

But riding with Beth was an entirely different experience. For one, there was her perfume, a
light, floral scent that beat the exhaust fumes per-
vading New York City any day. Then there was
the conversation. Beth was smart and funny, easy
to talk to. They joked about Stone Gap, caught up
on the current status of mutual friends from high
school and talked about his dog. The mutt was
growing on Grady, but not as much as Beth was.

"I'd forgotten how beautiful it is here, especially at the end of the day," she said, with a sigh in her voice.

He glanced over at her. Beth's attention was on the rolling blue-green hills passing by in a blur. The same setting sun that left mauve and amber kisses across the tops of the hills danced gold in the strands of Beth's hair.

"Absolutely breathtaking," he said.

"Isn't it? I clearly don't take enough time to appreciate the view."

"Neither have I." If he'd been braver in high school, maybe he would have been looking at Beth, right there at his side, for the past ten years instead of financial statements that made his eyes cross. He loved his job, loved the thrill of the hunt and the capture of another location, another sale, but there was something to be said for quiet moments. Something he hadn't realized he'd been missing until he had one with Beth.

With his last girlfriend, another corporate Realtor, they'd talked about work almost nonstop. They hadn't taken leisurely car rides or done family dinners on Sundays. When they broke up, he'd missed her company for a day or two, but then realized he'd had little in common with Marie outside of work and sex. But with Beth, it was different. They had a lot of common ground, just from growing up in the same area. There was no stress in being with her, no deadline pounding in the back of his head. Just the two of them, and something beautiful in their sights. It was nice. Very nice.

She shifted to look at him. "What's it like? Living in the city, nothing depending on you except maybe a potted plant?"

He chuckled. "Well, I haven't been able to keep a single plant alive, so I would say it's probably a good thing no family members are depending on me." When he'd first moved into his apartment, his decorator had filled the window shelves with plants she said were impossible to kill. Yeah, well, Grady had pulled off the impossible. At the end of the day, the last thing he wanted to do was worry about whether he'd remembered to water the ficus.

"I have no concept of that," Beth said. "I've had someone or something depending on me pretty much all my life." She smoothed her skirt across her lap. "You asked me about my life back in the diner and I ran out instead of talking about it. Avoiding the past means you are doomed to repeat it. I read that somewhere."

Grady would attest to that. He was doing his damnedest to not repeat the mistakes of his past. "I get that. I made a huge mistake last year, and now it has me second-guessing every decision I make."

"A huge mistake? What happened?" She flushed a moment later, seeming to realize that the question might come across as nosy. She waved off the words. "It's okay if you don't want to tell me. I mean, we're sort of in this weird not-relationship."

Did a man share his regrets with a woman he was in a not-relationship with? What would it hurt to tell her? She wasn't going to run to his competitor and spill the gory details. Plus, maybe telling her would take some of the burden off his own shoulders.

"I made a very good living buying properties and matching them with buyers. Sort of a flipping business, only on a corporate level," he said. "Then a senator friend of mine gave me the inside scoop on a new government research facility for the Defense Department. He all but signed the check, saying the deal was mine, if I could provide the building they needed. He had specs and everything."

For the first time since the ship went down, Grady didn't feel the same twisting, panicky feeling in his gut as he talked about what had happened. Maybe it was Beth, sitting beside him, listening without a drop of judgment in her eyes.

"So I rushed into the deal without thinking twice. My COO and CFO both told me not to count on government contracts." Grady could still remember that conversation, Dan's cautions, and his dismissal of the concerns. How would things have been different if he had listened? "I was so cocky, so sure. I went ahead and built the building—a massive thing, constructed on very specific guidelines—before I had a signed deal."

"That must have been a huge risk. What happened?"

"The program got cut from the budget before it ever got off the ground."

Beth gasped. "Wait…they didn't buy your building?"

Grady shook his head. "I was left with a fifteen-million-dollar research facility that had cost me everything I had—and that was so personalized for the Department of Defense that no one else wanted it. I held on to it for months, floating loans and juggling cash, so sure that the contract would come through any day. When it didn't…" He let out a breath. "I lost pretty much everything."

Beth's jaw dropped. "You did? But…but…" She gestured toward the interior of the new model but cheap sedan, the suit he was wearing.

"Rental car. Outdated suit, bought over a year ago. My grandmother's house. I don't own much of anything of value right now, except one very expensive building. I have some money left in the corporate account and a little in my retirement accounts, but I'm not taking any salary. And I won't touch what's there, no matter what happens to me."

"Where's the money going then?"

"To pay salary and insurance for my COO, who had a damned-near-fatal heart attack after this happened." Grady let out a long breath. "So you talk about guilt and regret, Beth? I have a few pages of that myself."

She sat back in her seat. "Wow. I'm so sorry."

He drove for a while, not saying anything. In his mind, he saw Dan in that hospital bed, pale and shaky, the machines keeping up a steady beat like a pounding hammer, driving home the blame. Grady had vowed then and there to fix this all, somehow.

Beth's hand covered his, and something in Grady's tough exterior cracked a little. "Thanks." It was the only word he could manage.

As they turned toward the ocean, a spectacular sunset appeared between the buildings and smattering of trees. Deep orange, mauve and blue painted the sky with an undulating brush. The water glistened with those last rays of sunshine that were disappearing in the west, and the briny scent of the ocean filled the car. "It's gorgeous," Beth said.

Grady glanced over at her. The spectacular masterpiece of sky faded from his attention. "Yes, it is."

She caught him looking at her and smiled. He loved her smile, loved the way it lit up every space she was in, better than any sunset he'd ever seen.

He pulled into the restaurant parking lot, but instead of going in, Grady parked the car and shut it off. He hesitated to remove the key from the ignition. "I had this great romantic night planned. Candlelit dinner on the water, dancing at a club I found online. But right now, all I want to do is keep on talking to you out here, with this gorgeous view."

Her features brightened and another smile curved her lips. "I'd like that, Grady."

"We can always get dinner later, and skip the dancing, if you want. Let's take a walk for now." He pocketed his key, came around the car and opened her door. She had her heels in one hand and put the other into his.

A simple touch. Something other couples did several times a day. Grady loved the softness of her hand, the closeness of her body. So he didn't let go.

The restaurant faced a long boardwalk jutting out into the water, dotted by moored boats. Two smaller piers flanked it, peppered with late-night fishermen and a dinghy here and there. Another wooden walkway curved along the shore, lit with Victorian-style lampposts. Grady and Beth ambled along the deserted path. A jazz band played outside one of the bars, while lights from the shops and restaurants cast a glow on the water.

"What happened senior year?" The question popped out of him, an intrusion, and he almost took it back. But then Beth answered, as if she, too, needed to unburden.

"My mother got sick and died. Even before that—for *years* before that—my life revolved around taking care of her. But that was when it got really bad." Beth scoffed. "I always say she got sick, but the truth is, she drank herself to death. She wasn't always that way, and there are times when my heart aches for how things used to be." They stopped and looked out at the waves softly lapping the shore. "I should have tried harder to get her to stop."

"You can't force someone to listen. I know that too well. I'm sure you did more than most people would, Beth." A car passed on the road behind them, the tires hitting the pavement with a soft pat-pat-pat sound. He listened to it fade into the distance before Beth spoke again.

"Maybe," she said, as she started walking once more, turning to head down one of the piers. She took her phone out of her purse and checked it for the tenth time since they'd left Stone Gap. Even though they were almost an hour away, her thoughts stayed with Reggie. "My father was never home when I was a kid. My mom had a lot of trouble with that. I think she just hated to be alone and got easily overwhelmed, especially with being a single mother. She struggled without my dad there, and started drinking at night. To sleep, she said. One drink led to two, led to three, led to a lifelong habit she didn't want to break. I think she was actually relieved when her liver began to fail because it was…a way out."

"That's so sad." Grady put his arm around her and drew her to him. His Beth—no, not his, not truly, but his for the night—was a caring, sweet person who had put her life on hold for a mother who hadn't been there for her, and was doing that again for her father, with zero resentment.

"It's life, Grady." She turned to him. "Sometimes it's great, sometimes it's bad. But you keep moving forward and doing the best you can."

Such a simple philosophy, but so hard to put into play. "Why?"

"Because the great parts are worth it." She smiled

again, and he realized that right now, right this second, was one of the great parts. If he could have taken a photo, he would have, but nothing, Grady knew, could completely capture this moment.

"Look, we're so close we can touch the sea." Beth dropped down to the edge of the dock and let her feet dangle in the dark water. "Join me."

"I've got dress shoes on."

She arched a brow. "And they don't come off?"

He laughed. "Okay, you're right." Grady bent down, untied his shoes and took off his socks. He set them to the side, rolled up his pant legs, then slipped into place beside her. The water was cool on his feet. It could have been a summer night at his grandmother's house. "I haven't been in a lake in a decade. My grandmother's place was where I learned to swim, to ride a bike and to really live. My parents' house was so quiet, I could hear the grandfather clock in the foyer ticking at night, even when I was lying in my second-floor bedroom. There were no arguments or deep discussions. Family dinners, when they happened at all, were lessons in etiquette, and our small talk centered around briefs and judicial decisions. The only time I was a kid was at my grandma's house. Me and my brothers…"

Grady shook his head. Even now, more than a

decade since those times at Ida Mae's, when he looked back on the summers, everything seemed infused with this golden glow. Maybe it hadn't been as good as he remembered, but it had always been better than being home. "We had a great time with our grandparents. My grandpa died when I was nine, and then it was just my grandma. My brothers and I spent most of our summers with her, when we weren't in summer school or taking piano lessons or learning French."

"French? Ugh. I hated foreign language in school."

He laughed. "Me, too. I know I should keep up with it—the business world is more and more global every day. But I've never really had a knack for remembering the words or how to conjugate the verbs."

"Good thing I work with dogs." She grinned and paddled her feet, sending up a little splash of cool water. "I haven't gone swimming in a really long time. I sort of missed that entire part of childhood, you know?"

"On the next warm, sunny day, come over to my grandmother's house. It leads down to Stone Gap Lake, and the pier is still there, perfect for jumping off of into the water."

"I'll have to take you up on that someday." Beth

leaned her head on his shoulder. Grady's arm stole around her, and a part of him wanted to hold on to this moment as much as he wanted to hold on to her.

Then her phone rang, and everything changed.

Chapter Seven

"What were you thinking, Dad? You could have killed yourself." Beth stood in the hospital room beside her father, who seemed to grow paler and thinner by the minute. After the doctor called, Grady had broken all speed limits rushing her back to the hospital outside Stone Gap. He'd dropped her off, then gone to park the car while she'd bee-lined for the emergency room and found her fa-ther, who looked far frailer than before. He had a bandage on his left arm from trying to put out the fire he'd accidentally started when he'd knocked a newspaper into the stove, trying to reach one of the upper cabinets for the good wineglasses he'd wanted to clean.

"I was just working on the house a little. Trying to stay useful." The cardiac monitor above his head displayed a steady stream of heartbeats, and a constant check of oxygen levels, blood pressure and resting heart rate. The nurse had just come in to draw more blood and run enzyme tests to see if her father's chest pains had been a heart attack.

Lord, please, no. His heart was already weakened from the first two heart attacks. How much could one man take? She dropped onto his bed and took one of his hands in hers, then leaned over and pressed a kiss to his temple. "You need to take it easy."

"I'm tired of taking it easy," Reggie said. "We have a big event coming up, and I want to be ready."

"Dad, it doesn't have to be a big event. Grady and I haven't even set a date yet—and neither of us want anything splashy." The lies slid off her tongue far too easily, leaving a trail of guilt running into her gut, piling onto the regret she felt about leaving him home alone tonight. She never should have agreed to the date. This was why she had no time for a relationship.

Her father leaned back and held her hand up.

"That's one hell of a beautiful ring," he said. "Grady did good."

Beth had forgotten about the fake engagement ring. The moment when he'd given it to her seemed ten years in the past, not a few hours. This charade was spiraling out of her control. Somehow, she had to end this entire thing. But...

Telling the truth was out as an option. The last thing Dad needed right now was another shock.

Her father's cardiologist came into the room, a young man with dark hair and dark glasses, and a serious expression that sent icy dread through Beth's veins. "You gave us quite a scare there, Mr. Cooper," Dr. McCall said.

Reggie waved that off. "Just doing some housework. I'm sure it was nothing."

"That's not what the EKG is saying." The doctor sighed. "We're running blood tests to be doubly sure, but you almost caused yourself another heart attack. When I say take it easy, I don't mean move a recliner or redecorate the kitchen."

"You tried to move your chair, too?" Beth let out a gusty sigh. "Dad! Why didn't you wait for me to get home?"

"Because I have put too much on your shoulders for way too long, Bethie. I was just trying to clean up the house, get things ready. So I can give my little girl the wedding she deserves."

Before it's too late. The words he didn't say, the words that everyone in the room was thinking. Her father was dying, and there was nothing she could do about it, no way to reverse the inevitable.

The doctor touched her shoulder. "Can we talk out in the hall?"

"Of course." She gave her father's hand a squeeze and put a hopeful smile on her face that belied the worry churning inside her. "Promise me you'll lie here and rest?"

"Do I have a choice?" Her father returned a weak smile. "I promise. Stop worrying."

Beth headed out of the room with the doctor, and shut the heavy door behind her. Grady came down the hall just then and stopped beside her. A little ripple of relief filled her, simply from his presence.

"Everything okay?" he asked.

"Not really." She quickly explained what had happened, introduced Grady to the doctor and then braced herself for what was coming next. She'd had enough conversations with the cardiologist to know by the look on his face that he was about to deliver news she didn't want to hear.

"Miss Cooper, you know your father is living

on borrowed time. His heart was already getting weaker by the day, and this incident didn't make things any better. He truly needs to rest, and build his strength up gradually. I'm going to start the physical therapy again, but it would be nice if he got some walks in around the neighborhood. Get him outside, let him enjoy some fresh air."

The words were ones she'd heard before, but this time the inflection in the doctor's voice had shifted. There was an urgency to his advice, and a hesitation in his sentences. "What aren't you saying, Dr. McCall?"

The man took a moment before he spoke. Beth reached over and slipped her hand into Grady's, needing someone there, someone to lean on, for just a moment. His larger fingers closed over hers, strong, sure, secure.

"Your father doesn't have a lot of time," the doctor said. "His heart is operating at about a tenth of normal strength. So get outside. Make some memories. Enjoy the days. And pay someone to move the furniture." His brown eyes softened. "I'm so sorry, Miss Cooper. I wish I had a different prognosis. I've always admired your father. Used to watch his fights with my dad on Friday nights."

"Isn't there anything else we can do?"

The doctor shoved his hands into his pockets

and rocked back on his heels. "One thing your dad has going for him is that he is a fighter. I've never known someone as stubborn as he is. There are times when that's hurt him—"

"Because he doesn't listen and tries to move a recliner." She still couldn't believe her father had done that. He knew better.

"Yes…but there are also times when that can be a good thing. If I was a betting man, I'd say you have a few weeks, maybe a month." He paused and Beth choked back a sob. "*But*…the reason I'm not a betting man is because I have seen the human spirit give some people months, sometimes years, more than anyone with a medical degree predicted they would have. Your dad has a strong spirit, and from what he told me, something big to look forward to with you getting married. Sometimes that hope and anticipation can do more than all the treatments in the world."

Beth thanked the doctor, and he headed down the hall to his next patient, promising to come back and check on her father again later. The hospital went on about its controlled chaos, nurses rushing from place to place, machines beeping, orderlies hurrying to deliver equipment and meds.

Beth leaned against the pale green concrete wall

and sighed. "I knew this was coming, but hearing the doctor say it…"

"He didn't say your dad is going to die tomorrow, Beth. You still have time," Grady said.

"Yeah, but how much?" Her eyes filled and her heart squeezed. For months, she'd been avoiding the full extent of the truth, trying her best to pretend it didn't exist. "I don't know what to do."

Grady glanced down the hall at the retreating figure of the doctor, then back at her father's name scrawled on the paper plaque outside his room. "Marry me, Beth."

It took her a second to process the words in her head. "Grady, you don't have to pretend," she said. "My dad's inside and probably asleep. He can't hear you."

"I mean it. Marry me, this coming weekend." Grady's brown eyes met hers. "We'll do it up right and let your father see that you're happy and taken care of. And maybe, like the doctor said, that will give him something wonderful to focus on, and that will change the tide."

Marry Grady? Now? That was the most insane idea she'd ever heard. The haste made it sound like a shotgun wedding, but this wasn't the Wild West, and she wasn't some teenage girl with a baby in her belly. "Why are you doing this? It's above and beyond what we agreed to."

"Because I wish like hell I had a father who loved me half as much as your father loves you." His voice was thick, but he cleared his throat and went on. "I like your dad. I like you. And it's a small thing I can do before I leave town, and not feel like a jerk for not having some medical miracle to give you."

She smiled, but couldn't work up a laugh at his joke. The offer was huge—too huge—and she couldn't possibly say yes, even to make her father happy. "Marriage means living together, Grady. We can't do that. And then you're going to leave and—"

"And I'll take a business trip. We'll tell everyone we had a fight and are separating for a bit, but let your father think we're still trying to work it out. As for living together, we don't have to do that. Your dad could stay at his house, you stay at yours and I stay at Ida Mae's. When I sell the house, we'll have that fight." He grinned. "In the meantime, your dad will think we're working on some grandkids. Long-term anticipation."

She shook her head. "We can't do that. Quite honestly, I don't know where my dad and I are going to stay. My dad set off a small fire accidentally. Now the stove is useless, plus there's smoke damage on one wall of the kitchen. He can't stay in his house, and my cottage is only a one bedroom."

"Then come to my grandmother's house and stay until it sells. There's plenty of room." Grady took her hand. "And a lake you can swim in."

The reference to their date made her warm inside. For a moment, she imagined swimming in that lake with Grady. Splashing him, dunking him, kissing him… Damn. Still, the crazy spiral she was trying to contain was expanding and moving faster by the second. Get married, now? "Grady—"

"We'll have a small wedding. Nothing formal or…"

"Binding," she supplied. Because this wasn't anything other than a way to give her dying father some peace, and maybe a reason to hang on.

He nodded. "That way we have nothing to undo legally later."

That was practical. Clinical. Not at all emotional or romantic. Which was exactly what Beth wanted. "So we just keep on lying," she said. "To my father. My friends. The preacher. The whole damned town."

"Or we don't lie. We get a real preacher, and have a real wedding. And get a real annulment later. People do it all the time, for much weaker reasons than ours."

Her heart had skipped a beat when he said *real preacher* and *real wedding*. For a second, she'd thought Grady was genuinely proposing to her. Then he'd added *get a real annulment*, and that little lilt had disappeared. But this was what she wanted, wasn't it? If that was so, then why did she feel like she was losing more than she was gaining?

Grady's brother stood on the doorstep of Ida Mae's house and glared at him. "What the hell are you doing?" Nick said.

He had the same dark hair and eyes as Grady, another inch of height, and the kind of smile that women fell all over themselves to see. Right now, there wasn't a hint of that smile on his face. Grady hadn't seen his brother in several months, and maybe it was a trick of the light, but he looked younger and brighter. Or maybe it was due to the wedding ring on his finger and the woman he had married.

"I'm doing what's smart for me," Grady said. "You got your inheritance and invested it in… something." Grady realized he had no idea what Nick had been doing for the last few months.

"You don't have a clue about my life, do you?" He shook his head. "You couldn't even be bothered to show up for my wedding."

"I was in China. It's not like it's a quick flight from Asia to here. And I sent a gift."

Nick rolled his eyes. "Yeah, the gravy boat was just as good as you being here."

Dealing with his brother was about the last thing Grady needed right now. His mind kept replaying his impromptu promise from the night before, to marry Beth in a week. All Grady kept hearing when the doctor was talking was "borrowed time." He had seen the way Reggie looked at him, felt it in his handshake when Grady had left after dinner the other night, and heard it in the older man's voice when he said, "Thank you for being in my daughter's life. That means everything."

The words had stuck with Grady, and when he'd been standing in the hospital hallway with Reggie hooked up to a bunch of machines a few feet away, he'd thought maybe it wasn't the craziest idea in the world to just marry Beth anyway. Maybe it was actually in his power to make this family happy.

He sure as hell wasn't having any luck with his own family. Exhibit A: his brother showing up, pissed as hell to find the for-sale sign on Ida Mae's front lawn.

Monster nosed past Grady's leg to greet Nick. The brother who was so angry a second earlier melted at the sight of the dog. He bent down and rubbed Monster's ears. "What's a nice dog like you doing with a guy like that, huh? You know he's going to leave you homeless on the streets, don't you? Did you see the sign?"

"I am not." Grady sighed and opened his front door the rest of the way. Might as well invite Nick in before the whole neighborhood heard their conversation. He'd missed his brother more than he realized. "Want some coffee?"

"I thought you'd never ask." Nick straightened, then marched into the house, with Monster on his heels. The dog clearly had no taste in humans, if he was siding with Nick over Grady. "By the way, I *don't* like what you've done with the place. Especially that sign on the lawn. Looks like crap."

Grady shook his head. "That sign is there because the house is up for sale. It's mine and I'm going to do what I want with it."

"You know you sound like a four-year-old, right?"

Grady scowled. "Since when do you care what I'm doing or not doing?"

"Since you put Grandma's house up for sale and didn't tell anyone. She didn't give it to you just so you could flip it, like you do everything else in the world."

Grady let out a gusty breath. His brother had no idea what was going on in his business. Nick had once worked for the company that took care of Jackson Properties' IT needs, but as an outside contractor, his brother didn't have the inside scoop on what the last failure had cost Grady in terms of his confidence and mental health. And he wasn't about to make that public knowledge.

It was bad enough one of his competitors was trying to buy him out. He'd looked over Jim's offer, and it was a reasonable one that another business owner might have considered. But to Grady, accepting the offer was tantamount to admitting he'd failed.

"I'm not having this argument."

"Good. Then we can take that sign to the curb and shove it in your trash can." Nick leaned against the counter and crossed his arms over his chest. Monster plopped down beside him, two against one. "Because I'm not letting you do this."

"You don't get a say." Grady sent the traitorous dog a glare. "Ida Mae left you and Ryder a bunch of money, and she left me the house. I'm not telling you how to spend your money. Don't tell me what to do with this place."

"That's because, even though you have thought your younger brother is less responsible, *I'm*—" Nick put a hand on his chest "—not doing something stupid like investing in a Beanie Baby collection or buying a worm farm. In another month, my restaurant should be open, and I'll have not just a place, but a new career. See? Smart."

"That's wonderful. I'm sure you'll do well. You're a great chef, Nick." He was opening a restaurant? Grady had known his brother loved to cook, but it was a pretty big jump into a chef career. "I'd appreciate if you understood my choices, too. Selling the house is smart for me. I can't live in Stone Gap. My business is up in New York and it needs my attention." Which wasn't entirely the truth, since the company was on shaky legs, but close enough.

"So? Move it here. You can work from anywhere. There's this awesome thing called the internet that lets you work from anywhere in the world."

"Are you part of the welcoming committee for Stone Gap or something?" Grady scowled.

Nick grinned. "Nah. But this place has grown on me. It might have something to do with a certain woman and the fact that I'm finally working a job I love, but…" He shrugged, and the smile only widened. "I'm pretty happy."

Envy curled in Grady's gut. What would it be like to feel that way, every day of his life? To have someone to come home to who brightened his world, made the stress melt away? Technically, he had that, but for only a whisper of time, and not for real, like Nick's marriage. "I'm glad for you, Nick. I really am."

"You should consider it, you know. Marriage, I mean. It's a pretty sweet thing if you find a woman you love." Nick nodded toward the percolator. "Wasn't there an offer of coffee?"

"Oh, yeah. Sorry." Grady put a filter in the basket, scooped in some grounds and turned on the pot.

"You know, I'm not surprised you want to sell— even if I'm hoping I can talk you out of it," Nick said, as the coffeepot dripped rich brew into the carafe. "You blew out of town as fast as you could, and never looked back. It's as if you left us in your rearview mirror."

"I call. I email. I text."

"How often? Because last I checked…" Nick pulled his phone out of his pocket. "…I heard from you three months ago."

Had it really been that long? Grady started to argue, then realized yes, three months had passed since he'd talked to Ryder and Nick, and it had

been over a year since the three of them had had
any kind of meaningful conversation. Even at Ida
Mae's funeral, Grady had been working from his
phone, trying to turn things around at the company. He'd run out of town as soon as the services
were over.

The coffee machine beeped, which gave Grady
a welcome excuse to abandon the conversation and
pour two cups. Just as he handed one to his brother,
the doorbell rang. Monster skidded down the hall,
barking his fool head off.

Grady opened the door and felt a smile curve
across his face when he saw Beth on his porch.
She looked a little tired from the afternoon spent
at the hospital, but even with her hair in a ponytail
and her face bare of makeup, she was still one of
the most beautiful women he'd ever seen. "Everything okay?" he asked.

"Yes, yes. I was just bringing your car back and
my dad here." She dropped his keys into his palm.
"Thanks for letting me borrow it this afternoon to
pick him up, because mine isn't the most dependable vehicle in the world. My dad is all excited.
He started talking to me about our wedding—"

"Whoa. You're getting *married*? Why am I the
last to know everything about my big brother?"
Nick poked his head around Grady and thrust out

his hand. "I'm Nick, Grady's younger brother. And you are…?"

"Beth Cooper." She gave Nick a smile and shook his hand. "Nice to meet you."

"Oh yeah, I remember you. You were a year or so ahead of me in school. You said you're Grady's fiancée?" Nick held up her left hand and let out a low whistle. "That certainly puts a dot on the exclamation point."

"Well…yes, we're engaged." She flushed under Nick's clear surprise and scrutiny. "It's complicated."

Nick arched a brow in Grady's direction. "Complicated? You're dating the right man for that. He didn't even tell his own family about this happy news."

Grady glared at his brother, but Nick just went on grinning. "Beth lives here in Stone Gap," Grady said, to fill the silence. "She's training the dog." Like that explained anything.

"So, you've got a dog, you've got a wife-to-be, and yet you're insisting that you're selling the house and moving back to New York? Sounds like you can't decide between coming and going. As for me, I've got a meeting with the builder, then a date with my own wife." Nick gave the dog a pat and Beth a nod before he strode down the porch steps. On the walkway, he turned back. "When's the wedding, by the way?"

"It's not—" Grady began.

"Sunday," Beth said.

"Sunday?" Nick gave a low whistle. "Well, hell, Grady, I guess you'll be extending your trip to Stone Gap by a few days at least. Let me know when to put on my tux and where you're registered." He shot him a grin, then hopped in his car and left.

Chapter Eight

This was a mistake.

Beth realized that the second she got out of her car in the driveway of Grady's grandmother's house. From the outside, Ida Mae's home looked huge. Two stories, plenty of bedrooms, and an expansive lawn out back. And yet despite all that, moving in with her father and Grady was surely going to feel cramped, if only because Grady seemed to take up all the air in the room, even when he was simply standing still. Anything that put him within a hundred yards of her felt too close, because it made her think about him altogether too much.

Then she'd met his younger brother, and the whole getting-married thing suddenly became real. Too real.

"I'm so sorry about the fire back at my house," her father said. "It was a stupid mistake."

"Dad, you already apologized fifty times. It's fine. The insurance will take care of it, and I'll hire a contractor to repair the damage." She made a mental note to add *look for reputable and inexpensive contractor* to her list of five million things to do.

Her father paused on the walkway and touched her arm. "Why don't you let me do that? I'm sitting around all day anyway, bored out of my noggin. I don't know what to do with myself these days. I'm used to being able to go to the gym, hang out with the guys, get on a plane and head to some other country for a showdown. Making some phone calls would at least help pass the time." He sighed. "In fact, if you'll let me, I'd like to plan the wedding for you two. I know it's normally something the bride wants to do, but you've got so much to do already, with your business and handling everything with my medical care…" His eyes softened. "Let me help you."

Maybe if it was a real wedding, she'd be more interested in being hands-on with the process.

But it wasn't, and if her father was offering to do something—and most especially, to do something for her—she wasn't going to turn him down. For months, Reggie had barely moved from the chair in front of the television. With the news of the wedding, he seemed more motivated, more positive. It might not be a miracle treatment that would restore him to his youthful strength, but the optimism sure seemed like great heart medicine. As long as they were all tasks he could do while comfortably seated, she didn't see the harm in it. And it meant he would be even more involved with her life, something she couldn't turn down. Beth's heart squeezed.

She covered her father's hand with her own. "That would be wonderful, Dad. Just remember, we don't need anything fancy. Small, private, intimate. Just me and Grady and you."

"And the preacher." Her father grinned. "I was thinking of Pastor Dudley from the Baptist church. Nice fella, and he did your mother's funeral."

"Sure, sounds great." Beth was already distracted. Grady was coming down the walkway to help her with her dad, and all coherent thoughts flitted away.

Yeah, this was a mistake. Because just looking at him, in jeans and a pale gray V-neck T-shirt, she wanted to touch him. Wanted to curve into his chest and kiss him again, like they had the other day. He was going to be in a bedroom just down the hall from her all week, and then they were going to be "married" and presumably sharing a room. With any luck, the repairs would be done at her dad's house by then. He would go back there, and Beth wouldn't have to play the charade of being Grady's wife. Because she wasn't so sure she could share a bed with that man and not want to do a whole lot more than kiss.

"Let me get the bags," Grady said, coming around to the trunk of the rental car. He retrieved the two bags Beth had packed—one for her and one for her father. He hefted them both into one hand, then hurried ahead of Beth to help Reggie up the porch stairs and into the house.

"I like this boy," her father said over his shoulder as he stepped into the house. "Nice and respectful toward his elders. Such a gentleman."

Grady did treat her father well, as he did her. He always opened the door, rose whenever she left the table, walked on the outside of the sidewalk so that she was in the safer, protected position. All the things her dad had told her a gentleman should do. What would it have been like to date him in high school? To be treated like this for the last ten years? To have someone there who understood her complicated commitment to her father, and supported her?

She'd dated, but most men didn't want the added responsibility that came with seeing a woman who was caring for a parent. They didn't understand when she canceled a date because her father was having a tough day, or when she was late because his physical therapy ran over. They wanted a woman who was at their beck and call, or ready to take care of them, and didn't like that she had responsibilities and a life that didn't revolve around them.

Whereas Grady...

Well, Grady had been different from the minute he walked into her shop with the dog he didn't want. A dog that now trotted alongside him, looking up at his master with adoration every few feet.

Grady helped her father down the hall to a first-floor sitting room that he had converted into a bedroom by moving one of the beds from upstairs into the space. It was a nice space, with a picture window that looked out over the lake and a king-size bed that faced a wall-mounted television. Beside the window, an armchair, a small bookcase and a little table invited a lazy afternoon of reading.

Beth almost cried. Grady had done all this for a

man he barely knew, and a faux fiancée who was going to be out of his life soon. It made her wonder what kind of husband he would make for someone he truly loved, because he was sure doing great in the faking-it department.

On the nightstand, Grady had set a couple water bottles, and a small green plant that was so new it still had the price sticker on the plastic container. A tiny gray box sat beside the television remote. "I put an intercom in here," Grady said. "In case you need anything, Mr. Cooper."

"Thoughtful. Thanks." Reggie sank onto the bed and let out a sigh. "Long day, but I'm glad to be out of that prison they call a hospital."

"Dad, they needed to keep you overnight to be sure you were okay." Her father had bemoaned every second he'd been there. She didn't blame him—simply sitting by his bedside in the sterile, noisy hospital was the opposite of fun—but complaining didn't change anything or make conditions better. And yet, it seemed he couldn't help himself. When her father was younger and healthier, he couldn't sit still. One day at home and he'd be itching to go to the gym, or get back on a plane. He'd keep busy with yard work or projects, but when the sun began to sink behind the horizon, a jittery wanderlust invaded her father's spirit. She remembered being a little girl, sitting at the kitchen table with a science project or an A she'd gotten on a test, wanting only for him to slow down, notice her and talk to her. Instead, Reggie would burst from the seat and head out the door, more and more often to a bar or to the gym as his career began to wane.

That had been one of the best parts, if there was such a thing, about him getting sick. He'd spent days in the hospital, weeks convalescing at home, and had finally had time for all the conversations he'd missed years ago.

Reggie kicked off his shoes, swung his legs up on the bed and leaned against the pillows. "Okay, you two can go be alone. And stop hovering over me."

"You sure?" Beth asked.

Reggie rolled his eyes at her mother-hen question. "I need a nap anyway. And you're interfering with my beauty sleep."

Beth followed Grady out of the room. He shut the door, then led the way down the hall and up the staircase, stopping between two doors. "Your room is the one on the right. I'm...well, across the hall. I thought of putting your dad in that room, but I didn't want him to walk any farther than he had to or climb the stairs. If this doesn't work for you, let me know and I'll see how I can change it up."

"It's fine, Grady, really. Everything you did for my dad was so thoughtful and sweet. I appreciate it a lot."

"No problem." They stood in the hall, awkward semistrangers. She glanced down at the ring on her finger, and thought the entire situation was incredibly ironic and weird.

Grady filled the silence first. "I…uh, ordered dinner from the café. I realized I have no idea what you like, except for roast chicken, and I didn't want to buy groceries without knowing." He chuckled. "I'm rambling, aren't I?"

"A little." But the admission warmed her, and erased a little of the uncomfortable air between them. "But I appreciate it. I tend to get quiet when I'm nervous, or out of my comfort zone. And this whole situation is on another planet from my comfort zone."

He leaned against the wall beside his door, his hands in his pockets, looking so casual and comfortable that Beth wanted to lean into him and soak up some of that. If this had been a normal relationship, she would have, drawing strength and warmth from her man.

"I've never done anything remotely like this before," Grady said. "I've never lived with a woman, and I've sure as hell never lived with one with her father under the same roof."

"And pretended you were engaged," she added softly.

"That, too." Grady scuffed at the wood floor. "Listen, I know this whole wedding thing and moving in with me was my idea, and you kind of got swept up into it, but you can call a halt to it at any time. I never meant to put you in an awkward position. I just—"

She put a finger over his lips in a quick, impetuous move. She'd meant only to stop his protests, but the movement brought her within inches of him, and as he cut himself off, his mouth moved against her finger. Her pulse accelerated, and it seemed every nerve ending in her body was in that touch against his lips.

"Don't, Grady. Please. This is the happiest I've seen my father in years. I would give up pretty much anything to keep him feeling that way. You've done something so…" she bit her lip "…selfless, and I can't thank you enough."

He cut his gaze away, as if he was embarrassed by the praise or uncomfortable with the emotion in her voice. "No problem. I, uh, have work to do, Beth. I'll see you at dinner."

Then he was gone, and Beth was left alone in the hall. She picked up her suitcase and ducked into her room, telling herself that she was more relieved than disappointed that he'd walked away without welcoming her into his home with a kiss.

As much as Grady had worried about running into Beth and having to pretend like they were madly in love, they were rarely in the same room, and so the need to pretend didn't come up as often as he'd expected. For his part, Grady stayed busy with work. He'd set up an office in the den, and spent most of his day on the computer or on the phone, avoiding another moment like that one in the hall. The house was on the market but there'd been minimal interest thus far, which Savannah said would change soon. Beth busied herself with training Monster, taking care of grooming appointments and arranging her father's doctor's visits and physical therapy. At the end of the day, she was often so exhausted that she went to bed soon after her father did, leaving Grady as the only one awake in a house that felt bigger and emptier in those dim hours. The only time they had to keep up the sham of being a couple was at dinner. Her father insisted on a family sit-down meal every single night, and that was where Grady and Beth flirted and feigned a relationship, while Reggie regaled Grady with stories about his fights.

The more time he spent with her, the more clearly Grady saw the toll everything took on Beth. She was constantly running between places, worrying about her father, trying to keep her clients happy, helping with the housework... It was a lot for one person's shoulders, so Grady opted to take over the meal planning and prep.

He was surprised when he turned out to be a pretty good cook. Maybe it was a trait he shared with Nick—whom he'd begun texting often for advice on recipes. For Grady, cooking proved to be a relaxing, enjoyable activity, and a means of rebuilding his bond with his brother. That was a win right there. Grady reached out to Ryder, too, and after a hiccuped start, the two brothers talked and texted and vowed to get together soon. Grady vowed to never let that much distance get between him and his brothers again.

Over dinner the first night, they'd talked about favorite meals, and Grady had made mental notes. Beth loved pasta, hated mushrooms, was allergic to raw onions, and was a fan of anything with cheese on top, even if Grady nixed the heavy layers of cheese as unhealthy. Her father was on a heart-healthy diet, which meant low in sodium and high in vegetables. Armed with that information, Grady had scoured the internet for recipes and how-to videos. By Wednesday, he was whipping up stuffed peppers with brown rice and a grating of parmesan on top, then a stir-fry for Thursday's dinner. With Beth just a few feet away at night, Grady rose before the sun and spent his time making breakfast, so he wouldn't think about slipping into bed with his wife-to-be.

He looked forward to the evening meal the most. There was something homey about sitting at Ida Mae's mahogany dining table under the soft glow of the chandelier, saying grace and passing the rolls to the woman across from him. It felt like it transported Grady into a whole other world than the one he'd always known. A world that was temporary, he reminded himself, when the dishes were done and the dining room was empty.

Every day, he talked to Dan, who was back at work, but with reduced hours. The deadline to buy the company in Manhattan was Monday, the day after Grady's "wedding." So far, he'd ignored Jim's repeated attempts at contact to talk about the buyout offer. There was no way Grady wanted to concede defeat or give up the company he'd worked hard to build.

A few people had come to look at the house, but

even though Savannah had created an aggressive marketing campaign, no offers had been made. Grady had lowered the price, and talked to the Realtor often, but except for one very lowball offer that was laughable, there was zero activity on the sales front. Grady couldn't understand it—a family home sitting on the water in a small town seemed like the quintessential purchase.

"Not sold yet?" Cutler Shay had asked this morning when Grady was outside, sweeping the driveway.

"Not yet."

Cutler smiled. "Probably Ida Mae's doing. I bet she's up there in heaven, shooing people away. She would want you to stay here, son."

Grady just nodded, instead of debating ghostly interference in real estate deals.

Friday night, two days before the "wedding," Grady couldn't sleep. Hell, he'd barely slept since Beth moved in. When he did, she starred in his dreams, long blond hair spread across his pillow, with her wearing that smile he loved so much… and nothing else. Those were the good dreams. The bad ones were about everything falling apart.

After an hour of fitful sleep, he'd jerked awake, caught in that spiral of panicky thoughts about Dan, the business and the deal. He paced his room, concentrated on his breathing. Read a little, but didn't retain a single word. Checked his email, surfed the web, but his mind kept drifting back to money and choices. Finally, he gave up and went downstairs. The house was silent, the world dark. The grandfather clock in the hallway ticked past two in the morning.

In the kitchen, he put two pieces of bread into the toaster and got the peanut butter out of the cabinet. While he waited, he poured a glass of milk, then set it on the counter and watched the toaster count down to zero. He wasn't even hungry, but figured maybe the carbs and dairy would make him sleepy.

"Can't sleep either?" Beth's soft voice filled the kitchen, and the tightness in Grady's chest immediately began to ease.

He pivoted toward her. "Nope. You, too?"

"I don't sleep, period. I'm either worrying or working." She nodded toward the carton of milk. He handed it to her, then reached past her head to retrieve a glass from the cabinet. When he did, he could smell the warm fragrance of her laundry detergent, and almost feel the softness of her T-shirt. She was wearing a pair of pink plaid pajama pants, slung low over her hips and secured by a drawstring. Her feet were bare, her toes painted

(nails)

a bright coral. There was something so intimate about those bare feet and this moment, so…long-term couple.

"You worrying about your company?" she asked.

"Always. And sleeping even less than normal." He shrugged. "Maybe it's all this fresh air. Or the sound of night birds outside my window instead of traffic." *Or the woman sleeping across the hall from me.*

"I toss and turn, always feeling like there are ten million things I should be doing and not nearly enough time to do them. And I worry that my dad is doing too much. I wish…" She shook her head. "It's not really your worry. Sorry."

He started to say *lean on me, Beth, that's what I'm here for,* when the toast popped and interrupted him. He'd lost the appetite for the snack, but assembled it just to have something to do. If nothing else, it would keep him from making promises he couldn't keep.

He poured some milk into her glass, put the container back in the fridge, then turned to go before he did something stupid like kiss her. Because he sure wanted to. He wanted to do a hell of a lot more, things that all began and ended with Beth in his arms and a smile on her face.

But this wasn't a long-term relationship. Come

next week, if all went well, Grady would be on a plane back to New York and Beth would be back in her little house, playing the part of a new bride with a husband in another state. What was the sense in starting something he couldn't finish? With the kind of woman who deserved more than just a few-nights stands?

"Sleep well, Beth." He started to walk away.

"Grady."

One word, a soft whisper in the dark. He turned back. "What?"

She dropped her gaze to the floor and paused a second before speaking. "I should say something before I lose the nerve. If you want to bow out of this whole thing, I'd understand."

"Bow out of our wedding?"

"You offered me an out, and I should have said the same to you." She nodded, her face serious, unreadable. "Marrying me, even if it's for only a day, is so far above and beyond what anyone would do for me, or my father. I think it's a great thing, I really do, and I'm incredibly grateful, but this isn't necessary. You have a life somewhere else. A life you are missing because of this. Truly, don't worry about me or my dad. We'll be fine regardless."

She was telling him to go. To head back to New York, and leave her and this town in his past. If he did, he'd be free to concentrate on his business again, instead of wondering if he should roast a pork shoulder for dinner or whether he took the trash out before coming to bed. Once the house sold, he'd be on his way back in his world of taxis, household help, and meals that appeared after a single phone call. It would take some time to rebuild, but eventually, he'd even have enough money to go back to his expansive thirtieth-floor apartment with a view of the Hudson. An apartment so empty that it echoed when he walked through it.

An apartment where he wouldn't run into Beth in the middle of the night. A dining room where he would eat his meals alone instead of with her and her father. A bedroom a thousand miles away from her. Yes, he was going back to New York. But he wasn't doing that today or tomorrow, and he didn't want to think about returning to the city until he was boarding a plane. Right now, all he saw was Beth, looking vulnerable and unsure. All he knew was how much he wanted to hold her tight.

"I don't want to bow out." Grady set his plate and glass on the counter, then crossed to Beth. He took her glass out of her hands and placed it on the counter in turn. She stared up at him, her eyes wide, and his heart flipped.

Damn. He was falling for her.

The realization hit him hard and fast. When had that happened? When had this whole thing gone from a business arrangement to something more? And what the hell was he going to do about that?

He took her hands in his and tugged her close. She let out a little squeak of surprise, but fitted into the space between his legs and against his chest like she was the other half of his body. In the weeks since he'd walked into her grooming salon, she'd become the other half of his thoughts, his brain, easing the parts of him that tightened and panicked.

Maybe it was the intimacy of the dark kitchen, or the fact that they were getting married in two days, but the words that his mind had been dancing around all those hours when he couldn't sleep, the words that had just formed in his head a second ago, slipped out. "I'm falling in love with you, Beth."

"You…what?"

Holy hell. Did he just say that out loud? *Way to leap without thinking again.* But this time, it felt different, felt right, to tell her what had been bubbling in his heart for days. He was falling for her, and leaving was going to be oh-so-complicated. Later, Grady decided, he would figure that out. For now, there was Beth.

"We've spent so much time together, and you're even more amazing than you were in high school," he said. "So different from any woman I've ever dated. You're not just smart and funny and beautiful, you're real and grounded. You ground *me*, when I'm ready to jump out of my skin with worry. I didn't even realize I wanted someone like that until I met you."

She backed up until she hit the countertop, her hands in the air and her head shaking from side to side. "Grady, we're not doing this for real. Whatever you're feeling is just an illusion created by all that flirting and close proximity."

"Is that what you think, Beth? Because that's not even remotely close to what I'm feeling right now. Or, I suspect, what you're feeling." He closed the distance between them again, reached up and cupped her jaw, then kissed her, slowly and sweetly. She yielded to him, clutching at his back, deepening the kiss until they were both breathing heavily and he couldn't see straight.

Damn, she was addicting and intoxicating. The desire that had simmered between them from that very first day came to a full boil, and Grady stopped giving a damn about what was real and what wasn't.

He hoisted her onto the counter, slid between

her legs and slipped his hands under the cotton T-shirt. When his palms cupped her breasts, Beth let out a gasp. He was already hard, desire raging in his body like a fire ripping through a dry forest. Every woman he had ever dated paled in comparison to Beth, who was the first woman he'd ever met who made him want—

More. More of her. More of this. More of *everything*.

He lifted the shirt, exposing her bare skin to the air. Her nipples hardened, inviting him to drop his mouth to her breast, tasting, then teasing the hard nub until her legs wrapped around him and her hands tangled in his hair, and all she could say was his name in one long, desperate breath.

He kissed her again, his hands lifting the pale gold tresses from her neck, then letting the silky waves run through his fingers. When that wasn't enough, he thought about taking this further, taking it—

Where? Upstairs? To his bed and a one-night stand? Hadn't he just been thinking that Beth wasn't a love-and-leave kind of girl? And if there was one thing Grady was doing next week, it was leaving. No matter how he felt, no matter what happened Sunday, he had to go back to reality on Monday. And yet, knowing that didn't negate what he could feel growing between them every time they connected. Something that neither of them could keep on denying.

He drew back. Beth's eyes were wide, her cheeks flushed, her breath coming in heavy gasps, and he wanted to kiss her all over again. Instead, he planted his hands on the counter on either side of her. "Was *that* an illusion?"

She shook her head, more in disbelief than in argument. "If it wasn't, then what was it? Because we're getting married Sunday and then you're leaving, last I knew. This isn't love, Grady, it's…something else."

"Come to New York with me," he said. "I sublet my place, but I can end that lease. I have plenty of room in my apartment and we can even keep that silly dog and—"

"My father is here, and I can't leave him when he's so sick and needs me so much. My business is here." She sighed. "And my heart is here, in this town, with my dad."

Which meant her heart wasn't with him. She wasn't falling in love with him, and she wasn't about to. To Beth, this was still a business deal.

He'd let himself get caught up in the moment, which had him acting irrationally. Believing something that wasn't true. Once again, Grady had taken a risk without thinking it through.

And it had backfired. Again.

"You're right." He stepped back, and cool air invaded the space where Beth's warm body had been a second earlier. He grabbed the milk and toast he no longer wanted, then headed up to his room.

Chapter Nine

Beth slipped into the white dress, feeling like a fraud. The reflection she saw in the mirror said *bride*—with her mother's A-line wedding dress accenting her figure—but her mind said *liar*. She could justify the dress and the ceremony all day by saying it was for a good reason, but the fact remained that the entire wedding was a sham.

After that night in the kitchen, when Grady said he was falling in love with her, a part of her had dared to hope the fiction might be turning real. Until he'd asked her to go to New York with him. That was when she'd realized that they were two very different people who wanted two very different lives. Grady wasn't the settle-down-in-a-small-town type, and there was nothing Beth wanted more than a place where she felt settled. She'd spent the first half of her life with her father gone, her mother incapacitated and her home anything but a place of refuge or comfort. Now that she had what she'd always wanted—time with her father to build a relationship—there was nothing that would get her to leave that behind.

She suspected her dad felt the same. For all his faults when she was young, he'd made up for it in spades over the last few days. He'd insisted on taking on the wedding planning. It had done him good, giving him a purpose that he had long been without. With the wedding details off her to-do list, Beth had put her head down, concentrating on her business and managing her father's appointments, and just agreed whenever Reggie asked her questions. Yes to flowers, yes to getting lasagna from Viv's café. Yes to a cake from the new baker in town. Whenever Beth offered to help, her dad told her not to worry about anything more than putting on her dress and showing up on time. "This gives me something to do, Bethie," he'd said. "Something that makes me happy. I haven't been this happy in a long, long time."

Now here she was, wearing her mother's wedding dress, which her father had pulled out of the attic and gotten dry-cleaned. It was Sunday afternoon, and she was about to marry a man she barely knew. This was crazy. She couldn't do it. She was going to have to go down the hall and tell her father the whole thing was made up and she wasn't going to marry Grady. Reggie would understand, wouldn't he?

I'm sorry, Dad, we're not getting married. It was never real. She whispered those words to herself, spoke them to the mirror. Maybe if she said them enough times, they would be easier to say aloud. And maybe they wouldn't break her father's heart.

Yeah, slim chance of that happening.

There was a knock on her bedroom door. "Bethie, can I talk to you?"

She pulled open the door to her dressing room—the first-floor bedroom at the Stone Gap Inn that Della had given her to get ready in. There was her father, wearing a dark blue suit from years ago that hung off his thin frame. The collar of his shirt gaped at his neck, but he was freshly shaved, with color in his cheeks and a light in his eyes that Beth hadn't seen in a long time.

"Oh God, you look so beautiful," he said. His eyes misted and his voice got thick. "So much like your mother."

And the words *it was all a sham* died in her throat. "Thank you, Dad."

"I can't believe my little girl is getting married today." He stepped forward and took her hands in his. "Everything's all set. I don't want you to worry about a single thing. Everyone's outside and—"

"Everyone?"

"I invited a few people from town. Nothing to worry about. Oh, and Grady's brother is here, too. Plus some guy Grady works with. Maybe they saw the announcement in the *Stone Gap Gazette*."

"You put an announcement in the paper?" This was what happened when Beth stopped paying attention. Everything careened out of control. "Dad, I wanted a small wedding. Just you, me and Grady. I thought that was clear."

"I know you did, but honey, I couldn't let you have a tiny wedding like that. I missed so much of your childhood. I missed graduation and birthday parties, and way too many important days." His eyes filled and his hands shook. "I might have gone a little overboard by booking the inn and all that, but it's not every day your only daughter gets married. I feel like I've gotten a second chance to be the dad I should have been, and I just want to make everything perfect for you."

How could she tell him that the intimate wedding had been so they could keep the truth about their "marriage" a secret from her father? So the breakup later wouldn't be as big a deal, and she could quietly erase her marriage? She loved her father too much to do anything other than nod and tell him, "Thank you for doing so much work."

"It's only work when you don't enjoy what you're doing. Though planning a wedding is a whole other world from strategizing how to win a fight." Her father leaned forward and kissed her cheek. "I'm so proud of you. Grady's a great guy, and clearly would do anything for you. He must love you very much."

"He must," Beth managed to reply.

I'm falling in love with you.

If that was so, he hadn't shown it in the last couple days. She'd seen Grady only in passing, and their brief conversations had been all business: *the dog seems to be doing well with his training; What time do you need me to be here for the wedding; How's your father doing?* It was almost as if that moment in the kitchen hadn't happened.

She should have been relieved. But as she glanced down at the wedding dress she'd once dreamed of wearing to marry the love of her life, she couldn't hold back the wave of disappointment. Tears stung

her eyes, and she prayed her father didn't notice—
or at least misinterpreted them as happy tears.

"Well, I'll let you finish getting ready," he said.
"I'll be in the hall, waiting to walk you down the
aisle whenever you are done."

"Dad, are you sure you want to do that? You
shouldn't be without your oxygen—"

"Got that covered." He stepped back and waved
at the normally plain green metal tank. He had put
a ring of flowers over the top and tied a big white
ribbon around the canister. "Nothing's going to
stop me from walking my girl down the aisle."

That part of her dream wedding would come
true, at least. And by the look on her father's face,
it was now his dream, as well.

"Give me five minutes, Dad." She kissed his
cheek. When he was gone, Beth drew in a deep
breath, then affixed her mother's veil with a pair
of tiny white combs, and slipped into a pair of low
heels. She stared at her reflection for a long time,
then took another deep breath, opened her door
and walked down the hall with her father.

She stopped short when she saw the scene beyond the window. Reggie had gone all out in his
planning, and clearly hadn't taken the words *small*
or *intimate* to heart. At all.

A small white tent was set up over a couple

dozen folding chairs on the rolling lawn of the Stone Gap Inn. Pink rose petals littered the hallway, then the path through the living room and out the front door. Flowers and white ribbons covered the posts and spindles of the porch, then formed a border for the white paper aisle that led from the porch and down the yard. A three-piece band was playing soft instrumental jazz while waiting to play the wedding march. It was all so surreal, all so elaborate. Guilt weighed her down. He'd gone to so much trouble, so much expense. "Dad…this is beautiful, but it's too much."

Her father shook his head. "Nothing is too much for you. I can't undo all those years I was gone, or how I left you to take care of your mother on your own when you were barely old enough to take care of yourself, but this is just a small part of me saying I'm sorry."

"You have nothing to apologize for."

"Oh, but I do, Bethie, I really do." His eyes shimmered with unshed tears. "Your mother and I loved you, and we loved each other, but we were terrible parents, and even worse spouses. I was too young and cocky when I got married, and fame just went to my head and made things worse. I thought the sun and the moon should revolve around me.

I realized too late that my world should have re-volved around you and your mom."

A single tear slid down his cheek. With any other man, the tear might have looked like weakness. But tears in the eyes of a man who had once dominated the world with his fists made him real and human and even more of a father to admire. "It's too late for me to be the husband I should have been to your mother, God rest her soul, but it isn't too late for me to try being a real father to you. Is it?"

She cupped his cheek and swiped away the tear with her thumb. "No, Dad, it's not. It never was." Beth worked a smile to her face. "Now let's walk down that aisle before I start to cry."

He nodded, then crooked his elbow. She slid her arm into his, and they began to amble down the flower-strewn path. The band shifted into the wedding march and the two dozen guests rose and faced Reggie and Beth. Every time Beth felt like a fraud, she glanced over at the joy in her father's eyes, and told herself she was doing this for the right reasons.

As they approached the folding chairs, her father patted her hand. "You ready?" he whispered.

Beth nodded. Her stomach churned, her breath was in her throat, but she took one step after another with her dad, passing Stone Gap residents she knew and loved. Della Barlow, with her husband, two of her three sons, her stepson and all their wives. Katie and Sam Millwright. Viv, the owner of the café; Grady's brother and a woman who must be his wife; and Ida Mae's old next-door neighbor, Cutler Shay. Several of her dad's friends and a few of hers from high school. Savannah and Mac Barlow sat in the front row, with Savannah sending Beth encouraging smiles. She'd told her best friend she was getting married, but not the truth about why. Instead, she'd chalked it up to some whirlwind relationship that made Savannah sigh at the romance of it all and rush the repairs on Reggie's house so that Grady and Beth could spend their wedding night alone. Beth didn't have the heart to tell her they weren't going to have the wedding night everyone expected.

At the end of the aisle, Beth saw Pastor Dudley, waiting with an open Bible. And Grady, wearing a dark suit with a cornflower-blue tie. When his gaze connected with hers, he smiled, and the nerves and stress in Beth's stomach eased. She had lied to him—or at least, she'd withheld the truth. She was falling for him, too, and even though she knew her heart would be broken later, today she allowed herself to feel every emotion.

She was getting married. To Grady Jackson.

It was a fairy tale come true—and Beth decided to enjoy the moment until reality hit at midnight.

His wife.

Grady looked over at the beautiful, incredible woman beside him, and repeated the words in his head. *His wife. Beth was now his wife.* And not a pretend spouse. They'd been married by a real preacher and signed a real wedding certificate.

That was all due to Reggie, who'd been so ecstatic over the wedding that he had taken the reins on the planning, and brought in a pastor he knew, hired a band he'd heard perform once before, and invited what seemed like every person he knew. Cutler Shay had showed up, and Nick had wandered in a few minutes before the ceremony started. Grady saw Viv from the Good Eatin' Café, Della Barlow and her husband, and a couple of the Barlow brothers. Even Dan, called by Nick, had flown down for the ceremony, a surprise Grady hadn't seen coming.

There were at least a dozen people Grady didn't know or recognize, but it didn't matter. The person who kept his attention riveted was his wife.

Beside him, Beth let out a long exhale. "Well, we did it."

"We did." He put an arm around her and drew

her close, all in the spirit of acting like two people who were deeply in love, but also because he was craving her touch. Five minutes ago, he'd been standing across from her and promising to love her until the day he died. In the back of his head, he'd thought how stunning she looked as a bride. The floor-length satin dress accentuated her curves. With the sun above her, and the picturesque setting of the lake behind them, it had been as close to a perfect wedding as one could get.

Even Grady had gotten caught up in the magic of the setting, the words he'd spoken. There was a moment after he'd slipped the band onto her finger when he'd held her hand a little too long, wanting to hold on to the memory, and to her, just for a second.

"If I haven't said so already," Grady murmured, "you are a beautiful, breathtaking bride."

"You've mentioned it. Ten times." She blushed. She'd worn her hair down and curled. The hazy fabric of the veil skimmed over the golden tendrils. She looked almost…angelic. "Thank you."

"I realize this isn't a prom, but we did get all fancied up and there will be dancing." If he had known all those years ago that Beth Cooper hadn't gone to the prom, he would have screwed up the courage and asked her himself. A woman like her deserved to be wined and dined, and to experience everything life had to offer. He made a mental note to come back to Stone Gap once he'd rebuilt his fortune, and whisk her away for a weekend in Paris or Rome.

Maybe this didn't have to end.

"No, it's not a prom. But it'll do." She pressed a kiss to his cheek, a sweet, light kiss that bordered on friendly. "Thank you, Grady. For everything."

He turned her to face him. Beth's eyes shone as she looked up at him, and the smile on her face made his heart skip. "You know, people are watching us. We're newlyweds and they're going to expect us to be kissing. A lot."

"Okay, we can kiss again." She rose up on her toes, and when their lips met, Grady wrapped an arm around her, then bent her backward in a dramatic dip before he swooped her up again, all without breaking the kiss. A few people laughed and clapped.

Beth stepped back out of Grady's arms. Her cheeks were flushed, her hair a little tousled. "That, uh, that was a hell of a kiss. People will really believe we're madly in love."

He kept his eyes locked on hers, hoping to see a sign of something, anything, that would tell him how she felt. "Too bad we aren't."

"Yeah. Too bad." Beth held his gaze for a minute, her thoughts unreadable. She was his wife, and still, in many ways, a stranger. "I should, uh, say hello to the guests."

Then she spun on her heel, snagging a glass of champagne as she crossed the lawn to greet Della Barlow. Grady grabbed a beer from the makeshift bar beside the dance floor, and watched his wife make the rounds.

His wife.

Two words that both touched his heart and broke it at the same time. Savannah had handed him an offer on Ida Mae's house earlier today, a fair price that Grady should take. He hadn't signed the papers yet, using the wedding as an excuse to put it off.

Dan headed across the lawn. "Congratulations."

"Thanks." His COO looked great, with some color in his cheeks and a few of the pounds he'd lost back on his thin frame. Clearly, the days off had been good for him. "I can't believe my brother told you about the wedding."

"Of course he would. He said I couldn't miss it. Called it the wedding of the century."

Grady scoffed as the two of them walked over to the makeshift bar, where Dan got a bottle of water. "I would have invited you myself, but it was all kind of last-minute and, uh, unexpected."

"You fell madly in love and couldn't stop your-self from popping the question, huh?" Dan tipped the plastic bottle against Grady's beer. "To making crazy decisions."

"I don't know if I'd toast to that." Grady took a long pull off the beer and let out a breath. "Lately, I've been jumping off cliffs without even looking below me to see if I'm landing in water or crashing onto rocks."

"Seems like it was a good choice to jump this time." Dan nodded toward Beth. She was talking to Savannah, laughing and smiling. Her face was animated, eyes bright, and the white dress made her stand out against the lush North Carolina landscape like a lily in a field.

Damn, she was beautiful. And his, at least for tonight. Tomorrow they could face reality.

"I hope that marrying Beth may prove to be as smart a move for you as me marrying Cathy," Dan said. His face broke into a wide smile. "I couldn't do what I do without her. She's a fantastic mom and a partner this old grump doesn't deserve."

The obvious pride and joy in Dan's voice struck a little chord of envy in Grady's gut. If his wedding today had been real, those could have been his words and his happiness. Maybe he was drinking too much of the water here, because a wife and kids and a Volvo in the driveway was never what Grady wanted. Yet right now, his gut craved all that with a ferocious need. "That's awesome, man. Congrats." He cleared his throat. "Anyway, I wanted to let you know I'll be back in the office tomorrow."

Dan's jaw dropped. "*Tomorrow?* What about your honeymoon? Work can wait, Grady. Seriously."

"No, it can't." Getting back to New York and back to work was the only way to move forward. And to forget. "I need to be there to make sure this deal goes through. I found a buyer for the medical device property, but he wants to meet with me personally to hammer out the details." An offer from a potential buyer would be enough to go to Bob and sew up the deal. If Grady had to float some money in between, selling Ida Mae's house sooner rather than later would do that. All he had to do was accept the offer he had in his pocket.

It was all good news. So why did the thought of his return to the city make his heart heavy?

"While we're on the topic, I wanted to talk to you about work." Dan put up a hand. "Just for five minutes. I have an idea I want to run past you."

"Okay. Shoot." Grady nodded in his brother's direction. Nick was talking to Savannah and Mac, and marveling at their baby. Nick's wife, a slender dark-haired woman with pretty eyes, looked happier than anyone Grady had ever met. Was that what his life would be like if he stayed—if this was real and Beth actually loved him back?

"I know you didn't ask me for my advice, but I'm giving it to you anyway. Sell to Jim," Dan said, drawing Grady's attention again. "Let him take on that albatross we built. Clear your debt and start over by buying something else, say, like…" Dan nodded in the direction Grady had been looking. "Mac and Savannah Barlow's solar company. I was talking to him before the ceremony and he's looking to bring on a partner so he can do the real estate and renovation thing full-time with his wife. But he wants to keep the business local." Dan fished a business card out of his pocket and handed it to Grady. "Since you might end up settling down here, it could be a good change of direction."

"Dan, I'm not settling down here. I'm not even staying here. Monday I'll be back in New York—"

"Do you remember what you said to me when I was in the hospital?" Dan was a foot shorter than Grady, but when he was determined and serious, that height difference seemed to disappear.

"Besides that I was an idiot who should have listened to you, and I'm so incredibly sorry I didn't?" That day in the hospital with Dan—almost losing his friend—had nearly killed Grady.

Dan waved that off. "You weren't an idiot. You took a risk. I respect that. Most people stand on the edge, but you jumped into the volcano."

Grady took another swig of beer. "Jumping into a volcano sounds like a pretty idiotic thing to do. That kind of stunt can get you killed. Or cause your COO to have a heart attack."

"Man, will you quit taking the blame for that?" Dan shook his head. "I smoked for twenty years, drank more than I should have, and burned the candle at both ends. Not because you made me work all those hours, Grady. Because I loved my job. I loved the thrill of not knowing what was coming around the corner. I loved watching you make decisions that I would have hemmed and hawed about for months."

Grady scoffed. "I need to do more hemming and hawing."

"No, you don't. You focus on that one bad decision, but there were dozens of times I recommended that you hold back—times when you ignored me and ended up with terrific successes. Successes that made our business thrive. If you'd done everything I told you to from the start, we would have failed years ago. The world needs people like you, who show courage even in the worst of times."

Grady spun back toward Dan. "How is losing everything I owned showing courage? Saddling the company with millions in debt. Laying off everyone. Stressing you out. That's not courage. That's idiocy."

"I think we're going to have to agree to disagree on that one." Dan grinned. "When I was in the hospital, you told me that it wasn't worth the adrenaline rush when there were such steep consequences. Grady, I'm telling you now that the adrenaline rush is what got me out of bed and back to work. If I wanted a boring job, I would have stayed at the financial services office you hired me away from."

"But—"

"But nothing. You aren't any more responsible for my heart attack than the grass is for a rain storm." Dan shook his head. "It would have been easier to blame you, but the truth is, that's all on me. Now, I've got to listen to my doctor's advice and get some exercise, and quit having steak on Saturday nights." Dan paused, sipped some water. A cloud passed over the sun, casting a wide shadow over the wedding for a moment. "There is one thing you could do for me, if you really wanted to make it up to me."

"Anything."

Dan spun in a slow half circle, and waved at the hill rolling down to the lake, the picture-perfect setting. "Buy a business in a place like this. It's my idea of heaven. A place where life is slow, weather is sweet and there's a little challenge to the days.

You do that, and I'll come back and work for you any day."

"Wait…are you quitting?"

"Yep. And so should you." Dan clapped him on the shoulder. "Quit feeling responsible for everyone else and quit looking at selling as failure. Look at it as closing one chapter and opening another." Dan gave him a grin. "Anyway, I heard there's some great lasagna over there. I'm going to try to sneak a bite before Cathy catches me. Oh, and look, here comes Mac. Right on time."

Right on time? Grady was getting the distinct impression that he'd been set up. Dan's grin widened as he left, having done his business matchmaking for the day.

"Congratulations." Mac shook Grady's hand. "I hear my wife had an offer on the house that she presented to you."

"It was a fair bid, too. I was beginning to worry it wouldn't sell." Relief washed over Grady, but with a chaser of cold reality that this was it. He'd done what he'd come to do, so his time in Stone Gap was nearing an end. Which meant he needed to get back to New York, and leave this town behind. "Dan says you're looking for a partner in your business."

Grady might be a man who was looking to leave

Stone Gap behind…but there was no harm in hearing Mac out, was there?

"Thinking about it," he said. "It was my wife's father's company, and I don't want to completely sell it, but I also want more time to spend with my family. I was thinking it would be a good fit for you." Across the yard, Savannah waved at Mac, beckoning for him to join her. He held up one finger, then turned back to Grady. "I hear you're smart as hell, and you're a risk taker, like me. And now that you're married to Beth, I assume you'll be settling down in Stone Gap?"

Grady couldn't say he was leaving for New York as soon as he could. There'd be questions if the groom ditched the bride too quickly, and the last thing he or Beth needed was those. It would get back to Reggie and all that they had done would be ruined. "We…we haven't decided on that yet."

"Well, stop on by the office on Monday and see what you think." Mac shook hands with him again. "I think it would be a great partnership. I don't know about you, but I'm always up for a new challenge."

Mac said goodbye, then crossed the lawn to Savannah. Her face lit as her husband approached, then her joy spread as he leaned in and kissed her. He placed a gentle hand on her back, whispered something in her ear, and the couple exchanged a private smile that seemed to shut out the entire world.

A part of Grady felt indescribable envy. As Mac and Savannah headed up to their car, he took her hand. She smiled and leaned into his shoulder. They were going to go home together, relieve their babysitter, then sit out on the porch and enjoy the last bits of sunshine together.

As for Grady and Beth, the "newlyweds"? They were going to keep up the charade until Reggie went home to his own house, then slip off to their separate homes and separate lives. A marriage in name only that would be over in less time than it took to binge *Game of Thrones*.

Grady crossed to the table where Reggie was sitting. His father-in-law was watching the people on the makeshift dance floor, a happy smile on his face. "Can I get you anything, Mr. Cooper?"

"Call me Dad, Grady. We're family now." Reggie reached out and clasped his hand. "I couldn't ask for a better man to be my son-in-law."

Guilt weighed heavy in Grady's gut. What would Reggie think about him if he knew the truth? If he found out the entire thing was an act, albeit one done out of good intentions? "Thank you, D-Dad." The word stumbled on his tongue.

But as soon as he said it, Grady realized Reggie was more of a father figure than his own father had ever been. In the week that Reggie had been living in Ida Mae's house, Grady had enjoyed dozens of conversations with the retired boxer. Reggie had been all over the world, and had hundreds of great stories, but he also had a sort of practical wisdom that he shared without judgment or condescension.

"I've seen the way you look at my daughter," Reggie said. "It's so nice to see her with someone who adores her."

Grady's gaze flicked to Beth, who was talking to Cutler Shay. Or rather, Cutler was talking to her, pouring out some long story that had her laughing. Adored her?

Yeah, he did. He hadn't been lying when he'd said he was falling in love with her. Beth Cooper—Beth Jackson now—was an incredible woman who intrigued him and challenged him and lingered at the edge of his every thought. A woman it was going to be hard as hell to forget. For a moment, he let himself fantasize that she'd change her mind about coming to New York with him. Then he glanced at her frail father, and knew that was a long shot.

"I do care deeply about her," he said to Reggie. "But then again, she's pretty easy to adore."

Reggie patted the seat next to him and waited

for Grady to sit. "Take some lessons from an old man who has screwed up his life," he said, "and don't take her for granted. Women like Beth— and her mother—don't come along very often. I made the mistake of abandoning my wife within a month of our wedding. I had stars in my eyes, and I was looking at what was ahead of me, instead of valuing what was right by my side. I left her alone, and I…" He let out a long sigh. "I broke her heart. Worse, I broke her trust. She couldn't depend on me to be there when I said I was going to, and every time a man does that to his wife, it puts a crack in the foundation of their marriage. A house like this one—" he waved toward the inn "—or one like your grandmother's can withstand a single crack in the foundation. It's strong, it's been here a long time, weathered a lot of storms. Two cracks, maybe even three, and it would still be standing. But every one of them weakens the base, and if the number goes up, then eventually it will be one crack too many."

"And the house will fall."

Reggie nodded. "It's the same with your marriage. All those little things—the trips away, the arguments over breakfast, the days where you forget to say 'I love you'—form cracks in the foundation, and before you know it, you don't have anything left to stand on. You wake up one morning and realize you are married to a stranger."

Reggie had no idea how true that statement already was. "I'll keep that advice in mind."

"It's too late for me to do it right for myself, but I'm not going to waste a chance to make my daughter's life happier. So forgive an old man's advice, and know it comes from having been there and screwed that up."

"I appreciate it, Dad, I really do." Grady folded and refolded the linen napkin on the table. "My own father has never been one to give me advice. He was too busy judging me and my brothers, and lecturing us about getting into Ivy League schools and becoming lawyers."

"Not all of us are meant to be fathers. And some of us figure out how to be parents way too late." Reggie sighed. "Anyway, I'm keeping you from your bride. Go take her for a spin on the dance floor. Bethie loves to dance."

Yet another thing Grady didn't know about his wife. But as he caught her eye across the crowd, he vowed to find out as much as he could in the little time they had together. When he went back to New York, he hoped that would be enough to get him through being there without Beth.

Chapter Ten

The last of the guests left the wedding in a flurry of hugs and good wishes. Jack Barlow offered to drive Beth's father home, so that Grady and Beth could get to their wedding night sooner, Reggie said with a grin. He was clearly thrilled with the wedding, and had spent the entire day energized and overjoyed. Every moment had been a celebration. Everyone who wished them well believed the couple was head over heels in love, and anxious to begin their new life together.

Beth was anxious, all right, but that anxiety was about what was to happen after this. She and

Grady were now alone at Ida Mae's house, with an exhausted-by-staying-at-the-pet-sitter's Monster sleeping in the corner of the kitchen. Beth turned on a streaming service, choosing some Michael Bublé songs to play on her phone speaker, then put on an apron over her wedding dress, started the water, and began to wash the few dishes left in the sink—breakfast dishes they'd been too rushed to take care of before heading to the inn.

Grady came in from taking the trash out and slipped into place beside her. He'd taken off his suit jacket and tie, and undone the top two buttons of his shirt. He flipped the cuffs up, and it was all Beth could do not to stare at the fine definition in his hands and the way his forearms flexed as he picked up the dishes and dried them.

"So, small talk seems pretty inappropriate now," he said.

Beth laughed. "Yes, indeed. I don't even know what one talks about when they've married someone in name only."

"Probably not how you want your eggs in the morning." He grinned.

She turned off the water and accepted the towel from him to dry her hands. For a second, she imagined herself waking up in his arms, with his smile the first thing she saw. "If this was real, I'd say scrambled with cheese and home fries."

"Sunny-side up, medium, with wheat toast for me."

"See? Not even close to the same breakfast." Beth wagged the towel in his direction. "That's exactly why we never would have worked out."

She tried to pass the words off as a joke, but underneath, her heart was cracking. Tomorrow was Monday—the first day of her married life, and also the day when her husband would get on a plane to move hundreds of miles away. And she'd be alone in her little house.

"I'm not so sure about that," Grady said as he placed the last dish in the cabinet. "You don't think we could have worked?"

At some point, he'd moved closer to her and now stood only inches away. Her gaze dropped to his hands again, those incredible muscular hands, then back up to his face. His brown eyes held hers, and a breath filled the space between them, then another.

"We live different lives in different places," she said.

"People do that all the time and still hold a relationship together." He placed a hand on the counter, shifted his body toward hers. "We could try that."

"New York and North Carolina are very far apart, Grady."

"They are. But we aren't right now." He leaned in, close enough for his lips to touch hers. Heat curled between them, awakening the desire that lingered on the edge of every conversation she had with him. "Mrs. Jackson."

The name sent a tangle of fear and joy through her. *Mrs. Jackson. Grady's wife.* This man, only a millimeter away and making her pulse hum, was her husband, for better or worse.

"We *are* quite close together at this moment." Her words were whispered against his mouth. Every breath inhaled the dark, woodsy scent of his cologne, the warmth of his nearness.

"We are. Quite—" he kissed her lightly, easily "—close."

Desire simmered inside her. She reached out and danced her fingers up his bare wrist, then tangled her hand with his. Their foreheads met, and Grady put his other arm around her just as the radio shifted to a love song. They began to sway to the music. The move was so intimate, so romantic, that the last little bit of reservation Beth had about getting close to Grady began to melt. She closed her eyes and allowed herself to be swept into the moment, the fantasy of being Mrs. Grady Jackson.

They were married right now, after all. What was wrong with enjoying a single night with her "husband"? Was she really going to leave here, go back to her empty cottage and spend her wedding night alone?

As if he had read her mind, Grady kissed her then, not a friendship kiss, not a just-met kiss, but the kiss of a man who wanted to make love to her, a man who desired her. And no matter how much she had tried to resist it, deny the feelings, pretend she thought of him only platonically, the truth was Beth's entire body craved Grady's touch. Ever since that late night in the kitchen, she'd thought about him, fantasized about him, sought out ways to be near him or brush up against him.

He'd looked at her as he spoke his vows earlier today with a depth of feeling in his eyes that shook her. *I'm falling in love with you*, he'd said the other day, and the proof had been right there at their wedding, when he'd promised to love her until the day he died.

"Grady," she said, and when his gaze met hers, she saw that nothing had changed. He still had that look in his eyes. She'd worry about the distance and the complications in the morning. "I… I don't want to go home tonight."

"Then don't. Stay with me." He rested his hands

on her waist. "Let's have just one night before we go back to scrambled eggs in North Carolina and sunny-side up in New York."

She nodded, because she didn't trust her voice, and he took the towel from her hands, laid it on the counter, then scooped her up. She let out a gasp of surprise, wrapped her arms around his neck and pressed her cheek to the hollow of his throat, where she could catch the combined scents of his cologne and the fresh starch in his shirt, warmth and restraint in one. He carried her out of the kitchen, up the stairs, then into the room on the left. His bedroom.

A queen-size bed dominated the space. She barely noticed the striped comforter or the view of the side yard, before Grady lowered her to the bed and lay beside her. She'd expected him to just go straight from kissing to sex, but instead he propped himself up on one elbow and brushed a tendril of hair off her cheek. The tenderness in that simple gesture melted her heart a little more. "You are an incredible woman, Beth. I should have asked you out in high school."

She laughed, but had to admit she was flattered, and wondered how things would have been different if Grady actually had asked her on a date years ago. "I probably would have said no then, too. My life was too busy for boys. It still is."

"Yet you've managed to fit me in."

"You kind of forced your way into my space." She smiled up at him. "Like your dog did to you."

"I want you to know that this isn't a one-night stand for me." He traced her face with a finger, and held her gaze. "I don't know what will happen tomorrow when I go back to New York, or what I'll do with Monster, or most of all, how we'll make this work in the future, but I don't want this to be it."

The thought filled her with joy, tempered with a dose of reality, but Beth pushed both out of her mind. She had this moment in bed with her husband. And right now, that was all she wanted to think about. "Tonight, Grady, that's all I want and need."

Grady leaned over and kissed her again, soft at first, then harder, deeper, stoking the fire inside her until she couldn't stand not touching him for another second. She fumbled between them to unbutton his shirt, then tug it over his shoulders and off. His broad back was warm under her hands, his muscular chest hard against hers. She could have stayed there forever, running her palms over his skin, but he rolled away, then tugged her into a standing position and moved behind her.

He lifted the hair from her neck and kissed the tender valley there while his hands roamed over her shoulders, skating along the V opening at the back of her dress, until he found the zipper. He hesitated for a second and she stood very, very still, her heart racing. "Grady," she whispered, "please."

The zipper made a soft snicking sound as it slid down her spine. Cool air rushed over her bare skin, as the satiny wedding dress parted and slid to the floor.

"You are beautiful, Beth," Grady whispered against her back. He hooked a finger under each of her bra straps, then slid the lacy fabric down her shoulders, unhooking the bra as he did. She leaned forward, and it dropped to the floor. Grady kissed a trail down the ridge of her spine, while his hands slid deliciously lower along her back with each kiss. "Absolutely beautiful."

Goose bumps of anticipation rose on her skin when he tugged the waistband of her panties, pulling them down her legs, kissing every inch of skin the thin scrap of material revealed. When she was naked, she turned to face him, reaching for the belt, fly and zipper that kept her from what she really wanted.

Because maybe if she had sex with him—mindless, amazing sex—she would stop thinking about how tender he was being and how it was melting her heart and making her wish they weren't going to settle for scrambled eggs in North Carolina and sunny-side up in New York. She let the roar of desire push those thoughts out of her head as she kissed him and urged his pants down and off.

He tugged a condom out of his wallet before kicking his pants to the side. Then he laid her on the bed and dipped his head to her skin. "I have wanted you since the first minute I saw you," he said. "I've wanted to kiss this—" he licked one breast "—and this—" he nuzzled the other "—and this." He slid his mouth down the valley of her belly.

She arched against his mouth, her hands tangling in his hair. "Later, we can talk," she said, the words half gasp, half breath, "but right now, all I want is you…inside me."

He smiled. "Exactly my thought." A moment later, he slid inside her body, matching his long, deliberate strokes with nibbles along her neck and sweet, sensuous words whispered in her ear. She couldn't get enough of him, clawing at his back,

wanting more of his delicious touch, the way he
almost revered her, and the way he stoked the fire
inside her over and over again, bringing her just to
the brink once, twice, three times, until she was
begging him to let her climax. And when she did,
it was like seeing stars, bright and hot and incredible. He came a second later, calling out her name
in one long syllable.

Afterward, she lay in his arms and curled against
his chest, sated in every way possible. She listened
to Grady's heartbeat as he traced lazy circles on her
bare back. He kissed the top of her head, a sweet,
reverent move, and Beth knew she was doing the
worst possible thing with her husband—

Falling in love with him.

Her father died the morning after the wedding, sometime before dawn. Beth had called and
checked on him one more time before she went
to sleep, and he'd chastised her for calling on her
wedding night. They'd had a lovely conversation
recounting the wedding day, and she'd told him
she loved him before she hung up.

The overnight nurse Beth had hired said her
dad went to sleep around eleven that night, and
simply didn't wake up. The news had come as a

shock, but in a way, Beth had been bracing herself for this day for months, maybe years.

Still, the days after his passing had been diffi-cult, filled with a million decisions to make, from flowers to hymns. Grady had been there every step of the way, a set of shoulders to lean on and a help-ing voice in making those decisions.

At the end of the day, going home to Grady and staying at Ida Mae's had somehow made losing her dad easier. Grady knew her dad, respected and maybe even loved him, and as they shared their memories and he held her tight, the grief seemed a tiny bit lighter. He'd been right beside her during the entire wake, and again today at the funeral, his mere presence a comfort.

Long after the other mourners had left, she stood over Dad's grave site, covered with flowers that reminded her of the ones at her wedding and the last time she'd seen her father, and thought none of it felt real. "I can't believe he's gone."

Grady's arm went around her waist and he pulled her to him. "He was at peace," Grady said. "I think he hung on all this time because he wanted to be sure you would be okay if he was gone."

A part of her knew that was true. Her father had said many times that all he wanted was to know she would be secure and safe. But still, the loss had hit her hard, especially coming on the heels of a beautiful day.

"All my life, all I ever wanted was for my dad to be there for me." She swiped at the tears on her face. "And the one night he needs me to be there for him, I wasn't there. I wasn't at his side. I wasn't… home."

"Beth." When she didn't look at him, he turned her toward him. "Beth, you can't blame yourself for not being there. Your dad was overjoyed to see you get married. He wouldn't want you to set a second of that day aside for him."

She bit her lip and nodded. Grady was right. Oh, how she wanted him to be wrong, but he was right. He'd loved her father, too, and had made her dad so happy in the last few weeks. The tears spilled over her lashes and down her cheeks. "Thank you, for staying, for being here."

He gathered her to him and held her tight. "There's nowhere else I'd rather be."

And just for this hard, awful day, Beth chose to believe that was true.

Grady woke up on Monday morning a month after the wedding, alone in his bed, and instead of booking a flight and running back to New York, something he had procrastinated on already a hundred times, he stayed in Stone Gap. Tuesday came and he was still there, still without a flight plan. Wednesday, same story, except it was getting harder to justify remaining in town. Every time he talked to Dan, he told him he'd be on the first flight the next day.

"I've known you a hell of a long time," Dan said. "And you never procrastinate on anything. What's it going to take for you to realize there's more than a house keeping you in Stone Gap?"

"I'll be back tomorrow. Just tying up some loose ends," he said. Last month, it had been his wedding night, then Reggie's death, the funeral, helping Beth with the house and the estate. Helping her deal with her new normal—a life without her father. This week, all that was done, and still he couldn't seem to leave. Grady turned on his laptop and opened up a travel website. He booked a flight for Thursday morning before he could change his mind.

Because there were no more loose ends to tie up. The house was under agreement, and pending an inspection and appraisal, would be sold in a matter of weeks at most. Savannah told him the couple buying it had gushed about raising their children there, getting a pontoon boat for the lake and maybe putting a hot tub on a deck in the back.

As for the dog, another young couple had answered the ad for Monster and picked him up just this afternoon. Maybe that was why Grady was at loose ends in a silent, empty house. He missed the noise and the company of that little mutt more than he'd expected.

But the real reason Grady had lingered in Stone Gap had everything to do with the woman he had married. The woman he had made love to twice on his wedding night, the same woman who had stayed in his bed for a week after their wedding. The woman who was gone—gone from his bed, gone from his life—right after the funeral.

He'd called her, but gotten voice mail. Texted, and got back short answers that said she was swamped with work but doing okay despite the loss of her dad. But when he swung by Happy Tails this morning to see her, the sign on the door said Closed. If Beth was inside, he couldn't see her through the window. He stopped at her cottage; no answer to the doorbell. Maybe she was at the diner, or with a friend? Or even something as simple as shopping?

Grady told himself she was grieving and wanted to be alone. Reggie's passing had been a hard thing to deal with, but Grady had taken comfort in the happiness of Beth's dad on their wedding day. Her father's life had been full, right up to the end.

His feelings about lying to a dying man were still conflicted. Had it been the right thing to do? Giving Reggie some peace, even if it was false? For a moment there—to be honest, longer than a moment—Grady had felt like the whole thing was real and true. Maybe because a part of him wished it to be.

Grady closed the laptop and dialed Beth one more time. The call went straight to voice mail, which meant she had either turned her phone off or hit Ignore as soon as his name popped up. What had happened? He'd thought things were great on their wedding night, and in the days after her father's death, they had been closer than ever. Had any of what she'd said been the truth? Or had Beth been keeping up the fiction with him, too?

Grady tossed the phone onto the counter. It landed with a clatter and skittered over to the toaster. Normally, Monster would start barking at the noise. Grady even glanced in the corner for the dog, but of course, the space was empty.

He'd dealt with most of the furniture in the house, scheduling a pickup with a local charity for Friday. Savannah had promised to be here to let them in, and wait while they carted out Ida Mae's sofa and dining room set and the bed where Grady had slept with Beth. He'd boxed up all Ida Mae's personal belongings and set them aside for storage.

But he had yet to tackle the garage. Maybe because he had so many memories wrapped up in that cool, dim space. When he'd been young, it had been a hiding place and a fort. A base of operations for playing soldier with his brothers. A place to escape when the sun got too hot or his father started calling his name. The garage had been where he'd built a birdhouse with his grandfather and where he'd sneaked a cigarette at age sixteen. Part of him wanted to keep it exactly as it was—but he knew that wasn't possible. It was time to handle this last detail, before he left Stone Gap for good tomorrow.

And left his house, his dog and his wife behind. God, his life sounded like a bad country-and-western song.

He skirted the house, unlocked the side door of the garage and slipped inside the dim building. The overhead light flickered to life, exposing a thick layer of dust and a few cobwebs. In the center of the garage, Ida Mae's beloved sky blue '69 Camaro sat under a cotton tarp. Grandpa had bought it and refurbished it for her as an anniversary gift more than thirty years ago. Grady pulled the fabric back, exposing a vehicle nearly as shiny now as the day it had rolled off the assembly line. He thought Grandma had sold it a long time ago, but no, here it was, just waiting for him to unveil it again.

He heard a low whistle behind him and turned. Mac Barlow stood in the entrance. "Nice looking car. I remember seeing your grandmother driving it before she…" The words trailed off, without mentioning the tragedy and the house that had brought Grady back to Stone Gap.

"Yeah, she loved this car. Drove my parents crazy when she'd take me and my brothers out in it, since it was too old to have all the safety features we take for granted. They pictured us all dying in some fiery crash on the interstate, but truth was, she treated this car like a baby and barely hit the speed limit in it." He ran a hand along the smooth, gleaming body. The light above the car bounced off the finish, making the chrome sparkle in the gray interior of the garage.

"You thinking of taking it out for a spin?" Mac asked.

Grady shook his head. "I really should sell it. A car like this is totally impractical in New York." Plus, shipping it there would cost a fortune. But the thought of selling it—

Pained Grady more than he wanted to admit. He'd packed up Ida Mae's clothes and dishes, and created a plan for the furniture, but when it came to this car, he almost couldn't bring himself to sever that last tie. It was little wonder he'd put this off to the last minute.

"Yeah, but it's fun as hell in sunny North Carolina, where the weather's good enough to drive around with the windows down ten months of the year." Mac stepped inside the garage. "As much as I'd love to ask for a chance to take this baby out on the road, I really came by because I wanted to know if you gave my offer any thought."

"Not really," Grady said, which was the truth. "I've been busy. The wedding, then the funeral, and now the house…" Procrastinating on going back to his real life… He had plenty of excuses.

"I don't get it," Mac said. "I saw the way you looked at Beth when you said your vows, and I would have bet every dime I had that the two of you loved each other. Yet she's down at the lake, crying, and you're up here, selling off your grandmother's house and heading back to New York."

"She's crying? Why? And how do you know I'm going back to New York?"

"Beth told me." Mac shrugged. "Actually, she told Savannah, and I overheard. The two of them went for a walk and I headed here to tell you my offer still stands, if you want to stay put and make something of this marriage, rather than making a stupid mistake."

He couldn't explain the truth to Mac. That the whole thing hadn't been a mistake, but it had been a foolish idea. Yes, Reggie had been happy and none the wiser before he passed away, and Grady could take comfort in that while he flew back to New York, leaving Beth behind. Except he hadn't gotten on a plane yet, and he didn't feel an ounce of comfort. "Is she still at the lake?"

Mac nodded, then pointed west. "Savannah renovated a house for us a couple miles down the road from here, and we just finished moving in, which was why Beth was there. Beth's car is in the driveway. If you leave now—"

Grady had already grabbed the closest keys— the ones to Ida Mae's car—and pressed the power button to lift the garage door. Mac stepped back and gave him a wave, then climbed in his own car. Grady backed out, turned left, and drove as fast as he dared on the windy lake road to Mac's house.

Chapter Eleven

The tires on Ida Mae's Camaro kicked up some pebbles when Grady parked. He hurried around the back of Mac's house and down the lawn to the dock, where Savannah and Beth were sitting and talking. Beth's shoulders were hunched and it was all Grady could do not to break into a run at the sight. When his steps made the dock creak, Beth turned. "Grady. What are you doing here?" She swiped at her face and feigned indifference. "I thought you already went back to New York."

He shook his head. "Not yet. I wanted to talk to

you before I left. But you haven't been answering your phone and you haven't been at work."

"I'm supposed to be on my delayed 'honeymoon.' Put off until after the funeral."

"If you were on a honeymoon, you'd be with your husband." It wasn't until just now that he realized how hurt he'd been that she had ignored him for the last few days. It was as if everything that had happened between them meant nothing.

Beth shook her head and turned back to the lake. Savannah got to her feet, and grabbed the stroller with her sleeping baby. "That's my cue to leave," she said. "I've got to start dinner anyway. You're welcome to stay, Grady, if you want. I think Mac's going to grill some steaks to go with my potato salad."

Grady muttered a vague maybe, then stepped aside to let Savannah pass. She paused and put a hand on his shoulder. "She cares about you, you know," Savannah said, too quietly for Beth to overhear. "Don't break her heart."

Then Savannah was gone, and Grady made his way down the wooden dock. Beth stood and leaned against the railing. "Hey," he said, which probably wasn't his best opening line. But he didn't know what else to say. If Beth truly cared about him, why had she left without a word, and shut him out of her life?

"Why are you still here?" she said.

"I didn't want to leave without saying goodbye."

"Well, you said it. Have a nice trip." She turned away and faced the water.

"What the hell happened, Beth? I woke up the morning after the funeral and you were gone. We'd spent all that time together, and then you just left without a word."

She still had her back to him, so he couldn't tell if she was mad or indifferent or hurt. "It doesn't matter, Grady. Just go back to New York."

"And what are you going to do?"

She spun around, and when she did, he noticed tears in her eyes. Damn. "Tell everyone that my husband and I grew apart and that it's over. The sooner I can do that, the better, because I'm not that good of an actress and I just can't—"

Her voice choked and she turned back to the water.

"Can't what?" Grady moved to her left and rested his arms on the wooden railing. Close enough to feel the warmth of her body, but not quite touch her. Everything about Beth said *keep away*.

Grady knew he had done this. He'd had a grand plan of marrying her and saving the day with her father, like he was some white knight. But instead, he'd made promises he couldn't keep and broken Beth's heart.

In that moment, he realized that all it would take to undo the tears in her eyes and the catch in her voice would be to stay here. And from where he was standing, "here" looked pretty good. Before him, Stone Gap Lake sparkled under the waning sun, and somewhere in the distance a fish jumped. Birds swooped over the water, skimming along the dark surface, looking for a snack. A couple boats dotted the landscape, fishermen hauling in one more catch before the day's end.

And then there was his wife, the most perfect part of the picture. But would that be enough for him? Could he stay, and leave everything he'd built in New York behind?

Beth worried her fingers together, lacing them in and out, but not saying anything.

"Can't what?" he asked a second time, more softly.

"Can't pretend that none of this meant anything." She drew in a breath, then pivoted to face him. "For a moment there, it was real, Grady. When we said our vows, I saw the look in your eyes. You cared about me. You meant those words. And then…when we made love, it sure seemed like you meant that, too. That whole last month, through everything, you were there, and it felt so real, like you really cared about me."

"I did, Beth. I still do." He brushed the hair off her face. She looked so strong, so determined, even as her eyes filled with tears that she held back with sheer stubbornness. "I didn't marry you out of pity for your father. It was much more than that."

"And yet you're still going back to New York."

"We have different lives. You knew that all along."

"We do? Because last I checked, the best part of your life was right here, in this town, on this very lake. Every time you talked about being at your grandmother's, you were happy. But I have yet to see you talk about New York the same way."

He shook his head. "Well, New York's a city. It's apples and oranges."

"Maybe so. Or maybe Grady the risk taker won't take a chance on what we could have here."

He threw up his hands. He'd taken chances ever since he'd walked into her shop. He'd taken a chance pretending to be her boyfriend, then her husband. But in the end, he'd been living a fantasy. He wasn't cut out for this town, or this domesticated home-for-dinner-at-five kind of life. He never had been. "What do you think I've been doing for the last two weeks? You were the one who made it very clear you don't have time to date. That your life revolved around your father."

"It did. He was sick and he needed me."

"But now that he's gone, you're still keeping that distance. Was it really about responsibilities or because you're just as scared of falling in love with someone? I'm not the only one who isn't taking risks." Grady was scared; he wasn't going to lie about that. The thought of uprooting his life for someone who wasn't fully invested... He'd had enough of living with people who barely tolerated each other. He didn't want perfection, but he'd thought for a little while that he and Beth had the kind of thing Dan and Cathy, Nick and Vivian, and Mac and Savannah had.

The little whisper in the back of his mind said, *You can't have that without fully investing yourself, too.*

"If I did that, and made time for you," Beth said, pushing off from the railing and taking a step closer to him, "and for us, would you stay in Stone Gap?"

"You know I can't—"

"You own the company, Grady. You can do whatever you want."

His gaze went to the lake again. The blue water shimmered under the sun, peaceful and still. When he'd been young, he'd imagined living here all year long, in the very house he had inherited. Then he grew up and built a company and suddenly had dozens of people depending on him to pay their mortgages and get their kids braces. He'd had to let those people go, but he still planned to rehire them, to keep all the promises he'd made. He couldn't just up and abandon that. "A company that's in trouble. I've got someone trying to buy it out from under me, and I'm spending most of my time trying to save it. If I'd been more cautious before I took a risk on that government project—"

"Did you ever think that maybe you undermined that yourself?"

Beth's question came out of left field. He'd worked tirelessly for years to build his business to what it was. He'd never done anything to purposely hurt the company. "What are you talking about? Why would I do that?"

"Because you're not as happy as you think you are." She narrowed the distance between them even more, and her stormy blue eyes seemed to bore into his. "You live a life with no ties, Grady. You're trying to unload your dog, and your grandmother's house and all her possessions, as fast as you can—"

"I need the capital to get my business back on track."

"Did you ever think that maybe, just maybe, your grandmother left you that house for a reason? I didn't know Ida Mae as well as you did, but one thing I do know is that she had ties. To this town, to the people in it, and to you and your brothers. Maybe she wanted you to have some, too."

He had no doubt Ida Mae had had something like that in mind when she wrote up her will. But she also would have supported him in trying to restore his business. She'd been the only one to encourage him and his brothers to go after something different than the law careers their parents had pushed so hard for. She had dared to be different in her own life, and had encouraged the same with her grandchildren.

Beth couldn't possibly understand that. All she'd known was this town. "I have to go back to New York, and have a flight out tomorrow," Grady said. Beth's face fell a little. "I would love it if you came with me."

She sighed. "We've been through this. My life is here. My business."

"They need groomers and dog trainers in New York, too. And you can fly down and visit your friends here anytime you want."

"I love my life here, Grady. I know you did, too. Boy, you really don't want to get out of your comfort zone, do you?" She shook her head. "Have a safe trip."

Then she brushed past him and headed down the dock. Grady started to hurry after her, but realized it was too late. It had been too late before he even arrived.

Beth stood on the porch of her father's house for a long time before she opened the door. The conversation with Grady on the dock at Mac's house had cemented a truth she'd been avoiding. There was no future between her and Grady. When Mac told her that he'd offered an opportunity to buy into the solar company, and Grady had turned it down, she knew it was pointless to hope for a better ending. Grady may have done something selfless in marrying her, but when it came to a relationship, he retreated from true commitment.

Her heart had broken then, and she'd known she had to have a conversation she'd been avoiding, because there wasn't going to be a happily-ever-after for Mr. and Mrs. Jackson.

She grabbed the huge stack of mail and went inside the house where she had spent so much of her life. The furniture was still there, the pictures of her father on the wall, but the home itself was empty.

Beth sighed, dropped onto the sofa and began sorting the mail. Some bills, a lot of catalogs and other junk, and then one big package, addressed to her dad.

She opened it, and pulled out what looked like a book. It took her a second to recognize what it was.

An album for photos. The kind that people used for scrapbooking. This one was a complete kit, with patterned paper and stickers and all kinds of little extras that had toasting glasses and wedding rings to tack on the pictures.

Her eyes welled. Her father had surprised her yet again by turning out to be more of a softy than she knew. If she'd had a list of a thousand people who would start a scrapbook after her wedding, her dad would have been the last person she thought of.

And yet here he was, even after he was gone, showing her how proud and happy he was.

Another package in the pile contained some photo proofs from the photographer her father had hired. Of course her dad would have asked for hard copies—while he still owned an ancient desktop computer, he'd never had the patience for keeping up with the latest software, never mind keeping any kind of digital frame.

Beth dumped out the photos and sorted through them, her heart breaking a little more with each picture. Beth and Grady at the altar, speaking their vows, then kissing, then turning to head back down the aisle, hand in hand.

Beth swallowed hard. How she wanted to believe in those pictures, in the happy couple they portrayed. Except the marriage was already over and the sooner she made that knowledge public, the better. She couldn't go on pretending that she and Grady were happy and in love. Because they weren't.

She got to her feet and crossed to the images of her father that filled the living room wall. Reggie in the ring, in the middle of a fight, or raising a fist with a victorious smile. A strong man, right to the end. "I'm sorry about lying to you, Dad. I really am," she said, her voice thick, the tears unchecked now. "You were so sick, and all I wanted to do was make you happy—to give you something to get excited over.

"When I was a little girl, you'd come home from a fight and swing me up in your arms, and carry me on your shoulders around the yard. We'd celebrate, you know? You and me. Sometimes you'd sit down at one of my tea parties and pretend to drink tea with me and Mr. Bear. And then…you just stopped doing all that."

She stared at the image of him with his promoter,

one from back when she was in high school. Her father had been gone so much, so often. "I missed you," she whispered. "I missed you so much, Dad. The only thing I ever wanted was a relationship with you, and after you got sick, and we started talking, and then…when you thought I was getting married…we finally had the relationship I wanted."

She sighed. He wasn't here, he couldn't hear her and he couldn't reply. But looking at his pictures and telling him all the things she wished she'd said before made it easier. A little.

Would Grady feel the same heartbreak about leaving her? She doubted it, and wishing it were so wouldn't make it happen.

The wedding had given her father something to look forward to, to hold on for, and for that, Beth would have done it a hundred times over, even with all the heartbreak that had followed.

For a moment there, she'd dared to believe it was more. Especially when Grady stayed through the wake and the funeral. *I'm falling in love with you.* If he'd meant those words, then why was he leaving? And why had he gone ahead with selling the house? That had been the clear message Beth needed that none of this was real.

She glanced at the clippings, pasted inside frames and hung on the wall. Dozens of fights over the years, different locations, different fighters. Her gaze lingered on one clipping of her father, fighting a man who was taller and had longer arms. Lenny Miller. The name rang a bell of some story her dad had told her years ago.

The fight had been in Georgia, in the early part of her father's career. He was unproven, green, and Lenny had ten years of experience on him. "Lenny had a reach that was like ten feet," her father said in the postfight interview. "I knew I couldn't beat him just by punching him. He would have creamed me in five minutes. So I went in there and did the only thing I knew how to do. I pretended I wasn't scared. I acted like I was the next George Foreman. All tough and unbeatable. Every time he hit me, I stayed standing, shook it off like it was a tap from a fly. He'd swing at me, I'd laugh after he hit my jaw or my head. And poor Lenny, he was standing there, confused as hell, trying to figure out what was going wrong."

She laughed at the story, thinking of her father doing that, acting brave even when he wasn't feeling very brave. She read over the stats of the fight, the round by round recounting by the reporter, who'd called it "incredible. A nail-biter."

In the last round, her father had used his lower height and his speed to sneak in a jab, then a second before Lenny recovered. The other fighter crumpled, and ten seconds later, her father had won his first major bout. And then there was a tiny article, from another paper, that had run a few weeks later. She'd never noticed this one before, maybe because the photos had been there so long they'd become a part of the wallpaper. The snippet talked about how Lenny Miller was glad he'd lost to Reggie, because his son had gotten sick, and the loss allowed him to be home and take time for that. "Everything happens for a reason," Lenny said in the interview. "Even losses."

"I'm having trouble seeing the reason for all this," she whispered to her father's picture. A short-lived joy that she almost wished had never happened. Then she wouldn't be struggling so hard to forget those moments.

Grady might already be gone, and all of this was over. He'd made it clear his life was hundreds of miles away from hers.

Beth stayed in the house for a long time, going through photos and memories while the clock ticked away the minutes and her husband got further and further away from the life she'd dared to hope they'd have.

Chapter Twelve

Grady didn't go straight back home after he left Mac's place. He couldn't face the empty house, the offer-pending sign that the Realtor had tacked up, and the glaring absence of the dog that had already gone to a new home. He should have been glad; all his plans had come to fruition and now he could go back to New York, give the business a much needed cash infusion, and turn things around. The deal to buy and resell that property in Lower Manhattan was nearly closed. A few more details to work out, and he'd be back on the road to success.

Technically, Ida Mae's house wasn't "home"

at all. And yet, in the weeks he'd spent here as a man, and all the weekends and summer days of his childhood, it had become home, or at least more of a home than anywhere else he had ever lived.

Beth had been right—he wasn't connected to New York. Yes, his business was there, and his apartment, but that world was so vastly different, with its skyscrapers and constant movement, from the quiet, rolling green hills of North Carolina.

He spent a lot of time driving around Stone Gap, not stopping anywhere, but passing by the storefronts that had names that sounded more like a family reunion than a downtown business district. Gator's Garage, Betty's Bakery, George's Deli. The park Jack Barlow had built to honor his friend Eli, who'd died fighting overseas. Ernie's Hardware, where Ida Mae had bought Grady his first fishing pole. Joe's Barbershop, with the black plastic stools Grady had sat in many times for the crew cut his father insisted upon.

Several people raised their hands in greeting at the familiar sight of Ida Mae's Camaro, but there was only one person Grady wanted to take for a ride right now—well, two, but one of them wasn't talking to him. He pulled up in front of the Stone Gap Inn, then went inside, hoping he wasn't too late.

Della Barlow poked her head out of the kitchen.

"Hello, Grady! What a surprise to see you. I thought you and Beth would still be on your honeymoon."

Instead of answering that, Grady asked, "Is Nick still working here?" His brother had told him about his chef job at the inn, but Grady had forgotten when his last day was supposed to be.

Della nodded. "For a couple more days. Then we'll lose him to his restaurant." She smiled. "You'll find him in the kitchen, of course."

Grady thanked her, then headed down the hall. The scents of roasted chicken, fresh rolls and something chocolate filled the air, making Grady's mouth water. When he entered the kitchen, Nick stopped in the midst of whipping up some kind of sauce.

"What are you doing here?"

"That seems to be the question of the night." Grady held up the keys to the Camaro. "Want to take a ride with me?"

Nick's gaze sparked with interest. "Are those for Grandma's car?"

"I thought we'd take her for a spin."

Nick grinned the mischievous smile that Grady remembered from their childhood. "Grandma would have loved that."

"Exactly my thinking. So, you in?"

"I've only got a few minutes, but hell, yes, I'm

in." Nick called out to Della that he'd be back in a bit, then the two brothers bounded down the front stairs and out to the car like teenagers. The sun had started to set, casting the town in hues of mauve and peach. The Camaro's engine was a dull roar beneath them as they headed to the more remote parts of town. Grady couldn't help but remember being on this road with Beth not so long ago. It seemed like a million years, back before everything went to hell.

"So, where's that pretty wife of yours?" Nick asked, as if he read Grady's mind.

"Honestly? I don't know." Grady sighed. All his life, he had kept to himself, sharing very little of his feelings, his struggles, with anyone. It wasn't until he was living under one roof with Reggie and Beth that he'd begun to see the value of a family connection. He envied what Beth had, and hoped to build some of that with his brothers going forward. That started with telling the truth. "It wasn't a real marriage. It's a long story, but we got married to make her dad happy."

"A shotgun wedding?"

"No," Grady said. Although a shotgun wedding would have meant he was having a baby with Beth, and for some reason, that idea didn't terrify him. "We were never actually together in the first place.

Her dad was sick, and had a bunch of heart attacks, and wasn't going to live much longer. He wanted his daughter to be settled and happy, and I kind of agreed to be the man to do that. Her dad died the next day."

"I'm so sorry for Beth. That had to be tough." If Nick was surprised by Grady's statement, he didn't say anything. "Since she's not in the car and you don't know where she is right now, I take it you aren't together anymore?"

"Not so much." Grady flicked on the headlights. Twin white beams lit up the long stretch of road ahead, an empty corridor that could take him far away from here if he kept on driving.

The woman Grady had just left on the dock was neither settled nor happy, and a lot of that unhappiness was his doing. "Can I ask you something? Why did you marry Vivian? I mean, you didn't know her more than a couple months, right?"

"That's an easy question." Nick rolled his window down and let the breeze fill the car. The air was fresh and clear, with a sweet, warm scent. "Because she brought me something I never found anywhere else. A…peace, I guess you'd call it. With who I am and where I'm going."

Peace. That was what Grady had found with Beth. She was the only person he knew who could calm his thoughts just by being in the same room. "I've been driving around for hours, trying to figure out what exactly has made me so averse to relationships. Beth said something about how I take risks everywhere else but there. Grandma told me the same thing today."

Nick looked at him askance. "Uh, Grady, are you hearing voices from beyond the grave? Because I'd really like to call an Uber right now, if that's the case."

"No. It's here." Grady leaned over, popped open the glove box and pulled out an envelope, then handed it to Nick. "She wrote that before she died, and left it there, figuring I'd take the car out—"

"And see if she'd left the ice cream money in there."

That had been the first place the boys had gone every time they got in the car. If Ida Mae had left money there—and she pretty much always did—that meant they'd all get a cone down at The Last Scoop, and eat it on the bench out front before going back home. Dessert was forbidden in their parents' household, so Ida Mae indulged her grandsons every chance she got. Grady had peeked in there for old times' sake, only partly surprised to find Grandma had tucked a note there.

"It's not that I needed a few bucks for a vanilla

cone," Grady said. "It was the memory. I was a kid again when I peeked in that glove compartment, you know?"

"Some of the best memories of my life were at that house and in this car."

"Mine, too." Grady gestured toward the envelope, as he turned around in an empty driveway and headed back to town. As much as he was enjoying the ride and the time with his brother, there was a dinner waiting to be served at the inn, and Nick needed to get back. "Anyway, go ahead, read it."

Nick rolled the window up again, then unfolded the letter and began to read aloud. "'Dear Grady, I knew you'd go looking in here, because you thought your grandma might have left you a few bucks for a sundae. I already left you the house, for Pete's sake. Go buy your own ice cream.'" Nick laughed. "That sure sounds like Grandma."

"Keep reading. Because I think you'll get something from the rest."

Nick cleared his throat. "Okay. 'I bet you're wondering why I left you the house and gave your brothers cash. Ryder and Nick loved the place as much as you did, but they are already on the paths they need to take. Breaking away from your dad and becoming something else. You did that too, but you did it by leaving behind everything you knew.

"'If Nick did what I hope he did, then he's as happy as butter on toast. Ryder will get there, and I'm hoping the money gives him the heave-ho he needs to find what he truly wants.'" Nick grinned. "She knows us boys well."

"She always did. Better than Mom and Dad."

"For sure." Nick made a big deal out of clearing his throat again and flapping the letter. "'Grady, you always needed something different. You might think it's the excitement of risk, but I think it's something more. The thing that scares you most.'" Nick glanced over at him. "I take it this is where it gets interesting."

Grady scowled. "I didn't ask for commentary."

Nick grinned, then dipped his head and started reading again. "'Of all the boys, you were the one who craved a home the most. I'd see you crying, looking out the back window of your father's car every time he pulled away from my house, and it near broke my heart. I know that this house was home for you when you were here. I wish that could have happened more often. So I'm giving you this house, so you can have that home you wanted so badly, and have a place to build a life in. Because all the success in the world matters not if you don't have a family to share it with. So live in my house, find yourself a smart and funny wife who can make cookies like your grandma did, and fill that house with children and laughter. Because, my dear Grady, jumping off the platform into a lake of love (I know, I know, but I really liked the metaphor) is the greatest risk of all.'"

Silence filled the car for a moment, then his brother murmured, "I gotta agree. That's how I ended up taking that leap with Vivian. Best choice I ever made." He folded the letter and put it back in the envelope. "So, what are you going to do?"

Grady gestured toward the scene ahead of them. Stone Gap lay at the bottom of the hill, a constellation of streetlights and porch lights. "I'm gonna leap."

Beth left her father's house and had started to head home when she saw a familiar dog attached to a leash, and two people she didn't know in the downtown area. She pulled over and got out of the car, looking down at the dog, then up at the couple. "Monster? What are you doing here?"

"We adopted him," the man said. "We saw an ad some guy hung up at the supermarket, on the bulletin board. We've been looking for a dog like this."

Beth knew that Grady had been looking for a home for Monster from the start, but she'd always assumed...

Well, that she would have taken Monster and given Grady an excuse to visit. The fact that he had given Monster away cemented what Beth had secretly hoped wasn't true. Grady was gone. For good.

"We have been looking for a dog, but not like this one." His wife's face pinched. "I've never seen a dog who misbehaves like him. He's in our house for twenty minutes and he chews all my shoes, then tries to eat the meat loaf I made for dinner!"

Beth knelt down to the puppy's level and cupped his face in her hands. His fur was soft, his eyes bright and eager. "Monster. What are you doing? I taught you better than that." The dog's tail wagged at a furious pace.

"Anyway, I think we're going to have to bring him to the shelter," the husband went on. "He's clearly not the right dog for us."

"A shelter?" Beth looked up, keeping a protective hand on Monster's collar. No way in hell was she going to let these people put Monster down or send him off to parts unknown. "I'll take him home. I know this dog, and he's not as badly behaved as you think."

"You can have him." The husband dropped the leash into Beth's hands. "Next time, we're going for a nice, quiet, elderly golden retriever."

Some people, Beth decided, shouldn't own dogs at all. She thanked them, took the leash, then helped Monster into her car. The puppy bounded into the seat, sat as primly as a schoolmarm and, panting, sent a happy smile in Beth's direction. "You did all that on purpose, didn't you?"

Monster just kept on panting. But his tail wagged a slow yes against the vinyl seat cover.

She should take Monster back to Grady, and tell him what had happened. But just as she went to put her car in gear, Beth's heart dropped. She couldn't. If Monster had been adopted out, that must mean Grady had left for New York. And they were over. She supposed he'd send her some annulment paperwork or something, and put the whole thing in his past.

Any last bit of hope she'd had died right then.

She drove home, grateful she knew the way by heart because she could barely see. She swiped away her tears, but they kept on coming. By the time she pulled into her driveway, the tears had become full-on sobs.

Before she could get out of the car, Monster bounded across the console and into her lap, barking and prancing. She tried to pull the dog back, but he wouldn't listen. "What are you doing? You need to sit, Monster. Sit and—"

And then she saw what Monster was so excited about.

Grady, leaning against Ida Mae's bright blue Camaro, looking so damned handsome under that streetlight she wanted to hit him. For being there. For looking so good and for setting alight her own foolish heart, which kept falling for him, over and over.

Beth opened the door and tumbled out of the car, with the puppy leading the way. Monster yanked his leash out of Beth's hand and bounded forward, barking with joy until he reached Grady. Then he leaped up, placed his paws on Grady's chest and licked his face. Grady laughed and gave the rambunctious puppy a hug. "Okay, okay, I've got you now. You can calm down."

"What are you doing here?" she asked.

He laughed again. "If I had a dollar for every time I've heard that question today, I'd be a rich man."

He hadn't answered the question. She wasn't sure she wanted to hear what he had to say. Chances were good he was here with the annulment papers. A man like Grady wouldn't want to leave in place a tie to a town he couldn't stand. "I've got to take Monster home," she said. "I took him from those people who adopted him. They said he was too rambunctious."

"I know. They just texted me." Grady kept on leaning against the car, a devilish grin on his face. "So you're taking Monster home. Meaning…back to our house?"

Our house? What did he mean by that? "You sold that house, Grady. There's no 'our' anything anymore." She picked up the leash and gave Monster a tug. "Come on, buddy, let's go."

The dog refused to move. He plopped his butt on the concrete and looked up at Grady with utter adoration. "Monster…" She tugged again.

"He doesn't want to go," Grady said. "Because he knows I don't want to, either."

Beth stopped midstep. What had he just said? She turned around. "What do you mean, you don't want to, either?"

"I'm selling my company," Grady said, pushing off from the Camaro and coming to stand before her. "Jim upped his offer, and it's enough to pay off my debts and send some severance to the people I had to lay off."

She blinked. "But…what will you do in New York?"

"Nothing." He grinned. "Because I'm not going to New York. I took Mac Barlow up on his offer."

Grady was buying Hillstrand Solar? To sell

it? Or to run it? "But…I thought you turned him down."

"I did. Then I changed my mind. I changed my mind about a lot of things tonight. Spent the last twenty minutes on the phone, working out a partnership with Mac, undoing the deal to sell the house, and texting with the people who adopted my dog. They told me some crazy woman took him home with her, and I knew that had to be you. Because you're the only one crazy enough to take in a wild mutt and a man who's been stupid for far too long." He placed a hand on her cheek, his gaze locking on hers. Her breath caught and she dared to allow hope to rise inside her once again. "I didn't realize what a coward I was being until I almost got on a plane and left. Which would have meant losing you."

"You weren't losing me." She had been here all along, and despite her brave speech to her father, she knew deep down she would have waited for Grady.

"I would have if I'd run away to New York." Monster nudged at his leg and Grady gave him an ear rub. "Logically, going back to the city made sense. I had an existing company there, an existing home, an existing life. But here's the thing…" He paused a moment. "When I was a kid, what made me happiest was going with my gut instinct. Jumping off the edge of something and knowing I could make it without getting hurt. I stopped doing that when my gut failed me."

"When that business deal with the government fell through."

He nodded. "It was a mistake, and it cost me everything. But it also taught me something none of my previous successes ever did. That sometimes, mistakes bring you exactly where you need to be."

"And where is that?" she asked, almost afraid to hear his reply. Even Monster was sitting still, as if waiting on the answer.

"To the biggest risk of all." He smiled at her. "Marrying a woman I barely knew. Pretending to fall in love, in front of an entire town."

Pretend he was in love? All this time, she'd thought maybe there was a chance that his words in the kitchen that night were real. She shook her head. "I should go home, Grady."

"Wait," he said. "Please."

She turned the leash over and over in her hands. "Grady—"

"You are the only thing in my life that makes sense. That…grounds me." He brushed a tendril of hair off her cheek. "When I'm around you, Beth, I get this sense of peace. Calm. Joy. I've been rich and I've been poor. I've been all over the world, and achieved things most men my age never do. But when I got in my grandmother's car today and started driving, I realized something. I've only been *truly* happy in two places."

"Where is that?" If he said Timbuktu or Paris, she was going to slug him. Her heart had begun to drop, and she didn't want it to break again.

"Here in Stone Gap and…" He closed the distance between them, then wrapped his arms around her waist. He was warm against her, solid, strong. "…anytime and anywhere with you."

Here. With her. Did he really mean that?

She put her head against his chest and listened to the soft thud of his heart. It was steady and dependable, and something she had come to treasure. "I've been so afraid to trust a man, so afraid to fall in love," she whispered. "Every man I've ever known has let me down. But then you came along and you did more than I asked for."

"Because I love you, Beth." He tipped her chin until she was looking at him. "I really do. You remind me so much of my grandmother, because you are strong and determined and the kind of woman the right person should see as his partner. But only if he steps up to the plate and becomes the kind of man you deserve."

"You were that person, Grady. You still are." Was he saying what she thought he was saying? That he wanted to stay married? "So…you aren't here with annulment papers?"

He laughed. "No, honey, not at all. I thought this was more appropriate for the occasion of me admitting I was almost the stupidest man alive." He reached in his pocket and pulled out a velvet box with the logo of a local jeweler. An almost perfect replica of the ring he'd given her was nestled in the dark blue interior. "This diamond is real. Because this marriage will be real. If…"

"If what?"

He took a breath, then held her gaze. "If you still want to marry me, Beth."

The question hung in the air between them. So much had happened in the last few weeks, so many twists and turns to a life that Beth once thought was as predictable as rain on a hot summer night. Then Grady came along and disrupted the quiet, scheduled world Beth had lived in, and asked her to be more, to dare more.

"I can't do that, Grady." She shook her head, and a shadow dropped over his features. "Because… I'm already married to the man I love."

A wide grin spread across Grady's face and joy lit his eyes. "That is one hell of a lucky man." He leaned down and kissed her, sweet and long, while Monster barked and twined his leash around their legs. The lost puppy had found a home, and now, Beth realized, so had she.

Epilogue

Beth had started to waddle. She put a hand on her aching back and gave Grady a grimace. "I look like a penguin."

He chuckled and pulled out a cushioned chair for her at the table on the deck. "No, you look like a beautiful woman who is about to have our first child."

Beth grinned. "There is that." She sighed as she sank into the comfortable chair and looked out over the lake. Grady had bought a small pontoon boat that was docked at Ida Mae's pier and ready to go for a sunset cruise later, although clouds had been moving in all day and threatening rain.

Grady had already put a swing set on the lawn, even though it would be a long time until their child was ready to use it. Monster snoozed in the sunny corner of the deck, his paws moving in a puppy dream of chasing rabbits.

The grill was sizzling with burgers and hot dogs, and there was cold lemonade in the pitcher on the table. They had just come home from the dedication ceremony for the Ida Mae Jackson Gazebo in the center of Stone Gap Park. The roof of the gazebo had been painted a bright blue, the same as Ida Mae's Camaro. Grady had hired the ice cream shop to hand out free cones for the occasion, and Cutler Shay had insisted on being the one to dish up the scoops.

The back door opened and Mac and Savannah emerged, their two-year-old daughter perched on Mac's hip. She had the same bright blond hair as her mother, and an infectious grin that clearly had Mac infatuated.

Nick and Vivian and their daughter strolled across the lawn. Nick had told Grady, and sworn him to secrecy until they had a chance to make it public, that Vivian was pregnant. Nick's restaurant was doing well, a busy and cozy place just outside of town that was gaining a reputation all along the East Coast for locals and tourists alike. "Hi, Nick," Beth said.

He leaned down and kissed her cheek, then deposited a brightly colored gift bag on the table beside her. "Bought my soon-to-be-nephew a noisy toy. Be sure to only let him play with it when Grady's in charge."

Beth laughed. "It might be a niece, and will you quit buying things? We're going to need to purchase a bigger house for all the toys and things you and Grady are bringing home. The baby hasn't even been born yet."

Grady chuckled and put a hand on his wife's shoulder. "You can't blame us. We're just excited. And you know me and my brother. We don't do anything halfway."

"You both are going to have to learn some restraint or our baby will be spoiled." She covered Grady's hand with her own and leaned her cheek against the warmth of his face. How she loved her husband, who made her life so much richer and better. She had no doubt he was going to be a fabulous, hands-on father, given how involved and present he'd been throughout the pregnancy.

"I have something for the baby, too," Grady said. He handed Beth a small bag and leaned down to whisper in her ear. "This is from someone special who couldn't be here today."

Beth picked up the bag, reached past the piles of bright blue tissue paper and pulled out a teeny tiny pair of boxing gloves. Her eyes misted and she looked up at her husband. "That is so sweet."

"I know your dad would want our baby to have a pair. And to tell him or her that it's never too early to learn how to fight for yourself." Grady gave a mock one-two jab, and grinned. "Okay, maybe a little early. Use them as a mobile for now, and then our baby can dream about his grandpa."

She brushed away her tears and drew her husband into a long, tight hug. The baby kicked between them as if he was just as ready to be here as everyone was to meet him—or her.

A minute later, Grady and Mac went to the grill, turning burgers and talking business. Monster woke up, grabbed his ball and crossed to Savannah and her daughter, begging for a game of fetch.

Just then, the clouds opened up and rain began to pelt the deck. The guests hurried into the house, shooing the kids in ahead of them. Grady helped his wife out of the chair. "Come on, honey, we need to get out of the rain," he said. "Monster, you, too."

The irrepressible Lab bounded past them, down

the deck steps and out into the storm. Beth sighed. "That dog's going to track in mud later."

"No, he won't. Watch this." Grady whistled and called Monster's name. "Come!"

The dog halted, spun around and barreled back up the stairs to the deck. Grady pulled open the door and the Lab trotted inside.

Beth laughed. "Whoa. When did he start listening to you?"

"About the time I started taking cues from my smart and talented wife. I finally started associating doing the right thing with a reward."

She ducked under his arm and into the house. Outside, thunder rumbled and the rain started to fall harder. Beth brushed off the worst of the droplets and gave Grady a grin. "Oh yeah? What reward is that?"

"This." Grady drew her into his arms and kissed her, sweet and slow. In the kitchen, their family and friends were laughing and talking, filling the house with joy and love. Ida Mae's home was alive again with the very thing she had hoped for when she'd bequeathed it to Grady. He had finally created the home he'd wanted his entire life. "All of this."

* * * * *

COMING SOON!

We really hope you enjoyed reading this book. If you're looking for more romance, be sure to head to the shops when new books are available on

Thursday 20th March

To see which titles are coming soon, please visit

millsandboon.co.uk/nextmonth

MILLS & BOON

Coming next month

ONE NIGHT WITH HER MILLIONAIRE BOSS
Kandy Shepherd

The rain was coming down so hard it had driven channels into the gravel, forming small gushing streams. The path was well lit, but it was getting more difficult to avoid the streams and save her shoes and she found herself jumping from side to side as if in a game of aquatic hopscotch. She cursed out loud when the umbrella suddenly turned completely inside out. She was left with only a light jacket over her dress for protection against the elements.

Then Ned was there. 'Seems like you could do with some help,' he said. He was sensibly encased in a long oilskin raincoat and held aloft an enormous black umbrella.

'This darn umbrella is useless,' she spluttered and threw it on the ground.

'Don't tell me—you chose it because it was purple.'

'It was the first one I saw,' she fibbed. Of course she'd been attracted to the pattern of purple iris. The possible sturdiness of the umbrella hadn't been a consideration.

'Come here,' he said.

Ned pulled her to him and under the shelter of his umbrella. Suddenly the stinging onslaught of the rain on her face stopped, but she was far too distracted by Ned's closeness to care. She was dry. She was warm. *He was hot.*

'It's great to get rain. We need it. Trouble is when it all comes down like this at once, so much of it runs off.'

'Hopefully it will ease off,' she said.

His chest was a wall of solid muscle. As he led her towards the house, steering her through the channels, she leaned in closer. Just, of course, to make sure she was completely under the shelter of his umbrella.

'We're almost there or I'd pick you up and carry you,' he said.

'*What!*'

'You're a little thing. Nowhere as heavy as a full-grown sheep to sling over my shoulder.'

Before she had a chance to reply, they reached the house. In one fluid movement, Ned ditched his umbrella, put his hands under her armpits, lifted her off the ground and up the steps, depositing her on the veranda. Freya was back on her feet, out of the rain, before she had time to protest.

'Did you just compare me to a sheep?' she said, mock glaring up at him, a smile twitching at the corners of her mouth. His hair was dark with damp and fat drops of water sat on his cheeks. He grinned. Her heart gave that curious lurch of recognition—she didn't know where it came from.

'A ewe, if I'm to be precise,' he said.

'I'm glad you at least amended that to be a lady sheep.' She couldn't resist his grin and responded with one of her own. 'Do you really lift and haul sheep around the place?' If so, no wonder the man was made of muscle.

'If needs be,' he said. 'I grew up learning to do everything that needed to be done with sheep. Rescue them, shear them, sometimes birth them. So yeah, I've had to haul around the odd sheep or two over the years. No special treatment for the boss.'

He sounded so laconic, so laidback, so *manly* she leaned up on tiptoe and kissed him on the cheek. 'Thank you, for rescuing me like a stray sheep caught in the rain.' She froze. *Why did she do that?*

Her lips tingled from the connection to his skin, cool with raindrops. For a crazy moment she'd wanted to taste them, taste *him*. Her gaze connected with his for a long, still moment.

Continue reading
ONE NIGHT WITH HER MILLIONAIRE BOSS
Kandy Shepherd

Available next month
www.millsandboon.co.uk

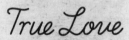

MILLS & BOON
MEDICAL
Pulse-Racing Passion

Set your pulse racing with dedicated, delectable doctors in the high-pressure world of medicine, where emotions run high and passion, comfort and love are the best medicine.

JOIN US ON SOCIAL MEDIA!

Stay up to date with our latest releases, author news and gossip, special offers and discounts, and all the behind-the-scenes action from Mills & Boon...

 millsandboon

 millsandboonuk

 millsandboon

It might just be true love...

LET'S TALK

Romance

For exclusive extracts, competitions
and special offers, find us online:

 facebook.com/millsandboon

@MillsandBoon

@MillsandBoonUK

Get in touch on 01413 063232

For all the latest titles coming soon, visit
millsandboon.co.uk/nextmonth